THE
BLOCKCHAIN
REVOLUTION

A TALE OF INSANITY
AND ANARCHY

ANDREW UPDEGROVE

To my brother Steve, who has spent his life serving others

By the same author:

The Alexandria Project, a Tale of Treachery and Technology

The Lafayette Campaign, a Tale of Deception and Elections

The Doodlebug War, a Tale of Fanatics and Romantics

The Turing Test, a Tale of Artificial Intelligence and Malevolence

Available as eBooks at Amazon and in paperback at your favorite online
book site as well as at http://andrew-updegrove.com/books/
They can also be ordered in paperback through your favorite local book store

The Alexandria Project, The Lafayette Campaign and *The Doodlebug War*
are available as audiobooks published by Tantor Media. You can find
them at Audible, Amazon, and wherever else audiobooks are sold

Prologue

"There's a fine line between genius and insanity. I have erased this line."

Oscar Levant

"There are only nine meals between mankind and anarchy"

Alfred Henry Lewis

THE PATTERNS ON the screen were mesmerizing. Beautiful, even magical. Squares silently appeared out of nowhere, multiplied, formed fractal shapes, and drifted away. Each square represented a new block of transactions. On a thousand computer systems, each block took its place atop thousands of others that had come before.

It was like watching life itself evolve before his very eyes. And it was his creation.

Our creation! the voice objected.

Yes, our creation, he agreed. It was best not to argue.

Ten years. Ten years ago, to the day, since he first proposed a new technology he called a blockchain, promising it would provide the foundation for a new financial world order. At first, only his fellow anarchists and a few libertarians knew of his discovery. When others learned of it, most laughed.

They aren't laughing now! the voice added.

Indeed not. But with time, recognition of his genius had dawned here and then there. As well it should have; his invention was elegant and self-reinforcing, disruptive and revolutionary. Soon, scores of companies adopted it to produce what the markets now called "cryptocurrencies." And then hundreds. Now more than two thousand. Multinational companies and governments everywhere were scrambling to adopt blockchains, casting their old ways aside and embracing the new.

And yet the secret of his identity remained secure. In all the world, only he knew from whose fertile brain this new technology had sprung.

And us! You must not forget us! a deeper voice boomed.

Yes, all of us, he conceded.

Everyone wanted to learn who was behind the blockchain. For all they knew, it was some sort of cyber wizard able to create unimaginable crypto-wealth out of thin air.

A Cryptomancer!

Why, yes! He smiled at that. A Cryptomancer. Perhaps that's what he was. But that sounded too theatrical, too formal. Crypto, though – yes, that might do.

Yes! Crypto! We approve.

But back to the business at hand. Ten years he had waited. It was time for "Crypto" to act.

Chapter 1

Mr. Cronin Will See You Now

FRANK WAS FIDGETING.

That was hardly remarkable. He was almost always fidgeting. Especially when he was in public. The mere presence of another human being invariably left him struggling to control whatever tic his mind had most recently devised to make his life miserable.

The human being setting him a-tremble at the moment was a well-dressed and strikingly attractive receptionist. Through the floor-to-ceiling windows behind her, Frank had a breathtaking view of Manhattan far below. Perched on the edge of a couch, he struggled to hold himself still while wondering why he was there. He was a well-recognized cybersecurity expert, so it must relate to those skills. But after that, what?

Just yesterday, life had seemed simple and neat. His most recent project had ended, and he was treating himself to a rare vacation.

For a few days, he'd even relaxed.

"Mr. Adversego?"

He looked up. "Yes?"

An austere woman in a conservative suit and dark-rimmed glasses faced him, her hair pulled back in a bun. Frank guessed she was thirty-five and wondered why she wanted to look fifteen years older. Something about her reminded him of a librarian he'd been terrified of in third grade.

"I'm Audrey Addams," she said. "Mr. Cronin will see you now."

Frank jerked to his feet and followed her past a dozen sumptuous, glass-walled offices. At the end of the hall, they paused outside an even grander corner office. A nameplate beside the door read *Benson Cronin, CEO*. Inside, a sixty-ish-year-old man sat behind a glass-topped desk the size of Frank's living room rug. His suit was obviously tailor-made; Frank wondered how much more than a thousand bucks it had set its owner back.

Addams tapped on the door. Cronin glanced in their direction, sizing Frank up. Frank could imagine what he might be thinking: *If this guy even owns a suit, I bet it cost less than my haircut.*

"Welcome!" Cronin said, sliding into sales mode as he walked around his desk, a broad smile on his face and his hand extended.

"I'm Benson Cronin – call me Ben. Mind if I call you Frank?"

"Sure," Frank said, waiting to retrieve his fingers from a thorough handshake.

"Great. Let's sit over here." Cronin gestured toward a couch and chairs. "Would you like something to drink? A cup of coffee?"

"No, I'm fine."

"Good, good," Cronin said. "So, I appreciate your making time to meet with me today. Audrey tells me you were on vacation. And pretty hard to reach, too."

* * *

Not intentionally. But if Frank hadn't been having breakfast that morning at one of the few places on the island with cell phone service, he wouldn't have ended up in Manhattan at all. Halfway through his fish hash and eggs, his phone had vibrated.

"Hello?"

"Mr. Adversego?"

"Yes?"

"Did you get Mr. Cronin's letter?"

Letter? Who sent letters anymore? Frank paid all his bills online and only opened his mailbox when the postman couldn't jam any more junk mail through the slot.

"Uh, no. I've been away for a while."

"I've also been trying to reach you by phone. You've already missed two appointments I set up for you. Mr. Cronin is a very busy man."

"I'm sure he is, Ms. …"

"Addams. Audrey Addams. Mr. Cronin's chief of staff."

"Well, the wireless coverage is spotty up here. Anyway, can you tell me what this is all about?"

"I'd like you to meet with Mr. Cronin at four this afternoon to discuss blockchains."

"Meet where?"

"In New York, of course." There was a long pause during which Frank imagined Ms. Addams grappling with the astonishing concept that someone might not know where Benson Cronin worked. "At the main office of First Manhattan Bank," she added.

Frank looked at his watch. "I'm afraid I can't. You see, I'm on an island off the coast of Maine. At this time of year, the ferry only runs every other day, and the next one isn't until tomorrow."

"What's the name of the island?"

"Matinahaven."

"Where are you staying? And where are you right now?"

Frank looked at his phone in astonishment. "The Slackwater Motel. And I'm having breakfast at a place called the Harborside. Why?"

"I'll get back to you. Stay by your phone."

And she was gone.

Frank shook his head as he set down his phone. Now, there was a chief of staff who didn't take no for an answer. She'd need to this time, though, unless she owned a lobster boat. And a fast one at that.

He was settling his tab when his phone vibrated again.

"Addams here. There's a car waiting for you outside."

"Excuse me?"

"There's a car waiting to take you to the airstrip. If you leave right now, you can catch the mail plane."

Frank frowned. "All the way to New York?"

"Of course not. The mail plane will take you across the bay to Fowlshead Airport. Mr. Cronin's private jet will pick you up there."

Seriously? "Okay ... but I'll need to stop back at the motel to –"

"No, you won't. I've already spoken to Mr. Gladman, the owner, and settled your bill. Your suitcase and laptop are in the car outside."

And once again, she was gone.

Ten minutes later, Frank was driving along the edge of a grass airstrip toward a ridiculously small airplane, its propeller already spinning. As he climbed in, the plane rocked side to side in a nasty crosswind. He started to feel queasy.

"Are you sure it's safe to take off?" he asked.

"Landin' were a bit interestin'," the pilot said in a thick Maine accent. "Takeoff's gen'rally easyah." He shoved the throttle all the way forward.

The plane lurched ahead, gathering speed as it bounced down the narrow lane carved out of the dense forest crowding the airstrip on either side. Frank clutched the arms of his seat as the light plane lifted off. Immediately, it drifted to one side, one wing dipping alarmingly toward the ground as the pilot compensated at the controls. Goggle-eyed, Frank watched as the trees reached out to grab them.

And then they were free and rising, the broad, shining bay spreading out before them, speckled with islands and dotted with fishing boats.

"Piece a cake," the pilot said. "You should come along when it's thick o' fog."

* * *

Now here Frank was – still in the same jeans and flannel shirt he'd been wearing while eating fish hash just six hours ago – anxious to learn why he'd been summoned from the wilds of Maine into the presence of the CEO of one of the most powerful banks in the world.

"So," Cronin began, "how much did Audrey tell you about what I'd like to discuss?"

"Nothing, actually, except that it has something to do with the blockchain."

Which had not surprised him. All you heard about these days was the blockchain. The concept was simple although the technology was not. Traditionally, banks controlled the global financial system, acting like hubs with thousands of spokes, each spoke connecting one bank with another. Everyone trusted banks to hold assets, keep proper records, and otherwise act on behalf of their customers.

With a blockchain-based network, banks weren't necessary. Anyone could send funds to anyone else in digital form using software they could download for free. That software would combine their individual transaction with a bunch of other ones to form a "block" of records. The software would link each package of data to the previous one, creating an ever-growing "chain" of transaction record blocks. But what if someone hacked that software and stole those digital funds before they reached their destination? How could you prove you'd sent them at all?

That's where the clever part came in: when someone set up a successful blockchain system, others created tens, hundreds, or even thousands of identical copies of the same chain of transactions. Each chain would live on a different computer in as many different locations. With so many duplicates of the same data, everything was supposed to be much more secure. Frank wasn't so sure about that.

"Ah – well," Cronin continue, "Audrey tends to focus on the immediate objective, which in this case meant tracking you down and getting you here. May I ask how available you are right now?"

The honest answer was "totally." Frank was currently – and, he hoped, temporarily – *persona non grata* with the government, because his last project for the CIA hadn't ended well. Not through any fault of his own, but it seemed everyone involved was guilty until proven innocent in the eyes of the CIA's congressional oversight committee. Anyone at the CIA, or the FBI, for that matter, would be crazy to hire him until the inevitable hearings were over and the blame assigned somewhere else. Thankfully, his name hadn't made the news. Otherwise, he was sure he wouldn't be having this conversation.

"I think it depends," Frank hedged. "What do you have in mind?"

"Well, I guess I'll just put my cards on the table," Cronin said. "How would you like to be First Manhattan's new Chief Risk Officer for Blockchain Technologies? Starting immediately?"

Frank stared blankly in response. "Me?"

Cronin smiled. "I guess that was a bit abrupt. As I expect you're aware, like every other bank, we're adopting blockchain technology. Specifically, we're moving all our financial processes onto something we call the Global Financial Blockchain System. For marketing purposes, we refer to it as 'BankCoin.'"

Frank nodded. "Yes, I'd be surprised if you weren't making a move like that. But I'd be lying if I said I was a blockchain expert."

"Understood," Cronin said. "But who is? It's all too new – as far as I can tell, everybody's making it up as they go along. Anyway, you needn't worry on that score; we've got plenty of bright people doing code development. What we don't have is someone with your ability to step back, take a hard look at complex technology, and figure out where the cybersecurity gremlins might be hiding. Are you game?"

I certainly should be, Frank thought. *I've been complaining for years how I never get any interesting private sector work. Now, this guy's offering me a fancy title at a huge bank.* But the same thought put him in a panic. Would he have to show up here every day in a suit and tie? They might even expect him to have an administrative assistant!

"I don't know," he said, trying to squelch the mad spasm of tapping his right foot had just embarked upon.

"If it's the compensation, don't worry. We've budgeted five hundred thousand dollars a year for base salary and up to a hundred seventy-five thousand dollars in bonus. On the equity side, we've allocated options to buy two hundred thousand shares of First Manhattan stock vesting over three years. By 'vesting,' I mean that the longer you stay, the more of those shares you'd be able to purchase at today's low price per share."

Frank's left foot had now joined the dance. "Well, that sounds great, but –"

Cronin leaned closer. "Okay, I can see you're a good negotiator. You're right, the position might not last three years. How about we say you can exercise all those stock options after just six months?"

Frank felt the walls closing in around him. "Gee, I don't know. I live in Washington, DC. That's too far to commute. And I don't think I want to move."

Cronin frowned. "Okay. So, I guess we could deal with that. Let's say you work remotely half the time and the other half here. We can provide a suitable place for you to stay when you're in town."

Frank stared back and opened his mouth, but no words came out.

"All right," Cronin said. "A two-year contract at six hundred thousand dollars a year, plus bonus, plus just six months to get all the stock options vested, and only two days a week here at the bank, but honestly, that's as far as I can go." He leaned back and crossed his arms, straining to keep the smile on his face. Who'd have thought the nerd would drive such a tough bargain? "So, what do you say?"

What should he say? Frank pressed his hands down on his knees, trying to pin his hyperactive feet to the floor. Just the first year's salary was more than he'd earned in the last five years combined.

"Well, I –"

Cronin could see Frank wasn't there yet. "Okay, I didn't mean to be pushy. Why don't you think about it and get back to me in the next day or so?"

"Sure," Frank said, eyeing his escape route to the CEO's office door. "Why don't I do that."

"Good!" Cronin said, standing up and clapping Frank on the back. "Here." He picked a business card out of a holder on his desk. "This is my direct dial number. Give me a holler any time if you have any questions at all."

"Great – thanks."

Cronin walked Frank to the door of his office. As if by magic, the receptionist materialized to escort him to the elevators. Before he knew it, Frank was walking up Lexington Avenue in a mental fog. Only after several blocks did he realize the Amtrak station was in the opposite direction.

* * *

Audrey Addams found Cronin sitting at his desk, staring out the window.

"Did he take it?" she said.

"Not yet."

"Do you think he will?"

"Dunno. He's a hard guy to read. Who else do we have on the list?"

"I'm afraid he's the last one. If he says no, we'll have to start the search all over again."

"Then this guy Adversego better accept," Cronin said with the tone of someone not used to being disappointed. "Our stock price still hasn't fully recovered from that big data breach last summer. I don't care who we get so long as next time the board has somebody else's neck to choke instead of mine."

He waved Addams out of his office and swiveled back to stare out the window.

Damn! he thought. *I should have offered the geek another twenty-five thousand options.*

Chapter 2

What Were You Expecting?

"SO, YOU'LL TAKE it, right?"

Marla, Frank's daughter, was pushing him hard.

"Well, I'm not sure. I don't know much about blockchain design. And I'd have to travel back and forth to New York City every week."

"For six hundred thousand dollars, you can't take a train or plane a couple times a week? And those options could end up being worth millions."

"Sure. But what would I use the money for? I don't spend everything I make now."

He had her there. Other than a faster laptop, Marla couldn't think of anything her father would want. It certainly wouldn't be new clothes.

"Well, you could travel."

"To where? I don't like cities, and it doesn't cost anything to camp in the backcountry."

Marla paused. What could make her dad realize a great opportunity was staring him in the face? "Well," she said hesitantly, "it would take your mind off Shannon."

"*What?*"

"I mean, you've been kind of mopey ever since she took that position with Boeing in Seattle."

"I have not been mopey!" Frank said. "And she did exactly what she should have — that was the dream job she'd always been hoping for. I couldn't be happier for her!"

"But you haven't seen her once since she moved."

"We both agreed we weren't long-distance-relationship types. And I've never liked talking on the phone."

Time to switch her line of attack, Marla thought. Truly, her father was impossible. Whether he admitted it or not, she thought he was lonely. Plus, he'd been whining that he might never get a good project again. Yet here he was, trying to come up with an excuse not to accept the golden egg laid in his lap. Then, she had a thought.

"Still there?" her father said.

"Well ... so, I guess you might think about setting up a college fund."

Frank's eyebrows shot up. "Is there something you want to tell me?"

"Maybe."

"Are you pregnant?"

"I wasn't going to tell you until after my first trimester, but that ends next week. So, yes."

Frank had been looking out the window. Now he plopped into a chair. *Wow.*

"So, Dad — are *you* still there?"

"Yes — you just took me by surprise. But that's wonderful! Do you know if it's a girl? No, scratch that. I don't want to know."

Marla smiled. She was looking forward to watching her father play with a grandchild.

"Anyway," Frank continued, talking faster. "That's great! I mean, that's really tremendous!" Then he frowned. "Are you okay? Is everything going well?"

"Yes, don't worry, everything's great. I like my obstetrician a lot. She says the baby and I are both doing fine. Except I'm gaining a lot of weight."

"As you should! That's normal. Don't forget, you're eating for two now!"

Marla smiled again. Her father had already switched allegiance to a grandchild he'd first learned of only a few seconds before.

"Anyway," she said, "I'm glad you know now. I don't like keeping things from you. And I've really wanted to share the news."

"I'm delighted you did! This is exciting."

"Absolutely." Marla pursed her lips and then continued. "So, we plan to have at least two or three kids. I can't imagine how we're going to put them through college, and maybe grad school besides. If you wanted to help out, it would be a huge load off our minds."

Indeed, it would, Frank thought. Marla's husband, Tim, still hadn't found his long-term niche in the world. Marla wasn't making much, either, working for a nonprofit. They had a small apartment and a used car. Things would have to be tight for them after adding a child into the mix.

That put things in an entirely different light. He made his decision instantly. "I'd love to. I'll take the job."

Marla felt simultaneously guilty, relieved, and concerned. "But only if you really want it!"

"Don't you worry about that. I don't have anything else to do right now except sit around and fret. This should be a really interesting project. I should grab it even without your news."

"Are you sure?"

"Completely. You've just helped me be realistic. Now, why don't you go lie down for a while? You're probably tired."

Marla grinned and said goodbye. It looked like she'd be enduring a lot of parental fussing over the next six months. Shipping her father off to New York City a few days a week might be as welcome as his help with tuition.

* * *

Frank's alarm went off. He squelched the annoying buzz and woke his phone to see what had washed up on his digital shores overnight. Uh-oh. Rather a lot. Then the phone rang.

"Hey, Dad – I see you're famous again!"

"Not so far as I know. What are you talking about?"

"Don't you have a Google alert set up for your name?"

"Of course not. Why on earth would I do that?"

"So, you'd know it when a big bank issues a press release announcing your appointment as Chief Risk Officer for Blockchain Technologies."

Frank groaned. "Really?"

"Really. Here's the quote from First Manhattan's CEO: 'With the bank's hire of the world's foremost expert on cybersecurity –'"

Frank sat up straight. "What? What did you just say?"

"Didn't you see the press release before they issued it?"

"No!"

"So, why did you give them a quote for it?"

"What quote? I didn't give them any quote for a press release. What does it say?"

"Let me scroll down ... okay, here we go: 'I'm delighted to join First Manhattan's world-class cybersecurity team,' Adversego said, –"

"I haven't even met them yet!" Frank said.

"Hold on, there's more," Marla said. "Your quote continues, 'Together, we'll personally guarantee that First Manhattan's customers will be protected against whatever criminals send our way.'"

"I'd never say that," Frank protested.

"That's probably why they didn't ask you for a quote."

"I'm sure. Look, I gotta go. I want to see what else they put in there."

Frank slumped back against the pillow and stared at his phone. It was crammed with new text, voice, and email messages. He opened the first text. It was from a coworker from his Library of Congress days: "So – I once shared a cube wall with 'The World's Foremost Expert on Cybersecurity.' If only I'd known!"

Frank groaned again. Just five minutes ago, he'd been blissfully unconscious.

* * *

"Next, I want to introduce you to your administrative assistant," Audrey Addams said. Frank had to hustle to keep up as she strode down the hallway on the sixty-fifth floor of First Manhattan's headquarters.

As he did, he glanced nervously to one side. Each admin he passed was more attractive and self-assured than the last. He wondered whether appearance outranked ability on the management floor list of qualifications when it came to female employees. That wasn't a good sign.

On the other side of the hallway, every office held an executive – almost always male – each expensively dressed in a suit and tie. He didn't even own a suit. He was wearing the only sports jacket to his name, and the last time his shoes had seen polish was a decade ago, before they left the factory. Frank began to perspire. He'd trade his first week's salary for an invisibility cloak right now.

They turned a corner, and Addams approached a drop-dead gorgeous young woman sitting at a workstation. "Margaret, I'd like to introduce you to Frank Adversego. Frank, this is Margaret LaCeroix. She also works with Hank Trammel, a vice president in the credit card group. His office is next to yours."

LaCeroix stood up. "Very pleased to meet you, Mr. Adversego. I'm looking forward to working with you." Frank wished his expression was as confident as hers. He gave her hand a quick shake.

"Very happy to meet you as well, Ms. LaCeroix."

"Oh, please. Call me Margaret."

"Yes, well, please call me Frank."

"And this is your office," Addams said, turning around to the glass wall on the other side of the hallway. It was furnished with expensive furniture, a computer, and a large, threatening plant he couldn't identify. Behind his desk was half of Manhattan and New Jersey beyond.

"Someone from IT will be by shortly to log you into our systems," Addams said, turning to leave. "If you need anything, tell Margaret."

Frank stared out the window for a minute and then eased himself into his new office chair. He'd never seen one before with electronic adjustment controls. People passing by in the hallway glanced in with mild curiosity. He turned on the computer and gazed at a login screen that required a password he didn't yet have. Tapping his fingers, he wondered what to do until the IT guy arrived. Margaret looked up from across the hallway and smiled. He gave a lopsided smile back. He was beginning to feel like a goldfish in a bowl surrounded by bored cats.

After two minutes, he couldn't take it anymore. He stood up and crossed the hall.

"Margaret –"

"Yes, Mr. Adversego? Oh – I'm sorry – Frank?"

"Would you point me towards Ms. Addams's office?"

"Of course. Go this way and turn left at the end. Her office is right next to Mr. Cronin's."

"Great, thanks."

He hurried down the corridor, turned the corner, and brought himself up short outside Addams's office. She was sitting, erect and brow furrowed, at a desk bare of anything except a telephone, computer screen, keyboard, and mouse. Periodically, her fingers exploded into a flurry of percussive keystrokes.

Frank bucked up his courage and tapped lightly on the glass wall next to her open door. Addams kept typing.

He tapped harder, and this time, Addams' head swiveled toward him, like an owl reacting to the sound of possible prey.

"Ah, excuse me, Ms. Addams. But do you have a minute?"

Addams looked at her watch, frowned, and grudgingly conceded she did.

"Yes, Mr. Adversego?"

Frank walked in and stood in front of her desk, feeling like a misbehaving student sent to the principal's office.

"Look," he began, "I appreciate the great office. But it doesn't make sense for me to be up here when the IT department is fifty floors downstairs. Most of what I'll need to do will involve the people and the equipment down there. So, how about giving me a place to work on the IT floor instead?"

Addams paused and considered his request. Frank certainly didn't look the part of an executive, and that offended her sense of propriety. She'd already decided to tell visitors Frank was a second-career intern if she couldn't avoid passing him in the hallway. Parking him downstairs with the rest of the disheveled IT mob would solve that problem most of the time.

"Very well. You'll still need the office up here, but let me see what I can do. I'll get back to you."

Frank found himself staring at Addams' ear as her head rotated back to the computer position.

"Great – thanks," he mumbled. He caught himself backing away and turned around to complete his retreat. Now what? Return to his office and fidget until someone arrived to unlock his computer? He took his time getting a cup of coffee on the way.

When he returned, Margaret caught his eye. "Oh – Frank. I have Ms. Addams on hold for you."

"Thanks. I'll take it here." She handed him the phone.

"Hi, Ms. Addams. Frank here."

"Someone from the IT department will be there momentarily to show you downstairs."

"Thanks. I appreciate the quick help."

"My pleasure," she said brightly. For the first time, he detected a positive note in her voice.

Before his backside reached his desk chair, Frank saw a portly, middle-aged man with a sparse salt and pepper beard arrive at his office door. In the pocket of his wrinkled shirt was a vinyl protector holding two pens and a mechanical pencil. Frank felt a rush of relief surge through his body. It was one of his own tribe.

"Frank Adversego?"

Frank stood up. "That's right."

"Hi. I'm Herb Fishbone, from IT. If you're ready, I'll take you downstairs."

Frank was more than ready. "Great! Thanks. Maybe you can show me around the department, too?"

"Sure. Happy to."

Frank heaved a sigh of relief as the elevator doors closed behind him, his cruel sentence of executive floor incarceration now largely commuted. They might be paying him a lot but not enough to live in a fishbowl.

When the doors reopened, it was as if they had been transported to a different building. No expensive carpets or glass walls here. There were almost no interior walls at all. Just a sea of cubicles from side to side and end to end. It felt great to be home again.

* * *

Ryan Clancy set the report aside and stared thoughtfully at nothing in particular. So, First Manhattan had hired someone named Frank Adversego to keep an eye on the BankCoin software. The name sounded familiar.

The special FBI investigations unit Clancy led was barely three months old, created in the wake of a growing number of cryptocurrency thefts. He'd been struggling to put a team together ever since. The technology was brand-new, so talent was scarce. And the private sector was paying triple what the government did. In most cases, the best he could do was establish liaison relationships with cryptocurrency projects and exchanges and hope they'd share what they should. It was not ideal.

Last week, the Department of the Treasury had made it even less so. BankCoin, they informed him, was now on the list of "critical infrastructure" covered by a standing presidential directive. Would the FBI be willing to coordinate with Treasury in protecting it?

The FBI would. More specifically, it was willing to add protecting BankCoin to Clancy's already over-long list of responsibilities. The higher-ups left it to him to decide what that meant in an operational sense, and he was still working that out. Should he invite Adversego in for a chat? Better check the FBI's records first to see what they had to say.

Hmm. Adversego first showed up on the Bureau's radar screen by pulling off a cybersecurity coup, thwarting a North Korean nuclear attack plot. All well and good. But then he co-wrote a best seller about it, and a lot of people at the FBI thought he could have made the Bureau look better.

Hmm again. Then he headed off efforts to hack the last presidential election. When the news leaked out, his co-author wrote another book, and this time definitely made the FBI appear inept. He titled the new book *The Lafayette Campaign* and in it he chronicled how Adversego saved the day in spite of the clumsy efforts of government agents. According to the author, Frank refused to be interviewed. But how could you believe that?

The file also said Adversego had a well-known independent streak. And there were unresolved questions concerning his son-in-law. Those related to a barely thwarted attack launched by an extremist group a few years back where once again Adversego played a key role. Clancy kept reading, shaking his head. This guy was like a Teflon-coated bad luck charm. Just a month ago, he was part of a CIA project that blew up. Once again, no one laid any blame at his door. But still.

Clancy walked to the window of his office. Across Pennsylvania Avenue was the anonymous, neoclassical facade of the FBI's old home in the RFK Building. He wished he'd had a chance to work there. It looked like every other federal triangle building of the same era, and in his business, it was better to blend in.

So, no, he decided, asking Adversego in wasn't an option. Even if he wasn't responsible for the botched-up CIA operation, it wouldn't do for his visit to be memorialized in Clancy's calendar. But on the other hand, the BankCoin platform was as big a target as a terrorist or foreign government could hope for. If someone hacked it, everyone would blame the Bureau for letting it happen, and he'd be the guy in the spotlight. If Adversego discovered anything, Clancy would want to know about it before it turned into something serious.

He made up his mind. Adversego worked for the bank with primary responsibility for BankCoin's security. The bank's management should be happy to assign someone on Adversego's team to communicate with Clancy. If he or she was like most people, they'd be a bit awed by the chance to work with the FBI. That usually made it easy to get them to agree to keep things quiet.

He told his administrative assistant to find out who to contact at the bank, and she connected him with Audrey Addams.

* * *

Ryan Clancy wasn't the only one who noticed the press release. *So, the other side has recruited the great Frank Adversego*, Crypto thought. The same guy who had played a key role in defeating some of the most potentially spectacular cybersecurity attacks of all time. So much the better. Without worthy opponents, victory couldn't be as sweet.

Still, having a skilled adversary increased the chance of failure. He'd need to give this new development some thought.

Yes, a voice said. *Yes, indeed you must.*

Chapter 3

You Want Some Fries
with Those Pies?

T HERE WAS A knock at Frank's new office door on the IT floor. It was Hank
Taylor, the BankCoin project manager.

"So – you ready to see the fusion room?"

"You bet!" Frank said. He'd been looking forward to this. "Fusion room" was
a name borrowed from the military. It referred to a highly sophisticated command
center set up to monitor and defend against attacks launched from anywhere
against a global network. Every major bank and payment card system had one now.

Frank followed Taylor down the hall to a steel door with a two-slot card reader
and a keypad.

"Okay," Taylor said. "So, there's no elevator stop for the fusion room, which is
one floor down. It's completely sealed off except for this single door and a couple
of one-way fire exits to the floor below it. Your card is already coded for entry, but
you'll need to come up with a unique password for fusion room entry only. That
takes two cards to set."

Taylor slid his security card into the top slot, entered his code, poked the hash key, added several more numbers, and pushed the hash key one more time. "Okay. Your turn."

Frank put his own card in the second slot, thought for a minute, and typed in a password. "All set," he said.

"Great." Taylor pressed the hash key one last time and removed his card. "You're all set. But we can only go through one at a time; an alarm will go off otherwise. You go first."

Frank did as instructed. The door clicked, and he stepped through into a cement-walled stairwell that only went down. When Taylor joined him, they clattered down a flight of steel steps and turned into a windowless room. Frank guessed it took up most of the floor. The entire space was filled with computer engineers sitting at terminals. Here and there, knots of them talked and pointed at wall-mounted whiteboards.

"Welcome to BankCoin Security Central, aka the fusion room," Taylor said. "From here, we have access to every system hosting a copy of BankCoin anywhere in the world. It's our job to know it if one of those systems is successfully hacked. Needless to say, there'll be hell to pay if we screw up."

"Focuses the mind, doesn't it?" Frank said.

"Indeed, it does. That's why we hired most of our senior personnel away from fusion rooms run by Homeland Security and CYBERCOM, the US military's central cybersecurity force. You'll find that most of what goes on here has a kind of military flavor to it. That's deliberate. We want people to feel like we're the last line of defense against terrible threats, because that's what we are. Based on past experience with financial networks, we expect we'll be fielding over a quarter million attacks a day – that's about one every three seconds."

Frank gave a low whistle. "That's quite a pounding," he said.

"Not when you consider the value of the target," Taylor said, "or the number of criminals in the business. Last year, cybercrooks made off with almost a half a billion dollars. And that's before you count cryptocurrency thefts."

"There's an awful lot of people here," Frank said, scanning the room. "Are you fully staffed?"

"Yup. Everything is in place for network-wide monitoring when we go live next week. We're tracking over three hundred major banks, so everybody you see here is scurrying around doing final testing."

"What's behind that door at the end?" Frank asked.

"Our next stop. That's where we have our simulated battle space."

"Cool!" Frank said.

Taylor used his card to unlock the door and flipped on the lights inside. Large digital displays surrounded the room, mounted high up on the walls. Taylor sat down at a terminal, and soon the screens began flickering into life. Many displayed maps, each showing a separate continent or region. Others showed various types of data, all graphically presented.

"Wow!" Frank said. "You'd think we were in the War Room in Washington."

"Yeah," Taylor said. "That's deliberate, too. Those big pew-pew maps are there to add realism when we run simulated attacks."

"'Pew-pew?'" Frank asked, frowning.

"Yeah. Like the sound laser guns used to make in old video games. You know: *'Pew! Pew!'*"

Frank laughed. "That's great. So, what do they show?"

It was Taylor's turn to laugh. "Most of them, nothing. Just a bunch of meaningless lights shooting around the world as if something important was happening."

"Because?"

"Because it impresses the hell out of the suits. We run tests and imagined attacks all the time in the big room with our guys and the techies from the other banks. But the bank execs sit in here when we run a massive attack scenario. Those exercises can go on for hours – sometimes, we simulate systems going down in dozens of countries. You see those phones over there? Professional actors playing journalists, regulators, and other bank managers ring those off the hook to build pressure.

"In the middle of all that commotion, the execs have to make really tough decisions. Someone might walk in from the other room, for example, and ask whether they can pitch a compromised member bank over the rail in order to protect the rest. Some execs make pretty good calls, and some make really lousy ones. Afterwards, we evaluate and critique their performance so, hopefully, they'll make better decisions when the real thing happens."

"I'd like to be a fly on the wall for one of those exercises," Frank said.

"I expect you will," Taylor said. "But not just a fly."

* * *

Frank assumed – correctly – that his arrival on the security floor of the bank was not particularly welcome. The Chief Technical Officer – or CTO – had already assembled a very capable group of experts to manage BankCoin cybersecurity. Frank could imagine them wondering why Benson Cronin suddenly decided to appoint someone from the outside to look over their shoulders. Frank found himself wondering the same thing.

The CTO told Frank he'd instructed Taylor to do whatever it took to make the arrangement work. Happily, it seemed Taylor had taken that directive in stride.

Toward the end of Frank's first day of work, Taylor had invited him out for a beer. Over their third one, he delivered his own message: don't make me look bad, and I won't make you look bad. If that works for you, we'll get along just fine. Frank assured him it did, and so far, they had.

Over the days that followed, Frank tried to learn as much as he could without getting in the way or passing judgment on anything. He was impressed with what he saw and found little to criticize.

* * *

Crypto decided that today he would learn more about First Manhattan's new hire, Frank Adversego. It was a name Crypto had been aware of for years. Who in the world of cybersecurity wasn't?

He soon discovered his subject did not fit the profile of a self-promotional technology rock star. No provocative, widely read blog; no highly paid speaking engagements; no nothing, really. The only exception was a co-authored, best-selling, true-life thriller relating how he'd thwarted a North Korean plot to set off a nuclear war between the US and Russia. Beyond that, all Crypto could find were random facts in articles about other attacks Adversego had helped prevent. The cybersecurity investigator must be something of a recluse, Crypto decided. Hard to fault someone for that.

Intriguingly, Crypto couldn't find any evidence Adversego had worked full time for anyone in years. Why then had he taken the offer from First Manhattan? Crypto shrugged and bought Adversego's book, as well as another called *The Lafayette Campaign*, written by Adversego's earlier co-author, describing a failed attempt to steal the last US presidential election.

* * *

It made no difference now where Frank was – at home, on the train, or in his much less lavish office on the fifteenth floor. If he was awake – and sometimes even when he was asleep – he was completely immersed in the blockchain. Day by day, he studied its origins, its evolution, and, most importantly, the many ways in which blockchains had already been successfully attacked.

But digging deeper didn't make it clear to him why the blockchain had such an extraordinary appeal to some people. Or why its fans had such a love affair with quirky jargon: in the alternative world inhabited by blockchain aficionados, you encountered *whales* and *bagholders*, used *dapps* instead of apps, solved problems by *sharding*, and made money when your crypto investments *mooned*. And you didn't hold cryptocurrency, you *hodl* it – that one was the result of a drunk-texted typo that caught on. Moreover, if you were a true believer, you would hodl on to your cryptocurrency no matter what. Even when its value was spiraling down the toilet.

Frank already knew an almost religious fervor drove many blockchain proponents. As he spent more time on the Reddit pages where the most zealous advocates hung out, he decided some of them were just plain possessed.

Indeed, the story arc of the blockchain recalled the rise of many religions. In 2008, an unknown developer calling himself Satoshi Nakamoto emerged on the web as the global financial system lurched perilously close to collapse. There, he posted a nine-page white paper describing a computer network capable of supporting the transfer of economic value without involving a bank or the use of an existing currency. Nakamoto never revealed any details about his personal life in any of his many electronic communications. A few years later, after "bitcoin" – the cryptocurrency he created – became a reality, he sank beneath the surface of the web as suddenly and mysteriously as he had appeared.

To this day, no one knew who the enigmatic cryptocurrency prophet was or where he might be now. Was Nakamoto in fact Japanese as his name suggested? Perhaps he was really a woman? Or even a secret cabal of anarchists obsessed with replacing the crumbling financial system? There were plenty of theories, but no answers. And though bitcoin enthusiasts yearned for the return of their crypto-messiah, he, she, or they never appeared again.

Frank became dimly aware of a loud rapping sound. He looked up and realized someone was outside his office. He wondered how long they'd been there.

When he opened the door, he instinctively stepped back, confronted as he was by a pair of eyes so wide-open that the great, dark pupils in their centers suggested hazelnuts stuck in marshmallows. Two sandy eyebrows embellished them like monochromatic rainbows. And below, as if reluctant to interfere, a set of rimless spectacles rode far down a long, thin nose.

"This is still a good time?" the owner of the eyes asked.

Frank wondered what time it was and then realized it didn't matter. He had no idea who the guy was or what he was there for.

"You wanted a briefing on the BankCoin project, yes?" his wide-eyed visitor added.

"Right!" Frank said, remembering now. "Yes! Come on in and have a seat." He took in the rest of the guy's appearance as he sat down: tall, lean, maybe forty-five years old. Instead of normal office attire, he wore a European soccer team jersey, thin-leg jeans, and long, black pointy shoes. But that was to be expected. This guy was a serious coder and an open source software hotshot to boot. He could wear whatever he wanted.

"So, I'm Dirk Magnus," Frank's visitor said, easing himself into a chair. He had a slight accent Frank couldn't place. "I'm the bank's lead developer on the BankCoin project. And you are the new blockchain security guy and also Vijay Patel's replacement on the BankCoin Foundation board of directors." It was a statement rather than a question, delivered in a curt voice.

"That's right," Frank said. "I just found out this morning I was replacing Vijay, so anything you can tell me would be a big help."

"I can do that," Magnus replied, his eyes locked on Frank's. "Please tell me what you already know about the BankCoin Foundation."

Frank shifted uneasily in his chair. The guy's gaze was extraordinary. Frank felt like he was pinned down by two searchlights in the no man's land between hostile forces.

"I know it's a nonprofit foundation formed to support BankCoin development. Also, that First Manhattan organized it about a year ago and that it's funded by members that include all the major banks plus many of the biggest technology vendors. But that's about it."

"That is not much, but it is all as you say, yes," Magnus said. "Where should I start?"

"How about briefing me on where the software came from to begin with?"

"Okay," Magnus said, "So, the answer is from the same person who runs the project, Günter Schwert. About a year and a half ago, he posted on GitHub the first copy of what is now BankCoin. Very impressive for one person to create such a large and complex piece of code. He named that version Venice, and we technical folks liked it a lot."

Frank had already checked out the BankCoin code on the web. Like most collaboratively developed software, it was hosted at a site called GitHub. Anyone could post code there and see if others took an interest in it. To date, more than sixty million programs had been uploaded to the platform and tens of millions of developers visited the site regularly.

"How come Venice?" Frank asked.

"When he posted the code, Schwert recalled that Venice is one of the Italian cities where banking as we know it first evolved. Anyway, Venice picked up support quite quickly in the developer community."

"What was the appeal?" Frank asked. "There were other financial blockchains by then."

"Venice solves many problems bitcoin and most other blockchains have, like poor capacity and speed. The bitcoin software allows a new block to be added every ten minutes, and a block can only contain so many transactions – usually about seventeen hundred. This is pathetic. A major payment card system like Visa can process sixty *thousand* transactions in the same amount of time. So, the banking system could never use the bitcoin platform to replace existing systems. Also, Schwert's architecture is most elegant. That attracted a lot of the best talent."

"Who does he work for?" Frank asked.

"No idea."

"But you work with him, right?"

"Yes, of course." Magnus sniffed. "But this does not mean I've met him. Everything is done online. And who cares? Schwert is brilliant."

Frank cared, but that could wait. "Okay," he said, "how about the rest of the top programmers? Do they all work for banks?"

"No. As I said, word spread that Venice was much better than any of the other blockchains. Once the banks became interested, even more programmers started contributing code. For sure, developers from most of the big banks are involved. But like every other really successful open source project, this one operates as a meritocracy. Anybody can offer to contribute code, and the best developers rise to the top. It does not matter who they work for. Some of the great ones are independent programmers."

"Why do they get involved?" Frank already knew the usual answer, but he wanted to confirm it applied to the BankCoin project, too   .

"Status, mostly. As with Linux, getting recognized as a top BankCoin developer makes you a big deal in the software development community."

"And very employable as well," Frank prompted.

Magnus blinked several times. "Yes, this also is true. With all the banks joining, good BankCoin developers are in great demand."

"Does the meritocracy apply to the Technical Steering Committee, too?" Frank asked, referring to the small group of developers that made all the important technical decisions.

"Again, of course. Several TSC members do not work for member banks or technology companies."

"Got it," Frank said. "So, let's talk about the code itself. Where do things stand there?"

"So far, we have made two major releases since Schwert posted the first version to GitHub. The last version was otherwise ready to go live but needed further work to handle a full volume of transactions. Schwert calls this release London –"

"Okay – I got it. Also, the name of a financial center."

"Yes," Magnus said. "May I continue now?"

"Sorry."

"So," Magnus said. "We have been cleaning this third release up and testing for weeks. It is now almost ready to go." Magnus's eyes somehow managed to open even wider. "Unless things slip, the banks will transition over to it next week."

"What's that version called?"

"Manhattan, of course," Magnus said.

By the time Magnus left, Frank felt reasonably well grounded in the history of the Foundation and BankCoin. But he hadn't learned much at all about Schwert, and his interest was very much piqued. Either there wasn't much of interest to be told about the project leader or Magnus just didn't care. Frank typed Schwert's name into Wikipedia. But all he found were a few references to him on the BankCoin topic page. One of those mentions noted that Schwert was an early bitcoin "miner." Under Nakamoto's system, bitcoins only came into existence when someone solved a difficult computer-generated problem. The first person to do so was paid a set number of bitcoins as a reward. That process came to be called mining, as if a bitcoin was a precious metal obtainable only through the expenditure of great effort.

There weren't many miners back then, and each was paid thousands of bitcoins when a block of transactions she tendered was accepted and added to the blockchain. Not that they were worth anything at first. What value did a bitcoin have if no one would accept it in payment for anything? It was another year before someone did for the first time, accepting ten thousand bitcoins from a Florida miner in exchange for two large Papa John's pizzas, delivered. The faithful still celebrated May twenty-second as Bitcoin Pizza Day.

Frank opened up a cryptocurrency tracking site. *Wow.* Those ten thousand bitcoins would be worth thirty million dollars today! And at bitcoin's all-time high, their owner could have cashed them in for one hundred fifty million dollars. Frank went back to the BankCoin Wikipedia page and saw Schwert was believed to be a bitcoin millionaire. Lucky for him. He must not have been fond of pizza.

* * *

Frank felt his phone vibrate. It was a text from Marla.

>*Did you see they're going to make a movie out of The Lafayette Campaign? Isn't that cool!?!*

Frank stared at his phone. No! It wasn't the least bit cool! It was bad enough his role in stopping the election hacking had become public, and worse yet, that his co-author had written a book about it without Frank's cooperation or blessing. Worst of all — until now, that is — the writer had concocted all kinds of melodramatic nonsense to fill in the blanks whenever his sources came up dry. Now a scriptwriter was going to take a crack at the story?

Frank clicked on the link from Marla's text and groaned. There were the dreaded words he feared he'd find: "Based on a true story" – meaning the scriptwriter would rely on the facts only when they were exciting and make up the rest.

His phone vibrated again.

>*I'm thinking Nicolas Cage to play you. What do you think?*

Frank thought he'd turn his phone off and leave it that way.

Chapter 4

Heads, You Lose, and Tails, the Banks Win

F RANK WAS FINISHING his lunch and a scan of the news when a headline caught his eye. It read *Your Bitcoin or Your Life*.

A pop-up alert opened on his computer, breaking his concentration. It was almost time for his call with Vijay Patel, the guy he was replacing on the BankCoin Foundation board. Okay.

He went back to the article. Apparently, cryptocurrency thefts were now occurring in the physical world, too. In each case, people foolish enough to brag about making a killing in a cryptocurrency were targeted. Typically, they answered their doors late at night to find armed men threatening to kill them unless they transferred hundreds of thousands, or even millions, of dollars' worth of cryptocurrency to the thieves' anonymous, untraceable, accounts. How about that? The perfect crime.

Frank shook his head. Everyone kept confusing ledger accuracy with system security. Just because multiple copies of a database existed didn't make it harder for a thief to steal from a digital wallet. Or any easier to get the money back after they did. Developers had made plenty of mistakes in creating cryptocurrency exchanges and the wallets where alt coins – i.e., electronic tokens used as alternatives to traditional currency – were stored, and thieves had exploited them to steal hundreds of millions of dollars' worth of cyber currency. A non-bank blockchain-based ecosystem might be secure someday, but that day hadn't arrived yet, at least as far as Frank was concerned.

The ringing of his phone startled him. "Hello?" he said.

"Hi, Frank. Vijay here. Hey – thanks for taking over the BankCoin Foundation board seat on so little warning. It seems like every time I blink the bank's doing another reorganization."

"Sure. No problem," Frank said.

"So," Patel said, "let me give you a quick overview. As you know, there are millions of open source projects out there but only a couple hundred with lots of corporate support. The big, well-funded ones have boards of directors to take care of the business side of things and a developer committee that calls the technical shots. That's the setup at the BankCoin Foundation, too, where we call the developer group the Technical Steering Committee.

"On the participation side, the Foundation has several membership levels. First Manhattan's a platinum member – that's the top tier – along with fifteen other companies, mostly banks but also some technology vendors. The five hundred thousand bucks we pay annually to be a platinum member buys us a guaranteed board seat. On top of that, platinum members have to commit two of their best programmers to work full-time on the project. All in, that sets us back well over a million a year after you take salary, bonus, benefits, and travel into account. So, you can see how important the bank thinks it is to keep a close eye on how the BankCoin sausage gets made."

"Any reason beyond wanting to be sure we end up with good code?" Frank asked.

"Actually, yes," Patel said. "We think there's no doubt every transaction in the future is going to take place on somebody's blockchain network. The question is whose. Will the banks be in the driver's seat making lots of money, or will they be on the sidelines, watching someone else rake it in? Plus, First Manhattan wants to be sure BankCoin is the only global banking blockchain."

"Why so?" Frank asked.

"Well, profit, of course. We'll make two basis points – that's two hundredths of a cent – every time a dollar changes hands on the BankCoin network. That's not much per dollar, but we're talking about a heck of a lot of dollars – a trillion a month pretty soon. That translates into almost two and a half billion dollars a year for First Manhattan."

"I know we manage security for BankCoin," Frank asked. "Are we doing anything else for that fee?"

"Sure. For starters, we made a big cash investment setting the whole thing up. And we've had ten of our best developers working on the software from the beginning. We also volunteered Dirk to be the chair of the Technical Steering Committee. A lot of the code that Schwert didn't write, one of our employees did. For the last six months, about half our BankCoin staff have been working – and they will keep working – full-time spotting vulnerabilities and fixing them. That sounds high until you remember the BankCoin Foundation keeps adding new code. We also fix vulnerabilities other banks find and tell us about on a confidential basis. When we do, we privately send a patch out to every other bank so no one ever knows there was a problem that could have been exploited. We'll only get one chance to move the banking world over to BankCoin, so we've got to get it right."

"What's happens if we screw up?" Frank asked.

"Well, think how this technology changes the marketplace," Patel said. "If the blockchain solves the problems of security, transparency, and speed without using a bank, who needs us? We realized that if we couldn't stop the blockchain, we better make sure we own it."

"Got it," Frank said, "But will people be comfortable switching over to a blockchain?"

"Why not?" Patel said. "Look what happened to stock brokerages. Once upon a time, if you wanted to invest, you had to use a stockbroker, because only brokerage firms had seats on the stock exchanges. The brokers loved that, because they could charge a hefty trading fee. They also gave advice, wrote research reports, and maintained retail offices all over the place so you could meet with your broker. All of which took a lot of money to support.

"But once the internet came along, some smart entrepreneurs figured out most people didn't care about the extra trappings any more. So, companies like eTrade built slick online platforms anyone could use to buy and sell securities really cheaply and without ever talking to a human being."

"So, I guess you're right," Frank said. "If I was launching a financial blockchain startup, I'd build a consumer app that looks just like the online banking software everyone's already using."

"Exactly," Patel said. "First Manhattan realized it needed to kill its old business model before someone else did. You've got to give Ben Cronin credit for seeing that and selling it to the board; that couldn't have been easy. Of course, brand-new startups are trying to do the same thing, but we've got advantages – our existing customers, our IT department, lots of regulatory expertise, lobbyists out the wazoo, longstanding relationships with other banks, and so on. In theory we should beat any startup that comes along, no matter how much financing it has. But if we don't do it fast and do it right, we can still blow it."

"Okay, thanks," Frank said. "I get the picture."

"Good," Patel said. "So back to my overview. The board of directors makes the strategic decisions, like how to promote the BankCoin platform and how to satisfy the regulators. It also takes care of the nuts and bolts stuff, like approving a budget and making sure the bills get paid, and, maybe most importantly, keeping the developers happy."

"And are they?" Frank asked.

"Ah, well, that's always an interesting question, isn't it?" Patel said.

"How so?"

"Hmm," Patel paused. "So, you're a developer, aren't you?"

"Sure. Why?"

"So, how to ask delicately? What's your opinion of the emotional maturity of the best developers you know?"

"Oh. Okay. So, you've got personality issues among developers?"

"That would be an understatement. Sometimes, it's a challenge keeping them focused on the current release instead of setting off flame wars or going down rat holes on things that don't matter."

"What about Schwert?"

"Oh, if it weren't for him, we'd be sunk. The guy's a rock. Always on message, always getting things back on track when they get derailed."

"Have you met him?" Frank asked.

"Me? No. There's no in-person interaction between the board and the developers. Or even among the guys who write the code, for that matter. But that's okay. Anyway, let's switch over to the Manhattan release. The banks have been testing it on a virtual platform for a month now, and we're satisfied it's stable. At midnight this Friday, we'll start running live transactions on it in parallel to our existing processes. If all goes well through Wednesday, every bank will shut down its old system and run all new business on the blockchain."

"That's a big step," Frank said.

"You bet! And it better go smoothly."

"But if we're going to have a problem, better sooner than later, right?" Frank asked.

"Well, I guess. One of the beauties of the blockchain is, no matter what happens, we could always go back to our old systems. Every transaction would be recorded on hundreds of copies of the same blockchain on bank computers all over the world. But it would be a nightmare."

"I bet," Frank said. "Still, it's awfully new technology. Doesn't that make you nervous?"

"Heck yes!" Patel said. "But it's too late to second-guess the decision now. Our best estimate is, next week, ninety-five percent of all international banking transactions will be completed on the BankCoin platform. And almost all the domestic ones, too."

* * *

Frank settled into his first-class seat waiting for his short flight to Washington, DC to begin. He wondered how much more the bank had paid for his wider armrests. This wasn't what he was used to, and it made him uncomfortable. But he reminded himself, if traveling in comfort was what it took to endow his grandchildren's education, well, he'd have to suck it up. Along with the scotch the flight attendant was handing him just now.

He turned and looked out the window. There was a storm in the distance; a towering thunderhead soared miles into the air behind the Manhattan skyline. The crown of the massive cloud mass gleamed eerily white, but its nether regions were a dusky orange, illuminated by the jagged bolts of lightning flickering inside. The jet-black skyscrapers silhouetted against them made him think of the towers and parapets of a medieval city, its gates barricaded against an approaching barbarian horde.

That image matched his mood. Patel's prediction had made a deep impression on Frank: ninety-five percent of all global banking transactions would soon be running on technology that until a few years ago was mostly used to complete illegal drug sales. Hackers had already made off with ten percent of all the cryptocurrency that ever existed! What were the banks thinking?

Well, he'd found out the answer to that question from Patel. For five hundred years, banks had grown wealthy by playing the middleman, always keeping something for themselves when money changed hands. Some financial intermediaries were even worse. When some poor immigrant sent a hundred hard-earned dollars home to his family in Honduras, Western Union charged him as much as ten percent. It was highway robbery. But there was nothing the immigrant could do, because the banks owned the highway. At least until now. With a blockchain, that same transaction could theoretically cost less than a penny. That made working for First Manhattan seem almost virtuous – assuming they kept their fees low. And it sounded like they would, if only in their own self-interest.

The plane started rolling, and the pilot told the flight attendants to take their seats.

The big surprise was that the banks were being so realistic, unlike all the businesses that had sat and watched as internet-based startups shoved them out of the way. If the banks played their cards wisely and had a bit of luck, they'd likely hang in there in the center of the financial world.

Well, so be it, Frank thought, as the plane swung around onto the runway. As usual, Wall Street banks would take the world wherever they wanted to, whether it was good for humanity or not. Would the blockchain prove to be a good direction? Who knew? The financial powers that be had dragged the nation into a recession or worse about every ten years for as long as Frank could remember.

And probably always would, he thought, as the plane rumbled down the runway, gathering speed, until it lifted off and thundered into the troubled sky.

Chapter 5

Happy Birthday to You!

"OPEN IT!" MARLA said over the phone.

"Don't you want me to wait till the next time you're over here?"

"No, today's your birthday, so go ahead."

Frank gave the package a gentle shake but heard nothing.

"I hope you didn't get me anything alive again."

"Well, not exactly. And anyway, you like Thor."

"Okay, I do. But I'm not interested in managing a zoo here."

"Quit whining and open it."

"Okay, okay." He removed the wrapping paper and frowned. "A bird feeder? Why a bird feeder?"

"Because you always got a kick out of Julius visiting you on your balcony. Maybe he'll come back if he sees the feeder. And if not, there must be lots of other birds in your neighborhood."

He did miss Julius. After the crow flew away with Frank's thumb drive, he'd never seen the bird again. So why not?

"Well, that's true. This is very thoughtful of you. I'll figure out a way to put it up this afternoon."

"Great. Let me know what kinds of birds show up. Love you."

"Will do, and you too." He hung up and took the bird feeder out of the box. It looked like you could either mount it on something or hang it up. He walked outside and found it clamped easily onto the railing. Back inside, he ordered a ten-pound sack of mixed bird seed online and promptly forgot about his present.

* * *

Two days later, he left for San Francisco and his first meeting as the bank's representative on the BankCoin Foundation board. Ever vigilant against the threat of a chatty seatmate on such a long flight, he donned his headphones before boarding.

But despite his precautions and downward gaze after he took his seat, someone nudged his shoulder. Just an accidental bump, he hoped. But then he was poked again. Absentmindedly, Frank turned and found himself looking into the bulging eyes of Dirk Magnus.

Frank grudgingly took off his earphones. "What takes you to San Francisco?"

"The same as you, of course. The BankCoin Foundation board meeting." Magnus saw Frank frowning. "The chair of the Technical Steering Committee is given an automatic board seat," he continued. "But not on behalf of their employer – to represent the developer community."

"Ah – got it," Frank said. "I guess I've heard of that practice."

"Yes," Magnus said, in his usual monotone. "For all my past sins, this is my reward."

"I don't follow you," Frank said.

"Where to begin?" Magnus replied.

Drat! Frank thought. *I set myself up for that.* He looked longingly at the headphones in his lap.

"First," Magnus continued, "I have the same duties as any other board member. But the developers think I am supposed to be their advocate to the board regarding every real and imagined issue, yes? Second, board meetings are confidential. I cannot share anything I hear with the other developers, but they refuse to believe that. And last, I am obliged to support each board decision whether I agree with it or not."

"Okay," Frank said. "Makes sense. How bad has it been?"

"Perhaps not as bad as I make it sound; I sometimes exaggerate a little. And it is amusing to see how willing the mighty directors are to kiss the butts of the technical folks. You would think the managers worked for the elite programmers rather than the other way around."

"Why's that?"

"Well, in any brand-new technology, the top programmers are in big demand. The best developers can name their price. They can even refuse to work on a project if they do not approve of it."

"What do you mean, not 'approve' of it?"

"Well, for instance: at the first BankCoin Foundation board meeting, an executive VP from one of the largest IT companies in the world said if the board did not pick the right open source license for the BankCoin code, he could never get his developers to work on the project. And he was probably right."

"Interesting," Frank said. "By the way, if you don't mind my asking, where did you grow up? I've been trying to figure out your accent and can't place it."

"Denmark. But I have lived in this country many years now. Will you excuse me? I have much to catch up on."

"Of course," Frank said, as they each donned their headphones. He was learning to identify with this guy, quirks and all.

* * *

After the board meeting, the directors adjourned to an expensive restaurant for dinner. As the Golden Gate Bridge bisected the blood-red, sinking sun, Frank settled into his seat and gratefully accepted the glass of wine offered to him by a waiter. It had been a long day in the company of businessmen he didn't know discussing things of which he was largely ignorant. Luckily, he'd been able to grab a chair at the end of the table next to the most taciturn person on the board. But there was one thing he wanted to talk about with his seat mate.

"So, what's Schwert like?" Frank asked.

Dirk Magnus turned his bulging eyes in Frank's direction, clearly disappointed that Frank had chosen conversation where silence would have sufficed.

"As I have said before," he replied curtly, "He is a brilliant programmer."

"Right, but what's he like beyond that?" Frank pushed.

"I would not know. We communicate exclusively by email, and we only discuss BankCoin when we do. Why does this matter?"

Because I don't know whether to trust him Frank thought. But instead he said, "Why? Doesn't it seem a bit weird to you that the financial wellbeing of the world relies on someone no one's ever met or spoken to?"

"I have also not met nor spoken with the US president," Magnus said.

"But you've seen and heard him. You know he exists. That's a big difference."

"Do I? The images and sounds you refer to could be computer-generated. It is very easy to do."

"Oh, come on now, Dirk. You're just being difficult."

"I do not think so. But let us agree the individual I would see on television, if I watched television, would in fact be someone given the name Henry Yazzi at birth. How would I know he believed what he was saying, or intends to do what he promises he will do? He is a politician, and a politician will say anything. And even if, by coincidence and as a result of self-interest, he does believe and intend to do what he says, the Congress must vote for it. So, how much difference does it make if I could shake his hand?"

"Well, it's a heck of a lot better than not knowing whether Günter Schwert exists. You've got to agree with that."

"And yet I do not. What I can understand and admire and even change is Schwert's software. That is what matters, and that is enough. Schwert himself is an unimportant detail. What the world should care about is that his code can deliver what the world needs. And I know it will."

* * *

Josh Peabody leaned back and enjoyed his view of the heart of Silicon Valley. He'd spent a long time in the business wilderness after his partners at TrashTalk LLP had tossed him out. Eviction from the venture capital fund he'd co-founded had been the ultimate humiliation. True, his investment in a company called iBalls. com had led to a debacle of epic proportions. But hey, here in the Valley, people said failure was the best learning opportunity of all. Bless their gullible hearts, the investor community even believed that. Like they did almost any other outlandish idea you fed them.

Anyway, it was great to be back on top, and he owed it all to Satoshi Nakamoto, whoever he was. Countless startups had issued cryptocurrencies, most within the last two years. One had raised four billion dollars that way! Many of these alt coins immediately soared in value. Even some of the most ridiculous ones. His favorite nonsense coin was created to pay for dental visits. Now, there was a problem the world never knew it needed to solve with a cryptocurrency!

Yes, without Nakamoto, Peabody could never have gotten back into the game. He'd jumped on the bitcoin bandwagon early, insisting bitcoin would be the investment opportunity of the century. When he turned out to be right, at least for the time being, Peabody was able to hit the restart button on his financial career and raise another venture capital fund. At half a billion dollars, CryptoBoom! LLP wasn't one of the biggest. But all that money was earmarked for investing in the cryptocurrency companies that kept popping up like crabgrass in a negligently tended lawn.

That made Peabody a big deal again, and he was enjoying every minute of it. So far, he'd invested in twenty-two companies, some issuing alt coins and others providing everything from digital wallets to crypto market analysis to cryptocurrency trading exchanges. He hadn't had such fun, or made so much money, since the heyday of the internet bubble.

Just like then, you could make a killing on any fool scheme. He swung back to his screen and opened his favorite cryptocurrency news site to check out how this week's ICOs – initial coin offerings of new cryptocurrencies – were doing. Yup! They were doing great. He loved ICOs!

It was like the Wild West. You could sell just about anything. And until recently, you could "pump and dump," too, and get away with it. Pumping meant spreading rumors about how high a cryptocurrency would rise. The dumping part, obviously, was selling out at the top of the market before the investors wised up and the price crashed.

Was this a great time to be alive or what?

Incredibly, the Securities and Exchange Commission had taken years to decide the obvious – that anyone buying alt coins was making an investment. And therefore, that alt coin offerings should be regulated the same as offerings of stocks or bonds. Still, lots of people were ignoring that news. Others were setting up new companies in places like the Cayman Islands even though that didn't make any legal difference at all when you sold to US investors.

And, there was a silver lining to the SEC's announcement itself. Now that the regulators were watching, entrepreneurs needed advice to stay on the right side of the law. Silicon Valley lawyers and accountants were all over that and profiting handsomely. But that left plenty of room for someone to advise on the nuts and bolts of promoting ICOs – the yin of salesmanship to the yang of legal compliance.

Peabody knew he was just the person for that job. As soon as his CryptoBoom! fund was off the ground, he launched an ICO underwriting firm he named ICOBoom! He used that venture to teach startups how to set up and hype their ICOs without going over the line – or not too far over, anyway. He was making money hand over fist with ICOBoom! helping to sell the most ridiculous concepts imaginable.

And entrepreneurs were coming up with concepts more absurd than even Peabody could imagine, which was saying a lot. Still, some ideas were dynamite. Take the ICO he'd underwritten yesterday for a ten percent cash commission. He had his CryptoBoom! fund invest thirty million dollars in that one because it just couldn't fail: the new company's alt coins could only be used to make anonymous purchases of pornography. What a stroke of genius!

Peabody clicked a few more keys at the exchange site. Sure enough, his BitchCoin investment had already quadrupled in value. *Ka-ching!*

* * *

Crypto's normal reading interests ran to the drily technical and theoretical. He was pleasantly surprised, then, to find himself intrigued by the accounts of Frank Adversego's past adventures. Both books were written in the same breathless style, making it obvious Adversego had authored little, if any, of the first book. Still, it was clear he was, like Crypto, a loner; one who drew exclusively on inner resources and avoided human contact like snakes. It was also obvious Adversego's intuitive approach was fundamental to his success, allowing him to discover plots and plotters that eluded everyone else. But this knowledge brought Crypto more pain than gain. There was not enough to lead him to any actionable conclusions, but plenty to alarm the voices that were his constant companions.

* * *

Ryan Clancy read the first report from his liaison at First Manhattan and was pleased. Some of his industry contacts filed breathless, jargon-filled updates, fantasizing that they were G-Men. This message was brief and to the point. True, the point was that Frank Adversego hadn't discovered anything useful yet. But Clancy's contact hadn't taken much of his time to tell him that, and that was good enough for now.

Chapter 6

I Have Met the Enemy, and He is Fang

F RANK RETURNED HOME dead tired from San Francisco after a sleepless night on the redeye flight. Under the mailboxes in the foyer was a large package with his name on it; it was heavy, too. What could that be? He carried it upstairs and opened it in the kitchen. Oh, right. Birdseed. After he got some sleep, he filled his new feeder.

For the next several days, he looked for birds whenever he passed the door to his balcony. But no luck. No birds, and the feeder was still full. Oh well. It had been a nice thought on Marla's part.

When he returned from New York the next week, the feeder was empty. So, the birds had finally found it. Maybe Julius was back! Frank refilled the feeder and looked forward to seeing who would visit.

But the next day, the seed was untouched. He sat down where he could keep an eye on the feeder as he worked, but then he got immersed in what he was doing. When he paused to get a cup of coffee a couple hours later, he was surprised to find the feeder half empty. No birds there now, but clearly, they must have been there today. He'd have to watch more carefully. But he didn't see a single bird for the rest of the day.

The next morning, the feeder was empty. He refilled it and vowed that whatever was emptying it wouldn't escape his notice again.

But the unknown visitor eluded him anyway, leaving the feeder empty for the third time. Frank began considering a web cam.

That proved unnecessary because the mystery was solved the next day. When he woke up, he saw the butt and twitching tail of a well-fed squirrel sticking out of the feeder. Hah! Caught him in the act. Frank tapped on the window to scare the moocher away. It ignored him. He rapped harder. Same result. Then he opened the sliding door.

"Scat!"

The squirrel withdrew from the feeder and perched on its hind legs on the balcony railing, staring at Frank. Then it unleashed a long and annoyed chatter, its miniature front legs tucked up against its chest. But otherwise, it didn't move.

"I said scat!"

More irate chattering.

It wasn't until Frank took a step forward that the animal bounded off along the railing before jumping on to the ivy vines covering the wall. And there it stayed, its tail madly twitching, bawling Frank out for his lack of hospitality.

Hmm. Frank had nothing against squirrels as such, but the goal here was to attract birds, not rodents. He stepped back inside and rummaged through a closet. Yes, he did have picture-hanging wire. He returned to the balcony with a chair, unclamped the feeder, refilled it, stood on the chair, and hung the feeder from a bracket supporting his upstairs neighbor's balcony. That should do it.

He sat down and waited to see what would happen. Sure enough, the squirrel came back. It hopped onto the railing and studied the situation, cocking its head to one side. Frank felt sorry for it and went into the kitchen. It wasn't the squirrel's fault it didn't have feathers.

What else could he feed it besides seeds? He found a granola bar and broke off a few pieces, opened the slider, and tossed one toward the squirrel.

After a few moments evaluating this intriguing turn of events, the animal approached the bit of food through a halting, zigzag series of hops. At last, it seized the morsel and retreated to the safety of the vine. Frank wondered whether he could get it to eat out of his hand, the way Julius used to. He stepped slowly outside and sat down.

The answer appeared likely to be yes. He threw another piece of granola bar, and this time the squirrel ate the morsel on the spot.

Frank broke off more pieces, tossing each one a shorter and shorter distance.

By fits and starts, the miniature beast zig zagged closer. Whenever it paused, it tucked its right front paw against its chest, cocked its head to the side, and gazed up at Frank as if to ask, *Is this some kind of trick?* Soon it was close enough for Frank to see it had opposable thumbs! How cool was that?

When only a corner of the granola bar was left, Frank leaned over and held it close to the floor.

The squirrel waited for Frank to toss it forward, but Frank held fast. Eventually, it began its final approach, one halting hop at a time, its tail erect and occasionally snapping back and forth. Frank had never seen a squirrel so close up and was fascinated by everything about the animal. It had bright black eyes and extraordinarily long black whiskers, and advanced with abrupt, sure movements. Frank noticed another curious thing: its tail sported two layers of hairs: a short, thick covering and a longer, sparser set. Each long hair had a white end and a dark middle. How did an animal manage to grow hairs that changed color as they grew longer?

It was only a foot away now. Each time it stopped, it froze for a few seconds, tense, almost on tip-toe.

Now, it was only six inches away. Would it be brave enough to close the gap? It would.

"*Yow!*" Frank yelled, jumping up, his index finger streaming blood. The infernal beast scampered off, its prize secured.

Frank stomped inside and ran cold water over his bleeding digit. *Okay, you little bugger. Game on.*

The next day, the feeder was empty again.

* * *

Yes! Crypto exulted. BankCoin had just gone live!

Yes! Yes! The voice agreed. It was a very great day.

And now we will set the countdown clock, Crypto thought. He tapped a few keys and two dials appeared on his screen, a large one above a small one. Under the small one was the fraction 1/100,000. Each clock had a single hand set at the Noon position.

What does the smaller one show? The voice asked.

That is to give us an idea of pace; it will spin a hundred thousand times before the main clock completes its single circuit. Now we must be patient.

For how long? The voice asked.

Eight months, more or less. An algorithm Crypto had created would drive the clocks, taking into account how many transactions were closed on the BankCoin network, the numbers of banks and countries participating, how much money was involved, and what percentage of all transfers was being transacted in BankCoin. When the hand on the large clock completed its journey to Midnight, the time would be ripe to launch his attack. Any sooner, and the global financial system might recover too quickly for his goal to be achieved.

Eight months! That is a very long time! The voice said.

Yes, but not when compared to the ten years we have waited already. Crypto replied.

But for most of that time, no one was paying attention. Now, everyone is watching! The voice said. *It will be risky to wait so long.*

Yes, but that cannot be helped, so we must be patient. There is no choice.

Crypto looked at the faster clock, wondering how long it would be before he could detect any movement.

It would be difficult for him to be patient as well.

* * *

Frank picked up his tablet to check on the news, scowling as his Band-aid-encumbered index finger swept ineffectively across the touchscreen. Uh-oh. There'd been another breach of a cryptocurrency exchange. He started the video to find out how big it was. One of two men in suits sitting at a news desk began to speak.

"Good evening. This is your host, Fred Marx. In what may be the biggest cryptocurrency theft to date, cybercriminals have made off with over one billion dollars' worth of the Delirium alt coin. Here to tell us what this means to the cryptocurrency markets is Karl Engels, our chief financial analyst. Karl, the alt coin sector has been soaring lately. Do you think this will bring it back to earth?"

"Well, Fred, normally, the theft of a billion dollars' of something would catastrophically affect any market. But we're talking about DTs here –"

"I should tell our viewers that DT stands for Delirium Tremens, the alt coin that was hit."

"That's right, Fred. Anyway, you'd expect a meltdown after an event like this. But this is the crypto market, where it seems like nothing – and certainly not reality – can spoil the party. And after all, this kind of crime isn't new. Six months ago, over one hundred million Tabbies –"

"The alt coin issued by PerpetualKitten.com, right?"

"Right again, Fred. Tabbies worth almost four hundred million dollars were stolen. And yet, the Tabby hit a new high just eight days later."

"But Karl, don't you think this will have some sort of impact on how the other cryptocurrencies are valued?"

"Of course. All the other cryptocurrencies are up dramatically."

The news anchor shook his head.

"That doesn't make any sense."

"Sure, it does. Part of Satoshi Nakamoto's genius was to launch a currency with a set number of alt coins. Unless a majority of the bitcoin miners agree to change the software, there can never be more of that alt coin than the number Nakamoto set back in 2008. Most other cryptocurrencies are capped, too."

"But what does that have to do with the Delirium breach, Karl?"

"It's supply and demand, Fred. Don't forget, before this breach, Delirium was second only to bitcoin in total value. Now that it looks insecure, everyone's flocking to the other cryptocurrencies."

Frank closed the video. Well, it did make sense, in a crazy, world-turned-upside-down kind of way. But only if you accepted that cryptocurrencies made any sense to begin with. And he didn't. Even if you could build a totally secure system for issuing alt coins and recording transactions, people would still need electronic wallets to keep them in and exchanges to trade them on, both of which had been hacked. Or you could "spoof" – that is, pretend to be – somebody else and get someone to send their alt coins to your wallet instead. Lots of people had fallen prey to that type of scamming. Since no one could reverse a transaction once it was added to a blockchain, they were just out of luck.

And that was only the start. If cryptocurrencies were to replace regular money – "fiat currency," in the jargon of economists – stores, restaurants, gas stations, and everyone else would have to start accepting them. If they did, all the usual ways bad guys used to clean out your bank account or run up your credit card bill could be used to steal cryptocurrencies, too. Only better, because everything was so new. Software flaws would abound, and the black hat hackers usually spotted vulnerabilities before the white hat developers did.

Frank's phone buzzed, and he saw an invitation. Oh heck. Cronin had called a meeting of the cryptocurrency team for eight-thirty a.m. tomorrow. Frank had just gotten home from New York, and now he'd have to be on the six a.m. shuttle headed back.

* * *

Crypto had been pleased to see that the hand on the faster of his countdown clocks had begun to move within minutes of being activated. Two days later he could tell that the hand on the large clock had begun its stealthy approach to midnight. Soon they were both progressing in a most satisfactory fashion indeed.

Checking in on his countdown clocks became the first thing Crypto did when he arose and the last before he retired. As well as a frequent diversion in between.

Chapter 7

On Second Thought,
Make that a Double

A FTER A FEW weeks on the job, Frank was feeling diligent but unfulfilled. He was now pretty well accepted by the IT staff, mostly because he'd been careful to keep a low profile. He attended meetings of the security team but rarely spoke. Once a week, he had a half-hour sync-up meeting with Hank Taylor, the manager of the BankCoin project. Frank sensed the purpose of the brief get-togethers was to reassure Taylor that Frank wasn't undermining his own authority.

Over time, both men loosened up, and their weekly exchanges grew more productive. Frank learned Taylor was a methodical engineer dedicated to ensuring that the bank's controls were redundant, scrupulously maintained, and constantly reviewed and updated. For his part, Taylor came to realize Frank had an intuitive approach to security and often made creative suggestions not to be found in any manual of best practices.

All of which was well and good but not enough to make Frank feel particularly useful. The more impressed he became with the team, the more he felt like a useless appendage. BankCoin had been up and running for several weeks now, processing over a hundred thousand transactions a minute. Everything had gone astonishingly smoothly for such an ambitious undertaking. And the only bugs he'd found on his own were minor glitches rather than real security flaws.

But new software always had flaws that took months, or even years, to surface. He decided he needed to come at the problem from a new angle to find where they were lurking in BankCoin.

* * *

Crypto had finished both books detailing Frank's exploits and found his mind turning often now to the First Manhattan Bank employee. As it was right now while he pedaled away furiously on a stationary bicycle. He rather loathed the unforgiving machine, but found he did his best thinking in the narrow, vibrating saddle, sweat creeping down his back as he propelled himself endlessly forward into the exact same place. Better yet, for some reason the voices seemed to be unable to monitor his thinking when he was gasping for breath.

In any event, he found his preoccupation with the First Manhattan employee to be curious, given that he was only one of what must be hundreds of bank personnel, contractors and government staff focused on maintaining the security of BankCoin. So, why always focus on him, and never them?

Part of the answer, of course, was because he knew Adversego's name. But all those others would have names, too. He just hadn't bothered to find out what they were.

Crypto considered whether he'd simply adopted Adversego as a proxy for all the other foes who might stand between him and victory. That made objective sense; from time immemorial, people and societies had projected their angers and fears on representative individuals. And also, their hopes and dreams. Scape-goating and hero-worship were as much a part of human nature as were the emotions that gave rise to them.

But that didn't seem to adequately explain his preoccupation. There must be something more.

He mulled over that question for days. If Adversego was more than just the personification of the defenders of BankCoin, what unique feature was it that explained Crypto's fixation?

In the end, exertion outran inspiration. He deferred resolution of the issue until another day.

* * *

Frank settled with a grunt of relief into the town car waiting to take for him to the airport. Access to a cushy ride was one of the perks that accompanied his exalted position at the bank. It had been a long day, and he'd spent most of it in a conference room on the sixty-fifth floor. And not just with Cronin and the cryptocurrency team. For the first two hours, Horace Nukem, the executive chairman of the board of directors, had participated as well.

Nukem was a heavy hitter: a retired four-star general who'd served on the joint chiefs of staff. He'd pushed everyone hard today – especially Frank and Dirk – on whether the bank's new blockchain platform was bulletproof. Cronin almost rose out of his seat when Frank observed that nothing deployed over the internet was ever one hundred percent secure.

"While Frank, of course, is right," Cronin interrupted, "You can be sure we're doing everything humanly possible to ensure the bank's assets are secure."

"That's not good enough," Nukem replied.

"Well, if you find an alien willing to do the job, send him my way," Cronin said, giving Frank a sideways look that said, "and I'll gladly give him Frank's job."

Yeah. Frank sighed. A long day indeed. Sometimes he worried whether he really had any idea how secure the BankCoin blockchain actually was. The bank's security team continued to find and patch flaws. None big or fundamentally worrisome so far, but weaknesses nonetheless. What worried him was he had no way to tell what hadn't been found yet. The bad guys were still finding great, big flaws in twenty-year-old programs, and BankCoin was brand-new. Who knew what little monsters might be lurking in it, waiting to unleash disaster?

One commentator had nailed it when he observed, "Blockchain technology is like a proof of concept that escaped the laboratory into the wild." Not that anyone seemed to care. People in all kinds of industries were jumping on board without thinking the security concerns through. Or in many cases considering security at all. People were even ignoring some vulnerabilities everybody knew existed.

Most famously, Satoshi Nakamoto's original white paper admitted that anyone owning more than half the number of copies of the bitcoin blockchain could take over the system. Then they could reverse a transaction or steal anyone's bitcoins. That was still as true for bitcoin a decade later as it was for many other blockchains. The likelihood of such an event occurring – it even had a name: a "fifty percent attack" – was simply ignored by bitcoin enthusiasts as an inconvenient truth.

And then there was Etherium, one of the most popular cryptocurrencies in the world. Almost immediately after Ether, its alt coin, began to circulate, somebody launched a crowd-sourced venture capital fund to invest only in Etherium-based startups. The fund founders slapped together a blockchain system to manage the funds, pulling in a hundred and fifty million dollars in no time. Almost as quickly after that, someone made off with forty percent of it! More and bigger hacks of alt coins followed.

But that hadn't slowed down the cryptocurrency movement at all. *Some things would never change*, Frank sighed as the town car rolled to a stop at the edge of a fancy awning running out to the curb.

A uniformed doorman opened the door for him.

"Good evening, Mr. Adversego. I hope you've had a pleasant day."

"Sure, sure. Thanks. Hope you have, too."

"Yes, thank you, sir," the doorman said.

Frank gave a tight smile, embarrassed he'd forgotten the doorman's name again.

The two-story lobby he crossed to reach the elevator was all milky travertine, brushed aluminum, and glass. Abstract paintings in muted colors ran from floor to ceiling. Indirect lighting and soft ambient music completed the understated atmosphere of expensively modern elegance.

The elevator took him to the forty-eighth floor, where only six doors opened on to the lengthy hall.

What he could see from his bank-provided apartment was almost as impressive as the view from the management floor at work. He wasn't as high up, but that made it easier to appreciate Central Park through the glass walls of his living room. He could enjoy the same view from his bedroom, which was twice as large as the room he slept in back home. Five classic, tailored suits lived in his closet here, one for each day of the full week he never spent at the bank. Each was partnered with a matching shirt, tie, belt, and shoes, all selected from posh Fifth Avenue stores by a personal shopper under the personal direction of Audrey Addams. Frank was under strict orders from her not to be seen on the sixty-fifth floor unless he was inside one of those outfits.

He flopped on a couch he knew must have cost more than all the furniture he owned and contemplated the well-stocked credenza against the wall. Like a hotel wet bar, it was replenished daily. Unlike the hotel version, he never received a bill for what he consumed. The bank saw to that, as it did each of his other New York living expenses. As ridiculously expensive as his Big Apple apartment must be, he decided he could get used to the place so long as someone else picked up the tab. The truth was, he was starting to appreciate living somewhere that was comfortable, cleaned by someone else, and not reminiscent of a Goodwill Industries showroom.

Not forever, of course. But if the job demanded it, well, what could he do? Besides, he reminded himself, the only reason he was putting up with such outrageous luxury was for his grandkids-to-be.

He walked over to the wet bar and poured himself a shot of fifteen-year-old scotch. He'd checked its price at the liquor store around the corner. Seventy bucks a bottle! He'd never dream of paying that for a bottle of hooch, no matter how much he was earning. But he *was* learning to appreciate good scotch on somebody else's nickel. He decided he could get used to that, too. And then he added another shot to his glass.

Chapter 8

Quizzing Dirk, Gently

FRANK STARED AT his computer, looking for trends in reported cryptocurrency attacks. On his screen was a breakdown by category of every significant theft since bitcoin first erupted on to the scene. Most heists involved successful phishing exploits, which meant fooling someone into thinking an email came from a sender they knew. The email would ask the intended victim to click on a link they shouldn't or get them to send their valuable cryptocurrency to the disguised address of the criminal.

The next most common exploit involved hacking into wallets holding cryptocurrencies. Last came attacks against the exchanges where alt coins changed hands. Only rarely had an attacker successfully exploited a vulnerability in the blockchain software itself, and then the hack usually occurred early in the life of a new network, before all its bugs were worked out.

Frank tapped his fingers. Was that because blockchain architecture was as secure as its fan boys claimed? Or was it that other parts of a cryptocurrency ecosystem were so much easier to exploit? He suspected the latter, but there was no way to tell for sure.

And then there was this: sometimes it was possible to reverse the effect of an enormous theft. That was because the software of some blockchains permitted a majority of the ledger owners to agree, in effect, to a "do-over." What that meant was going back to a place in the blockchain before the crime occurred and starting again from there.

This was referred to as "forking," because it resulted in two different copies of the same blockchain – identical up to the point in time just before the theft occurred and then diverging. The branch with bogus transaction would usually be abandoned, the other would continue, and *voila*, it was as if the crime had never been committed. Messy and difficult to agree upon, to be sure, but effective. So, at least when an enormous theft occurred, there was a chance everybody would get their money back.

So, the potential security of a properly designed and executed blockchain architecture did seem strong – maybe stronger than that of the traditional banking system. With the BankCoin platform, it was even more robust: the entire global network lived on the highly protected servers of major banks, there were no third-party exchanges involved, and only participating financial institutions hosted wallets. Was he letting paranoia overcome reason? Perhaps he was looking for a fatal flaw that did not exist.

Still – what if someone *did* figure out how to hack the BankCoin software? In just its first few weeks, it had already handled a hundred times more transactions than all other blockchains combined. What an unholy mess it would be if anyone ever took it out, even for a day.

* * *

Frank stopped by Magnus's cubicle, and Dirk turned, his bug eyes training themselves on Frank's normal ones like a pair of headlights.

"Frank," he said. It was an acknowledgment, not a greeting. "What is up?"

"Would you have time today to review the BankCoin architecture with me? I'm trying to take a fresh look at it to see if there are any flaws I'm missing."

Magnus stared at Frank for a second, reminding Frank of a computer processing a particularly difficult equation. Then he blinked twice and said, "There are no flaws in BankCoin."

Frank tried again. "Well, sure, it's really secure. Still, I'm supposed to be worrying about it one way or other, so would you be able to find the time today?"

Magnus stared some more. But at last he said, "Yes. What would you like me to cover?"

"Well, that's part of the problem. I think I understand BankCoin pretty thoroughly, but I don't want to take anything for granted. Maybe I don't know what I don't know. Or worse, perhaps I think I've got something right that's actually wrong."

Magnus considered that and blinked again. "How about ten o'clock? Does that work?"

"That would be great."

"In your office?"

"Perfect."

"I'll bring Ruth."

"Ruth?"

"Yes," Magnus said, "Ruth Kim." He turned back to his computer.

Magnus walked into Frank's office on the hour and sat down without speaking. A young woman stood behind him, looking for a second chair that wasn't there. Magnus treated her as if she weren't either. She wore round, black-framed glasses and a bowl-cut hairdo. *If you put her in a Chairman Mao era tunic*, Frank thought, *she'd be a dead ringer for Honey*, Duke's ever-loyal assistant in the Doonesbury comic strip.

Frank hopped up and held out his hand to shake the young woman's. "You must be Ruth. Let me find you a chair."

She followed him out onto the floor where Frank commandeered one from an empty cubicle.

"So, you work with Dirk?" Frank said.

"I'm not sure 'with' is the right word. I sit in a cubicle next to him, but we only communicate by email."

"I see," Frank said with a laugh. "Are you a developer?"

"Yes, but not for this job. Dirk's tired of the bank sending him everywhere to explain BankCoin, so he's training me to stand in for him."

"What specifically do you want to know?" Magnus asked when they returned to Frank's office.

"Maybe you could start at the top and work down," Frank said, "as if I knew nothing about the BankCoin blockchain. I'll try to listen in the same way and maybe pick up something new."

Magnus blinked. "Am I allowed to assume you understand what a blockchain is?"

Frank laughed. "Sure. Just not anything about the BankCoin blockchain. How about this – tell me how it's different from bitcoin? Especially from the security point of view."

"Yes," Magnus said. "But first, to set the stage. BankCoin is a transactional payment platform, like bitcoin. As is typical of a blockchain ledger network, it creates blocks of transactions linked by unique numbers called hashes, one to the other. So far, just like bitcoin. But there are also differences.

"First, the BankCoin token is a proxy for the US dollar. This means the participating banks agree a BankCoin will always have the same value as the dollar.

Such a cryptocurrency is referred to as a 'stable coin.' And BankCoin is exchanged only among member banks."

"Let me stop you there a second," Frank said. "Let's review how that works."

"Ruth," Magnus said, without taking his headlights off Frank.

"It's actually easy," Ruth said. "The token in this case is just a packet of data that can pass back and forth between participating banks. So, if I want to send you one hundred dollars, here's what happens: the wallets you and I maintain at our separate banks exchange security keys and information about the transaction.

"After that, copies of BankCoin at other banks confirm the transaction, and one of them includes it in the latest block. Once that happens, my bank's total assets on deposit will have been reduced by one hundred dollars while your bank's will have increased by the same amount. Also, the balance of BankCoin in your wallet will be higher by one hundred dollars, and the balance in mine will be lower by the same figure. Now, we're all done. No more need to wait days for the check to clear or for the banks to confirm that funds have been transferred through the banking system."

"Yes," Magnus said, nodding. "Also, there can be no volatility in BankCoin independent of the dollar and no speculation."

Frank frowned. "How can you stop speculation in BankCoin? People haven't been rational about any of the other cryptocurrencies."

"Ruth," Magnus said a clipped voice, like a verbal snap of the fingers.

"Schwert has a very clever answer for that," she said. "It's a closed system. Although BankCoin can pass back and forth between banks, it can never leave the banking system. If you want to withdraw from your bank wallet, you must take it in a fiat currency – dollars or Euros or whatever – or in a different cryptocurrency. In fact, when people look at their banking statements, all they'll see will be a balance in their local money."

"Quite," Magnus said. "Now, back to differences between BankCoin and bitcoin. BankCoin is not a public blockchain – one where anyone who wants to can maintain a ledger. As you know, only banks are eligible to keep BankCoin ledgers. Also, BankCoin is not, like bitcoin, a 'proof of work' system, where trust is based on solving power-intensive, increasingly difficult problems. Instead, it is derived from what the blockchain world refers to as 'proof of stake.' In this case, the 'stake' is the significant assets of each network bank. And there are no mining fees because there is no mining.

"But still," Magnus continued, "not only First Manhattan makes money from BankCoin. When two member banks handle a transaction between their customers, they split a very small fee – three hundredths of one cent per dollar transferred. Each bank deducts its share from the money that is changing hands. The fee was set at this low rate to discourage others from launching competing blockchain-based financial systems. Charging for a transaction is not totally different from bitcoin because Nakamoto assumed his system would operate on a fee basis after all the bitcoin he authorized have been mined."

And thank goodness, Frank thought. Bitcoin mining already occupied the resources of vast data farms of computers. Together, they consumed more electricity than Denmark.

"Got it," he said. "Let's talk about transparency and anonymity next. How do BankCoin and bitcoin compare?"

"Ruth," Magnus actually snapped his fingers this time.

Ruth shot Magnus a dirty look he couldn't see. "They're quite different," she said. "Everyone with a BankCoin account holds her funds in a wallet. But unlike bitcoin, the host of the wallet – always a bank – is required to verify the identity, address, and other details of the wallet owner. That's because the bank regulators insisted the BankCoin banks follow the same 'know your customer' rules they're bound by for regular accounts."

Magnus nodded.

"So" Frank, said, "roll all that up together, and you get something that's as close as possible to the current banking system with just a few major differences, those being hundreds of identical distributed ledgers and transactions that are verified almost instantly."

"It could be mostly summarized that way, yes," Magnus said. "What you have described is not unusual for what is called a 'private blockchain.'"

"How about on the security side? What's different and the same between bitcoin and BankCoin?" Frank asked.

"Here, we are not so very different from bitcoin," Magnus continued. "The core goal of Nakamoto's proposal was to provide trust with no central authority required to monitor the network and guarantee security. BankCoin incorporates many of the same basic concepts, but it does not need all, because the banks already trust each other. So, the BankCoin software does not require validation of every block by fifty percent of the banks. We only require a representative subset – twenty network members. So, this is a big difference from bitcoin."

"I can see how that makes sense," Frank said. "You couldn't process a hundred thousand transactions a minute otherwise. How do you select the banks to confirm each block? Randomly?"

"Not quite," Magnus replied. "One might say random in a predetermined fashion. The algorithm that selects the banks to verify a block makes sure no two financial institutions in the verifying group are controlled by the same person or company. A hacker cannot interfere with the validation of a block because he cannot anticipate which banks will confirm that block."

"That's clever," Frank said. "What else?"

"Ruth."

"As we mentioned," Ruth said, "Only banks can host wallets, and the design of those wallets tightly integrates with the BankCoin software. With bitcoin, there is no such linkage. Anyone can develop bitcoin wallets any way they want to and then market them."

"Just so," Magnus said, nodding.

"That all sounds good," Frank said, "but what if a customer didn't like the new system?"

"Why should they know or care," Magnus said, "so long as the regulators are happy? Every customer's account balance has now been transferred to a BankCoin wallet. In the US, federal insurance covers the contents of each wallet up to the usual amount, just like a traditional bank account." He crossed his arms and began to tap his fingers on his biceps, one after the other. *One, two, three, four* … "Are we finished soon?"

In fact, Frank was running out of questions. It all sounded pretty solid. "Almost. So, let's say I wanted to steal some BankCoin, how would I do that?"

"You could not," Magnus said.

"Really?" Frank said.

"Of course not. There can be no theft because BankCoin does not exist outside of the member banks." The fingers were tapping faster now, *one-two-three-four...*

"How about the software generating the BankCoin blockchain?" Frank asked. "Could someone steal by compromising that?"

Magnus blinked four times rapidly and sat up straight. "I have never met anyone who could hack the BankCoin blockchain or the BankCoin software. I do not believe such a person exists."

Shades of Jerry Steiner, Frank thought. But instead, he said, "That's a mighty strong statement. All software can be hacked."

Magnus's eyes looked like they might leap out of his skull and attack Frank. "Is there anything else you wish to ask?" he said, standing up.

"No, that's it. And thanks. I feel a lot better."

"I am pleased you feel better," Magnus said stiffly and left with Ruth in tow. At the door, she looked back at Frank over her shoulder and shrugged, as if to say "What can I do?"

Well, Frank thought. There it was, almost as if it had come from Schwert himself, channeled by Dirk Magnus, his apostle. Frank expected no one else understood BankCoin better. Not only was Magnus the chair of the TSC, he'd written more lines of BankCoin than anyone but Schwert.

Still, no one would convince Frank that BankCoin, or any other code ever written, was invulnerable.

Then he had a troubling thought. What if the code that supported the BankCoin blockchain had already been hacked? Trillions of dollars changed hands every year through the global banking system. Maybe someone was just biding their time, waiting for more banks to sign up before pulling off a massive theft.

Could that be so? How could he find out?

Chapter 9

I'm Shocked!

I T HAD BEEN a while since Crypto last scanned the web to see what the technical press was saying about Günter Schwert, the reclusive genius behind the blockchain Crypto was preparing to destroy. He wondered whether there was anything new to learn?

Surely not, the voice whispered.

Yes, he agreed. *But it cannot hurt to check.*

The voice was right. The pundits continued to believe Schwert was leading the life of a latter-day Howard Hughes, the multi-talented industrialist/film director/aviator who retreated into a reclusive life as phobias took control of his mind. No one knew if Schwert suffered from similar issues, but clearly, he shunned publicity with the kind of success, the press assumed, only vast wealth could achieve.

Some were convinced Schwert owned penthouse apartments in multiple locations, moving from one to another as his whims or paranoias dictated. San Francisco, Dubai, and London were often mentioned although no one had ever confirmed a street address. And the emails Schwert sent to project members always came from untraceable Dark Web addresses.

Still, there was a wide tolerance for Schwert's behavior. And why not? Look at the popularity of bitcoin, and Nakamoto hadn't been heard from in years. Naturally, many wondered whether Schwert *was* Nakamoto – or vice versa. Or that each was in fact someone else.

Predictably, a few techies were obsessed with discovering Schwert's identity. Some used sophisticated artificial intelligence programs to compare sets of emails from Schwert to messages from Nakamoto – or from other open source luminaries, like Linus Torvalds – looking for telltale similarities. But no matches were found. Others were unwilling to let a little thing like lack of evidence stand in the way of an interesting theory. Perhaps whoever it was who called himself Schwert covered his trail by using Google Translate to convert his draft emails into another language and then back again. After that, he'd clean up any awkward wording, and off the email would go. That could work! Must be true!

Enough, Crypto concluded. There was nothing to be found but rank conjecture. More searching would be a waste of time.

Just a waste of time. The voice was not whispering now. *Now as to this Adversego person – that is another matter!*

Crypto had been preoccupied with Adversego for some time now, but more as a person than a threat. Yes, the First Manhattan investigator was skillful, but so was Crypto. He was not convinced that anyone, including Adversego, was an adversary he must take seriously.

But he is! The voice was strident now.

Crypto moved uneasily in his chair. It was better when the voice whispered.

You cannot take Adversego for granted! The voice was louder still.

Very well then. He would follow Adversego more closely. *Now leave me be.*

* * *

To be strictly accurate, what Crypto first became aware of when he was much younger were not voices at all. The intrusions were more like questions that came from nowhere and hung like peaceful clouds in his mind. He could see as well as understand them although, strangely, he was unable to make out the individual letters in the words. He was sure they weren't his questions and had no idea whose they were. It was very curious, but did not trouble him.

After a while, they did. Instead of floating, the questions darted in and out of his brain, as if someone was probing his mind. The first time this happened, he was sitting in the university library. Alarmed, he looked up, hoping to see where the intrusions were coming from. But all he saw were the bowed heads of other students studying their books. He felt as much as heard an urgent humming in the air.

Breaking into a heavy sweat, he stumbled to his feet, knocking over his chair. The heads surrounding him rose as one in slow motion. Their faces looked identical, and their eyes bored into his brain in annoyance.

Suddenly, the questions were no longer silent. A cacophony of voices replaced them, attacking him from all sides, as if from a hundred loudspeakers. But not ordinary ones: these could transmit pure energy into his skull. Once there, the beams morphed back into voices he could neither ignore nor understand.

With hands that shook uncontrollably, he shoved his books in his backpack. Then he fled, hoping to leave the barrage of sensations behind him. Running, stumbling, he managed to descend the library steps, grabbing the railing to save himself from tumbling into the street. The voices were laughing now.

And then, as abruptly as the attack began, it was over. He stood shaken and terrified, stock-still on the sidewalk in the gently falling snow, as the silent echoes of laughter faded inside his skull. He vividly remembered people passing him by as if he wasn't there.

* * *

Crypto spent the two months after this crisis in a state of limbo, fearing the voices would attack again, yet afraid to tell anyone lest they think he was crazy. As indeed he feared he was. And then the voices did attack. And attack again.

He researched what he was experiencing and was horrified at what he read in the psychiatric literature. His symptoms were most consistent with schizophrenia, and the prognosis of those afflicted with that illness was dire; medications were few and their side effects often severe; he would almost certainly never have a career or even a job; the odds favored his spending the rest of his life in some anonymous, heartless institution.

Terrifying as that prospect was, the increasing frequency and violence of his delusional episodes eventually forced him to seek help. With trepidation, he turned himself in – there was no other way to think of it – to the behavioral physicians of the student health service.

And so began the long and painful process of seeking a formal diagnosis and proper treatment. On good days, he attended classes and kept his appointments at the medical center. On bad ones, he cowered in his room, forgetting to shower or brush his teeth. Or, really, to do anything at all except suffer through the paranoid welter of thoughts and sounds rushing through his brain. During those episodes, he realized he had strange powers. He could, for example, kill with his mind – already had, hundreds of times. He knew this to be true when the fit was upon him.

Meanwhile, his delusions continued to evolve. Individual voices emerged and then faded away as others took their place. Over time, two became more distinct, mostly crowding out the rest. The first was female and by turns soft or shrill, argumentative or demanding. The second and less frequent visitor's intonations were deep, male and strident. The rest of the voices gradually merged into a sort of Greek chorus that appeared erratically. When present, they reminded him of the sound that might escape a full-to-capacity stadium, their volume rising and falling in response to invisible actions on the field hidden inside.

The defining moment of this dark period came as he rode a packed subway car. It began when the two familiar voices whispered that the strangers pressing against him on all sides were hideous, carnivorous aliens, masquerading as ordinary commuters. Any moment now, they would attack, tearing him apart with tooth and nail. He began to tremble and dart glances at what, until a moment before, had been blank faces staring at newspapers or at nothing at all. Now, he saw hellish eyes glowing bright and cruel, their owners clearly plotting their assault. He had to escape.

When the train approached the next station, he made his move, lunging toward the doors, striking out at the demons surrounding him, desperate to gain the platform before their fangs sank into his defenseless neck.

Those around him swore at him, struggling to avoid his flailing fists and kicking feet. But there was nowhere for them to go. A bull of a young man standing behind him grabbed Crypto, now shrieking in anger as well as fear, in a bear hug and lifted him up, staying upright with difficulty as the train lurched to a stop. As soon as the doors opened, passengers fought to get out, allowing enough room for Crypto and the man restraining him to crash to the floor. A few commuters joined his captor and together dragged Crypto off the car, barely able to control his wild, thrashing bid for freedom.

Crypto could not recall what happened after that. It was clear he had not escaped. The passengers restraining him must have summoned the police, because the next thing he knew, he was drifting in and out of consciousness in a white room. When he became more aware, he realized he was in restraints; the straps holding him down cut into his arms and legs whenever he struggled to sit up.

He grew more frantic by the hour to recover his freedom. When at last an attendant entered the room, Crypto recognized him as a demon, too, and screamed in terror. The attendant injected Crypto with something, and once again, Crypto lost consciousness. Over the weeks that followed, Crypto spent more time in restraints than free to move about in what he learned was a state institution.

His captors were understaffed and underfunded, but they had the means to maintain strict control. To his horror, Crypto found himself defenseless in a madhouse of antiseptic smells and callous attendants, populated by sometimes violent patients who often terrified him. Not only could his keepers restrain him and drug him, they had the power to condemn him to solitary confinement. And they could interrogate and probe him at will.

Worst of all, when the masters of his fate were not satisfied with his progress – and for months they were not – they could raise the stakes. There were many treatments at their disposal, some of which were unlikely to help but which they were free to try, anyway. The worst of these was electroconvulsive therapy; he had horrific memories of writhing in agony as the electrodes fired, his back arching almost to the point of breaking against the cruel bonds holding him down. Yet it was the electroshock treatments that finally brought him a degree of mental clarity. Only then was he able to work out how to play the game and eventually escape.

It was months before he emerged from the soulless, dingy, haunted wards of his prison. When he did, he was a changed man, one who had learned that the path to freedom lay in concealing his thoughts and controlling his actions.

Still, the doctors had given him one thing of value, and that was a diagnosis. While dire, it was not as hopeless as he had feared. They concluded he suffered from schizoaffective disorder rather than schizophrenia, a severe but less harrowing fate. Some high-functioning sufferers, he read, led lives that appeared outwardly normal, despite the inner turmoil they often experienced. And together with a diagnosis came medications that finally helped control his delusions. When they fully took hold, he was at last released.

With his newly regained freedom came a resolve to learn everything he could about anything that might help him maintain his equilibrium. He became fanatical about his diet, his sleep patterns, and his exercise. He kept a journal in which he recorded his daily medications, external stresses, and mental state. He pored over this data and fine-tuned his habits to what he thought was the best effect.

Also, he wrote rational statements to read when he was irrational in the hope they would help him resist madness when his sanity was under attack. Whenever he felt himself slipping, he would recite these pronouncements like the credo of a private religion he hoped would save his rational soul from delusional hell: *I am not evil. I can't control others with my mind. Neither can they control mine.*

Most critically, he trained himself to give nothing away even when he was most ill. Medical authority, he had learned, could be as dangerous and abusive as political authority, and just as obsessed with asserting control over the individual. He spent endless hours in front of his mirror, acquiring the ability to remain blank-faced no matter what his state of mind. He set up a web cam to record himself when he was delusional and studied the recordings when he was sane. He came up with elaborate strategies he hoped would persuade his unreasoned self that outward tranquility was essential to prevent attacks by imaginary enemies. In short, he became the stage director of the daily performance of his life.

So it was that he eventually felt able to return to his studies, telling anyone that asked that his long absence was due to a severe physical illness from which he was now fully recovered. His hard-won ability to feign normalcy when he was manic served him well. It also helped him establish a manipulative relationship with a psychiatrist in private practice.

Crypto grew adept at persuading the compliant doctor to maximize the dosages of his prescriptions and to allow him to try new drugs as they became available. This allowed Crypto to gradually amass a stockpile of medications and to adjust dosages and drugs as he pleased. He learned to do this with what he believed was great success.

Above all, he was committed to a singular goal: under no circumstances would he ever again allow himself to lose his freedom. Better to die insane than to find himself once again strapped, helpless, to a gurney, surrounded by white-coated ghouls attacking him with syringes and electrodes in order to bend his mind to their will.

Chapter 10

From Russia, Sans Love

"**N**ICE OF YOU to call to check in on your old dad," Frank said.
"Of course," Marla replied, "and anyway, I wanted to find out how the feeder's working out. What kind of birds have you seen so far?"

"None. Just Fang."

"Fang?"

"That's right. Fang. The squirrel that's eating me out of house and home."

Marla giggled, appreciating the situation immediately – her father outsmarted by a tiny ball of fur. She couldn't resist the urge to tweak him.

"Well, I'm sure you can figure out a way to stop him. What have you tried so far?"

"Well, I bought a baffle online to stop him from climbing down the wire."

"And?"

"He switched to jumping up from the railing."

"So? Did you try moving the feeder?"

"Of course, I did."

"And?"

"He just finds a new launch pad. My balcony isn't all that big, you know."

"Yeah, I can see how that would be a problem. Anyway, why Fang?"

"Because the little devil slashed me."

"Slashed you? How in the world did he do that?"

"I was trying to feed him by hand," her father admitted.

"Well, don't do that again!"

"You can bet I won't. Anyway, I'll figure out a way to beat him."

Marla smiled – this would be fun to follow. And she was putting her money on Fang.

* * *

A news update popped open on Frank's phone as he sat in the silent comfort of one of the bank's town cars. *Hmm.* He poked the link and saw an empty podium on a stage backed by a blue flag with a white compass rose. He turned up the sound to hear the voice-over.

"In just a minute we expect NATO spokesperson Colonel Allan Bradley to provide an update regarding Russia's latest ZAPAD military exercise – and it looks like that's him now."

A uniformed man with a stern face and a short military haircut stepped up to the podium and adjusted the microphone.

"Good afternoon. I'll begin by reading a statement.

"Earlier today, the Supreme Allied Commander Europe issued a warning to the Russian Federation to discontinue its build-up of military forces in Belarus. The Kremlin responded that its actions are part of a long-scheduled joint military exercise involving Belarusian and Russian land and air forces. The Kremlin maintains these exercises comply with protocols agreed upon by NATO and Russia under the Vienna Document, which since 1990 has required the exchange of certain military information between Russia and most European nations.

"Under other sections of the same protocols, each side has the right to place on-site observers to monitor military exercises involving more than thirteen thousand military personnel. The purpose of these protocols is to lessen tensions and thereby stop preventable outbreaks of hostilities between East and West.

"Based upon reliable satellite data and other information, NATO believes over twenty-eight thousand Russian ground forces are now in place close to Belarus's borders with Latvia, Lithuania, and Poland. These troops are supported by more than one hundred fighter and bomber aircraft, as well as extensive tank, artillery, and mobile missile launch assets. Because the Russian Federation misrepresented its troop numbers in the pre-exercise information supplied to NATO, we have no observers in place. NATO regrets that the Russian Federation has opted to ignore long-standing protocols, thereby increasing tensions in nations bordering Belarus.

"That's the end of the statement. I'll now take questions. Okay – over there."

"Thank you, Colonel. Trevor Quinn, *The London Times*. Can you tell us why Russia would under-report the number of troops involved in these exercises?"

"We can't know for certain what is motivating these actions, but I can give you some historical context. One purpose of the reporting protocol is to limit a country's ability to amass a force sufficient to launch an invasion under the guise of conducting military exercises. Violating this protocol was part of the playbook the Russians followed before invading Crimea and South Ossetia. Okay, over there."

"Julie Penbrook, *NPR*. Colonel, is there a real concern Russia is planning another invasion? Are tensions really that high?"

"On your first question, I have no information indicating that is the case. On the second, keeping tensions low is another reason for the protocols. Throughout history, aggressors have blamed their victims, claiming severe provocation or that the other side attacked first. The list of examples is almost endless: Hitler's invasion of Poland, Russia's aggression in Ukraine, and so on." The colonel pointed to someone on the other side of the room. "Your question, please," he said.

"Ralf Menning, *Die Zeit*. If not as a prelude to an invasion, Colonel, why would Russia under-report its troops? Is this simply theater for a domestic audience?"

"As I stated previously, we don't know the specific reasons for Russia's actions. That said, Russia's economy is suffering badly under economic sanctions imposed in response to previous Kremlin aggression. Sergei Denikin, the Russian president, has a long history of saber-rattling to increase his popularity, and he's been quite successful in achieving that result. Seeming to put one over on NATO always plays well for him at home.

"I also expect President Denikin wants to show those abroad that he can force Belarus to come to heel. A year ago, the Belarusian president signaled he might back out of the close alliance that has bound his country and Russia for decades. The current exercise sends a clear signal to the people of Belarus that Russia can rapidly deploy extensive forces into their country any time it wants. These exercises demonstrate to NATO as well that Russia is capable of sending a large force into the heart of Eastern Europe at will.

"But I say again we can't know for sure what Russia's true purpose here may be. That means we need to be prepared to respond to all contingencies. Too many wars have been launched on this continent on false pretexts. We don't want to allow another situation to get out of hand."

We sure don't, Frank thought, closing the browser. Russia had been growing more aggressive ever since Georgia, a former Soviet Socialist Republic, announced it wanted to join NATO. Among those actions, Russia had pulled out of European arms agreements, expanded its military, and launched other exercises like this one on NATO's doorstep. How far was it planning to push things this time?

* * *

"Frank?"

He looked up from his desk on the IT floor at the bank. Now what might she want?

"Hi, Ruth. What's up?"

"Nothing, I just wanted to apologize for Dirk's behavior the other day. He could have been more helpful."

"Well!" Frank replied, "That's hardly your fault. That was just Dirk being Dirk. He's not the easiest guy to get information from."

"I know," Ruth said, "That's the other reason I thought I'd stop by. I'm getting up to speed pretty quickly, so if there's ever anything you'd like to know, feel free to ask me. I might know the answer."

"That's very kind of you – thanks. I might take you up on that." Frank waited, wanting to get back to work. But Ruth was still standing at the door to his office. "And?" he said.

"I hate to take your time, but I'm not a security person by training. There are a couple things that aren't making sense to me with BankCoin. If you have ten minutes sometime, I'd love to ask you about them. Dirk doesn't seem willing to spend time with me on anything other than what I need to know to cover for him."

Frank sighed. "Sure. Now's as good a time as any. Have a seat."

To Frank's surprise, he found it easy to talk with Ruth. When she left, he realized half an hour had passed and that he'd likely gotten more out of the conversation than she had. Despite his perpetual unease with people, he knew he did his best thinking out loud. And Ruth was an exceptionally good listener.

* * *

President Yazzi did not like being pushed. He especially didn't like the corner his advisers were trying to maneuver him into right now. True, there was the chance for a big win, but only at a significant cost. If he approved the plan his national security adviser was pitching his pro-environmental supporters were sure to howl. And he wasn't convinced it would put enough economic pressure on the Kremlin to bring Russia to the bargaining table.

To the good, the plan was based on a strategy that had worked before, when an aggressive, decades-long arms race had helped bring an end to the Cold War by pushing the Soviet Union to the brink of bankruptcy.

Of course, the fruits of that Reagan-era military spending didn't last forever. A decade after the Soviet Union collapsed, leadership passed to a Russian president who bitterly resented his country's loss of superpower status. When the skyrocketing price of oil later refilled the Kremlin's coffers, he used it to rebuild the military and reassert Russian influence abroad. Russia's gross domestic product was still only eight percent of the United States' – less than the annual output of Italy, South Korea, or Canada. But what the Kremlin lacked in economic power it made up in shear cussedness. And it had thousands of nuclear weapons.

Yazzi couldn't pretend the economic sanctions already in place were working. So, what more could he do? According to Jim Wakeman, his national security adviser, the answer was to artificially depress the price of oil and keep it there until the Russians buckled. And he had a point. Without some new way to put the screws on, Russia would remain a pain in America's behind.

Yazzi snapped out of his reverie and frowned at the waiting faces around the table. Besides the members of the NSC, his chief of staff had invited the secretary of the interior and the administrator of the Environmental Protection Agency to join today's meeting. Now everyone was looking at him, waiting for his decision. Well, they could wait a little longer.

"Hugh," he said, turning to the secretary of state. "How much can we count on the Saudis if we do this? They'll take a big financial hit. Are you sure they'll hang in there for as long as this takes?"

"They're all in, Mr. President. Luckily, the OPEC alliance has been in a shambles lately. If it weren't for that, we wouldn't be making this proposal. Anyway, the Saudis are furious that Russia never pulled out of Syria after ISIS was defeated. They're even more concerned over Russia collaborating with Iran. The crown prince wants everyone to acknowledge the House of Saud as the dominant power in the Middle East, and he rightly figures that won't happen if Iran can rely on Russian support. Plus, this will give him another chance to show everybody how tough he is."

"Did you get down to specifics?" Yazzi asked. Hugh Calhoun had not been his first choice for secretary of state or even his second. He hadn't wanted a politician to fill such an important post, because they were big on talk but short on execution. But the process of getting his nominees through a fractious Senate had worn Yazzi down, and Calhoun had served four terms in the Senate, allowing him to sail through with the support of his cronies and colleagues. "If we go forward with this," Yazzi continued, "everyone's going to have to agree to stick it out for as long as it takes."

"The Saudi ambassador assured us they're willing to help hold the price of oil below thirty-five dollars a barrel until the Russians come to the table," Calhoun said.

"And how long will that be – on the outside?" Yazzi asked.

"The Kremlin's back is already pretty much against the wall," Calhoun said. "The price of oil hasn't topped forty-five dollars a barrel in twenty-one months. Natural gas prices are at historical lows, too, so their cash reserves must be running dry. And then there's the acceleration in alternative energy sources coming online. That's starting to have a significant effect. Even without further technological advances, alternative energy sources should push oil prices down about a dollar this year and accelerate from there."

"That's not what I asked," Yazzi said. "We won't be able to get US oil companies to keep oil prices down forever. How long will it take for this to work?"

"That's where the concessions on drilling on public lands come in," the secretary of the interior chimed in. "We've come up with a list of the least environmentally-sensitive public land tracts and offshore areas that are currently off-limits to drilling. If we agree to drop those restrictions, almost all the oil companies say they'll play ball. Of course, we'll have to give them a waiver from antitrust prosecution, too. An agreement between competitors to cap prices would otherwise be a criminal activity."

"Right," Yazzi said. "But now tell me this. How am I supposed to justify opening public lands for drilling after I promised to be pro-environment? Why won't this look like a sellout to special interests?"

Wakeman took a deep breath. This was indeed the tough part. "We're certainly not going to make everybody happy with this plan, Mr. President. But I think most voters will understand if we explain three things clearly. The first is the Russians are a major threat to world stability. That's got to stop, and the current economic sanctions haven't been enough.

"The second is we can't expect private companies to lower profits now unless there's a way to earn them back in the future. Boards of directors are responsible to their stockholders, so they really don't have a choice about that.

"And the third is that this is temporary. Alternative energy is going to claim a bigger and bigger share of the market. That will eventually lead to an oil and gas glut, so many of the areas we open up now will likely never be touched. The oil companies want guaranteed access to them in case oil prices go up, but they're not fools. They're not going to drill wells they can't pump at a profit."

"Okay," Yazzi said, "let's set that aside for the moment and get back to my first question. I still want a clear answer on how long Russia can hold out. The last thing I want to see is oil prices going back up before Russia cries 'uncle.'"

"Sir, the anti-government demonstrations in major Russian cities are the biggest we've seen in years," Wakeman said. "Poking a thumb in our eye with military exercises in Belarus will only buck up the government's popularity for a little while."

Yazzi waited.

"All right," Wakeman said, taking a deep breath. "Not more than eight months. That's the longest we think Russia's cash reserves can last even with a good deal of belt-tightening. After that, they'd need to start cutting pensions and take other measures the people won't tolerate."

"Good," Yazzi said. "You can count on me to remember that answer, so you better be right. Who else can we depend on?"

"Canada, Kuwait, Oman, and the Emirates are on board; we're still working on Brazil and Qatar. After that, there aren't any big producers we can expect to help. China uses all its domestic reserves, so they're a buyer, not a seller. Venezuela, of course, would side with Russia even if it could afford to see prices go down, which it can't. It's not worth contacting Iran, and Iraq said no."

"How about domestically?" Yazzi asked, turning to the secretary of energy.

"Four out of the five biggest oil companies are in, and the last one will have to price-drop to stay competitive. If Congress lets us open up the onshore and offshore tracts we've asked for, the oil companies will hold their production levels down now for a reasonable amount of time."

"Didn't you hear what Hugh just said? We need a firm commitment from them for at least eight months."

"Yes, Mr. President. We'll get back to them, and then to you."

* * *

Everything was proceeding according to plan. Not that Crypto was surprised. The actions of capitalists were nothing if not predictable. Provide an opportunity for profit and it would be taken as surely as the sun would rise tomorrow.

More surely! the voice echoed.

Yes, yes, Crypto responded.

And, of course, the voice was correct. That a capitalist cared only for his own self-interest was a lesson drummed into Crypto almost from birth. As it was to everyone attending school in the German Democratic Republic – or East Germany, as it was known to those in the West – before the fall of the Berlin Wall. Only much later did it occur to Crypto that his teachers had focused as much on indoctrination as education.

Be that as it may, everything he'd seen since the Soviet Union collapsed had confirmed that what he'd been taught about evil capitalists and the puppet governments they controlled was largely true. Indeed, he decided East Germany had delivered more fully on its promises of social equality than Western governments had lived up to theirs – and certainly more than the overlords of the United States with their "land of opportunity" myths and discriminatory realities. Not that he could pardon either system for the abuses it perpetrated against its own citizens. Governments, he concluded, existed solely for the benefit of the governors, regardless of the ideologies they promoted.

Indeed, earlier in life he had been one of the beneficiaries of that reality. Life might have been bleak for most people on the eastern side of the Berlin Wall, but not so much for a child of the elites. His father, as haughty and distant at home as he was at the office, was a high-ranking official in the much-feared-and-loathed Ministry of State Security – known to everyone simply as the Stasi. The families of those in power, like his father, had access to large apartments, luxury foods, and many other privileges denied to those they supposedly served.

Their children received special care, too, to ensure their proper ideological orientation. Not only to groom them to become loyal apparatchiks in the communist bureaucracy, but to protect their parents against the possibility that an errant child might attract the attention of one of the hundreds of thousands of informants the Stasi maintained everywhere. Regardless of who you were, where you lived, or what you did, there was an informant in your building, your club, your classroom. Often enough, even in your bed.

Then the wall came down, more abruptly than anyone could have imagined, breached in a day by cheering crowds wielding crowbars and anything else they could turn to that purpose. Once the celebratory flood of East Germans had surged through the gaps in that hated symbol of oppression, there was no turning back. Soon, the governments of Soviet Socialist States were falling all across eastern Europe and central Asia. Almost overnight, half the post-World War II world order crumbled like the wall into rubble.

At first, his father was contemptuous of the change. Working covertly with other Stasi officers, he sought to orchestrate the creation of an interim government that publicly would promise fair and open elections while privately ensuring that authoritarian business would continue as usual. But the flood of euphoria of the masses in East Germany and throughout Eastern Europe was too great. Soon the Stasi was dissolved. Ten days later, Nicolae Ceaușescu, the much-hated dictator of Romania, and Elena, his equally despised wife, fled and were promptly captured. Within hours, they were convicted of high crimes, stood up against a wall, and executed by an impromptu firing squad. Truly, the world was turning upside down.

Not long after, Crypto's own family found itself in danger when a mob surged into Stasi headquarters to stop the feverish shredding of millions of pages of files going on inside. Those records included the names and identities of the decision makers whose orders Stasi jailers, torturers, and executioners had carried out. One of those decision makers was Crypto's father.

Then things grew worse. Before a year had passed, nearly destitute East Germany was reunited with rich and powerful West Germany, dashing the hopes of East German elites to retain any real influence at all. The very same Western leaders the Stasi had sought to manipulate were now their masters.

Before the end of the year, Crypto's family was evicted from its comfortable apartment. Soon after, Crypto's father decided they must move again, this time to Slovenia, leaving behind almost all of their possessions – even their names. Crypto was both horrified and disgusted to learn their flight was the result of his father's fear of revenge at the hands of those he had persecuted and their survivors.

It might have been easier for Crypto had he been older or younger. One moment, he was a pampered teenager of fifteen, assured of a privileged job and career. The next, or so it seemed, he was on the run, no better than a rat scurrying one step ahead of the exterminator.

East Berlin might have been grim, but it was luxurious compared to the primitive rural village they removed to in Slovenia, where donkey carts outnumbered cars. Crypto didn't dare approach his father now. Daily, he grew more prone to unleashing torrents of abuse. At the slightest provocation, his voice rose and his face grew flush. Worse, the veins in his forehead bulged and throbbed in a way that alarmed Crypto's mother. Always a quiet woman, subservient to her husband in every way, she now lived in terror of his rages.

Throughout the long Slovenian winter, his father rarely left the tiny, squalid house, and neither did Crypto. He was unable to attend school, much less look forward to a career in a country whose barbaric language he could not speak and refused to learn.

One day, he woke up to find his father gone, away on a trip whose purpose his mother would not share. Eight days after his father's disappearance, she shook him awake an hour before dawn, telling him to dress as quickly as he could. Ten minutes later, a strange man hustled them into a waiting car and once again they fled, leaving behind the few belongings they still possessed. A day and a night later, they were in Los Angeles, California, where the bright sun, lazy palm trees, and capitalist opulence of Hollywood stunned Crypto. His father, Crypto's mother told him, was somewhere on the East Coast of the same country.

Later, he would learn his father was in Washington, DC, telling the Americans everything he knew about the Stasi, the Soviets, and anything else he had not already told them in Berlin in exchange for the family's safe passage to the US. It was three months before he rejoined the family and only a week after that when he died of a massive stroke. With all the heartless certainty of a sixteen-year-old, Crypto thought it was just as well.

Chapter 11

(Oops!)

SARAH SWITT SAW two black SUVs drive slowly through the intersection ahead and glanced at her watch. Drat. She'd seen this movie before. Now, she'd be late to work.

She slowed down as a third black SUV coasted to a stop, blocking her lane, and a fourth sealed traffic headed in the opposite direction. Several men jumped out of each car, darting glances in every direction. Oh well. She picked up her cell phone, set it to video, and got out to get a better view.

Sure enough, a minute later, two joggers in dark glasses and identical running gear trotted by, scanning the scene ahead. Two more followed, this time in unmatched clothes. She immediately recognized the tall, serious-looking one with a full head of dark hair. Sarah zoomed in on him, ignoring his partner and a third pair of runners who could have been doubles of the first. Once they cleared the intersection, the glorified crossing guards hopped into their SUVs and rolled on.

Switt stepped back in her car and resumed her commute. At the next light, she replayed the video. Excellent! She'd gotten a good clip of the president of the United States, out for his morning run. That would look great on her Facebook page.

* * *

Chief of Staff Carson Bekin was happy to be the president's running companion. Otherwise, he'd never fit in any exercise at all. And that wouldn't be good, given all the late-night junk food everyone ate at the White House.

"So how many more votes do we need in the House?" Yazzi asked. Reluctantly, he'd agreed to the plan to depress global oil prices.

"It looks like eight. We should pick up that many if we add increased oversight of offshore drilling platforms and promise new regulations on disposal of fracking wastewater. As usual, the problem is hitting a balance where we gain more votes on one side than we lose on the other."

"I don't need 'should,' Carson. Before we ask the Speaker to take this to the floor, I have to know for sure she can get it approved."

"Well, Henry, you know this is a heavy lift. You had a strong environmental plank in your platform. A lot of candidates rode your coattails into Congress supporting you on that. How do you expect folks up for election to support more drilling on sensitive public lands?"

"By pointing out the bill caps the new wells at a reasonable number and reminding them this is a once in a generation chance to get Russia to play ball. All we need to do is push oil and gas prices a bit lower and hold them there and Denikin will have to come around."

"I don't know, Henry. To the environmentalists, every new well is a bad well. And you know most voters don't care about foreign policy."

Bekin hated it when the president got worked up; it always made him pick up the pace. How did the guy manage to talk so much and run so fast at the same time?

"Okay," Yazzi said, "then tell the voters this: for every cheap, new well that comes into production, an oil company will probably take an older, more expensive one off-line that's more expensive to operate. If prices stay lower than they are now, those wells will never start pumping again. And we're standing firm on keeping alternative energy tax credits in place. Over the long-term, that will make oil less competitive, and that will shut down still more wells."

True, but so what? Bekin thought. Anything that couldn't fit in a soundbite would go over most voters' heads. But this wasn't the time to disagree too strongly with the president, even if he was an old friend. Especially when Bekin was struggling for breath.

"Well," Bekin huffed instead, "that might play with the moderates. But we'll still catch hell from the hard-core Greens. And nobody will like it when we rely on a bunch of ultra-conservative congressmen to get over the line."

"But you're forgetting one thing, Carson, and that's cheap gas. A voter will need to be mighty green not to like seeing gasoline under two dollars at the pump again.

And anyway, at this point, it is what it is." Mercifully, Yazzi ran in silence for half a block before adding, "What's the latest on that Russian cryptocurrency project?"

"Which one?" Bekin asked. "The public or the private one?"

"The second."

"I don't know anything beyond what's been in the Daily Brief."

"Well, tell Helen to find a half hour in my schedule ASAP for a CIA briefing. I want to know just how much Russia is making selling embargoed goods for cryptocurrencies. If they can unload enough goods for Russ, they may offset a lot of what we hope they'll lose on oil sales. I don't want to catch hell from our base if we're wasting our time."

With that, he picked up the pace again, this time leaving Carson Bekin lagging behind.

* * *

Walter Hansen, the young CIA analyst charged with monitoring Russian blockchain intelligence, shuffled his papers and cleared his throat. He could feel sweat trickling down his back and hoped his suit jacket didn't show it – he'd never briefed a president before.

"Good morning, Mr. President," he began, "let me start by summarizing the blockchain activities the Kremlin acknowledges." *Slow down*, he thought, noticing the frown on his boss's face. *Take a deep breath*. "Sberbank, one of Russia's largest financial institutions, leads those efforts. Since January 2018, much of that activity has occurred inside what it calls the Blokcheyn Laboratiya. According to the Lab's public statements, it's several years away from rolling out a commercial bank platform.

"But as I understand you already know from the Daily Brief, the private efforts supported by the Kremlin are much more advanced. Most notably, they have an operational blockchain. It supports an alt coin they call the Russ."

"Private efforts meaning what?" Yazzi asked.

"Good question, sir," Hansen said. "Like a lot of their offensive cyber activities, the Russians claim the Russ blockchain isn't a government project. The party line is it's an open source software initiative like bitcoin, staffed by volunteers. But we know that's not true. Our informants tell us the government controls and funds RussCoin, the private company that supports Russ development. That's who most of the Russ programmers work for. Those that don't are employed by various foreign shell companies owned by it. Most of the coders are in Russia, but some live in former member states of the Soviet Union."

"Where does the funding come from, specifically?" Yazzi asked.

"It's quite a mouthful, sir, even in English. The supervisor of the project works for the Finance Ministry's Department of Information Technology in the Sphere of Budgeting and State and Local Finance Management."

"So," Yazzi said, "The government has indirect control, but the actual coding is done by programmers who are spread out across the map, some even outside the jurisdiction of the Kremlin? That sounds risky. I understand they want deniability, but that's a high price to pay."

"I take your point, sir. But the Russians have a long history of using private sector black hats to conduct cyberattacks, run fake news social media campaigns, and meddle in elections. A lot of those partners live in countries that are non-Russian but happy to do business with the Kremlin. To some extent, the Russians are up to so much mischief they've painted themselves into a corner."

"How so?" Yazzi interrupted.

"Sorry, sir. What I meant was financially. These private sector companies and individual hackers are in great demand, so they command high fees. Plus, the Kremlin protects the Russian ones when they engage in cybercrime on their own account. Between working for the government on a contract basis and hacking foreign targets for their own profit, these guys make far more than they could as public sector employees. So, no surprise, the Kremlin can't directly hire enough top cybersecurity talent to do its own dirty work."

"That could be good for us," Yazzi said. "Do we have anyone inside the Russ blockchain team?"

"Yes, sir. We have a mid-level operative in Crimea."

"How about on the commercial side?" Yazzi asked. "Do we know how much money's changing hands in Russ?"

"We've got several agents in a position to monitor that, sir. We aren't able to see individual transactions, because they're encrypted, and the transfers are between anonymous electronic wallets. But by combining the information we get from multiple sources, we can come up with a good estimate of the Russ transaction volume."

"And what does that tell us?"

"That business is booming, sir. The Russ blockchain only went into operation three months ago, but well before that the Kremlin started lining up orders of embargoed goods they can't get through conventional channels. So, there was a backlog ready to ship as soon as the payment channel was in place."

"And there's nothing we can do to clamp down on the individual companies involved?"

"Difficult, sir. With no bank in the middle and anonymous wallets, the Russ blockchain provides the perfect means to get around our sanctions. Even the payment terms and shipping details are encrypted and included in something called 'smart contracts.' Blockchain technology supports those, too. So, if we intercept a transaction, we may not be able to decrypt the information to tell who's doing business with the Russians, what they're selling, and how much they're being paid."

"Give me numbers," Yazzi said. "How much is getting around the sanctions?"

"We believe the Russians are currently using the Russ blockchain to sell goods worth about six billion dollars a month, mostly shipped in bulk out of Black Sea ports to destinations in Myanmar and Somalia. Once they get there, the cargoes are broken up into smaller lots, redirected, and shipped to their ultimate destinations."

"Do we know what they're using the profits for?"

"Yes, sir. Our best estimate is the Russians are spending about half the Russ they receive to support the Russian economy generally. They're using the other half to procure goods we're embargoing in the other direction, like advanced computers. They buy those through shell companies around the world and then ship them back through the same channels they use to avoid the embargo when they're on the sell side. The sales volume in both directions is going up fast."

"Unbelievable," Yazzi said.

"Excuse me, sir," Hansen said, "the Russians are receiving another major economic benefit I should mention."

"What's that?"

"The Russ has become a darling of cryptocurrency speculators. Right now, only bitcoin sells for more, and sometimes, the Russ tops it."

"Where?" Yazzi asked.

"Everywhere – even in the United States, sir, because it's a much less risky alt coin. The price of Russ does fluctuate, just like other alt coins. But not as much, and mostly upwards, because the Kremlin controls the supply. When the value of the Russ starts to slip, the government buys it back to shore up its price. None of the free market cryptocurrencies enjoy that kind of support because there's no country backing them. So, the upside opportunity for speculators is unlimited while the downside risk is covered. That makes Russ a uniquely attractive investment of any kind. All kinds of financial institutions, including the biggest hedge funds, are building up significant Russ positions."

Yazzi shook his head. Businessmen were signing on to make a quick buck even though it meant trading with the enemy. He turned to Calhoun. "So, while we're planning this grand oil strategy to bankrupt Russia, our own investors are propping it up?"

Hugh Calhoun cleared his throat. "That would be one way to put it, Mr. President. But I doubt the appreciation in the value of the Russ and the sales of embargoed goods can offset a big drop in the price of oil." He hoped he was right.

"How much impact will it have?" Yazzi asked.

Calhoun turned to the aide sitting beside him. Flustered, the younger man said, "Can you give me a moment to work that figure out?"

Hansen knew how it felt to be in that spot. "Shall I go on, sir?"

"Continue," Yazzi said.

"As I was about to say, sir, the Russians not only buy back Russ to prop it up, but they can issue and sell more when it's value is moving up. Unlike bitcoin, the Russian technology doesn't cap the number of alt coins that can be issued.

"The Russians don't have to worry about causing domestic inflation, either, because the value of the Russ isn't pegged to the value of the ruble – the two are separate, and their values fluctuate independently. In effect, that means it doesn't cost the Russian government anything to buy embargoed goods using their blockchain. And they can keep selling as much Russ as they want so long as the speculators keep buying up the new coins."

"It doesn't cost them anything at all!" Yazzi echoed, turning back to his secretary of state. "So, tell me, Hugh. How are we going to drive the Russians to the bargaining table if the Kremlin is making a laughingstock of our trade sanctions?"

"Excuse me, sir," the aide interrupted meekly, "I've got the numbers you wanted now. Dividing the Kremlin's monthly profit from selling embargoed goods for Russ by the number of barrels of oil it exports each month gives an offset of about eighty-nine cents. So, from a bottom line perspective, it's as if Russia is selling oil for an extra eighty-nine cents per barrel. If embargoed product sales and the value of the Russ increase for six months at the rates they are now, that number goes up to approximately two dollars and nineteen cents per barrel."

"That's it!" Yazzi snapped, turning back to Calhoun. "That means we'll have to go back to the oil companies and get them to agree to push the price of oil well below thirty-three dollars a barrel to break the Russians. Hugh, what do you think of that?"

There was nothing Calhoun could think of, other than to wish his aide had taken longer to come up with those numbers.

"It's a hell of a situation," Yazzi fumed, "when I'm the one who finds a critical flaw in a strategy my team asks me to approve. We're in too far to turn around now, so I strongly suggest that before our next meeting you and Terry" – he gestured to Terrence Dougherty, the CIA director – "come up with a deniable plan for busting the Russ blockchain. I expect you'll need to bring in Defense as well. This will be at the top of the agenda of our next meeting."

* * *

Frank desperately wanted to scratch his nose, but Fang would notice the movement. He needed the squirrel to get a little closer to be sure to reach him with the full force of the Super Swoosher water gun he was holding.

There! Fang was tensing to make his leap from the railing to the feeder! Frank drew and fired, catching the little bandit in midair. *Hah!* Take that!

But Frank's act of defiance had unexpected consequences, altering the animal's trajectory by more than Frank had anticipated. He watched in triumph, and then in horror, as his diminutive nemesis flew past the feeder and out into the void. It disappeared downward, hurtling toward the street and the traffic below. Frank dropped the Swoosher and edged up to the railing, afraid he'd see a small, still, two-dimensional form pasted to the pavement below. But Fang was nowhere to be seen. Had he crept away, injured?

Frank slumped into his chair. Could he have actually killed Fang? He felt terrible. Then he remembered that squirrel tails acted like parachutes, protecting the furry aerialists from the otherwise lethal consequences of their occasional slips. As if on cue, a fierce chattering attracted his attention. Sure enough, the infuriated rodent was back on the ivy next to his balcony, giving Frank a thorough dressing down. *Just you wait!* It seemed to be saying.

The next day, the feeder was not only empty but lying on the balcony. Fang had gnawed through the wire.

Chapter 12

The Decider in Chief
Makes Up His Mind

PRESIDENT YAZZI WAS not looking forward to this meeting. He was as mad at himself as he was at the situation. If he'd never brought the Russ up, he wouldn't have to decide whether to take it down.

For the hundredth time, he told himself that when you took the oath of office, you made a deal with the devil. On the one hand, you were expected to have a firm moral compass and the will to stand by it. But on the other, you had to be willing to get both hands dirty when the situation demanded it. The tricky point was figuring out when that was. Only you could make the call, but anyone could – and would – second-guess you when things didn't work out as planned.

He envied the more straightforward roles of his advisers. John Hightower, the secretary of defense, would surely argue today for taking out the Russ, and more power to him. That was the position he should be pushing. And Hugh Calhoun would counsel caution, just as he should, to make sure the president didn't start something he couldn't finish.

But when their little debate was over, it would be him – Henry Dodge Yazzi – the first Native American president of the United States of America, who would have to call the coin toss. Liberals had ridiculed George W. Bush's folksy way of phrasing it, but the forty-third president had nailed it: when you came down to it, he'd said, the main job of the chief executive was to be "the Decider in Chief." The guy where the buck stopped even when all the alternatives were equally terrible. The one that had to decide which acts were over the line, and which ones weren't.

Yazzi found it particularly tough to make those judgments in matters involving spy craft. After all, espionage was by definition based on lies and trickery. Once you were on that slippery slope, was there any logical place to stop? Why not just slide all the way to the bottom and stay there?

But Yazzi rejected that conclusion. He didn't know for sure where the dividing line was, but he was still convinced there was one.

Which secretary of state was it, he wondered, who had said, "Gentlemen do not read each other's mail," and then disbanded his department's highly effective "Cypher Office"? Yazzi plugged the quote into his phone browser. Right. Henry Stimson, way back in 1929. Well, that was a far simpler time, although not for much longer. Stimson's high-mindedness had died a rapid death once the Axis Powers unleashed World War II, and things had been decidedly ungentlemanly ever since.

An aide arrived at the door to the Oval Office to remind Yazzi it was time for his meeting. Time to go. The Decider's chair was waiting for him at the head of the table where it was easy for everyone else to watch, fascinated, as he twisted in the wind.

* * *

"All right, let's get started," Yazzi said, rapping his knuckles on the table.

The side conversations halted, and the National Security Council meeting got underway.

"First up on the agenda is Russia. As you'll recall from our last meeting, the Kremlin has rolled out a financial network based on a new technology, called a blockchain, to generate a virtual currency they call the Russ. They're using that system with increasing success to evade our economic sanctions. This in turn undermines our strategy to force the Russians to back off on their aggression in Eastern Europe and the Near East. I've asked State and Defense to evaluate how we might disrupt that system to the point of collapse. Gentlemen, which of you drew the short straw?"

"Thank you, Mr. President," Hugh Calhoun said. "That would be me. I'll start the presentation by placing your request in the diplomatic context. By that, I mean, what are the consequences you're willing to accept from disrupting the

Russ network? I pose this question because the greater our tolerance for Russian retaliation the more technical options we have while, conversely, if our tolerance is low, the approaches we can consider become much more restricted.

"For example, if we launch a cyberattack that severely disrupts or destroys the Russ payment network, the Kremlin might interpret that as an economic act of war that demands a stiff response. What might that be? Well, our banks use a somewhat similar blockchain system called BankCoin. That network carries virtually all financial transactions within the United States and between us and our trading partners. That would be the logical and symmetrical retaliatory target.

"If the Russians took BankCoin down, the disruption to our economy would be immediate and severe. Then we'd have to decide how to react, which would be tricky. This is a new type of warfare, and therefore, each act of cyber aggression and response needs to be looked at much more carefully than other, more traditional exchanges."

"Explain," Yazzi said.

"Well, Mr. President, as you know, whether, and how far, to escalate a hostile situation is always a difficult decision. We want to send a message that will be well-understood so the enemy can tell exactly how serious we are and therefore does not itself overreact. We and our enemies have had lots of experience with traditional forms of pressure and response, like imposing sanctions, stopping and searching a ship on the high seas, detaining foreign nationals, and so on. Everybody has a sense of where each one of those actions falls on the scale of aggression as well as what types of response might be of appropriate magnitude. But we don't have much to go on yet when it comes to cyber warfare."

"What about by analogy?" Yazzi asked. "Aggression is aggression. It's just old wine in new bottles."

"I take your point, sir. But so far, our record in calibrating those analogies has been poor, at least if having second thoughts is a good indicator. For example, when the North Koreans hit Sony, the big entertainment and electronics company, with a major cyberattack, all we did was impose a few minor sanctions. Similarly, we waited a long time to react to Russian meddling in the 2016 election. When we did react, many thought our response was far too mild – we ordered the Russians to abandon a few facilities in Maryland everyone knew supported their espionage activities and we deported some known Russian agents. That limited retaliation may have encouraged our enemies to be more aggressive in their cyber war planning.

"So, the bottom line is we don't know how Russia would react to an attack on the Russ that was traceable to the US. They might want to make a point by retaliating aggressively – we know President Denikin hates to look weak, either at home or abroad. Then it would be our turn to decide whether to escalate, and if we did, we could have a major crisis on our hands with no easy way to avert further escalation without looking soft."

"Then the answer on traceability is no," Yazzi said. "The only reason we're talking about the Russ at all is to prevent it from undermining our oil price strategy. And even that's just a stepping stone. Our end goal is to bring Russia to the negotiating table, and I don't want to do anything that would work against that goal."

"Exactly," Calhoun continued. "That was our conclusion as well. So, to sum up the diplomatic context, our recommendation is to address the Russ situation by persuading our allies to join us in imposing additional sanctions. However, if you believe a more aggressive response is required now or in the future, we urge you to consider a cyberattack that is untraceable to the US or at least one that is so deniable that Russia would hesitate to retaliate in kind. And with that, I'll pass the baton to John."

"Thanks, Hugh," the secretary of defense said. "Mr. President, we believe a forceful response is called for although I do agree that deniability should be preserved. Given our recent history of lackluster responses, we think we need to let the Russians know your administration will not hesitate to meet serious cyber aggressions with serious cyber responses.

"Consequently, my recommendation is that we urgently begin work on an exploit modeled loosely on Stuxnet, the malware attack we developed with the Israelis to disable Iranian nuclear efforts back in 2010. As you'll recall, when it was introduced to the Iranian systems controlling the production of weapons-grade uranium, Stuxnet caused centrifuges to spin so quickly they self-destructed. Importantly for current purposes, the malware was designed to suggest a system malfunction arising from preexisting software defects.

"This accomplished three goals. First, it made it extremely difficult for the Iranians to figure out what the problem was and fix it. Second, it took a long time before the problem was traced to malware. And finally, it was impossible to prove the bad code came from us or the Israelis. Adopting a similar approach in the current case would minimize the risk of retaliatory escalation while maximizing the time it would take the Russians to find and fix the problem."

"And how would you go about that?" Yazzi asked.

"While blockchains are by their nature difficult to attack in some ways, a variety of approaches should be possible. We might, for example, try to develop malware that introduces random errors into the transaction process. The result would be that some Russian trading partners would be underpaid and others overpaid. This would cause the system to become untrusted and likely force the Russians to take it off-line until they can figure out what's wrong. Given that the Russ blockchain is running fine now, they'll suspect we're behind the problems but won't know for sure. By the time they do, we should have forced them to the bargaining table, where the need to reach a broader resolution of outstanding issues should make them decide that retaliation for the Russ attack is not in their best interests."

"Thank you both for your recommendations," the president said. "Comments anyone?"

Of course, everyone had comments. Yazzi had already made his decision, but he let the discussion run until all who wished to weigh in had done so. "Okay," he said., "All good thoughts. Now, here's what we're going to do. First off, Hugh, I want you to persuade our allies as quickly as you can to add purchasing or holding Russ to the prohibited activities list.

"Now, regarding what's already invested in Russ: this one goes to the CIA. Terry, I want your folks to get access to a Russ node somewhere or even set one up under cover of a fake trading partner, if that's easier. Then I want your best cryptographers to figure out how to decipher the transaction data so we can tell who owns Russ and who's violating the trade sanctions. And before you say it, yes, I know you can't predict how long that will take.

"That takes me to task three, which is one for Treasury. Carson, get in touch with Jack over there and tell him I want his people to draft regulations that prohibit banks, investment houses, and so on from hosting accounts holding Russ or wiring funds to Russ exchanges.

"If those steps don't go a long way towards chopping the value of the Russ, I'll be surprised. But just in case, I want to be able to launch a cyberattack against the Russ as a last resort. If a few private investors get burned because they're still holding Russ in violation of the law, well, tough luck for them. Coming up with an attack sounds like a job for CYBERCOM, so John, I'd like you to start work on that.

"If it's not obvious, these tasks are highest priority. Each of you will keep me apprised of your progress on a frequent basis. Now, let's take a break."

As the room emptied, Yazzi congratulated himself. Sometimes, the Decider's job was easy – pick both options, especially when one might work before the second was ready to go. And, he reflected, there was at least one big advantage to being the Decider. Once the decisions were made, it was somebody else's problem to carry them out.

* * *

Crypto's interactions with the voices were typical of what one might find in any dysfunctional family. When life was smooth and conflict free, the voices were nonthreatening and tolerable. But when times grew tense, they became strident and distracting, like agitated insects buzzing around his head. They had never introduced themselves, so early on, he labeled the most consistently present one voice A. During difficult times, she became insistent and hysterical. The second – naturally voice B – only visited when times were bad. B was always loud and over-bearing. During a particularly trying period, Crypto renamed the exasperating, buzzing, circling voices A Bee and B Bee.

The presence of his Bees was not always unwelcome, though. The fact was, he had no one else to talk to. He'd never allowed anyone into his adult life, and his mother was a broken woman who rarely left the small tract house the CIA installed them in. When they arrived in the United States, Crypto spoke no English; Russian was the automatic second language for the son of a Stasi officer. The US government resettlement bureaucrats were not unsympathetic, but Crypto spurned the tutor they offered, even after he was lagged two grade levels to give him time to learn the language of his new country.

But why should he? There was nothing he wanted to learn from the capitalists who had pushed communism and his own family's fortunes to the brink. Instead, he sat silently in the back of the classroom, scowling over the heads of his smaller, younger classmates. They, of course, were quite content to leave the out-sized, ill-tempered stranger alone. Notwithstanding the sins of the Stasi, Crypto became more committed than ever to the communist ideology of his childhood.

Which, for a while, served him well, because in time, it led him to change his approach to education. He decided he wanted revenge, and the first step toward achieving that goal must involve learning English in order to infiltrate the capitalists and beat them at their own game. There was a delicious irony in that realization, and he turned himself to his studies with a vengeance, doing well enough to later earn a free ride through Stanford, earning both undergraduate and graduate degrees.

But halfway along this path his new strategy collapsed. In college, he enrolled in every Cold War history course he could find, hoping to determine why communism had failed; perhaps, next time, there could be a different result. He did not like what he saw. At first, he rejected what he read as American propaganda. But then he concluded that the accounts of corruption and mismanagement, deceptions and betrayals, were largely correct. And not just in the GDR but throughout the Soviet bloc as well. Yes, there were many true believers. But those at the top parroted the teachings of Marx and Engels only to keep the proletariat in check. Communist leaders could be brutal, too, and not just Stalin. It was his successors who brutally put down the Hungarian uprising of 1956 and sent tanks into Czechoslovakia in 1968 to crush the Prague Spring.

Nor were the Soviets alone in their abuses. The Chinese experience under Mao Zedong was likewise a debacle. In the early years, his ill-considered priorities led to the starvation of millions. Later, the Chinese chairman purged millions more during the Cultural Revolution. North Korea's overpowering government was if anything even worse. And the butchery Pol Pot unleashed on the Cambodian people rivaled Hitler's most terrible atrocities. How could so many communist disasters be explained away? Was Marxist theory flawed in some strange way that invariably led to authoritarian abuse?

Crypto concluded he'd been an idiot and a fool. It was foolish enough to swallow the party line as a child surrounded by puppets. It was ridiculous to self-indoctrinate as a young adult. Clearly, communism held no promise for him or anyone else. Therefore, his determination for revenge made no sense. Revenge against what? And for what? He had no answers to those questions.

That was when the voices emerged, leading to his initial and most terrifying bout with mental illness. It was not until he was halfway through graduate school that disaster struck again. For the first time in his life, he had allowed himself to believe a certain young woman might have taken an interest in him. For a few months, he felt a lightness of being he had never before experienced. But when at last he hesitantly made his belief known to her, she tactfully, but firmly, disabused him of that notion.

Crypto had suffered from bouts of depression since adolescence. Now, he sank into a deep, immobilizing despair. He blamed his doctor, since depression was a known side effect of his medications. Perhaps he could lower his dosage just enough to lift the heavy veil of hopelessness while still keeping the voices in check? No, he decided. That was too risky.

But then his depression and sense of isolation deepened. What did he have to lose? Maybe he could have the best of both worlds – a stable relationship with those who populated the world around him and a controllable one with the denizens that inhabited his own mind? Why not?

Like many afflicted with his disease, when Crypto was stable he was prone to over-estimate his ability to control his demons. And he had grown used to the voices over time, absorbing them into his own identity. Indeed, when they were too long silent, he looked forward to their return. The worst times of the past seemed less harrowing to him now. Was it not also true that their pressing and probing stimulated his thinking? Surely, they had led him to thoughts and places he might never have explored on his own. And he could pursue ideas with the Bees he would never dare discuss even on anonymous internet bulletin boards.

The harsh truth was, without his Bees, the loneliness was more than he could bear. Certainly, he should be able to ease off on his medications. Surely, there was a balance to be found.

Ultimately, his black depression left him no choice. Part of him knew it was crazy to allow himself to be half-mad. But living in deep despair was madness, too. And was a life with the Bees so different from thinking to himself? Or talking to a physical person? Could he not monitor his mood and his dosages and have the best of both his worlds?

And so, he did.

Over the years, new and better medications came along, and his own skills at self-medication improved. When his existence was relatively calm, he succeeded in keeping his mood positive and the voices bearable and even companionable. When he became anxious, his vulnerability increased. Sometimes, it was difficult to regain control. So, there would always be a risk. But what of it? This was the life he was born to lead.

Chapter 13

Welcome to the Club

"HEY, FRANK," A familiar voice said. "Got time for coffee?"

"Are you calling on a disposable phone? I thought I was still on the pariah list."

"Yeah. Well, as they say, that was then, and this is now. Also, as they say, something's come up. Anyway, can you fit me into your busy schedule? Or are you spending all your time in your swank New York penthouse these days?"

Frank paused. How would George Marchand, his former boss and sometime handler at the CIA, know he had a fancy apartment in New York? It wasn't public knowledge. Was the CIA keeping an eye on him?

"It's not exactly a penthouse, George, but sure. I'm only in New York two or three days a week. How about Thursday? Same place and time as usual?"

"It's a date. See you then."

And so, Marchand did. But not before Frank spotted him first, standing at the cash register of the coffee shop: tall, balding now, thin, and a little hunched over.

"Hey, Boss," Frank said when George turned around.

"Hey," George said, handing him a cup of coffee. "Lovely day for a walk, isn't it?"

In fact, it was pouring buckets outside, but Frank nodded and pulled the hood of his coat back over his head. "Never seen better."

"Great." Outside, Marchand opened a golf umbrella large enough to cover them both and walked off at his usual fast clip.

"So, am I back in from the cold?" Frank asked.

"Not really. At least, not as far as our congressional oversight committee's concerned. But the president's asked us to put together a top-notch task force to advise him on an urgent project. And the big guy gets what he wants. Interested?"

"Why bring someone in from the outside? Can't you find enough folks in-house?"

"It's too new a technology," Marchand said, a little stiffly. "We're not completely out of our element, but this is an area the FBI, Treasury, and SEC have been focusing on, not us."

"Ah," Frank said. "The pieces all just fell into place. So, it's the blockchain, right?"

"Bingo."

That first guess was easy but not the next. "Offense or defense?" Frank asked.

"Offense," Marchand said. "In a nutshell, the Russ, an alt coin the Russians are issuing, is going gangbusters. The speculators can't get enough, and that's shoring up the Kremlin's finances just when the administration very much wants them to be going in the other direction. And the anonymity of the Russ blockchain allows the Kremlin to get around all those sanctions we so painfully negotiated with our allies. The president wants to be able to kill the Russ within six months."

"Kill it? How?"

"That's up to you. Make the speculators abandon it so it's worthless. Scramble it with malware. Whatever. The one absolute requirement is that the attack not be traceable to the United States. That's why it's necessary to put together this little brain trust to come up with a plan to give Yazzi what he wants. So, are you game to join the team?"

"If it's just a few hours a week, sure. Under the contract I negotiated with the bank I can do limited work for other clients so I can keep my consulting practice alive."

"Yes, I know."

Frank grabbed Marchand's arm and stopped. "George, is the CIA watching me?"

"You're not being tailed every day, no. But you are a valued asset, and you also have a high public profile; we'd hate to see anything happen to you. The other side of the coin is you've earned yourself a reputation as kind of a loose cannon, and we like to know who we can trust and who we can't. Sorry. I don't make the rules. And I'm not the guy who manages that part of the operation."

They started walking again with Frank pondering what he'd heard. Had George just tipped him not to do anything stupid for the bank that might embarrass the administration? Otherwise, why would George reveal something Frank didn't have to know?

"Anyway," Marchand continued, "can you be available for a face-to-face meeting a few hours a week? For security reasons, this isn't a project you can participate in remotely; you'll have to meet at NSA headquarters."

"Leaving aside scheduling, yes. Any chance the meetings can be on weekends?"

"That's the plan. Most of the other team members are also employed full time. How about Sunday afternoons?"

It wasn't as if Frank had anything else to do, other than pursuing his vendetta against Fang. "Sure. That works."

Frank hadn't paid attention to where they were walking and now realized Marchand had circled back toward the coffee shop. "Who else is in the group?" he asked.

Marchand handed him a thumb drive. "You can find all the particulars here. The first meeting will be this Sunday at three o'clock p.m. at Fort Meade. Do you have a car these days?"

"No, it finally died. I guess an Uber driver can drop me at the guard gate?"

"He can take you all the way to the check-in building."

"Great. Will you be at the meetings?"

"No, I'm just the messenger on this one." Marchand held out his hand. "Now, go have fun."

As his old boss strode off, turning into a blurry silhouette and then disappearing entirely into the gathering mist, it occurred to Frank that Marchand's career with the CIA must have begun in the depths of the Cold War. Frank wondered whether his old mentor wished he could help tuck it to Ivan one more time.

* * *

Frank studied the material on the thumb drive with interest. It was a small group he was joining. He'd heard of several, and the credentials of those he hadn't intrigued him. And then there was Lawrence Dix, the chair, a full colonel from CYBERCOM. Frank mused over that datum. If the CIA was playing catch-up on the blockchain, CYBERCOM must also be scrambling to figure out what the heck this blockchain technology was all about.

Frank tapped his fingers on his desk. It was interesting CYBERCOM, one of the ten unified commands of the Department of Defense, was leading the task force alone, instead of teaming with the CIA. No wonder George was unhappy; with the work order coming directly from the president, the turf wars on this one must have been interesting. But it made sense. CYBERCOM had been formed in 2009 to centralize cyber defense response across all the service branches. Its remit had been growing ever since, eventually taking on the same role for offensive operations. And there was no way to pretend the task force wasn't charged with designing an attack against a foreign power, and a nuclear one at that.

Frank leaned back and folded his arms. Maybe this project would get him back in the good graces of the powers that be. There would be lots of glory to go around if they were successful. Or maybe banished for good if they were not. If the task force couldn't produce an exploit that worked – or, worse yet, designed one the Russians could trace – the powers that be would look for a scapegoat. He wondered whether they'd look all the way down to him?

But there was no point going down that road. He went back to his laptop to read the full bios of the task force members, starting with the colonel's. West Pointer, number three in his class. Must be about fifty-four years old now, based on his graduation date. Picked up a master's degree in computer science and another in advanced warfare strategy a few years later. Several tours in Iraq and Afghanistan. For the last eight years, attached to CYBERCOM. Sounded like he should know strategy, but how about cybersecurity? Would he be an asset or an obstacle?

The rest were as different as could be. One was a computer scientist with dozens of patents and an endless list of academic papers. One was a blockchain startup cowboy. One looked to be a real blockchain fan boy, and the other was a reformed black hat who'd served hard time for hacking banks. And the last one was Dirk Magnus.

This would be interesting.

* * *

Wow! Frank thought, looking at the news alert on his phone. The headline read "White House Announces Strict Price Controls on Oil and Gas to Stop Russian Aggression." That was something different. He opened the article and read on.

"A spokesperson for the administration has just read a statement to the White House press corps announcing a new initiative aimed at curbing Russian hostilities and interference in Eastern Europe and the Middle East. All NATO allies, and several oil-rich countries, including Saudi Arabia, the United Arab Emirates, and Kuwait, have committed to supporting these latest concerted actions against the Russian Federation. Russia is the largest exporter of natural gas and the second largest exporter of oil in the world and derives most its foreign trade income from sales of those products.

"Under the initiative, participating countries and oil companies have agreed to offer oil to the marketplace at or below twenty-eight dollars per barrel. Regarding natural gas, for which prices vary significantly on a regional basis, the parties have committed to price caps ranging from two dollars and fifty cents (in the US) to six dollars (in Japan) per million BTUs.

"In a first-of-its-kind agreement during peacetime, four out of five of the largest US oil-producing firms have signed on to the same commitment; the fifth is expected to commit shortly. The White House statement included details on a new Oil and Gas Supply and Pricing Board (OGSPB), which will coordinate supply and delivery logistics among US companies to achieve the desired price goals. The Department of Commerce and each participating US-based oil company will take part in the OGSPB.

"As part of its negotiations with the oil companies, the White House has agreed to ask Congress to make certain public lands and territorial waters available for exploitation that had previously been off limits. According to the statement, the speaker of the house and the senate majority leader have promised to bring appropriate legislation before Congress as early as next week …"

Frank paused. So, his Russ Task Force was part of a much bigger plan than he'd realized. Maybe an attack on the Russ would never be necessary at all. That would be good. He went back to the article.

"In response, the Russian president, Sergei Denikin, has called for an emergency meeting of the United Nations Security Council and placed Russian military forces on alert."

Frank closed the article. Then again, maybe it would.

* * *

Frank was drumming his fingers as he took stock of what he had learned about an opponent who was proving to be as wily as any foe he had ever faced.

For example, from his extensive online research, he now knew it was almost impossible to keep a squirrel out of a bird feeder once the beast had committed to its objective. Squirrels, he had read as well as observed, were worthy opponents. Clever, single-minded, and highly motivated; right up there with raccoons. The web was full of despairing tales of anti-squirrel devices purchased and then found wanting. Those few tools that seemed up to the task, like baffles capable of preventing a squirrel from climbing up a pole or down a wire, were of no use where the enemy could jump directly on to the object of its desire. Regrettably, that described his balcony.

What to do?

His phone dinged.

Who's winning? You or Fang? Marla's text read.

Very funny, he typed.

Sorry to hear that, she responded.

Admitting defeat was clearly not an option.

Chapter 14

Be Careful What You Ask For

TELEVISION SCREENS ACROSS Russia switched abruptly from their regular programming to the news studio of the Public Television of Russia network. An announcer behind a news desk promptly began to speak.

"Welcome to this special broadcast from the Kremlin. In just a few minutes, we expect the president to emerge from a meeting of the Council of Ministers."

As he spoke, a video clip shot earlier in the day played on a large screen behind the announcer. The footage showed Sergei Denikin, president of the Russian Federation, striding through the gilded halls of the Kremlin, guards in ornate uniforms snapping to attention as he passed, their backs arched into almost impossible angles of deference. As intended, the spectacle recalled the glory days of the Russian Empire. It also linked Denikin to the absolute power of the czars who for centuries had held the fate of the Russian people in their hands.

The announcer continued as the last pair of guards closed a set of enormous, golden doors behind the president.

"According to a statement issued earlier today, the president convened today's meeting to discuss the latest joint efforts of Western enemies to damage the Russian economy. Specifically, he is informing the ministers of the actions he will take in reaction to Western efforts to artificially depress oil prices.

"It appears that the meeting has just ended. We will now turn to live coverage of the president."

The camera switched to a full screen shot inside the Kremlin where the uniformed guards were reopening the doors of the council meeting room. Denikin walked out as decisively as he had entered, the cameras following him as he stepped behind a podium flanked by Russian flags. Gazing into the eye of the camera, he began to speak.

"Citizens of Russia! I have summoned the council today in connection with a development that is of vital, historic significance to us all. At issue is the continuing effort by the United States, together with its NATO allies and certain oil-producing countries, to destroy the economy of Russia and the well-being of you, the Russian people.

"These provocations clearly violate established norms of international law, as well as the explicit terms of treaties of which we are common parties, including the agreement establishing the World Trade Organization. The United States would have other nations believe it is responding to prohibited Russian deeds. But, every one of our actions has been a normal and necessary exercise of the sovereign rights of the Russian people in defense of our legitimate interests and historic borders ..."

* * *

Later that day, President Yazzi clicked the pause button at that point in the Russian president's speech, freezing Denikin in mid-sentence. "So, what do you think he'll do?" he asked Carson Bekin. "Did you catch that last bit about 'historic borders?' Which ones do you suppose he's referring to? The Soviet Union's? The Russian Empire's?"

"I don't know for sure, but it sounds like he's planning something – it would be hard for him to walk back from such a tough speech. If we keep the pressure on, he'll have to act, or he'll look weak right before his election. The question is, what does he have in mind? It's not like he can impose trade sanctions on us or the other countries involved. There's almost no trading going on with Russia right now – at least through legitimate channels. Recalling some ambassadors wouldn't make any difference to anybody at home or abroad. And China's the only UN member that might support him if he brings a protest before the security council."

"Agreed," the president said. "You'll recall he ends his speech this way –" Yazzi picked up a transcript from his desk and flipped through to the last page. "Here we are. He says that 'he will consider all means of retaliation to be appropriate and available to me in this crisis and that the United States and its allies must not underestimate the will of the Russian people to respond in kind to the outrageous behavior of its enemies.'"

"Sure," Bekin said. "But that's pretty much what we would say, too."

"That's what I'm thinking," Yazzi said. "Anyway, we've come way too far to back down now just because Denikin stages a photo op in the Kremlin."

* * *

Crypto was halfway through college when his dis-infatuation with communism set him intellectually and motivationally adrift. He met that crisis by switching his major to computer science, for which he had both an aptitude and an interest. The former made it easy to excel, and the latter provided a safer and more practical intellectual pursuit to immerse himself in. Unlike political philosophy, mathematics and science were reliable. X plus Y always yielded Z, regardless of human frailties or failings, and no demagogue could make it otherwise. For the rest of his college career, he largely left his fascination with ideologies behind.

Then he stumbled on a book about anarchy in a used book store. Not anarchy as in chaos but in the ideological sense. He bought it and was captivated by the idea of a society free of central governmental interference. With no leaders, there would be no one to delude and betray the people. He decided anarchy provided the only rational antidote for the insanity he'd observed in his own life. Why shouldn't a modern society try it?

Why not indeed, the voices agreed.

He began to study the history of anarchism and discovered there were almost as many theories as there were theoreticians. He particularly resonated with an extreme branch that favored returning to the purity of tribal life. At that level, equality and fairness could rule rather than advantage-taking and oppression. Anthropologists and archaeologists agreed the tribal form of self-governance had been universal and must have worked quite well for ninety-five percent of the time the human species had existed. In some remote jungle areas, it still did. That sounded promising.

He delved deeper, looking for examples of more complex societies to see if the same principles could hold true, and was surprised by what he found.

Iceland in particular intrigued him. For almost four hundred years after its founding by Scandinavians during the Middle Ages it had existed as a commonwealth with no army, no taxes, and no central government at all in the modern sense. Instead, each local community selected its own non-hereditary leader. Only at intervals of several years did representatives of these communities convene to address issues of common concern. The closest thing to national leaders that existed were individuals charged with memorizing and reciting the laws for the benefit of the non-literate Icelandic society.

And in Russia, before communism there were communes – villages governed by the serfs, who were otherwise the near equivalent of slaves during the autocratic age of the czars. These lowest of the low were nevertheless empowered to allocate land among themselves, settle local disputes and otherwise administer their own society.

Even Thomas Jefferson had agreed with the general premise, arguing for an agrarian democracy based on local control. That most democratic of all founding fathers had believed a central government was a dangerous necessity at best that should have as few powers as possible and no standing army at its command. Even then, it must be monitored with suspicion by the yeoman farmers that were the best exemplars and truest guardians of the virtues of the people.

But perhaps Crypto was deluding himself once again. Now there were billions of people, complex trade relationships, and competition for resources. How could such a community-centric system suffice today?

Perhaps technology could provide the answer. Look at open source development, and Linux in particular. Thousands of programmers all over the world contributed time, effort and code to the Linux kernel, all for free. And there were no elections or bureaucracy. Advancement was based purely on merit and by recognition of one's peers. And look at the Wikipedia – another common enterprise to which thousands of volunteers in scores of countries contributed their time and efforts. Again, for free. And once more, without any complex trappings of governance.

Or standards? Voluntary organizations to create those had existed for more than a century now. By now they had created more than a million technical, health and safety standards. Businesses, individuals and even governments everywhere voluntarily complied with them, with no need for police forces, courts or prisons to achieve that end. Legislatures around the world had adopted tens of thousands of those same standards. With the substance of so many laws already created without the participation of government, why have legislatures and government agencies at all? The enormity of that realization left Crypto's head spinning.

Very good! The voices were jubilant.

It was a stunning realization for Crypto. With it, at long last, came a goal and a purpose to which he could dedicate his life.

But there were limits, of course. Anarchy wasn't something you could talk about in twentieth-century America with anyone other than the voices in your head; people would think you were crazy or dangerous and most likely both.

Especially if you suggested it might be necessary to blow up all the governments in the world – metaphorically at least – so every person could make her own way forward in the resulting wreckage.

Yes! The voices loved the idea.

Crypto eased off on his medications to pursue a dialogue on the topic further with the Bees. Perhaps the communists had it half right but then lost their way. Maybe small collectives were the answer? Individual communities, each the master of its own destiny as of old?

A return to Eden before the fall!

He followed that train of thought enthusiastically for a while before once again concluding he was a fool. Anarchic theory was a pointless mental exercise. Even if his vision could succeed, there was no conceivable way to persuade a democratic government to disband to allow anarchism to take over, or to wrest control from an authoritarian regime, or even to sell an anarchic utopia to modern voters.

Forget it. Back to his computers. The voices were not happy, and for a time, he banished them by raising the dosage of his medications, leaving him teetering for a while on the brink of black depression.

But he never quite gave up on the dream that an anarchic society might somehow, someday, be possible. The world was becoming ever more dependent on technology. Perhaps that dependency could be exploited to thrust humanity into such a state of chaos that anarchy could rise from the ashes?

It was an interesting thought. That time was not yet. But perhaps in some distant tomorrow.

* * *

With Crypto's desire on hold to lead the world to ruin and then reason, he occupied himself exploring the expanding riches of the internet. From the beginning, he'd visited bulletin boards on every topic imaginable. Anyone could find like-minded individuals with odd aliases, like Yoda. With the invention and build-out of the web, Crypto's technical horizons and interests widened. His distrust of governments and every other type of institution led him to investigate concerns such as security, privacy, and anonymity. In his computer science master's thesis, he proposed a new method of authenticating identity online while preserving anonymity.

After graduate school, he followed technical advances that might allow computers to take over roles governments had often abused in the past. Happily for him, the marketplace had a strong interest in privacy and security for commercial rather than philosophical reasons. He found his developing skills were always in high demand and short supply, giving him his pick of opportunities. He gravitated to the creative havoc of the startup companies that emerged endlessly in Silicon Valley.

Over the next ten years, he switched jobs more than a dozen times, working for a company for as long as it held his interest, and then moving on to another that offered more challenging problems to solve. He cared not at all about money or material goods and lived in rented rooms. Most of his pay piled up in a direct-deposit index fund that was easy to ignore.

One day, he received an official-looking envelope. A huge information technology company had paid an enormous sum to acquire a company he'd worked for when it had a half-dozen employees and no money in the bank. That startup had granted him a generous sign-up bonus of vested stock. According to the letter, he was now a millionaire many times over. He shook his head in wonder. He'd worked there such a short a period he barely remembered its name.

Now he did not need to work at all. When he deposited the check in his long-ignored index fund, he realized with a shock from its balance that this had already been true. What to make of that?

He let that question percolate for a few weeks before deciding to quit his current job and take some time off to decide what to do with his life. He toyed with going back to school to study political philosophy. But why bother? He already knew which governing theory appealed to him most.

He'd taken up running years before in an effort to combat his depression, and spent the summer competing in marathons. The long stages gave him plenty of time to think, and the voices left him alone.

As he ran through the golden grass of the hills bordering Silicon Valley, he wondered what to make of all he had experienced and learned. His life was a tapestry of contradictions: he was a wealthy man who despised capitalism. A former true believer in one of the most controlling regimes on earth who now embraced anarchy. Even his brain hosted a debating society of thoughts and voices. The passage of miles beneath his feet was not matched by any progress in his mind.

Partway through his stint of politico-economic navel-gazing, his mother died after a long illness, the seriousness of which she had never revealed to him. The impact of her passing took him by surprise.

He hadn't visited her often in recent years, but she'd always been there for him. She satisfied the few needs he had for human contact, and she believed in him without reservation. Always had, no matter where his thoughts led him or what he did. Listened to him patiently, admiringly, even, as he delivered his earnest monologues. Now she was gone.

He had long prided himself for his ability to be solitary. Now he realized he had once again deceived himself: his mother had filled a greater need than he had been willing to admit. Now, that space was empty.

It did not help that he was not working, with nothing but his own thoughts to occupy him. He turned his attention to wrapping up her meager affairs and disposing of her few worldly goods. Among them was a stack of letters from his father, tied with ribbon. And he found diaries.

He debated burning them unopened. Would it violate her trust to read them or be a betrayal to dispose of them unread? She could have destroyed them before she died, but had not. Alone and lonely, he decided to see what they would reveal about her sad, quiet life.

Reading them, all in German, plunged him back into the throes of his fall from privilege in 1989 and the emotionally turbulent years that followed. Worse, they provided new and upsetting details. He learned his father had been an ardent Hitler Youth member. To his astonishment, he also found that the cold, indifferent man he remembered had once been passionately in love with Crypto's mother. He learned, too, that his mother's grandparents on one side were Bulgarian, which explained her dark complexion and hair.

All too soon after her marriage, the tone of her diary entries grew insecure, and then anguished, as it became obvious her husband's affections were withering on the altar of his ambitions. She had lost her figure and looks early, and her blond, blue-eyed husband no longer wanted to be seen with her. The Nazis might be gone, but the same biases lived on in the post-war government hierarchy. It struck Crypto like a brick to his head that the same would have applied to him – dark as his mother and pudgy and unathletic back then besides. His father must have been ashamed of them both.

The revelations were enough to throw him once again into a deep depression. He struggled to regain his mental balance, but this time, it was harder. To function at all, he was forced to dramatically reduce his medications, accepting that the voices would play a larger role in his life. They seized the opportunity to harass him into devising strategies to bring anarchy, finally, to the world.

At first, that seemed like a harmless if time-consuming request, a theoretical puzzle without a workable solution. But the voices were insistent, and the problem had always intrigued him. One day, an idea came to him that made achieving that unrealistic aim seem possible.

For several years, he'd taken part in an online forum dedicated to developing a way to anonymously transfer money outside the banking system. Many interesting proposals were offered that inched toward that goal, but all had fatal flaws.

The technical approach that occurred to Crypto addressed each of these issues. He called it the blockchain and decided it might provide the means to achieve the ends the voices insisted he pursue. But to do so, he would have to be cautious. He adopted a new online identity – Satoshi Nakamoto. It amused him and gave away nothing. The rest, as they say, was history.

It took two years of hard work before he decided bitcoin was firmly enough established that he could disappear from the scene. Establishing bitcoin as the first alt coin was, after all, only the initial step toward achieving his ultimate goal, and his need for secrecy was paramount. Bitcoin's progress from that point forward was not constant, but the long-term trend line was always positive. Five years after his disappearance, the results exceeded his highest hopes.

But not those of the Bees. *You must go further*, they insisted. *Don't stop now. Seize the opportunity. Complete your strategy and launch our attack!*

Their urging became incessant, and the medications could no longer rein them in. The best he could achieve was to maintain an outward appearance of calm. Internally, though, he felt as if he was losing control. The price of peace, let alone sleep, was pressing forward with the master plan the voices drove him to complete.

There were a few concessions on their part, to be sure. He could disregard the developing world, for example. Also, those countries controlled by dictators, as well as China. The latter's vast holdings of US securities and enormous appetite for foreign food, fuel, and commodities would guarantee that it, too, would fall if he was successful in taking down the developed nations. From that point forward, there would be no stopping the collapse of every economy across the globe.

The logic was irrefutable. Crypto bought into a strategy that could take down the power brokers of the United States and Russia, the two societies he hated most in all the world. With that concession, the urgings of the Bees became more welcome and affirming. It seemed acceptable to lower his dosages even at the price of giving the Bees unimpeded access to his mind. The prize and the challenge were each enormous, and in the end he was not sure he could go it alone.

Chapter 15

Hello in There!

DIMITRI FEDOROVICH USTINOV, superintendent of blockchain activities for the Department of Information Technology in the Sphere of Budgeting and State and Local Finance Management – a name that fit on his business card solely through the magic of acronyms – was feeling both self-congratulatory and insecure. The former, because the deputy director of the ministry had recently commended him in writing on the success of the Russ blockchain. And insecure, because he knew how little credit he deserved, an inconvenient truth he was sure must become apparent with time. Worse, he had only a general idea how that success had been achieved or to whom the real credit was due.

Today, he hoped to reduce his insecurity by forcing the issue with Mikhail Semyonovich Filitov, the managing director of RussCoin. Until today, they had communicated exclusively by telephone and email. Now Ustinov wanted to meet face-to-face.

The flight to St. Petersburg had been smooth, and the rental car had even been ready for him at the airport. Now he was approaching number fifty-two Savushkina Street, which proved to be a four-story building with blinds slatted shut behind every window. The street address sounded vaguely familiar, but he could not say why.

Ah! Ustinov recognized a building across the street and a few doors down. There had certainly been enough pictures of it in the news. It was purposely unremarkable, just like the rest of this street. Or it had been until Western journalists proclaimed it the home of a troll factory that had – allegedly – disrupted a US presidential election. Perhaps he should not be surprised to find RussCoin's offices in the same neighborhood.

He walked up to a glass door under the portico of number fifty-two and found it locked. There was no guard sitting behind a desk in the lobby inside and no tenant list outside with helpful intercom buttons to push. It seemed pointless to bang on the door; no one was likely to hear him. He dialed Filitov's number on his cellphone and with relief heard his voice after two rings.

"I am standing outside," Ustinov said. "Will you please let me in?"

"Yes. One moment."

It was cold, and the portico was open on both sides, funneling a bitter wind past him. What was keeping Filitov?

At last, the elevator inside opened, revealing a short man whose voluminous beard rested on a plaid shirt spanning an even more ample stomach. He took his time trundling across the lobby to open the door.

"Ah, Dimitri Fedorovich, so good to meet you in person at last."

"And the same to you. May I come in?"

"Of course, of course. You look cold. But do not worry, I put the kettle back on in my office when I received your call."

Ustinov followed him into the elevator. He was surprised when it descended to a bare hallway giving access to several drab metal doors, one of which Filitov opened.

"Welcome to RussCoin's world headquarters," Filitov said grandly, ushering Ustinov into a single, small room.

There was little to be seen inside except for an open laptop on a folding table. And in a corner, a small cupboard with a random assemblage of objects on top, one of which was a hot plate upon which a kettle was just beginning to sing.

"Sit, sit!" Filitov said. "I will make tea."

Ustinov decided his trip to St. Petersburg was a grave mistake. Now he could never deny knowing what he was seeing in Filitov's office.

Filitov turned and set a steaming cup of tea in front of Ustinov, together with cream and sugar. "Now," he said, "we shall get down to business, yes?"

Ustinov cleared his throat. "Yes, indeed. Mikhail Semyonovich, I hope you will forgive me if I observe you have always given me the impression RussCoin was a more substantial enterprise."

"But it is!" Filitov protested. "You should not judge a software project by its office. And after all, have we not exceeded your expectations?"

It was true. And more importantly, the deputy minister's expectations.

"Fair enough, my friend," Ustinov said. "But you must acknowledge that should someone less familiar with your enterprise ask to visit RussCoin, your world headquarters would create a most unfavorable impression. It is for this reason in general that I have come to visit with you today. The success of RussCoin has attracted notice at the highest levels of government, and because of this fact, I must ask you to provide explicit information regarding all aspects of its staffing, internal governance, operational locations, and more. The deputy minister expects me to present a full report on these topics by next Wednesday."

Filitov stroked his beard. "Yes, I see. It is quite understandable." He took a sip of his own tea and woke up his laptop. "Come, then. Sit next to me, and I will show you."

Ustinov moved his chair around the table as Filitov opened several windows on his laptop and began to explain them, toggling from one to the next.

"Here, we have the developer list. You can see each name, and after it, a letter or letters. CT stands for contributor. That is anyone who is able to suggest bug fixes and submit other input to the project but can do no more. CM stands for committer – this is a developer that has the authority to add code to the software supporting the Russ blockchain. A contributor may be invited to become a committer when he or she is recognized as being sufficiently skilled and dedicated to be trusted with the ability to commit code. M stands for maintainer. That is someone responsible for one of the significant sets of functionalities making up the code base. For example, those that create a new block or that verify a proposed block is legitimate. Any developer can rise through the ranks as his or her abilities are recognized by consensus among the committers and maintainers."

Ustinov squinted at the names. "These do not look like proper names."

"Indeed," Filitov said. "Most developers identify themselves by online aliases."

Ustinov sat upright. "But surely, Filitov, you know their real names and nationalities?"

Filitov smiled and sipped his tea. "But in fact, not always, my friend. Is this a problem?"

Of course, it was a problem. Filitov could scarcely be ignorant of that. The Russ blockchain was important enough that the Federal Security Service – successor agency to the KGB of the Soviet era – would want to open dossiers on the key developers, if they had not in fact done so already. And RussCoin was a nominally independent company. Filitov might not be held accountable for any disasters, but Ustinov certainly would.

"Yes, indeed," Ustinov said. "We will need to return to this. For now, please go on."

"Very well," Filitov said, turning to another screen. "Here, you see the log of all additions to the Russ code base – commits, as we call them. And here, the Wiki where the developers can discuss any issues. And now here, a history of each release of the Russ software."

Filitov continued his virtual tour of the Russ software project. Ustinov was a bureaucrat, not a technologist, but Filitov was patient. For the first time, Ustinov began to realize that these databases, as well as the blockchain code itself, were all there was to the Russ enterprise. The lack of developer names aside, perhaps that was neither more nor less than there should be. But still, he was troubled.

"Very good, Mikhail Semyonovich. I appreciate your very clear review of the Russ technology development process. I have a few more questions. First, is the technology secure?"

Ustinov stroked his beard. "The perennial, paradoxical question! The answer is both yes and no. No, in that, like any other software, it is impossible to ensure its complete security. Anything connected to the internet, as a blockchain necessarily is, can be penetrated given sufficient time, skill, and resources. But yes, in that the blockchain recording all Russ transactions is duplicated on seven hundred sixty-seven separate servers spread out across Russia and its trading partners. Currently, they may be found in thirty-four countries in all.

"Also, the software has been created in such a way that Russ exchanges can only be set up within the borders of Russia, and those exchanges are run by entities owned by RussCoin. The central development of the blockchain technology itself is tightly controlled by the small number of dedicated maintainers. Not all of these are Russians, but each is an employee of RussCoin or another company which RussCoin owns. Most importantly, no update to the software can be released without the approval of the overall project manager."

"Which is you, I assume?" Ustinov asked.

"Me?" Filitov said, laughing. "You would not want me to approve anything. I am not a programmer. I am simply the business person who manages the funds your ministry so kindly provides. No, the final and essential approval can come only from Oleg Borisovich Lupanov."

"And who is he?" asked Ustinov.

"He is the founder and leader of the project. Without him, we would be years behind where we are now."

The Federal Security Service would certainly want to keep an eye on him, Ustinov thought. Thank God there was a full name attached to him, at least.

"Good," Ustinov said. "We are fortunate then. I assume that a good deal of the Ministry's money has found its way to him?" The implication of that question was obvious. This was, after all, Russia. If sixty percent of the funding the Kremlin provided to any covert project reached those doing the actual work, the middlemen were considered to be exceptionally honest. Ustinov wondered if that much had made it past Filitov.

"None, in fact," Filitov said. "Lupanov is a true believer. The most dedicated blockchain people, you must understand, are libertarians and even anarchists. The hope of developers like Lupanov is that, through the blockchain, the central bureaucracies and authorities of existing nations – and perhaps even the countries themselves – will no longer need to exist."

It chilled Ustinov to even hear such words; certainly, this information would never make it into his report.

"Such beliefs," Filitov added quickly, "are all nonsense, of course. But the blockchain itself is not." Filitov smiled into his beard and waited for a response.

Very well, Ustinov thought. The idea for the blockchain project had come from the deputy minister himself. Ustinov could scarcely be held accountable for following through on his directions.

"I see," he said. "But I will need every bit of information you have regarding Lupanov for my report."

"That is easily done," Filitov said. "Do you have a business card?"

"Why yes," Ustinov said, withdrawing one from his wallet. "Why?"

Filitov accepted the card and wrote something on the back. "Here. Now you have his email address. That is all I have."

* * *

Crypto was assaulting his exercise bicycle, feeling like the poor, doomed schoolboy in D. H. Lawrence's short story, *The Rocking Horse Winner*, madly driving himself to rescue those who were ignorant, and perhaps unworthy, of his sacrifice.

The subject of his meditations today was once again Frank Adversego. Why was it the First Manhattan employee preoccupied him to such a degree?

Doubtless it must arise in part from the additional details about Adversego's past he had been able to assemble. Reclusive though the investigator might be, curious journalists covering his exploits had achieved some success in fleshing out his background.

Crypto had been intrigued, for example, to learn that Adversego had also led a solitary, unhappy childhood. He had, for all intents and purposes, lost his father at about the same age as Crypto. And both of them had drifted for many years from job to job, often working for startups along the way.

But the parallels ended there. Adversego had been a selectively successful student at best while Crypto had always excelled. Each was brilliant, but Frank had squandered his gifts for decades before finally hitting his stride. Crypto had switched jobs frequently, to be sure, but had invariably outperformed expectations. But for many years, Adversego had always been fired. And though each had lost a father in adolescence, Adversego was reunited with his decades later.

So where did this contradictory – both fraternal as well as competitive – sense of connection he felt with Adversego come from? Crypto could agree that each of them was engaged, in his own fashion, in efforts to save the world. But how different were the paths each had chosen! Crypto had selflessly dedicated himself to work alone and in secret in the service of humanity, perhaps never to receive credit for his many sacrifices. Adversego, on the other hand, was simply a commercially inept small businessman who had a knack for attracting assignments relating to threats to society.

No, that wasn't quite fair. Adversego had impressive technical abilities. He was determined, too, with a history of sinking his bulldog teeth into difficult problems and worrying them into surrender. And Crypto couldn't care less about Adversego's fancy bank title and presumably outrageous compensation. But still: why was Adversego celebrated while Crypto must skulk, rat-like, to avoid discovery and destruction by those he was trying to save?

But enough. Crypto decided he bore Adversego no ill will. Different as they were, the two were similar enough for that to make no sense, regardless of the very different paths destiny had assigned to them. What remained to be seen was what fate had in mind for them now that their paths were converging.

Chapter 16

Come Into my Web, Darkly

T RUE TO THE commitment he'd made to the Bees, Crypto had been
monitoring Frank Adversego's BankCoin interactions on GitHub for a month
now. Happily, nothing Adversego had done to date suggested he was on the way to
discovering anything of concern. But the possibility of his doing so was not zero.

Not zero! Not close to zero! A Bee's voice was disturbingly loud.

He waved his hand in the air. Sometimes, he could shoo the Bees away for a
little while.

Which was helpful because today Crypto needed to concentrate. It was time
to launch the next critical step in his plan, which was to raise the perception in
the marketplace that BankCoin was far more secure than any other alt coin. That
would reassure Adversego and his overseers as well.

But there was no need to act in haste. Only methodical care and a fanatical
attention to detail had allowed Crypto to remain hidden for more than a decade.
Over that span of years, a slow, careful approach had become second nature to him
– a source of pride rather than of impatience at the extra time and effort such care
required. But it was clearly time to put the next phase of his plan into operation.

He began by accessing the Tor Network, the most popular manhole into the
mysterious netherworld referred to as the Dark Web. Dark, because unlike its

everyday counterpart, data on the Dark Web was invisible to the indexing crawlers of browsers like Chrome and Firefox. Dark, too, because of its almost impenetrable anonymity: the Tor software automatically encrypted every message sent on the Dark Web and then encrypted it again, down through the multiple layers of scrambling that had produced the Tor acronym – short for The Onion Router.

Crypto loved everything about Tor, and especially the fact that the thousands of systems comprising its network were maintained by volunteers – it was a perfect demonstration of anarchism in action! Not only could you send massively encrypted email, chat messages, and files wherever you wished, but Tor separated your identity from the message or document itself. When you hit the "send" command, it directed each package of information separately caroming across the vast expanse of the Dark Web until Tor decrypted and reunited it with its peers at your intended destination. It was a wonderful resource for anyone – a whistleblower, for example – anxious to protect their online anonymity. It was even more useful to someone engaged in an illicit activity, whether it be drug dealing, fraud, or – in Crypto's case – taking down governments.

Still, one had to be careful.

But yet act – without action, there is nothing! A Bee's voice was growing more urgent.

Yes, yes. He waved his hand again.

A Bee had been friendly and supportive for so long; Crypto hoped the voice was not on the verge of unleashing another episode of torment.

In any event ... The Tor technology was powerful indeed. Still, that most venerable of all top-secret skunk works – the Defense Advanced Research Projects Agency, or DARPA – had helped fund its development. There was therefore reason to fear it might have weaknesses only the US government knew how to exploit.

So, you must be careful! Very careful!

Yes, yes, of course, he replied. Act or not act? He wished A Bee would make up her mind.

Crypto felt comfortable enough engaging in the type of quick hit-and-run activities he had in mind for today. It took only minutes to load his offer to several sites where zero-day exploits were bought and sold. A zero-day exploit was an attack designed by a black hat to take advantage of a program or system flaw that only he had thus far discovered. Such an exploit was hence still at "zero days" from the time the honest world would learn of its existence.

If a criminal bought the exploit, he would likely launch it immediately. But a government agency might also purchase it, Israel's Unit 8200, perhaps, or the NSA in the United States. Such agencies were constantly buying zero-day exploits to hold in reserve against the day they wished to infiltrate or compromise a foreign government or criminal enterprise. All these would-be buyers competed against each other on the Dark Web until the highest bidder won.

But not this time. Crypto was an anarchist, not a capitalist. He wanted to make sure at least several black hats purchased each of the exploits he was about to offer. For that reason, he would offer them to anyone for a fixed price, not just to a single successful bidder. That way, there would be as many attackers as possible, each one racing against the others to steal as much cryptocurrency as possible before the vulnerability upon which the exploit was based was found and patched.

The profits were irrelevant to Crypto. But he must require payment to avoid arousing suspicion. Why would anyone give something so valuable away for free? But he would take no chances. He would accept only bitcoins payable to a blockchain wallet he created solely for that purpose and would never access.

He logged on to the first site.

Now! Finally, now! A Bee enthused.

Yes, now. Crypto smiled. The voices had been mostly patient with him since he had committed to his plan. They were welcome to share this moment with him now.

Watch! he thought, hitting "enter" after uploading the first zero exploit offer, *This is how it's done!*

Yes! Now on to the next site! A Bee rejoiced.

Bravo! B Bee agreed.

Half an hour after logging on, Crypto's work was finished, and the Bees were ecstatic. For once Crypto and they were in emotional sync.

* * *

Josh Peabody was at his office, hosting a cocktail party for CryptoBoom!'s biggest investors when the telephone in his pocket went berserk. He ignored it for most of a minute because he was speaking to the chairman of the fund's valuation committee. But at last, the angry vibrations unsettled him.

That sense of unease was nothing compared to the sinking sensation he experienced when he looked at the phone's screen. With a sick smile, he left the room as rapidly as he could without attracting attention.

Once in the hallway, he dashed to his office and logged on to the site of the largest cybersecurity exchange. To his horror, the price of BitchCoin was plummeting on the breaking news that over twenty-two percent of the tokens in its initial coin offering – including CryptoBoom!'s entire position – had been stolen.

* * *

Discovering vulnerabilities in so many cryptocurrency blockchains had required great time and skill on Crypto's part. But the time between his posting them to the Dark Web and the resulting attacks was trivial. Greed had seen to that. It was amusing to watch the feeding frenzy as black hats snapped up his exploits and raced each other to launch their assaults and even more diverting to observe the desperate attempts of his victims to comprehend what was happening to them.

This time, the message was too clear to be ignored, even by alt coin fanatics. In a matter of hours, the value of untouched as well as affected cryptocurrencies alike had dropped catastrophically. Most importantly, the credibility of private blockchains – including BankCoin – was on the rise. And that was the sole purpose of the exercise.

Chapter 17

All Fall Down

F RANK WAS ONCE again sitting in the main conference room on the management floor of First Manhattan Bank. At the head of the table sat a grim-faced Horace Nukem, waiting for an update on the wave of assaults that had nearly destroyed alt coin markets. To varying degrees, everyone else looked shell-shocked.

The door opened, and the receptionist ushered in the last attendee, a middle-aged man wearing the expensively tailored uniform of someone who advises similarly dressed people. Nukem stood up to greet him.

"All right, everybody," Nukem said. "Let me introduce you to Henry Gould, from Bingham & Dana, the analytics firm advising us on cyber securities. Henry, please dive right in, and tell us how your people are reading the situation."

"Hello, everyone," the analyst said. "I know you've all read a lot about the chaos roiling the alt coin markets over the last two days. What I'll do this morning is try to quantify the losses and give you B&D's take on the possible short- and long-term impacts on BankCoin.

"Let's start with the high-level numbers. The attackers hit six cryptocurrencies, including bitcoin and the three alt coins with the next highest market values, other than BankCoin. They made off with seven to twenty-five percent of the total number of each of those alt coins, depending on which one we're talking about. Taken together, the stolen coins have an aggregate value of over twenty *billion* dollars – yes, that's 'billion' with a 'B' – based on their trading values at the time of the attacks. That's a truly staggering amount – far higher than all previous coin thefts combined.

"But that's just the tip of the iceberg. In reaction, the market valuations of all major exchange-traded alt coins plunged, dropping between fifty-six to eighty-two percent, depending on the coin. That amounts to a loss of another one hundred fifty billion dollars of value."

A hand went up. "Yes?" Dana asked.

"Why was the impact so great on coins that weren't hit? That's new."

"You're correct. The difference is that, previously, only one type of coin was stolen at a time. In this case, six were hit. The market presumably decided that if six different coins could be compromised at once, every other one must also be vulnerable. I expect they're right. Regardless of the motivation, we know a lot of people moved some or all of their money out of the blockchain ecosystem and into traditional investment alternatives, like stocks and bonds, or even cash. It's too early to tell whether those reallocations will be temporary or long-term.

"At its lowest point, the main alt coin index dropped below twenty-seven percent of its pre-attack value. So far, the same index has only recovered about ten percent of those losses. Assuming no more events occur, we expect index values will gradually move up, but it's too early for us to guess how far or how fast. You'll notice I didn't use the word predict there, either."

"Happily," Cronin interjected, "the value of BankCoin couldn't be affected, since it's pegged to the dollar. And our blockchain remains secure. Can you confirm that, Dirk?"

"This is correct," Magnus intoned. Frank noted that Audrey Addams had not yet succeeded in paper-dolling the crotchety Dane; he was lounging as usual in a soccer team jersey and jeans.

"And just as I would expect," Magnus continued, "because the BankCoin system is not set up in the same manner as other blockchains. We are a closed network. This is fundamental to maintaining its security."

"Can you tell whether the same attackers tried to take us down?" Nukem asked.

"There is no evidence to that effect," Magnus responded.

To Frank's embarrassment and Magnus's obvious annoyance, Nukem turned to Frank. "Do you agree?"

"I do," Frank said. "We've seen no increase in the frequency of BankCoin attacks."

"Well, thank God for that," Nukem said. "Here's hoping it stays that way."

Sure, it was great the criminals had spared BankCoin, Frank thought. *But why?*

Was it because the BankCoin blockchain was as secure as Magnus believed, or were the attackers simply saving BankCoin for later on?

That possibility troubled Frank. And another thing did, too: each of the six successful attacks had exploited a blockchain flaw and not a vulnerability in some supporting part of its ecosystem, like wallets or an exchange. That was unnerving as it undermined the prevailing wisdom that the blockchain was an inherently secure architecture.

At the same time, Dirk's point was valid. Any Tom, Dick, or Harry with a powerful enough computer could download a copy of most blockchains, become a miner, and start validating new blocks. Because there was no central authority, there was no minimum level of security required for any of those platforms. If some Dick wanted to set his password as "password" or "123456," there was no one to stop him. That was crazy. And since every miner had a copy of the blockchain, each represented a point of vulnerability that might allow a black hat to break in, mess with that copy, and then try to export the malware from there to other copies.

"So, where does that take you, Frank?"

Frank jolted back to attention. Nukem, and everyone else, was looking straight at him.

Frank had no idea what had just been said, so he ran for what he hoped was safe ground. "It's certainly a credit to Dirk and the rest of the BankCoin coders that BankCoin wasn't hit. That said, the fact we weren't breached this time is no reason to be complacent. Even if we're more secure today than the competition, we can assume the best of the other alt coin projects will up their game to plug the gaps, or investors won't come back to them. That means over time we'll become a more attractive target, on a relative basis, unless we figure out some way to maintain our security lead."

"Nonsense!" Magnus snorted. "You are all looking – what is your saying – the gift mule in the mouth. There is a reason every major alt coin scheme was hit except BankCoin. That reason is because BankCoin is far better protected. Unlike the other blockchains, it was designed with security against theft as its highest priority, not as an afterthought. Instead of sitting here wringing our hands, we should be telling the world how BankCoin is the only safe blockchain in existence. I do not understand why we are not doing this."

Cronin grabbed the lifeline thrown to him from such an unexpected quarter. "Dirk is spot-on, Horace. These attacks are an opportunity, not a disaster. We should do exactly what he said. Not inappropriately, of course. We don't want to sound like we're exploiting other peoples' misery for our own benefit. But we shouldn't be shy about pointing out that not one penny of First Manhattan customer assets was stolen."

Nukem paused and frowned. "Fair enough. I'm as happy as the next man to ride a gift horse – or even a mule, for that matter – for all it's worth. But I'm also with Frank. If anyone gets complacent about BankCoin security, they'll be doing it somewhere else if I find out. From now on, I want a weekly update on everything we can learn about these attacks – how they were carried out, who might be behind them, and what the vulnerabilities were."

* * *

Crypto's grudging regard for the ill-at ease, cybersecurity-fixated expert that was also his nemesis was beginning to take on Stockholm Syndrome-like properties. Once, while wrestling with a particularly knotty bit of BankCoin code, Crypto caught himself wondering how Frank might work his way through the same problem. But that was nonsense. BankCoin was software to be destroyed, not improved. And Adversego was someone to be defeated, not befriended.

* * *

An exhausted Josh Peabody turned off his computer and slumped back in the office chair he'd scarcely left in thirty-six hours. Exhausted but triumphant: he could still call on the old magic when he needed to. Truth to tell, he'd been coasting for the last couple of years, taking advantage of investment waves anyone with reasonable savvy and flexible scruples could ride to a wealthy result. But pulling off the thousands of complicated puts, calls, and swaps he'd just executed in the face of plummeting alt coin prices had taken real skill, not to mention balls. Now that the dust had settled, he could congratulate himself on snatching a small profit out of the jaws of a major disaster.

Yes, he thought, rolling his sleeves back down and watching the first light of dawn coloring the coastal mountains in the distance, *I do believe that Elvis has reentered the building.*

Chapter 18

Don't Worry, Be Happy

F RANK FELT UNEASY as he and Magnus left the meeting on the sixty-fifth floor. True, BankCoin had been spared, but what about the future? Now that such spectacular sums had been stolen, wouldn't many more criminals want to stick their greedy hands into the cryptocurrency cookie jar? And not just criminals. North Korea, chronically short of hard currency, was suspected of stealing more than a hundred million dollars from South Korean banks through cyber theft.

"You know," Frank said to Dirk as they walked to the elevator, "it's tough for me to feel as confident as you about BankCoin. There's a ton of bad guys out there, and only so many alt coins to go around."

"Only so many, yes," Magnus replied, "but that is not the same as 'not enough.'"

"Okay, I'll grant you that," Frank said, "but how about this? The more the valuations of the other alt coins go down, the bigger the prize BankCoin becomes in comparison."

"Yes, but so what? When speculators lose money, people say 'Who cares? What should they expect?' But if criminals hack the global banking system, every law enforcement service will say 'Oh my! We must catch these very bad guys!' Does that not make the criminals stop and think?"

As always, Magnus made sense, Frank thought as they went their separate ways. Still, while higher stakes might give some black hats pause, others would certainly be up to the challenge. Also, not all member banks were in developed countries. Some of those in emerging economies might not be as sophisticated when it came to cybersecurity controls or as diligent in paying attention to them. A successful attack against a single bank would not take down the entire BankCoin network, but it would undermine its credibility.

That type of risk was clear. Hackers had penetrated the Central Bank of Bangladesh in 2016. At first, they laid low and watched how the bank managed its electronic transfers. After they'd seen enough, they followed the same steps to instruct the New York Federal Reserve Bank to transfer a billion dollars to the criminals' accounts. The Fed wired over eighty-one million dollars before it caught on and turned off the tap. And that was only because they grew suspicious when the hackers misspelled "foundation" as "fandation" in an instruction.

If black hats could do that with the traditional inter-bank transfer system, why couldn't they figure out how to misdirect payments from BankCoin accounts as well? So, no, he didn't feel nearly as confident as Magnus. Now what was he going to do about it?

* * *

Crypto was back at work, more cautious than ever. He expected some law enforcement officers might not have worried much about thefts of alt coins owned by speculators foolish enough to put good money into invisible tokens. But they could scarcely ignore the financial bloodbath Crypto had just unleashed.

He would need to be particularly careful regarding BankCoin. Surely, the banks would push their cybersecurity experts as hard as possible to make BankCoin invulnerable. They would also look hard to discover what someone like Crypto might be up to.

What if they are successful? A Bee interrupted. *WHAT IF THEY SUCCEED?*

Hush! Crypto thought. *You know I've considered that possibility a hundred times.*

But what, A Bee persisted, *if this Adversego person is as good as his bank keeps trumpeting?*

If he is, then you must stop him! A deeper voice boomed.

Oh no, Crypto thought. B Bee was back. That was a bad sign.

Then both Bees went on the attack, each with unexpected fury. He would have to appease them. But how? He had already considered one possibility ...

Yes! Do that! You must do that! the Bees called out in unison.

But to do that, he would need help ...

Then get it!

Crypto looked back at his screen. He hated it when the voices grew so insistent; so confident. Sometimes too confident. But often they were right.

Do it!

Ah. He sighed, wavering.

The Bees had a point. He could not risk Adversego noticing something. But if Crypto sought assistance, there was also the risk that whoever he entrusted with the task might be careless. Or even betray him.

What to do?

Do it! Do it NOW!

It was growing hard to separate his thoughts from the words of the voices. Perhaps he should embark upon a measured response. Greed was a powerful motivator. There was no stronger glue to keep lips sealed than the promise of money. He could afford to pay well, and he would need to expose little to gain much. Maybe that would be all that was needed. And he could, after all, instruct one of his lieutenants to act as a middleman on his behalf.

Yes. DO IT! A Bee shrilled.

We'll be watching, the somber voice of B Bee intoned.

The background stadium sound Crypto could usually ignore ratcheted up to a sullen roar, as if the home team had just been defeated. He hoped it didn't signal the beginning of another difficult period in his life.

* * *

By "one of his lieutenants," Crypto was referring to a member of the cadre of Dark Web co-conspirators he referred to as his general staff. It had taken him years to gather them, and most of the rest of the decade for them to build his vast network of true believers in anarchist political theory. In the beginning, he had spent countless hours at radical chat sites, observing but never taking part. Doubtless the security agencies of many nations were monitoring the same web locations, and he could not risk being noticed by governments he hoped someday to overthrow. Instead, he lurked and listened, assessing the comments of regular participants and paying equal attention to how they expressed them. He was looking for zeal, to be sure, but also for maturity and for people he sensed he could trust. When he decided someone met those requirements, he added them to his list of potential allies.

When his list was lengthy enough, he turned to the next laborious step: contacting and further assessing each person on it. Then began a slow dance, much like the recruitment of a spy where the first step was to establish trust and plumb the true beliefs of the prospect. From the far smaller group that emerged from that process, he selected those with the most talent. Many, but not all, rose to the call. Necessarily, the invitations he extended were vague: simply to become part of a secret cabal dedicated to the goal of someday bringing their political convictions to fruition. And in truth, at that time, he could promise nothing more. Only as the years and the blockchain movement matured did he come to believe his master plan could indeed succeed.

Now he had thousands of loyal followers although, of course, he had no idea who any of them really was. For that matter, he didn't know the true identities of his own general staff; he could scarcely demand their names while withholding his own. That was as it should be. Like any spy apparatus or insurgency network, his troops were rigorously segregated into groups arranged in a pyramidal structure. Each cell of a half a dozen conspirators was separate and anonymous from all other cells. If any individual was caught, he could, at most, expose only the other members of his own cell. And therefore, the cause would live on.

For the same reason, information was rigidly restricted on a hierarchical basis. Not even his general staff knew the details of his master plan or even what his intended targets would be. But they understood the need for secrecy and had faith in him. Each staff member had his or her own role. Some were generals while others held directorships with responsibilities such as communications, recruiting, or reconstruction. Their subordinates, in turn, were privy only to the data they needed to perform the specific function of their division of responsibility. By the time you got down to the foot soldier level, all anyone understood was that a day was coming when they would receive their orders, and a new world order would arise from the ashes of the old.

To be sure, there was a danger that his plan would fail from lack of coordination as a result of such rigid compartmentalization. But the alternative risk was to fail if discovery preceded action. And so, he had no choice but to rely on the assurances of his general staff that the same anarchic convictions that drove them were shared by the thousands of true believers they commanded across the world.

Until now, Crypto had rarely called on a member of his team to take a direct and confirmable action. But if the Bees were right, he had no choice. And he could not risk that they were wrong.

* * *

Frank's phone rang; the frosty voice of Audrey Addams was waiting for him. Neither knew they were not the only ones on the line.

"Do you know what time it is?" Addams asked.

Frank was briefly bewildered; he stabbed at the keys on his laptop and pulled up his calendar.

Darn it. He should be upstairs in a meeting. "Sorry! I'll be right up!"

By the time he was leaving the elevator on the sixty-fifth floor, someone was slipping unseen into his office and closing the door.

As the intruder expected, Frank's tablet computer, with its thumbprint sign-in sensor, was in his backpack, sitting as usual on the floor next to his desk. *Good.* But his desktop was a mess. *Not so good.* The intruder stood on the desk chair and took a picture to record the exact placement of everything. Then she climbed down and donned a pair of latex gloves before clearing a space in front of the chair. *That was better.*

She removed a plastic tablecloth from her bag and spread it on the desktop before easing Frank's tablet out of his pack and placing it in the middle of the cloth.

Working quickly but carefully, she removed several more items from her bag: two sheets of plastic, one with an adhesive backing, a container of fine pink powder, an old-fashioned shaving brush, a magnifying glass, and scissors. After sprinkling the powder on the glass screen, she used the shaving brush to lightly whisk most of it off again on to the tablecloth. Peeling the backing off the adhesive-coated sheet, she placed the sticky side lightly on the glass surface of the tablet. Then she removed it and placed the same side down on the second sheet of plastic.

Now came the tricky part. She hoped Frank Adversego didn't have unusually dry fingers. A few seconds with the magnifying glass confirmed he did not. There were two satisfactory thumbprints to choose from trapped between the sheets of plastic, each with its unique whorls faithfully reflected in powder. She cut the best print out.

Only one more step to go. For that, she removed a laptop from her bag. Then she powered Adversego's tablet up and pressed his borrowed fingerprint on its sensor. *Yes!* The icons of Frank's apps popped into view.

By the time Frank returned from his meeting, his desk was as he had left it and his tablet was once again nestled in his computer bag, exactly the same as before. Or almost so. Now it had some interesting new software installed. That malware would use the tablet's microphone and on-screen keyboard to record everything Frank said and typed, and then transmit that data to its secret recipient. She also had a copy on her laptop of everything archived on Frank's tablet.

* * *

Crypto was pleased. The chance he had taken had paid off well. Within a few days of the intruder's visit, the malware now hiding on Adversego's tablet had captured and transmitted much of value to him. Of particular importance was the login information he needed to access all the software the intruder had copied from Frank's tablet.

From there, it was an easy step to compromise Frank's laptop, to transfer the same malware to that device, and then to examine everything he found there. Since Adversego used his laptop rather than a desktop computer to log on to the First Manhattan computer system – and BankCoin – nothing that Frank would do in his office, at home, or on the road would escape Crypto's attention from now on.

Chapter 19

We've Got to Quit Meeting Like This

ALEKSANDR ISAYEVICH SHUKOV was following familiar corridors on his way to the monthly meeting of the Joint Cyber Strike Council (JCSC). He was also following the director of the Federal Security Service, walking a step behind his boss, as was appropriate to his own inferior status. That was a gap his pride yearned to close. Although Shukov was Superintendent of Cyber Activities within the FSS, his position was based merely on ability, not political connections. If all went well, perhaps the director would nudge the public perception of Shukov's standing a bit higher by engaging him in conversation as they left the meeting.

That would be helpful. Like the Soviet administration before it, the Russian government was filled with secure bureaucrats who contributed little and were paid much. That was a fine system for those with political patrons, but alas, Shukov had no well-connected mentor. He could only advance on real achievement.

Like most such inter-agency gatherings, the JCSC meetings were largely meaningless bureaucratic exercises, valued mostly by their participants as opportunities to assess each other's influence and weaknesses. But beneath the surface was a real purpose. Last year, the president of the Russian Federation had elevated the status of the JSCS's mission to highest priority. Among other knock-on results, the minutes of each meeting were now sent at once to his office, depriving directors of their accustomed opportunity to request the removal of anything that might make them look bad.

All of which put great pressure on those like Shukov, who sat at the right hands of their directors and would be responsible for answering any question their bosses wished to dodge, which was to say all the difficult ones. Woe to Shukov if he was underprepared, allowed his agency to appear to be behind plan, or, worst of all, if he should say anything that didn't cast his director in the best of all possible lights.

Shukov's job was high stress, to be sure. But it was also meaningful. Whether his role was meaningfully good or bad was an interesting question that seemed to have a different answer every day.

In principle, the concept of cyber conflict could be seen as a positive advancement in the age-old art of war. With a few keystrokes, a well-prepared attack could darken a city or even an entire nation, degrading its ability to respond to a physical assault. Through such means, a small country might be overrun in a matter of hours with almost no casualties. That was a more humane way to gain territory or punish an enemy than softening up targets with thousands of tons of bombs before putting your own troops at risk.

And much more economical. To overcome the opponent in cyber war, a nation mostly needed brains, not cash. Russia might not have the riches the Americans enjoyed, but it had always excelled in math and sciences. Not to mention chess.

But cyber weapons could also be as lethal as traditional arms. In the first and second World Wars, the carnage was horrifying, yet the enemy had killed or wounded only a fraction of any combatant's population. Even in the Soviet Union, with its twenty million casualties, the great majority of the people survived. Often hungry, yes, and miserable, always. But alive.

Consider, then, the consequences of taking down an enemy's power grid and keeping it off-line for several weeks in the middle of winter. Most of the population would die of exposure, thirst, or hunger. Everything ran on or was managed by devices reliant on electricity – the pumps that moved petrol into the trucks and trains that transported food, the computers that controlled the delivery of water and the removal of sewage, even the heating system of every home. Take away a nation's electricity and you would transport it back into the Stone Age.

A cyberattack could therefore deliver the same punch as the neutron bombs developed during the Cold War – nuclear weapons that released enormous bursts of sub-atomic particles able to kill everyone within range while leaving buildings and infrastructure intact and radiation free, ready for the attacker to take over. Even during those tense and dangerous times, both sides decided not to deploy devices so obviously suited for naked aggression alone. If something as horrible as nuclear weaponry could be justified at all, it must be for defensive purposes only.

But there was no consensus, or even dialogue, on whether and how cyber weapons should be restricted. That was in part because the field was still evolving, and in secret at that. No one knew how far the potential to wreak havoc with cyber weapons could be extended. To the extent the military of any nation was having success in pushing that envelope, it was hardly likely to share that knowledge with its enemies. It helped that the pundits of the press were preoccupied with other computer-related hobgoblins – whether people might be run over by self-driving cars, for example, and if governments could use "big data" techniques to invade privacy.

Like every meeting of the JCSC, today's would therefore be held in the paranoid shadow of an insecurity that recalled the Cold War: the fear that the other side might be ahead, tempting it to use that advantage to launch a preemptive attack. For all intents and purposes, the nuclear arms race had been replaced by a cyber one, and the last arms race hadn't ended well for Russia. Shukov and his compatriots were determined that this one would.

He was now in the meeting room, which was dominated by an endless table that turned a corner four times to form a long rectangle surmounted by microphones and surrounded by chairs. At the far end were two Russian flags, and between them, the high-backed chair that would be filled by the Chairman of the JCSC. Shukov watched idly as the chairs around the table were occupied. The heads of the military forces were already in their seats, sweating in their heavy uniforms, each one flanked by his own deputy. Shukov knew most of the other number twos. Some were technical experts, like himself. Others were political favorites who could only parrot what their more knowledgeable subordinates had briefed them on before the gathering. Shukov naturally preferred the former as they could be engaged in useful discussions. The others could only repeat what they had been told, over and over if necessary, never giving an inch or agreeing to anything.

On most occasions, Shukov had little reason to be concerned before a monthly meeting. But today was different. True, the JCSC agencies were jointly charged with designing and deploying credible cyber strategies and weapons. But the authority to establish priorities and designate targets lay elsewhere. Those decisions were made by bureaucrats giving as much weight to economic and political concerns as military considerations. This resulted in uncertainty, and sometimes, his agency was taken by surprise. Just two months ago, that had happened, when BankCoin was added to the high-priority target list, and the FSS – meaning, for all intents and purposes, Shukov – was assigned primary responsibility for devising a way to take it down. As yet, he had no progress to report. And there was the Chairman now, a small, grim man sporting a Lenin-esque beard, flanked by two aides carrying his briefcases. Shukov wondered whether either actually included any papers at all. The chairman immediately banged the gavel placed in front of his throne-like chair and called the meeting to order.

It did not help that everyone understood these monthly meetings were largely theater. If agencies needed to cooperate on a target strategy, that would occur elsewhere through discussions among staffers who actually knew what they were talking about. The real objective for each meeting was to reach the motion to adjourn without looking like a donkey. Shukov could almost feel the subliminal message beaming from his boss today. That message was, "Don't screw up!"

Thankfully, there were a few tools at his disposal to avoid doing so. Most notably, the shared goal of surviving a meeting unscathed had inspired the development of a collection of evasive code phrases. Each was designed to sound convincing while saying and committing to as little as possible. They were particularly useful for an agency behind in fulfilling its assignments. Naturally, everyone in attendance wanted to report only good news. And if not, to blame somebody else.

No one was fooled by any of those phrases. But at the same time, everyone knew the day would come when they would need to employ the same verbal gimmickry, so it was in no one's interest to point out the missing clothes of whichever emperor might be speaking. Shukov had been boning up on those phrases all morning.

He stole a look at his watch. Soon it would be the FSS director's turn to make his presentation. He would certainly dip into the non-answer phrase book regarding BankCoin before moving on as quickly as possible.

And now it was time. The chair asked Shukov's boss to begin his report, and he began ticking through the items on his list. In the middle of the most sleep-inducing part of his presentation, he slipped in the following:

"I will next mention the western blockchain-based financial network known as BankCoin. I am pleased to report that my agency is advancing aggressively in devising a strategy to detect vulnerabilities in the BankCoin system that can be exploited on command to disable, or destroy, that network. Turning now to –"

"One moment," the chair interrupted. "BankCoin has been assigned a 'highest urgency' priority. It has been months now since –"

"Two months," the FSS head interjected quickly.

"Very well, two months," the chair repeated testily, "since you were given this task. Please be more explicit about what you have accomplished so far."

Naturally, the director turned to Shukov.

"Of course, Mr. Chairman," Shukov said. "First, I must note that this is a very new area of technology, so new that there are few experts in it. Indeed, it is evolving so rapidly that someone who is an expert today may be behind the times tomorrow. That said, FSS is proceeding on multiple fronts to uncover any vulnerabilities that may exist. Those efforts include assigning our best cyber staff to analyze the BankCoin software for weaknesses and enlisting the best talent in the extensive network of private sector contractors we support. We have often used these resources in the past to develop and launch attacks that have been both successful and deniable."

Shukov and his boss sat very still, hoping the dodgy answer would suffice.

The other attendees watched with mild interest as the chairman stared down the room at Shukov and his boss for what felt to them, at least, like a very long time. Would the chairman publicly humiliate them or let them off with a warning? "Very well," he said at last. "But I place you on notice that next time you will present a detailed report describing exactly what is being done, what you have achieved, and the projected delivery date – a delivery date in the near future, I must emphasize – for a credible attack that can be launched immediately if the president wishes to do so."

The message was loud and clear. Sufficiently so that Shukov's director, who knew nothing at all about cyber warfare but did know a month could pass very quickly, walked an extra step ahead of Shukov as they left the meeting.

* * *

Frank was returning to Washington from another long day in New York. But his fatigue disappeared when he entered the foyer of his building. There, on the floor below the mailboxes, was the package he'd been waiting for. He grabbed it and almost ran up the stairs.

When he lifted the contraption from the box, he felt a deep surge of satisfaction. It hadn't been cheap, but he'd found the ultimate anti-squirrel device: a clear plastic, cylindrical feeder surrounded by a round cage hanging from springs. A bird could stand on one of the small perches attached to the cage and reach the seeds through holes in the cylinder. But not a squirrel – its weight would stretch the springs and drag the cage down until it blocked the access ports.

Frank filled the feeder with seed and hung it from his upstairs neighbor's balcony. He couldn't wait to see the frustration on Fang's face as he tried and failed, and tried and failed again, to reach his reward, just like the squirrels in the video at the vendor's website. Revenge would be Frank's. And it would be sweet.

The next morning, he was astonished to see that his magnificent new, guaranteed squirrel-proof feeder was empty! How in the world could the little monster have pulled that off?

He stalked out on to the balcony and examined the feeder. It seemed perfectly fine. So, how?

He'd have to catch Fang in the act to answer that. He set the feeder on the balcony floor and refilled it. After replacing the lid, he picked the feeder up and watched as eight pounds of seed poured out onto his feet. He turned it over, and there was the answer: the miserable rodent had gnawed through the plastic bottom while hanging upside down from the cage.

So much for the best that American industry could offer. It was time to take anti-squirrel technology to a new level on his own. For the rest of the afternoon, he decided, the financial world would just have to protect itself.

Chapter 20

Cheers!

A WEEK HAD PASSED since the big wave of cyber currency attacks. Ben Cronin was updating Horace Nukem on how the global financial dust kicked up by the massive attack had settled for the BankCoin network.

"So, that's where things stand, Horace," Cronin said. "Everything seems shipshape. We've had the best white hat hackers hit BankCoin with everything they've got, and they weren't able to get inside."

"Yeah, well, tell that to the analysts," Nukem said. "They're all talking about whether they should change their 'buy' recommendations on First Manhattan stock to 'hold' or even 'sell.'"

"Well, you can't blame the markets for being jittery after something like this. All things considered, I think our stock price has held up very nicely. The longer nothing bad happens, the more it will firm up."

"It's not just me, Ben," Nukem replied. "The other banks are worried, too. We're the central security authority, and we're charging big bucks for that service. They're looking for something more from us to help rebuild confidence. What can we give them?"

Benson Cronin looked at Audrey Addams. But she shook her head – no, she had no bright ideas, either. "Well –" Cronin began. But Nukem cut him off.

"How about getting our cybersecurity guy out there? Isn't this why you told the board we had to hire him?"

"You mean Frank?" Cronin said, frowning. "Frank Adversego?"

"Sure. If everybody thinks he's such a genius, why don't you trot him around to tell everybody why BankCoin is different – why no one has anything to worry about? Have him hold a press conference – visit with the big pension plan gatekeepers – make the rounds on the financial cable news shows."

Nukem was warming to his own idea. "And hit up the analysts. We could schedule cocktail parties here and in San Francisco – let's add DC, too. I don't want the regulators breathing down our neck. Yeah. Let's do all that. Gosh knows we're paying him enough."

Audrey Addams's eyes were wide. Nukem wanted them to use the next best thing to a mute idiot savant as a spin doctor?

"Good!" Nukem said. "It's settled then. Send me a draft schedule by the end of the week."

Then he left.

"Well," Cronin said, looking at Addams, "I guess we have our marching orders." It was clear that by "we" he meant "you."

"But, Ben," she said, "using Frank makes no sense."

"Then you'll need to figure out how to make it make sense. Have our public relations people come up with some good talking points. Then have one of our lobbyists prep Frank the way they would if he was going to do a round of tough meetings on the Hill. They can rehearse him with some mock interviews, too, until he sounds good."

Addams nodded reluctantly. "Okay, I guess that would be a good way to start."

Cronin continued. "And we can assign one of our PR folks to work with him directly until this is all over. They can hover at his elbow wherever he goes. Don't worry. You can make this work." Cronin smiled, trying to project a comforting sense of assurance he didn't feel. Then he looked at his watch. "Looks like I need to get ready for my next meeting."

Addams stood up, resolving to make the best of this unexpected situation. She was already planning the additions to Frank's wardrobe.

* * *

Two days later, BankCoin's new cybersecurity poster boy was sitting in a conference room on the sixty-fifth floor. There was a knock at the door which opened to reveal a striking young blonde woman. She walked straight toward him, and he scrambled out of his chair to accept the hand she thrust forward to be shaken.

"Hello, Frank. I'm Lola Logan from PR Outreach."

Frank shook the offered hand lightly and quickly, stifling the urge to reply, "Hi, Lola. I'm Frank Adversego from PR Hell." He settled for "Pleased to meet you."

"Perfect timing, Lola," said Ted Miller, the public relations manager assigned to set up Frank's schedule. "We just started reviewing Frank's meeting schedule. Here." He slid a sheet of paper across the table to her.

"So," Miller continued, "Thursday morning we've got Frank giving the keynote presentation on the second day of the big investor conference at the Javits Convention Center – nice work grabbing that slot when the Wells Fargo guy canceled out, Lola. That night, you and Frank will cover the cocktail party we're hosting at a three-star restaurant. That runs from seven o'clock to nine thirty."

Frank's head popped up. "Two and a half hours? Really?"

"Don't worry," Miller said. "Lola will be at your side the whole time. She'll worry about the list of people we want you to chat up. She'll spot them in the crowd and walk you over and introduce you. All you'll have to do is be yourself."

Frank cringed when he heard the phrase "chat up." True, he'd made some headway in recent years; he could actually hold a conversation with a stranger for as much as two minutes before desperation set in. Still, "being himself" at a cocktail party full of Wall Street types would mean hiding in the darkest corner he could find, possibly in a fetal position. He decided to water that down a bit and make a joke out of it.

"If you really mean 'be myself,'" he said, "I'll be in a cab on my way home before Lola is halfway across the room."

Miller didn't laugh, but Lola generously gave him an appreciative smile.

"Now, on Friday ..." Miller continued.

When the meeting was over, Lola and Miller hung back after Frank left.

"So, what do you think?" Miller asked.

"I'd say he's all you said on the sociability scale and less."

"Think you can make this work?"

"Sure. I enjoy a good challenge."

"Well, thank goodness for that. Let me know Friday afternoon how everything went."

* * *

Lola was already in the town car when Frank got in. She was smartly dressed and gave him a warm smile.

"I hear your keynote went great today!" she said.

It had, actually. Frank was pleased with himself. But then again, it was much easier to talk to five hundred anonymous faces dozens of yards away than a single person up close. He'd been well rehearsed, and there hadn't been many follow-up questions from the audience.

"I guess it went okay," he said. "Better than I expect I'll do tonight, anyway. This isn't really my kind of gig," he said.

"Oh, you'll do just fine," she said, reaching over and patting his hand. "I've got a list of points I'm supposed to look for an opportunity to make, so you don't have to worry about the conversation stalling." That list didn't exist, but she was sure she'd come up with something on the fly if the need arose.

"I'm glad to hear that," Frank said. The last thing he wanted to do was make a fool of himself repeatedly in front of her.

"And don't forget," she said. "You've spent plenty of time prepping. You'll do fine." Another pat. Frank was starting to feel like a golden retriever.

He gave her a strained smile and looked out the window. He was already feeling tongue-tied.

"Let me look at you," she said when they got out of the car. She cocked her head to one side and adjusted his tie. "There!" she said. "Now you're ready for anything."

Lola spotted a direction placard on an easel inside. "Here we go. Off to the left." Frank walked dutifully beside her to a large table covered with name tags.

"Hi, Lola," said the young woman sitting behind the table. "We've got a nice crowd already." She found two tags with red ribbons along the bottom and attached a lanyard to Lola's. "Here you go."

Lola took both and pinned Frank's to his lapel before looping hers around her neck. "It was great when these lanyard things came along. You can't imagine how many dresses used to get ruined when your name tab caught on something."

And then they were inside a large room filled with professionally dressed men and women. "Nice crowd indeed!" Lola said. "Now it's time to get to work. All set?"

"Sure," Frank said, smiling weakly. "Can't think of anything I'd rather do."

"There's the spirit!" Lola said and dove in.

* * *

Frank was feeling positively smug as he rode the elevator up to his midtown flat later that night. Of course, Lola deserved most of the credit. She'd been masterful at ensuring each conversation flowed well, not least by charming all the men and making friends with all the women. But still, he thought he'd held up his end well enough.

Inside, he gratefully poured himself a drink; he'd stuck to club soda all evening.

He was drinking the Distillers Edition of his favorite scotch now. According to the label, it had enjoyed, "a second life experience in VSOP cognac seasoned casks to add exquisitely subtle flavor notes." He suspected that was utter nonsense, but he did like the result. He was becoming quite the scotch connoisseur if he did say so himself. His closet was becoming rather full, too, what with all the new custom-tailored clothing Addams had sent his way.

He loosened his tie and turned to face the sparkling city beyond his grand windows, swirling the scotch before bringing the glass up to his nose to appreciate its aroma. No ice in his scotch now! Who'd have ever thought he could ever become such a man about town?

Chapter 21

Call Me Doogie

F RANK SHOULD HAVE been reviewing his thick briefing book on the way
to NSA headquarters for his first Russ Task Force meeting. Instead, he was
gazing out the window, distracted.

Why hadn't he spent more time considering the risk of attack by a foreign
state? True, at a technical level there was no difference between a state actor and
a criminal, but that was no excuse – motivations might matter, and certainly the
goals of both types of attackers could differ. With global banking now dependent
on BankCoin, wouldn't the Russians have a task force of their own charged with
crafting a way to take down its opponent's financial blockchain? Of course, it
would, if only so it could retaliate in kind if the US ever took down the Russ.

It wouldn't have to be Russia, either. North Korea, China, and Iran all possessed
formidable cyber weaponry. It could even be a smaller nation, like Venezuela
or Cuba. The briefing book included a detailed report on the use of proxies to
stage deniable attacks – not just smaller countries but companies and criminal
enterprises, too. All types of stand-ins were used during the Cold War. Even if a
country lacked a technical team capable of pulling off an assault, most could afford
to hire one. Over a hundred and fifty nations fit that profile.

The use of proxies was ancient, too, as the paper pointed out. From the days of the ancient Greeks forward, nations had hired mercenaries to reinforce or replace standing armies. At sea, countries with weak navies, or no navies at all, could take an even easier and less expensive route, by issuing "letters of marque" to private ship owners, authorizing them to arm their vessels and seize enemy ships. If such a privateer was captured by a foreign warship, holding that simple piece of paper meant the difference between being treated as a prisoner of war and being hung on the spot as a pirate.

The privateer analogy struck him as being particularly applicable. All kinds of criminals were stealing money, identities, and priceless corporate intellectual property at will under the protective umbrellas of Russia and China. Sometimes they acted on behalf of one of those governments and at others for their own benefit.

Clearly, Frank decided, he needed to worry about more than hit-and-run hackers out to steal low-hanging alt coin fruit. Serving on the Russ Task Force would help him reorient his thinking to do just that.

Half an hour later, he was sitting in a conference room at NSA headquarters. Waiting for the others to arrive, he strolled over to the window and saw a dozen deer grazing on the lawn in the distance. Those must be the safest, deer on earth.

The door opened behind him and Frank heard a familiar voice. "Ah, Frank. Fancy meeting you here."

"Hi, Dirk," Frank said. "Interesting we should both be on the same task force."

"Not so much, I think. You have the big name, and I am heavily involved in BankCoin, so why not?"

"Why not indeed, I guess. Hi."

The "Hi" was directed at the uniformed man who had entered the room a few steps behind Dirk.

"Hello," the officer responded, shaking hands. "Colonel Lawrence Dix. And you are?"

"Frank Adversego. And this is Dirk Magnus."

"Glad to have you both aboard. I'm sure you'll be making a key contribution to the work of the task force."

Frank settled into the chair with his name in front of it and examined Colonel Dix and the other newcomers as they arrived. Dix seemed businesslike with a face that looked older than the age Frank had guessed from his bio. There were bags under his eyes, and his cheeks sagged down on either side of his chin. He reminded Frank of a basset hound in uniform.

The middle-aged professor who sat down behind the Arnold Lerner name tag looked out of his element – he was dressed much the same way Frank would have been had Audrey Addams not restocked his closet. Lerner was alert, taking everything around him in with interest.

Joel Rosen, the hacker who'd done hard time, looked like he'd rehabilitated well. He was wearing a blue blazer, open-neck shirt, blue jeans, and expensive shoes. Obviously, he'd gone native in Silicon Valley. And why not? The venture capitalists must be paying him a lot more than he'd ever made outside the law.

Douglas Petrie, the last task force member to arrive – late – was clearly the ghost of Rosen's criminal past. He was skinny and young, wearing sneakers, old jeans, and a black T-shirt with "Code Crusher" emblazoned on the front. The cover of the over-sized laptop he opened in front of him was covered with colorful decals.

"All right," Colonel Dix announced as Petrie sat down, "I'd like to welcome you all to the Russ Task Force and thank you for your service. I can assure you this project is of the highest priority. Regrettably, you won't be able to disclose your participation or share any of the details now or in the future, but your work will be of vital importance to our national security." Those around the table seemed appropriately impressed except for Petrie, whose eyes were locked on his computer screen.

"Password?" Petrie interrupted.

"Excuse me?" Colonel Dix said.

"Password for the Wi-Fi network? My phone's hotspot isn't working."

"That's right. The building's shielded," Colonel Dix replied.

"So, I need a password so I can log on to your network. I'll need to access my tools and stuff if you want me to do anything useful."

Colonel Dix pointed at the credenza behind Petrie. "Look over there."

Petrie swung around and spotted what he wanted. Colonel Dix glowered as Petrie set the laminated card next to his laptop and started typing.

"So," Colonel Dix resumed. "I think we can forego introductions. Your briefing books include full particulars on each task force member. Before we get down to business, though, does anyone have any questions?"

"Yeah," Petrie said, still typing. "So, what do you have against alt coins?"

"Nothing, Mr. Petrie, but –"

"Doogie," Petrie interrupted.

"Excuse me?" Colonel Dix said.

"I go by Doogie. Call me Doogie."

Colonel Dix gave him a hard look. "Okay – Doogie. As I was about to say, the government has nothing against alt coins. As you may be aware, many government agencies have blockchain projects in progress. Also, Treasury, the Federal Reserve, and Commerce have all expressed their support for BankCoin. Our focus here is exclusively on the Russ, which is being used by Russia to evade the sanctions imposed by the United States and its allies in response to Russian aggression. Does that clarification help?"

"Maybe," Petrie said, his eyes locked on his computer screen. Frank wondered what allowances had been made in completing his background check? Presumably someone at the CIA was keeping a close eye on him.

"Colonel," Joel Rosen said, "I think what Doogie may be saying is if we want to succeed, we'll need to be sensitive to the way the global blockchain community thinks about alt coins. If you have anyone in the field that doesn't display real enthusiasm for the blockchain, they'll be viewed with suspicion." *Good*, Frank thought. It never hurt to have a peacemaker on a team.

"Understood," Colonel Dix said. "So, let me continue. I think we should try to be as informal here as circumstances permit. Further to that goal, I'm not going to kick things off with the usual hundred slides. Instead, I'd like to hear your initial reactions based on your briefing books. Who wants to start?"

Nobody broke the silence that followed, so eventually Frank did. "What struck me most was that although the pre-reads do a good job of laying out the landscape, they don't suggest any particular way to go about devising a strategy for undermining the Russ. Was that on purpose?"

"Exactly," Colonel Dix said. "Our goal in setting up this group was to give you a clean slate rather than bias your thinking with anything that's already gone on inside CYBERCOM. What we're looking for is the maximum amount of creativity and ingenuity from you all." The colonel turned to Petrie, who was still clattering away at his keyboard. "I assume you're taking notes, Doogie?"

"Sorry," Petrie said, folding his arms as he pushed back from the table. "Just something I had to finish up."

Colonel Dix glared at him until Petrie reluctantly closed his laptop. Dix turned back to Frank. "Did anything occur to you as a promising place to start?"

"Nothing concrete," Frank said. "I tend to think from the top down. So, my usual approach is to start by categorizing things."

"I'm not sure I follow you," Colonel Dix said. "Can you elaborate?"

"Well, I started with the assumption that two types of attack were worth considering. The first is to attack the viability of the Russ as a cryptocurrency. So, for example, we could launch constant dedicated denial of service attacks against the Russ exchanges to make it difficult to do business. Or we could steal so many Russ that no one would want to risk owning it – rather like what happened recently with the big attack against cryptocurrencies. They all suffered for a while."

"Yes, but then they all came back again," Joel said. "There have been lots of thefts, none of them with lasting consequences."

"Agreed," Frank said, "And that led me to the second approach, which would be trying to come up with a cyberattack capable of disabling, destroying, or scrambling the Russ platform."

"Difficult," Dirk said. "That is the beauty of the blockchain. Once created and put into operation, it is very hard to change."

"Yes," Frank said, "But that conformity can also be a weakness. If we can find a way to monkey with the Russ software, it may take a long time for the Russians to redesign their system so we can't do the same thing again. And if we come up with several strategies, every time they get it up and running, we'll pull it back down again."

"Indeed," Dirk said. "But first we must find a flaw to exploit. And if they have done their job well, that is not so easy."

* * *

As he'd hoped, Frank took a lot away from his meeting of the Russ Task Force. He had a whole floor of engineers at the bank to discuss BankCoin security with, but they were all down in the weeds, looking for flaws a criminal could exploit. They were good at that – probably better than he was. To the extent he could be useful, it would be at the big picture level.

So, it was great to be working with a group of hotshots who were all focused on how to massively disrupt or take down a blockchain-based cryptocurrency. What more could he – or the bank, for that matter – have hoped for? Too bad he couldn't let First Manhattan know.

What he could do while the task force discussion was fresh in his mind was consider how an enemy might conduct a target analysis of BankCoin. The result was an outline that began like this:

Target could be:

– individual bank or banks

– banks in an individual country

– banks within an allied group of countries (e.g., European Union, NATO, etc.)

Goals might vary based on type of target, but could be to:

– make a political or other point

– undermine credibility of the BankCoin network

– disrupt financial operations

– stop financial transactions entirely

Attack types could include:

— traditional attacks to harm or punish specific banks temporarily (e.g., dedicated denial of service exploits, or hacking into a single bank's systems to do damage)

— multi-bank attacks, exploiting a common vulnerability in the BankCoin software itself

That looked good as far as it went. It also helped him decide what to think about and what not. There was nothing he could do to influence how well a bank other than First Manhattan managed its own security, for example, so he'd concern himself only with the BankCoin platform itself and not how any individual bank could protect its unique hardware/software systems.

Where to next? Ah — attack vectors. That is, what means could the bad guys use to get access to the global BankCoin network? Back to his outline:

Attack methods affecting entire system could include:

— Attacker plants malware on a new version of BankCoin

— Attacker penetrates participating bank as a first step in penetrating BankCoin

He stared at the words. The first approach would be the cleanest. If the bad guys could install malware in a new release of the BankCoin software, it would end up at every bank when the new version was distributed. How about the other route? He started typing again:

Attacker penetrates participating bank and then:

— distributes the malware via phishing attacks launched from that bank

— plants the malware in a block that bank helps validate

How workable were those alternatives? Well, the phishing attack scenario was certainly plausible, at least in theory. People blithely clicked on links and files from criminals pretending to be coworkers all the time. Here, the message might come from an email account the hacker set up on a participating bank's system. And the web page the black hat wanted the email recipient to visit might exist on the sending bank's site, too — just hidden from the view of the site's administrator.

But no. That kind of attack was technically possible, but it would be terribly difficult to pull off. For starters, participating banks were supposed to firewall BankCoin away from general software, like email and accounting programs. So, a phishing attack might get you inside a bank's general firewall, but it shouldn't give the attacker access to that bank's copy of BankCoin. Even if the bank botched its firewalls, a hacker would still have to find a vulnerability in BankCoin to exploit, and everyone involved was trying as hard as possible to make sure such a vulnerability did not exist. Finally, at least somebody at one of the hundreds of BankCoin banks should recognize the email as part of a phishing attack and then raise the alarm. So not impossible, but close to it, and therefore, not likely to be the route an enemy state or terrorist would choose.

The other possibility, though, looked worrisome. Every bank could create transaction blocks and submit them for validation by other banks, after which those blocks were added on to all copies of BankCoin. So, a viable channel to distribute malware throughout the BankCoin network was built right into the system. Surely, the Foundation, or at least First National, must be scanning each new block to prevent such an attack. This was important enough to check right away.

It only took five minutes for Frank to see that Schwert had covered that concern in a surprisingly simple way. If any single transaction block had more than two hundred lines of information above the average found in the last thousand blocks, the validation software would trigger a virus alert so the anomaly could be investigated before the block was approved.

Not only a simple solution but an elegantly practical one, Frank mused. Elegant, because it was hard to imagine designing a truly dangerous payload using such a small number of lines of code and also because Schwert's virus scanner could perform a line count almost instantaneously. That was crucial, because BankCoin needed to handle well over a hundred thousand transactions a minute if it was to be usable at all. Lastly, the few lines of code Schwert had written to perform the test were able to self-adjust as the marketplace and the technology evolved.

That ability to autonomously adapt was also elegant, because one of the neat features of BankCoin, like many other blockchains, was the ability to include "smart contracts" in blocks along with their related transactions. These were simple computer programs that could specify, for example, preconditions that must be met before a payment would follow. Because the terms of smart contracts would vary, the number of lines of information in a block would necessarily differ as well. Blocks would therefore not always be the same "size," from a computing perspective. And because smart contracts were so new, you couldn't know how complex they might become over time.

That solution appealed to Frank. Most programmers defaulted to complexity. Only the really good ones came up with simple solutions. This guy Schwert just might be as good as Dirk and everyone else seemed to think he was.

He turned next to what would clearly be an attacker's preferred strategy: tampering with the master version of BankCoin hosted by the BankCoin Foundation with the goal of adding malware to a new release of the software before it was distributed. If the enemy could get away with that, it could compromise every single bank. Clearly, this was where Frank should focus his attention. Then he paused; no, there was one other approach. He added a third possibility to his outline:

– attacker adds the malware to an interim security patch which is then distributed to the network

Frank stared at his screen. Yes, any enemy would certainly decide to use one method or the other to launch its attack through the Foundation itself. As with all the other big open source projects, anybody could commit code if they earned the respect of the rest of the developers. That's the way the world of open source software development worked, so if you wanted to attract the best programmers, you had to play by the community rules.

All of which Frank knew. But it still amazed him the banks had bought into such a vulnerable practice. He would have expected at least some kind of added vetting – most obviously, background checks. But, to be fair, that ship had already sailed. Just about everything in the world ran on open source software now, from telecommunications to automobiles to cloud computing to the Internet of Things, and all of that software was created through the same open process.

He shook his head. This was just another reflection of a mindset he'd always marveled at: once a risk became familiar, people forgot about it. Like driving on the highway even though you knew tens of thousands died there every year: you ignored the risk not because it was acceptable but because you got used to it.

Okay, back to business. He'd just have to work with the fact that hundreds of BankCoin programmers were spread out across the globe, any of whom might try to plant malware or install a "trap door" in BankCoin they could later use to launch an attack. The challenge would be to ensure the BankCoin Foundation and First Manhattan each had processes in place capable of detecting something evil before it was pushed out into the network.

That was a sobering thought and one he should expand on in his outline. He added the following:

Embedded malware could include:

– a trap door

– ransomware

– spyware

– error-inducing software

– destructive software

There were a lot of disturbing possibilities there. Installing a trap door in each copy of the platform would allow the enemy to cause mischief on a targeted basis, attacking as many or as few banks as it wished.

Ransomware – software that encrypted or wiped a system clean unless a payment was made – wasn't employed just by criminals. Terrorists and nation states also used it to destroy enemy systems; the payment demand was purely camouflage to cover the attacker's trail. North Korea had employed that gambit in a massive attack that crippled hundreds of targets including, for some strange reason, many hospitals. Of course, adding collaterally damaged target types could provide cover, too.

Now, how about spyware? Certainly, that was a possibility – maybe even an inevitability – because the entire global banking system ran on BankCoin. But Schwert's software encrypted all data, so there wouldn't be much point to that, assuming the encryption was strong enough. And anyway, Frank's job was to head off a devastating attack, not protect data.

Error-inducing malware was a real concern, though. And so was destructive software. The task force had spent a fair amount of time considering each of those attack approaches. Could he reverse that perspective to spot something malicious before it was triggered? He wasn't sure about that yet.

He tapped his fingers and reviewed his list. Done? No. He started typing again.

Specific destructive approaches could include:

– disable the ability to create new blocks

– disable the ability to verify new blocks

– erase the blockchain

He stared at the last entry. What a disaster that would be. And it wasn't out of the realm of possibility. Back in 2012, persons still unknown had wiped the hard drives of thirty-five thousand computers owned by Aramco, the state oil company of Saudi Arabia. The impact was devastating.

Well, that was enough cheerful thinking for the moment. He shut his laptop and went to bed.

* * *

Crypto, meanwhile, was reaching the end of what had been a very good day. The hand on the main countdown clock had passed the six o'clock position – he was half-way there. The fact that the acceleration of the smaller clock's hand had long since plateaued was also good news, because it confirmed that the entire global banking system had converted to BankCoin more quickly than Crypto had hoped. It was now impossible for any bank, or for any bank customer, public or private, large or small, to do business except in BankCoin. For months now, the hand on the smaller dial had spun swiftly and inexorably, bearing visual witness to the speed with which the apocalypse he had prepared was approaching. It was both soothing and gratifying to stare at the little clock face as its hand spun inexorably onwards.

Day by day, the world was being drawn deeper into his trap, like spiraling matter disappearing into the all-consuming maw of a black hole. Crypto smiled – it was an appropriate comparison. The gravitational force of such a cosmic abyss was so intense that within a certain distance – astrophysicists called it the event horizon – not even light could escape. With the developed world now universally committed to BankCoin, its event horizon was at hand.

Yes! You're right! The BankCoin event horizon! A Bee cheered.

Not quite yet, Crypto thought, *but very soon.*

Chapter 22

What's in a Chain?

FRANK WAS FEELING better about his job lately. He'd discovered several flaws in BankCoin now, some of which could have led to significant mischief if a black hat had found them first. They were pretty subtle, too. He figured that must have raised his stature some with the security team.

And the bank events he was expected to attend were turning out to be okay. Being squired around by an attractive and intelligent woman with a talent for putting people at ease – him in particular – rendered the events nowhere near as stressful as he had feared. Just last Friday night, for example, he'd attended a gala fundraiser, wearing a custom-tailored tuxedo that now held pride of place in his wardrobe. The next day, Lola sent him a link to a photo of the two of them from a newspaper story about the event. If he had a Facebook page of his own, he might have been tempted to post that one.

Ted Miller, Lola's boss, was also pleased. Frank was turning out to be a better cybersecurity front man than Miller could have imagined. At Lola's urging, Miller had begun promoting Frank as kind of a likable IT innocent abroad in the field of finance. Humanizing the security face of the bank couldn't hurt, Miller decided.

When the inevitable next breech came along, it might provide a modest reservoir of sympathy the bank could draw upon.

So, all in all, it was nice that Frank and Ted were feeling better. Sadly, the real world had other plans for their immediate future.

* * *

Gordon Greer settled in behind his Bloomberg terminal, hoping for another quiet day. Yup. Maybe he could catch lunch with some of his Wall Street bros and watch some curling on the TV over the bar.

But first, it was time to buy and sell some oil.

Except no. He squinted at his screen: it looked like nothing was trading. That was odd. Was it a problem with his computer? He moved his mouse around. Nope, his cursor was live, so his system wasn't frozen. So why were all the price and volume fields filled with zeroes? The exchanges couldn't all be down. He clicked over to a financial news site.

Wow! They weren't down – but for some reason, the exchanges couldn't access any data to trade on. What a mess! If this didn't get sorted out soon, he could take the rest of the day off.

* * *

At the headquarters of Baher AG in Zurich, Switzerland, the absence of information was causing far more anxiety. As the second largest oil trading company in the world, Baher's empire of storage facilities, refineries, pipelines, shipping terminals, and tankers spanned five continents and every ocean. Now all those assets were suddenly invisible.

That was bad enough, but Baher was also the manager of the recently activated Global Petro Blockchain Network – or the GPN, for short. And the hundreds of corporate members of that network were jamming Baher's switchboard with demands to know what the heck was going on.

At the center of the storm sat Jonas Baher, youngest son of the company's founder and the one in charge of the new network. Uncomfortably for him, he was also the one who had convinced the global commodity trading elite to buy into the GPN. Not that it had been a tough sell. His proposal met with immediate interest because of the complex route a barrel of oil took between the well and the ultimate customer – the type of path industries referred to as a supply chain.

That journey typically included time in pipelines, ships, barges, and trucks with layovers in collection facilities, refineries, port terminals, and distribution centers. Everyone – or at least their chief technology officers – agreed that a blockchain would provide a far better tool for tracking the billions of barrels of oil products that changed hands each year. And a superior tool for handling the financial terms that lubricated that supply chain, too.

Everyone also agreed that streamlining the process with a blockchain network would save a fortune for all involved: commodities took up space, and a supply chain was linear – barrel B couldn't be shipped to the next link in the chain until barrel A moved on to make room for it. But the owner of barrel B was in a hurry because storing oil was expensive. Empty tanks cost money but earned none, so the owner of a storage facility wanted to keep that asset topped off all the time.

Therein lay the beauty of the GPN. When it was up and humming, every barrel of oil that wasn't in the process of being refined was likely to be in motion, passing as quickly as could be from production to consumption, filling the tills of the petroleum industry as fully and efficiently as possible.

Of course, when you redesigned a system to resemble a gigantic, global network of dominoes, you needed to accept that interrupting the flow of oil anywhere would mean stopping it everywhere. With the GPN now down, the only question was who would be the first to say "I won't take your oil."

In Findlay, Ohio, the general manager of operations for Athens Petroleum Corporation, the largest owner of refineries in the United States, was preparing to say just that. With the GPN down, he could no longer document it when he shipped anything out of his facility and, therefore, no basis upon which to bill a customer for doing so. Since all of his far-flung storage facilities were at or near capacity, he couldn't take in new crude oil either.

Reluctantly, he gave the order to shut down all sixteen of the company's massive refineries. Then he sent notices to all his suppliers and customers that Athens would neither accept nor ship any products until the GPN was once again up and running.

With that single act, three million barrels a day of gasoline and other refined petroleum products dropped out of the system, and an equal amount of crude oil in transit between the wellhead and Athens refineries came to a halt wherever it was at that point in time. As the day progressed, all the company's competitors followed suit. By close of business, eighteen million barrels of US refining production had fallen off-line. As had the output of almost all refineries elsewhere around the world, because the owners of those facilities were members of the GPN network as well.

With the center of the petroleum supply chain shut down, the stoppage spread: backward to the oil fields and forward to the distributors. Oil tankers nearing terminals anchored offshore instead, unable to off-load their cargoes. Pipelines began shutting down everywhere.

* * *

The next day, Tom Bunker heard a ping and glanced at the phone mounted on the dashboard of his sixteen-wheeler. The subject line read "Read Now." That didn't sound good.

He opened the email and confirmed it wasn't. The message wasn't very enlightening – all it said was "Pickup on hold. Await further instructions" – but it didn't need to be. He'd been following the news all day. He took his next exit and coasted to a stop on the first wide shoulder he found. He'd spent enough time on the road to know any unexpected down time might as well be nap time.

The same email, or one much like it, was on its way to petroleum product truckers everywhere. Within a few hours, thousands of semis, engines idling, were piled up in rest areas and truck stops across the United States, their drivers waiting for messages that would in the end instruct them to go home. Meanwhile, the stocks of oil companies and related industries plummeted on exchanges across the globe. Just about every other type of stock and bond headed in the same direction.

By the next day, service stations were closing as they ran out of gas. As word spread, lines of cars formed at those that were still open, their drivers anxious to fill up while they still could. In response to rising howls of anger from consumers and business owners alike, US senators and representatives promised to hold hearings. But without knowing who had taken the GPN down or why, it was not clear what the purpose of the hearings would be, or who to call as witnesses.

Among all those made furious or frustrated by the attacks, perhaps the most anguished was President Henry Dodge Yazzi. That was because the only major oil producer in the world that had chosen not to participate in the GPN was the Russian Federation. By all reports, its supply chain was humming. And it was filled with crude oil that was now selling for seventy-five dollars a barrel. Was the Kremlin behind the attack?

* * *

Frank heard a knock and looked up to see Ruth at his office door, holding an open laptop.

"Can I come in?" she said. "I think you'll want to hear this."

"Sure," Frank said, pulling his guest chair next to his own.

Ruth restarted the video she'd paused, bringing the faces of two commentators back to life.

"... to this breaking news update. I'm Steve Thibeault, and with me is George Hurwitz. We've just learned who is responsible – or at least who claims responsibility – for the cyberattack that's brought the global petroleum supply chain to a halt."

On a screen behind the commentators, a bizarre smock-clad figure appeared, wearing a wide brimmed, flat-topped hat. An enormously long, down-curving beak protruded from the mask that hid his face. Ruth pushed the pause button.

"What in the world does that guy have on?" she asked.

"I think I've seen that get-up before," Frank said "It's what plague doctors wore during the Middle Ages. I guess Guy Fawkes masks have gone out of fashion." He started the feed again.

"Less than an hour ago, the Reuters news agency received a video statement. In it, the strangely disguised person you see behind me introduced himself as the spokesperson for a secret organization calling itself the Nakamoto Anarcho-

Syndicalist Liberation Army, or NASLA. He goes on to claim it was NASLA that destroyed the software used to support the Global PetroBlockchain Network, or GPN, which took over management of the petroleum supply chain earlier this year."

"Did he give a reason, Steve?"

"Yes, George. NASLA is apparently made up of blockchain purists. According to the statement, they believe Satoshi Nakamoto, the original inventor of the blockchain concept, made a great gift to the world when he created a way to make central authorities – banks, suppliers, even governments – irrelevant and unnecessary. According to NASLA, evil business interests like the promotors of the GPN have corrupted that gift and must now be punished."

"Corrupted it how?"

"By putting a central authority back into the equation while taking advantage of the rest of Nakamoto's blockchain concept. NASLA says taking control of the blockchain away from the people is a crime against developer humanity. NASLA has assigned itself the mission of shutting down every blockchain with a central authority."

"Are there a lot of blockchains like that out there?"

"We're researching that in depth right now, George. But the quick answer is yes – there are scores, if not hundreds in use. The ones that have central authorities and operate on an invitation-only basis are often referred to as 'private blockchains.' Mostly, they're used for tracking things from the point of production all the way to a consumer. For example, there's one that tracks gems so consumers can be sure they don't end up with a so-called 'blood diamond' when they buy an engagement ring. Others track goods and services like drugs, advertising, sustainable timber, and a lot more. Pretty much everything now, it seems. Including petroleum products, which is what the GPN tracks."

"But I thought blockchains were supposed to make everything more secure?"

"So did I, George. And on that score, it seems NASLA has a point, of sorts. The reason they could take down the GPN is that, just as the spokesperson said, it doesn't incorporate all parts of Nakamoto's vision. It's true there are hundreds of identical copies of the GPN blockchain around the world – comprising what Nakamoto called a 'distributed ledger.' But there's only one copy of the GPN software capable of producing new blocks.

"A Swiss company called Baher AG, based in Zurich, controls that copy. Baher receives all the data generated by the rest of the network, packages it into new transaction blocks, and then sends those blocks back to the rest of the network so that everyone has a complete local copy. Now that NASLA has destroyed the Baher copy of the GPN software, there's no easy way for any supply chain data to get from one point in the network to any other point."

"I've got it now, Steve. The copies are still intact – or, I guess I should say, intact up to the point of the attack – but the command center, if you will, is gone. I guess that means that until it's restored, there's no way to transact business."

"Exactly. As the NASLA spokesperson went to great pains to point out, the petroleum industry created its own vulnerability by subverting Satoshi Nakamoto's grand design."

"So, what happens next, Steve?"

"According to NASLA, they won't rest until they've taken down every private blockchain in existence."

* * *

A pop-up reminder appeared on Frank's laptop: it was seven p.m. He wasn't an evening news kind of guy, but he found the unfolding chaos caused by the NASLA attacks to be morbidly fascinating – not least because the aftermath of a successful attack on BankCoin would look much the same. Only a hundred times worse, since it would affect all goods and services. He logged on just in time to see the video cut from a view of an anchor at a desk to a reporter standing, microphone in hand, in front of a milling mob of would-be passengers at an airport. Turning to the camera, she spoke:

"Good evening, Bob. I'm reporting tonight from Terminal C in LaGuardia Airport, where carrier after carrier is terminating its outbound flights as it runs out of fuel."

The camera swiveled up to the flight board where the word "CANCELED" glowed angrily just about everywhere a departure time should have appeared,

"Almost no flights will leave until further notice, and fewer are landing."

"I'm sure the people there aren't too happy, Jill."

"Not at all, Bob, and no wonder. Passengers are furious at the carriers for not letting them know of the cancellations before they left for the airport. But to be fair, the airlines had no warning either. The government's decision earlier today to commandeer civilian jet fuel supplies took everyone by surprise."

* * *

Across town, President Yazzi muted the sound of the same broadcast. "Tell me again what I did to deserve this?" he said to Carson Bekin. "Would people be happier if we had no way to defend ourselves against an attack?"

"Nothing to deserve it, of course," Bekin said. "You did what you had to do. It's just bad luck this is happening on your watch. And the media are making it worse. They make it sound like the Air Force could use the strategic oil reserves instead. Of course, that's crude oil stored in underground salt dome formations, but why pay attention to the facts?"

"We've got to get ahead of this, Carson. What's the latest?"

"Well, we're making progress with the oil situation, anyway. The payment guarantees the Treasury and Transportation Departments announced yesterday are helping some. Everybody in the supply chain is feeling somewhat better knowing they'll be paid sooner or later. That doesn't help with the logistics though. Depending on where you're looking, only about five to ten percent of what should be moving actually is.

"The problem is, we're dealing with something less like a flexible chain and more like a train on a track – you can't push or pull one car faster than any other car in the same train. Without the GPN, everybody is scurrying around using telephones and spreadsheets to get things unstuck. It's one epic mess."

"How about the GPN platform itself?"

"They're hoping to get a new copy of the system up and running sometime after midnight tonight. But that's just the first step. Once it's stable, they'll have to pull in all the data from all those quick and dirty spreadsheets, consolidate it, and push it back out to the hundreds of GPN sites that need to update. Until that happens, the network won't be able to function again the way it's supposed to."

"So, you're telling me the more we do now to keep things moving, the longer it will take to get back to normal?"

"Sorry, Henry. I'm just the messenger."

"What about the attack?" Yazzi said. "Have they figured out how NASLA got into the Baher system?"

"They think so. And they've fixed the vulnerability. But there's no guarantee the GPN will be bulletproof once it's online again. NASLA may have installed a back door to let itself in again – heck, maybe lots of back doors. If so, the Swiss forensic team may not have found them all. Another concern I've heard is that NASLA could have planted a timebomb program disguised well enough to escape detection until they trigger it."

"Why hit the same system twice?" Yazzi said. "They've taken the pharmaceuticals blockchain down now, too. Isn't it more likely they'll keep moving on to new targets? Not that that's a good thing, but hitting just about anything else would be less disruptive than taking the petroleum chain down again."

"There's no way to know," Bekin said.

Chapter 23

Don't Tell Me What I Don't Want to Hear

A GRIM HORACE NUKEM sat at the head of the main conference room table on the sixty-fifth floor of First Manhattan's offices. Seated before him were Benson Cronin, Audrey Addams, and the bank's senior BankCoin technology and PR team members: Frank, Hank Taylor, Dirk Magnus, Ruth Kim, and Lola Logan.

"Okay," Nukem began, "I'll keep this meeting short. Obviously, the topic is NASLA. Yesterday, the cyber terrorists hit a third crucial blockchain. That means we need to assume they can and will take down every private blockchain. Given their success so far, we also need to conclude they have the skills and resources to do just that.

"Now I want to make one thing perfectly clear, so listen closely: as you know, this bank got hit – badly – by a cyberattack almost a year ago. The board brought me on as executive chairman with the specific mission of making sure that never happened again. I accepted that charge, and I'll be damned if I'll fail at it.

"Further to that goal, we'll meet here at this time every week until the feds catch up with this NASLA group. The agenda of each meeting will always be the same: item one is convince me you're individually and collectively doing everything in your power to prevent NASLA from taking down BankCoin. Item two is to make sure our messaging is effective at convincing the public of the same thing.

"Any questions?"

Nukem stared briefly at each of them in turn. "No? Good. In that case, I'll see you all next week. Ben, a word with you before you go."

Cronin frowned as the others filed out of the room. What did Nukem expect him to do? He wasn't a techie. If Nukem wanted to tell him to instill the fear of God in the bank's personnel, well, the executive chairman was a lot scarier than he was.

"Okay," Nukem said, when they were alone. "So, how secure are we really?"

"I'm not sure how you want me to answer that, Horace. We think we're as safe as we can be. We've got teams inside and outside the bank trying all the time to find a chink in our armor. If they do — which is extremely rare now, by the way — it's always very minor and fixed the same day. But everybody's human, and humans make mistakes."

"You mean like starting BankCoin in the first place?" Nukem snorted.

"No! I emphatically do not mean that! What would you have preferred? Letting another bank take the lead instead or, worse yet, getting replaced by some startup with a billion dollars of venture capital? Like it or not, we were going to end up on somebody's blockchain. I saw a big opportunity, and I took it. That's what the board expects of me. And don't forget, they voted unanimously to approve BankCoin."

Cronin's slight emphasis on the word "unanimous" did not escape Nukem's notice.

"Unanimous indeed. The question is whether you sold us a bill of goods. Ending up on a blockchain is one thing. Taking the fall for the entire global financial system if someone takes it down is another."

"Nothing ventured, nothing gained, Horace. Don't forget that every single time a bank transaction takes place anywhere we get a fee — that means that all other things being equal, we'll always be more profitable than any other major bank in the world. This was a once in a lifetime opportunity. Wall Street understood it completely, and our stock's been up ever since."

"Hah!" Nukem snorted. "Have you looked at Baher's stock price lately?"

Cronin had. And what he'd seen was ugly.

* * *

It had been obvious to all what Nukem would want to discuss, so Hank Taylor, Frank's boss, had booked a conference room for Frank, Dirk, Ruth, and Lola to meet after Nukem released them. They were sitting there now.

"So," Taylor said. "Anyone have any bright ideas how we prove the negative every week to Nukem? What does he expect us to do beyond what we're already doing?"

"Strictly speaking," Dirk said, "He did not ask us to do anything new. His exact words, if I recall them properly, were we are to 'convince him we are doing everything possible.' So, if we are already doing everything possible, we can do no more. Where is the problem?"

"The problem," Taylor said, "is in making him believe us. If we don't come up with something new each week, he'll be furious."

"So, every week, we will tell him something different," Dirk said. "I'm sure there are lots of ways we can spend the bank's money if we set our minds to it."

Taylor frowned. "But wait a minute, Dirk –"

"Ah!" Dirk smiled. "But he did not mention giving us any more budget to spend, did he? Perhaps that little item slipped his mind."

"Look," Lola interrupted, "let's cut to the chase. What we've got here is a marketing problem, not a technical one. We all agree we're covering every base we can already, right? Great. So, all we have to do is what Nukem asked us to: convince him and convince the customers and Wall Street we're on top of things. Nukem's not a technical guy. He doesn't have a clue what you guys do to maintain security. So, every week why don't we just bore him to death with some aspect of what we're doing now. It doesn't have to be anything new."

Heads nodded. "Yeah, we could do that," Taylor said.

"It sounds like a plan to me," said Dirk, standing up. "In which case, you will have to excuse me now. It seems I have some previously unscheduled busy work to do before this time next week."

* * *

Crypto played the NASLA video over and over, enjoying the spokesperson's costume and performance.

Yes, the sudden appearance of NASLA was a welcome surprise. Not only was Crypto supportive of the mysterious group's mission, but he was sure the NASLA attacks would help camouflage his own actions. True, law enforcement agencies around the world were now monitoring blockchains and scrambling to their defense. But the limited supply of skilled cyber investigators was stretched dreadfully thin: every few days now there was a new attack to investigate, and so many blockchains seemed equally at risk. How much time could the defenders spend on each one?

Surely the FBI and others would assume BankCoin must be the best designed and defended blockchain in existence. That BankCoin had not been NASLA's first target would reinforce that conclusion. He could not have planned things better if he was the leader of NASLA itself.

* * *

"So, what's the deal?" Doogie said, not waiting for Colonel Dix to call the task force meeting to order. "Why the extra get-together all of a sudden? And are we getting paid for this?"

"We're meeting," Dix said, "because the president has issued an executive order directing appropriate federal agencies to divert all available resources to the pursuit of NASLA. I'm sure you're aware of the attacks the group has launched. It's knocked four different industries flat so far, and there's no telling how many more are in its sights."

"No kidding," Doogie said. "It took me forever to get an Uber out here and cost me an extra ten bucks when I did. So, what about our pay?"

"I don't have the details on that yet. It may take a while to sort that through. But I'm sure you appreciate how great the threat NASLA poses to the national interest."

"I only appreciate what I'm going to be paid!" Doogie said, looking around for applause for his little joke. He didn't find any.

"All right, everyone," Dix continued. "Thank you for meeting today on such short notice. As you just heard, the scope of our engagement has been expanded. Specifically, we are now additionally tasked with reviewing all NASLA attack data as it becomes available. The object of our analysis is to identify elements common to each of those attacks with the goal of hardening potential future targets. This effort will be in addition to our existing work, which will continue as before.

"With that by way of introduction, let's turn to the briefing books you were handed as you arrived for today's meeting …"

Frank wondered what he would find inside the thick binder he was now leafing through. Was he about to experience an *Oh My God* moment, realizing that BankCoin shared a common vulnerability with one of the blockchains NASLA had already hacked? If so, it would be an excruciatingly long and fidgety meeting before he could flee back to the bank and start developing a patch.

Chapter 24

Abracadabra

"OKAY," PRESIDENT YAZZI said. "Enough on that one. What's next?" The National Security Council meeting was halfway through its agenda.

"That would be Jim Wakeman, Mr. President," Carson Bekin said, referring to the national security adviser, "With this week's summary of Russian actions."

"Right. Jim, what do you have for us?"

"More of the same, I'm afraid, Mr. President. Broadly speaking, they can be summarized as working aggressively to undermine NATO and the European Union and to further destabilize the Near East with the aim of keeping oil prices high. Here are the details.

"First, the Russians have added another category of disinformation to their campaign to undermine popular support for NATO throughout Europe. Now they're planting fake news on social media claiming NATO troops, usually Americans, are engaging in violent behavior in host countries, such as assault and rape. We've had tens of thousands of troops stationed in Europe since the end of World War II, so, unfortunately, such acts have occasionally happened in the past. That inclines some people to take the fake stories at face value. The Russians are pushing similar propaganda in Ukraine to discourage it from considering closer ties with, or joining, NATO.

"The Kremlin is also stepping up its funding of reactionary, populist candidates everywhere in Europe. Covertly, of course. They've been particularly generous to those advocating more autocratic, anti-democratic governments and those calling for countries to leave the European Union. Most recently, we're getting reports Russian agents are attempting to revive and arm formerly violent movements, like the Basque separatists.

"In the Near East, the Russians are using a combination of approaches to further inflame relations between the local governments and the Kurds in Turkey, Iraq and Syria. For example, they're spreading fake accounts of atrocities by both sides. Again, though false, it's hard to squelch such stories, because there is a history of real crimes. Lots of people would like to believe what they're being told, whether it's true or not.

"In summary, for the last six months we've seen a consistent increase in Russian interference throughout Europe and the Near East."

"Hugh," Yazzi said, turning to the secretary of state. "Is there anything new on the diplomatic front? Any back-channel indications of a change in Russia's intentions?"

"Nothing, Mr. President. It appears the Russian government is largely focused on maintaining voter support through next year's presidential and State Duma elections. The worse the Russian economy gets, the more President Denikin relies on rallying public sentiment against NATO in general and the United States in particular. And the harder we push him, the harder he pushes back."

"How about after the elections? Are you getting any indications he might discuss a thaw after that?" Yazzi asked.

"None, Mr. President," said Calhoun. "And frankly, I'm not surprised. The hotter the Kremlin rhetoric gets, the less possible it becomes for Denikin to do an about-face."

Yazzi turned to the secretary of energy. "Howard, how about the oil companies? Are they still solid?"

Blaine frowned, "Not as solid as we'd like. The NASLA attack on the petroleum supply chain has been a nightmare for them, and it took longer than we expected to get the new drilling leases through Congress. Then there's all the law suits. Environmental groups are trying to block drilling in over sixty percent of the new tracts we auctioned. Finally, you can imagine how they feel watching Russia selling oil for more than twice as much as they're allowed to. So, all in all, the oil producers aren't what you could call happy."

"Well, what did they expect?" Yazzi said. "Anyway, what's the bottom line?"

"I'd say we can get them to hold out for another three months, but that's it."

"Okay, the last question's for you, Terry. What's happening with the Russ?"

"Mixed, Mr. President," the director of the CIA replied. "Its value dropped as expected when we added it to the embargo list. We and our major trading partners have been pretty successful squelching speculation in it. But the Russian government is still propping it up, so the amount of trade in violation of the trade restrictions has continued to increase."

"So, there we are," Yazzi said, glaring around the table. "We're stuck in the same rut we've been in for months now – stay the course and keep the pressure on until they crack. Except the Russ trade keeps extending Russia's resources while we're facing a three-month deadline."

"That's the most obvious conclusion, Mr. President," Calhoun said, "which is why I believe we should consider privately signaling the Russians we'd like to work out a way to avoid further escalation on both sides," Calhoun said.

"Meaning what?" Yazzi said.

"We've been engaging in an internal exercise at State where we have a 'pro' and a 'con' team – something we do fairly often to help develop and evaluate policies. Essentially, we hold a debate as another means of testing policy alternatives to see which one stands up best.

"In this case, the 'con' team has made some good points recently. The first is that the harder we push the Russians, the more difficult it becomes for us to predict the result. That's for several reasons, including the possibility that factions and pressures within the Kremlin may shift, leading to decisions we didn't expect. And if there's an internal shake-up, our assumptions could go out the window entirely.

"Another point is that we don't want to end up with no choice but to take down the Russ. Granted, we have a task force designing just such an attack in case we decide there's no other way to bring Denikin to the negotiating table. But if we do go that route, we'll have legitimized a form of cyber aggression we're more vulnerable to than the Russians are. Or the Chinese, or, really, any of our enemies. To date, no one's taken down a financial system. Once we do that, the genie will be out of the bottle. Even the fact our attack can't be conclusively traced back to us will complicate our defense in the future, because it will prove how successful such a ploy can be."

"So, what would you suggest?" Yazzi asked.

"That we send a message to the Russian foreign minister stating we would be open to discussing a package deal in exchange for lifting all economic sanctions. Those discussions might be directed at signing a treaty addressing a variety of topics: barring social media interference, extradition of cyber criminals, adopting mutual policies of no first use of online weapons, and so on. Privately, it would also require them to stop baiting and undermining NATO."

"What do you expect the response would be?"

"There's the hard part," Calhoun responded. "At this point, we don't know how such an offer would be received."

"Mr. President, if I may?" The NSA director interrupted.

"Yes, Jim?"

Wakeman chose his words carefully. "While I applaud Secretary Calhoun's objective, I must go on record as advising that sending such a signal would be seen as a sign of weakness. We're already teetering on the edge of failure in our efforts to bring Russia around using economic pressure. The Russians must know the oil companies aren't going to cooperate much longer. Giving any indication we may be ready to break would incentivize Denikin to hold out until the last possible minute on the assumption he can outlast us. Then you'd have to choose between launching the Russ attack or backing off."

"Hugh?" Yazzi asked. "What's your response to that?"

"Well, Mr. President," Calhoun said, "there's nothing magic about today. We can wait and watch on a week-by-week basis and see what happens. But we can't dither for too long. This is one of those strategies you have to initiate early or not at all, because putting out a diplomatic feeler has its own time line. If you look hurried, you lose leverage. Once you've raised the topic, you've got to wait for the other side to respond at its own speed, and that can take time."

"How much time would you need?" Yazzi asked.

"Generally, I'd say three to six weeks. But if we think the oil companies are weakening, we can't wait too long if we want to give this a try."

Yazzi frowned. So, now there was a third option, albeit briefly. But that was no reason to act in haste.

"All right," he said at last. "Thank you all for this input. I'll take both viewpoints under advisement. What's next on the agenda?"

* * *

It was very late, and the light of a single window broke the dark silhouette of the cavernous headquarters of the Federal Security Service. Suspended between the blackness outside and the darkness of the hallways inside sat Aleksandr Shukov, hunched over his drab, metal, government-issue desk. The sole furnishing in the brightly-lit office was a small picture that sat on that desk. It showed Shukov's three-year-old son, laughing and holding a stuffed animal.

Shukov did not appreciate being assigned a one-month deadline to pull a cyber rabbit out of a hat, particularly since he wasn't convinced the hat contained any rabbits at all, given how secure the blockchain was supposed to be. Like Frank, he saw only two potential ways to take down a financial system based on a blockchain. And, like his counterpart across the globe, he had ended up in more or less the same place.

The first approach he had considered was to design an attack that could compromise the entire BankCoin network. That would mean penetrating the defenses of hundreds of different computer systems, each with its own unique security controls. Then he'd need to plant malware capable of compromising each of those systems.

Designing such software might be possible. But gaining access to every single system would be a different matter. It would take thousands of staff to find at least one vulnerability in each of those systems, and, in any given week, the hosts of some of those systems would discover and patch their vulnerabilities. If he failed to compromise even one bank, then the entire attack would fail, since every other bank could reboot its systems from the surviving one.

And then there was the second approach: find a flaw in the part of the BankCoin software that created the blocks. Again, before someone in the network spotted that vulnerability and patched it first.

So, in reality there was only one way: his people must find a needle in the BankCoin software haystack and then exploit it to compromise the entire BankCoin system.

If he could do all that, and he had no reason to assume he could, it would turn the security advantage of the blockchain upside down: instead of needing to hack every bank, he could penetrate just one system – the one that hosted the master copy used for updating the system. That would be an elegant solution to a difficult problem. Perhaps it might even be possible.

Very well. So, what more could he ask his team to do to devise such an attack? His top programmers were already deep in their review of the BankCoin software, conveniently available as open source code at GitHub. Others on his staff were monitoring the sites on the Dark Web where exploits were sold, ready to place the highest bid for anything interesting that might pop up.

He had also assigned field agents to join the BankCoin open source project itself, and they were working their way up the meritocracy ladder at the BankCoin Foundation. At some point one of those coders might rise to a position where he could plant malware on the authoritative version of BankCoin. But that would take months, and Shukov was not sure it would be possible to disguise malware to the point where it would not be recognized as such by other developers. This was, after all, a development process that allowed everyone to see everything, and bragged that "many eyes make all bugs" visible.

Finally, and perhaps most discouragingly, there was the risk that any flaw his team discovered or bought would be discovered and patched before it could be exploited. Most of the banks must have experts assigned to look for such weaknesses. So even if some day Shukov could report to the Joint Cyber Strike Council that the FSS was ready to strike, he would be unable to guarantee how long that capability might last.

It was all very challenging and depressing.

Chapter 25

Stop That!

F RANK WAS HAVING one of the professional insecurity attacks that from time to time snuck out of nowhere to bite him. He frowned as he watched the familiar monuments come into and out of view as the commercial jet climbed, circling over the nation's capital before heading off to New York. Everything looked the same as it always did – of course. Just as everything did for him every day at work. He'd been pulling down his huge salary at First Manhattan for months now, and except for finding a few flaws, what had he really accomplished? Not much. Not that anyone seemed to care, so long as he continued to let Lola trot him around like the rental pony at a grade school birthday party.

He scowled at the clouds and drummed his fingers on the arm rest. What should he be doing that he hadn't done yet? NASLA had everyone on edge, and for all he knew, his time to head off a huge disaster might be running out. Between the massive alt coin attack months before and NASLA's all-out war now, he'd had plenty of wake-up calls. The next assault might be Iran making off with a trillion dollars in BankCoin.

So, what would an enemy nation do, besides put its best people on the project? Then he had a disturbing thought. He'd never asked Hank Taylor whether someone at the bank was monitoring the Dark Web sites where zero-day exploits were sold! The National Security Agency and its equivalents around the world scanned those sites daily. That might explain why there hadn't been a successful criminal attack yet – government buyers could have been buying all the vulnerabilities anyone had found so far. But what if the winning bidder was an *enemy* government?

He opened his laptop. Darn! The Wi-Fi on the plane wasn't working, and they had just taken off. *Calm down.* There was no way Taylor wouldn't have covered that base a year ago. And anyway, another hour wouldn't make a bit of difference.

But he didn't calm down until he landed and put a call through to Taylor to confirm that yes, of course, First Manhattan had been watching the Dark Web all along. Better yet, they'd never spotted anything to worry about. Mostly reassured, Frank decided some redundancy couldn't hurt and spent his town car time spinning up a little program of his own. By the time the driver reached the bank, Frank was well into coding a piece of software that every hour would log onto the most popular sites selling zero days and alert him if it found the word "BankCoin."

By midafternoon, his bot was up and running and the brief therapeutic bump he'd enjoyed from feeling like he was getting somewhere for a change faded. Now what?

What indeed? What if BankCoin was already infected with malware, just waiting to go off? Or maybe a black hat had added an as yet undiscovered back door into the code? How should he go about finding something he might have missed ten times already?

He'd asked himself the same question often, but this time, an approach occurred to him that should make his quest more manageable. He could compare a current copy of BankCoin with the original version supported by the Foundation and focus just on what had been added since then. That would dramatically decrease the amount of code requiring scrutiny. And he could narrow his review still further by ignoring changes too small to be dangerous. He was sure he could think of some other rules that would allow him to limit his search. That all made good sense.

What else? Yes. He should keep the early version disconnected from the internet – "air-gap" it, in developer lingo – so it would never get compromised. That way, he'd always have an uncorrupted benchmark to compare against. No breakthrough, certainly. But at least he could be more efficient going forward.

Two hours later, he had a factory-fresh server sitting in his office, linked to nothing other than a monitor, a keyboard, a mouse, and the electricity outlet in the wall. Now to download the earliest BankCoin Foundation version of BankCoin.

Using his laptop, he logged on to the BankCoin libraries at GitHub and downloaded the BankCoin release he was looking for. Then he ran every anti-malware program he had to ferret out anything nasty that might be lurking there. Or at least everything the programs could spot. As expected, the scanning software found nothing. The final step would involve transferring the software to the air-gapped server in a way that minimized the chance that any malware he'd missed would come along.

That process began with unplugging the ethernet cable connecting his laptop to the bank's network. Next, he double-checked to be sure his Wi-Fi card was disabled. Then he did something he hadn't done in years: he plugged an external DVD burner into his laptop. Malware was a lot more likely to make a jump across a hard-wired connection than it was to hitch a ride on physical media. He transferred the BankCoin code and the compiler Schwert had provided, along with his own favorite code compiler and a bunch of developer tools, onto a series of DVDs.

Just one step more to go. He connected the DVD burner to the air-gapped server and transferred all the software once again. *Done.*

His new system now had as clean a copy of BankCoin as he could provide, and everything else he'd need to work with. Of course, if he'd allowed any malware to reach his air-gapped system, the whole exercise was just a fool's errand. But that couldn't be helped. One challenge at a time.

* * *

Ryan Clancy looked up from the latest report from his liaison at First Manhattan Bank. So, Frank Adversego had set up an air-gapped system. Why would he do that?

Clancy wasn't sure. On the one hand, he could imagine there were experiments that shouldn't be run on the live version of BankCoin. But on the other, the regular First Manhattan security team wouldn't be able to monitor what Frank was up to. *Hmm.*

And then there was the fact Adversego hadn't found much yet that was truly worrisome. Did that mean that BankCoin was unusually secure software or that the bank's star cybersecurity expert wasn't as good as he was supposed to be? Or what about this: could Adversego have spotted a vulnerability and never told anyone?

Clancy decided he was creating a suspect out of thin air; he'd seen nothing so far to make him suspect Adversego of anything other than trying to do his job. And his contact at First Manhattan seemed comfortable with Adversego's role and actions. Just because someone didn't match Clancy's buttoned-down view of how an employee should work didn't mean he was up to something he shouldn't be.

Of course, Clancy reminded himself, it also didn't mean he wasn't.

* * *

A Bee's voice was shrilling in Crypto's brain.

What is he doing?

Crypto stared at the information scrolling down his computer screen. What was Adversego doing indeed? He'd just downloaded the source code to the first public version of BankCoin and then disconnected from the bank's system. The Wi-Fi on his laptop was turned off, too. What could he be up to?

No good! You know he's up to no good! A Bee hissed.

Hmm. What would he be up to if he was Frank? This could be a dangerous development.

Of course, it is! What are you going to do?

I don't know yet. This would take some careful thought. He waved his hand in the air, trying to concentrate. Silence followed. *Good.* But not for long.

You'll have to kill him!

Crypto lurched back from his computer. *Kill him? What?!*

Yes! Kill him!

I can't do that! That's absurd.

Of course, you can! Do it before he figures out anything more.

No! Crypto stood up and began pacing, both hands fluttering helplessly in the air now.

Fool! Fool! FOOL! B Bee boomed, his attack echoed and amplified by the roar of the suddenly-returned chorus.

Crypto collapsed back into his chair. The Bees were spinning up in intensity to a fury he hadn't experienced in years. This was getting out of hand. If he couldn't calm them down, he'd need to increase his daily medications right away.

No! Don't do that! A Bee screamed.

Ha! B Bee bellowed. *That won't stop us! You know it will take weeks to take effect.*

B Bee was correct; where were his emergency meds? He sat down and fumbled with a desk drawer. Where were his sedatives?

Where you can't find them, so don't bother!

He hoped the voices were bluffing. And the howling of the chorus was becoming unbearable. When he finally located the two pill bottles, his hands were trembling.

Are you listening? Pay attention! B Bee thundered.

He shook a capsule from each container into his hand and swallowed them dry. He desperately needed some air. He stood up unsteadily from his desk and stumbled outside.

But he found little relief on the sidewalk as he shambled forward, waiting for the sedatives to take effect.

Pedestrians walking toward him swerved to the side, quickening their pace to get past the strange mumbling figure waving his hands in the air as he walked.

* * *

Two days later, Crypto was struggling to adapt to the newly furious Bees, working his way through the series of exercises he'd painfully developed over the years to train himself to project normalcy during times of severe mental stress. At the moment, he was hunched over, reciting a nursery rhyme into his laptop's video camera and focusing all his attention on just his lips as he pronounced the words. Doing so made it easier to separate his thoughts from the incessant swirling, yammering of the Bees. With luck, he would soon be able to be around others again without giving himself away.

After an hour, the Bees were back under some degree of control; their voices were fainter now, and better behaved. *Good.*

He progressed to the next exercise. This time, he watched his entire face on the screen instead of just his lips, forcing himself to look normal. Then he sat up straight so he could watch his bodily movements as well. *Also, good.* He no longer betrayed his inner turmoil. It was time to take the next step: interacting with someone in a store. For this exercise, he would need to not only focus on ignoring the voices but on communicating normally with another person. *Difficult.* But he'd pulled it off so often before.

He stood up and allowed his thoughts to turn to the other concern that had been tormenting him. There was still the problem of Adversego. Given the stakes, he had decided, he could not totally reject the use of threats of violence.

Yes! A Bee cheered.

But it must absolutely be used only as a last resort. He was as profound a pacifist as he was a committed anarchist. Compromising one value in the service of another was a betrayal of principle he was not ready to commit.

Suddenly the Bees were upon him again, more ferocious than ever. *Fool! You have no sense of the danger.* A and B Bee bellowed in unison, backed again by a rising stadium roar.

Stunned and shaken, he slumped back into his chair. He would have to start all over again, with his simplest exercise of all. Shoving his face into the screen, he started to speak, every muscle taut as he fixated on his lips. But the Bees were unrelenting.

"Humpty Dumpty sat on a wall," Crypto recited. *Steady!*

What if you fail? What if your foolish soft-headedness ruins everything? A Bee screamed.

"Humpty Dumpty had a great fall," he continued. *Focus! Focus!*

Fool! Idiot! B Bee echoed.

"All the king's horses and all the king's men,

Couldn't put Humpty –"

YOU MUST ACT!

It was too much. Crypto clutched the edge of the table and threw back his head. "All right!" he cried out to the ceiling. "If it comes to that, yes! But we're not there yet! There are still alternatives. Give me some peace!"

There was a brief silence. Then he heard A Bee again. *Peace?* Her voice was suddenly, jarringly, soft and caressing. *Perhaps. But only during good behavior. And you know we will be watching.*

Exhausted, Crypto snapped the laptop shut. He had to rest. When he recovered enough to go outside, he would need to exercise more self-control than ever. And he must convince the Bees he was making progress.

Chapter 26

I Just HATE it When that Happens!

TITUS STEELE, RANKING member of the House Department of Homeland Security Subcommittee on Cybersecurity and Infrastructure Protection, was striding forcefully through the Capitol, pursued by a scrum of reporters. As usual, each was calling out the kind of curveball questions they hoped he'd take a swing at but never did. So far, he'd ignored the reporters, other than to present his leonine visage to best advantage to their cameras.

With the committee room just down the hall, a BuzzFeed reporter decided to pitch the chairman a slow ball he might take a crack at. "Mr. Steele," she called out, "what about these NASLA attacks? Shouldn't we have caught whoever's behind them by now?"

And indeed, that one sailed right into Steele's sweet spot. He stopped short, and the reporters shoved their cell phones forward, microphones on, even as they bumped into each other.

"Absolutely! With all the resources at our disposal, it's a travesty this administration has failed to bring these cyber terrorists to justice. Congress has given hundreds of billions of taxpayer dollars to the Department of Homeland Security, the NSA, CYBERCOM, and countless other public and classified agencies to develop the means to keep this country secure. If President Yazzi can't deploy those resources properly, we need to replace him at the next election with someone who can."

Another reporter chimed in. "We've heard rumors the Global Petroleum Network will go back into operation later today. Isn't that a good sign?"

"Is it? The pharmaceutical blockchain is still down. Now there's no way for the Food and Drug Administration to know whether products in the supply chain are safe to use. That means, thanks to this president's incompetence, my constituents are facing life-threatening situations – from the little boy whose inhaler is running out to his grandmother, who can't pick up the heart medication she needs to stay alive. And now, just an hour ago, we learned the real estate transaction networks in New York, Los Angeles, Chicago, Atlanta, and Dallas have all been wiped clean. Apparently, those realtors started using a blockchain-based recordation system back in January. NASLA, I say, is making a laughingstock of this president!"

"But, Congressman," the same reporter persisted, "isn't the real problem that blockchains are being rushed into operation before the security issues are fully understood? When the president asked DHS to propose regulations to increase blockchain cybersecurity, you were one of the most vocal opponents. Why was that?"

"Now just a minute, young lady. I'm pleased and proud that the most active blockchain incubator in the world is in my district, and it's creating lots of fine, high-paying jobs for my constituents. Safety is one thing, but the role of government is not to cut down on jobs creation ..."

* * *

President Yazzi's tie was being straightened. In just a moment, the camera pointed in his direction would go live, and he would update the nation on the ongoing NASLA crisis. The opposition had been beating him black and blue for two weeks now over the impact on the economy and the quality of American life. And the media hadn't been much kinder to his press secretary during the daily White House briefing.

But still, he'd held off on addressing the nation personally, waiting until he had at least some evidence of progress before stepping in front of the cameras. With the GPN becoming fully operational again, he finally had some good news to report. Although not much.

He disliked having video cameras in the Oval Office and tried to ignore the last-minute preparations. As he often did, he ran his hand approvingly across the surface of the desk first used by Lyndon Johnson. Most people assumed he'd pulled it out of storage to underline the transition of power, but that wasn't it. The real reason had to do with Yazzi's Native American identity. Johnson had done more than most US presidents to recognize Native American rights. Yazzi would have preferred the Hoover desk though. The thirty-first president was the only chief executive who had ever lived on an Indian reservation. For his time, Hoover had been very progressive in supporting Native American rights. But using his desk would have been too obvious, and the press would have made too much of it.

"Ready, Mr. President?"

He looked up. "All set."

As the videographer stepped behind the camera, the White House media coordinator held up one hand; in just a moment, he'd fold one finger after another into his palm, counting down the five seconds before they would go live.

But before he could, an aide hurried into the Oval Office and placed a note on the Johnson desk directly in front of Yazzi. It read:

NASLA just took the GPN down again.

* * *

Frank's blockchain task force was meeting Saturdays and Sundays now. On the latter, the members continued to craft their plan for destroying the Russ, and on the former, they took part in the all-available-resources, all-out war the administration was waging against NASLA. Today was a Saturday.

Colonel Dix was running late. As he waited, Frank was fully occupied by two mental exercises, the first, as usual, being fidget suppression. The second was puzzling over how the meeting might unfold. As far as he could tell, the task force's Saturday efforts had been completely unscripted with no fixed aim other than the stated task of analyzing whatever data had become available during the preceding week. He wondered whether a coherent master plan coordinating the federal agencies even existed. It seemed more like his task force's efforts were part of a general effort to throw as much expert cybersecurity mud against the wall as possible with the hope that something resembling a solution might stick. If so, it was probably a long shot that anything generated by such an uncoordinated effort would bail the country — and the president — out.

Dix arrived and apologized. After he sat down, he still looked apologetic, as if hoping someone would pipe up with a suggestion about where to go next. This did not occur.

"All right," he said finally. "As you've likely guessed, no real progress has been made since our last meeting. NASLA seems as brazen and successful as ever. They've already taken down the oil network — twice — the pharmaceutical supply chain, and six other, less essential blockchains. There are scores of other private blockchains that haven't been hit yet, and we have to assume they're all at risk.

"Neither the FBI, the NSA nor anyone else has any solid leads, so this week we've been asked to look for technical clues that might lead somewhere. Further to that objective," Dix clicked on a projector remote control, "here's what the Baher AG engineers saw when NASLA hit the GPN the second time." The video clip opened with a shot of a computer screen displaying a software control dashboard; a cursor dodged back and forth across the screen, highlighting buttons as it clicked on them.

Then the screen went blank. After a few seconds, a computer company logo displayed, indicating that something had made the system reboot. When the sequence completed, the screen refreshed, only to show the unmistakable image of a plague doctor. For a few moments, the bizarre figure shook its staff in their faces. Then it walked off camera, and the screen went blank again, this time, for good. Along with the GPN system.

* * *

Frank's assigned duties – such as they were – at the bank never changed. Perhaps that was why he was becoming increasingly fixated on triumphing in a war he still thought he could win: outsmarting an eighteen-ounce rodent.

He was pursuing that quest with single-minded resolve. And there was plenty of information to work with. He had never paid much attention to squirrels before making the acquaintance of Fang. Poring over anatomical diagrams of his nemesis, he saw the beast had very large and muscular rear legs, for leaping, and smaller front ones with clever paws, for getting into mischief. When a squirrel stood up on its hind legs, Frank decided, it resembled a miniature tyrannosaurus with fur. Only more evil.

There was little now that Frank did not know about the eastern gray squirrel, including its Latin name, which was *Sciurus carolinensis*. He knew, for example, how much larger the average male squirrel in Washington, DC was than its cousins in Orlando, Florida – eleven-point-five percent – the average distance an adult squirrel in the mid-Atlantic states could leap from a stationary start to a landing place at the same height – thirty-seven inches – and even the last time squirrels were commonly kept as house pets in America – the Colonial Period.

He had brought all that knowledge to bear in making his latest advance in anti-squirrel technology. He turned his creation around and admired his handiwork. It looked something like an old-fashioned light shade from a bordello. But instead of red satin and black tassels, all the parts were shiny metal.

The starting point was a commercial squirrel baffle made out of aluminum and shaped rather like a Hershey's Kiss chocolate candy. The concept behind the off-the-shelf baffle was that a squirrel crawling up a pole would be unable to reach its rim, and would be able to find no purchase on its smooth surface if they did. If it tried to leap from a tree instead, the wobbling baffle would shake the squirrel off before it could grab the pole above.

All well and good. But that configuration was no use to Frank because Fang could leap directly to the feeder itself. To avoid that, he had drilled holes every inch halfway around the lower rim of the baffle. From these, he hung thin, stainless steel rods, forming a jiggly curtain that resembled a set of emaciated wind chimes extending the full length of the feeder but only halfway around it. And instead of installing the baffle below the feeder, he attached it above.

He hung the feeder, wearing its new baffle hat and cloak, from the balcony above his, with the curtain of rods in. That left the rod-less side facing the street and available for birds to feed from without difficulty. Assuming a bird ever arrived.

So tough luck for Mr. Fang. If he tried to get to the feeder from above, he would slide off the baffle and land on the balcony every time. That would be fun to watch! If instead he leaped toward the feeder from the wall, the dangling bars would deflect him. Nor could Fang grab on to the rods themselves – Frank was sure they were much too thin, jiggly and slippery for that.

And then there was the feeder itself, which now sported a thick, gnaw-proof iron shield on the bottom, as well as a brass tube protecting the wire holding it up. Frank took a picture of his creation and then hung it up. He wondered whether there was some sort of anti-squirrel technology Hall of Fame he could send the picture to?

He worked at home the next day, waiting for Fang to take up the challenge. But the squirrel never put in an appearance. Or the next day. Perhaps Fang was studying the situation from a hidden location, assessing his options. Well, good luck with that!

The next day, Frank left for New York, secure in the knowledge that Fang had finally met his match.

When Frank returned two days later, the feeder, along with his magical, mystical invention had disappeared, without a trace.

It was time to go nuclear.

Chapter 27

Inside the Box and Out

T HE LONELY LIGHT of Shukov's office window was once again gleaming like a beacon from the upper reaches of the FSS headquarters. Shukov had spent many hours now trying to devise a way to take down the BankCoin network, and he was not pleased with the results. Or, more accurately, lack of results. He'd decided that if the design for an effective attack existed at all, it would be novel and not like anything he'd ever come up with before. In short, to use a Western metaphor, he would need to "think outside of the box."

Thinking in such a fashion was not part of the Russian bureaucratic tradition, which made it doubly challenging. He massaged his face with both hands. The lateness of the hour was also not helpful. How should he get a fresh start? He wasn't sure.

He stood up and stared into the black void outside his window. One way might be to take nothing as a given. Perhaps that might lead to a useful insight.

He sat down and started a list, beginning with factors he'd identified as dead ends up until now:

— FSS does not have enough resources, using traditional means, to penetrate the defenses of every bank hosting a copy of the BankCoin blockchain

– It would be impossible to disguise a malicious program to the point where it could avoid detection when reviewed in source code form

– No vulnerability will remain undiscovered forever

The statements seemed incontrovertible. He massaged his face again, and then with some effort added a few more items to the list.

Now what? How about this – he could try and come up with an exception to each statement on his list. He tried that and failed. So, this approach must also be a dead end. His face ached from fatigue.

He stared at the items. Was there another way to think outside this box?

Maybe this: he could attempt to turn one of these dead ends into an advantage. He gave that a try.

And got nowhere the first time he reviewed his list. But the second time, an idea came to him when he reached this item:

– No vulnerability will remain undiscovered forever

The idea was this: what happened when a flaw was discovered? It was patched, of course. But if he had adequate, ongoing access to the master copy of BankCoin, he could remove that patch, and then the flaw would propagate back to every copy of the blockchain with the next release. Then it might remain there forever. And if it did not, the same trick could be played again, exploiting a different flaw. Or he could wait to reverse the fix until just before an attack was launched. *Hmm.* He would also need to devise a way to prevent GitHub from reflecting the process of removing the patch. Or to disguise what he had done. He made a note.

It was an exciting idea. He stood up and began walking around the perimeter of his small office to stretch his legs. He would immediately instruct some of his staff to review all earlier changes to BankCoin, looking for ones that might be security patches. He would tell others to monitor all future alterations with the same goal. After that, he would either need a mole with the authority to alter that particular part of the software, or a way to spoof the identity of someone who did. Or perhaps he could recruit a senior BankCoin developer to do the job. His budget would be adequate to that task.

Progress. But not a complete solution. Any time you went about correcting vulnerabilities, you needed to worry about a criminal exploiting the flaw before everyone applied the fix. There were always many users that ignored security notices. It made no sense, but there it was. Certainly, the big, multinational banks would patch their systems immediately.

But others might take a few days to apply the fixes. So, knowing this, those who maintained BankCoin would not want to identify a change as a patch needed to plug a security hole. Otherwise, since the source code was posted at a public website, criminals would notice and unleash bots against every member bank, searching for any that had not updated immediately. He logged on to GitHub to see if his suspicions were borne out.

He was right. There were no public notices of security fixes. But such patches must exist. Perhaps the BankCoin network mixed vulnerability corrections in with normal bug fixes as camouflage? If that was the case, how would his people be able to tell one from the other?

There would be a way, he was sure. Finally, he was on to something. He stood up to go. Despite the hint of dawn now illuminating the horizon outside his office window, he felt more energized than when he'd arrived the morning before.

* * *

"I just don't get this," Nukem said at the third weekly meeting of his NASLA defense team. "Who are these guys, and what do they have against the modern world? It's not like they have another planet to hang out on. They must be suffering from the effects of their attacks along with everyone else."

"Allow me," Dirk said. "I have been on the blockchain discussion sites since Nakamoto posted his famous white paper. You must keep in mind that all the true believers back then were anarchists and that coming up with something like bitcoin was their common goal. They are still around, and their goals have not changed."

"All well and good," Nukem said, "but what's the link between anarchism and blockchains? I thought anarchism was about getting rid of governments entirely."

"That can also be so – there are many branches of anarchist theory. Americans are not so familiar with anarchism today. Also, I think the concept goes against your national identity. Americans are taught that democracy is like revealed truth from up above – and that it is your country's great gift to the world. What is the phrase? 'American exceptionalism,' yes? As in, 'if only the rest of the world was like us, everything would be okay.'

"But the rest of the world, it is not so sure. Most countries have not had so much success making democracy work if they have tried it at all. What people in Europe have seen since, oh, let's say, forever, is governmental systems coming and going, often several times within in a single lifetime. Take the long view, and they all fail. So, those who grew up under czars, kaisers, emperors, and then duces and fuehrers – their lives taught them there is no good authority. So, some of those people say, 'I want to live in a world where there is no big guy who can tell everyone what to do. I want a political system where no one can unleash the

Cossacks on my village, or ship me off to a 'reeducation' camp, or compel me to fight in their imperialist war."

"Okay, I guess," Nukem said. "But what does that have to do with NASLA?"

"Oh, everything!" Dirk said. "Many anarchists think getting rid of every kind of authority – not just governments, but banks, too – will be the salvation of mankind."

"Well." Nukem snorted. "I don't know a lot about anarchists, but I do know they've never had much success in the past."

"Yes, but that is why the blockchain is such a big deal to them," Magnus said. "Wanting an anarchist society didn't mean there was any obvious way to get one. But since Nakamoto, some think there is now a way to take authority out of the center of everything forever."

"Oh, come on now," Nukem snorted. "They can't believe that. How could they?"

"Perhaps they are encouraged by what they have already seen," Magnus said. "Even without blockchain, look at all the fundamental, disruptive changes technology has accomplished just recently: Amazon puts more big merchants out of business every year. Uber is killing the taxi companies. Now we see millions of scooters popping up like mushrooms on city streets in many cities. Unless Uber builds scooters, too, or self-driving cars, maybe, will it be the next one to go?

"Also, countries: some governments are abandoning radio spectrum allocation and broadcast regulation – who needs them with internet broadcasting? Others are trying to get rid of cash entirely. The list goes on, and all these were unimaginable just a decade ago!"

"But why," Nukem asked, "would anyone think the new people running things would be any better than the old ones?"

"Because NASLA-type people say there will be no new guys." Dirk said. "The blockchain, they think, makes them not only obsolete but unnecessary. The algorithm is the only 'guy' there is."

"So, let's say I accept that a lot of the world could be run by software," Nukem said. "Why is that so much better than having governments and banks doing the job? This country may not be perfect, but I think it runs pretty damn well. We've never had a czar or a fuehrer here."

"But the anarchists do not see it that way. They would answer, 'Not yet, no. But wait and you'll get your turn.' They have a profound distrust of authority. For thousands of years, people have trusted leaders who then betrayed them. To anarchists, authority is bad, even in a theoretical sense. And it is so much worse when you give it to real people because real people do bad things.

"Technology, though, is different. Ones and zeroes cannot decide to be either good or bad. They just are. You set a program up, you let it go, it runs and does not care who you are. With blockchain, the anarchists have found a way to take people out of the system and place their trust in the computers. Does this help make NASLA easier to understand?"

"I'm beginning to be sorry I asked," Nukem replied, "but let's assume everything you're saying is what NASLA is thinking. What does that mean for BankCoin?"

"Oh, it's very good for us."

"Really?" Nukem said, perking up. "Please explain."

"Sure," Dirk said. "All the blockchains NASLA has hit so far are basically dumb distributed ledger networks. Every participant has a copy – 'their own personal copy of the truth,' as the blockchain fans like to say – but that is all they have, because only one company has authority to make new blocks. So, they are just like traditional database systems controlled by a single entity who everyone must depend on and trust. But BankCoin is mostly like bitcoin – no block of transactions is trusted unless multiple banks confirm it first. True, only some rather than all. But even the bitcoin zealots admit bitcoin is too slow. BankCoin should not look too bad to an anarchist, because the basic principle is maintained. So, we would not be perfect in the eyes of NASLA, but with so many worse actors, perhaps they will find more appealing targets elsewhere."

For the first time, Nukem looked interested. "So, you're telling me we may not have anything to worry about?"

"Well," Dirk said, "I cannot know what goes on inside the heads of the NASLA people. But so far, it is the central authority blockchains they have been harping on. With so many of those to target, we can hope they will leave us alone."

Nukem turned to Lola Logan. "What do you say, Lola? Can you make something of that? Put out a big PR blitz explaining why BankCoin is the safest place to keep your money?"

"Hold on, Horace," Cronin interrupted. "Let's not claim we're immune. That may sound like a dare to these NASLA crazies. I don't think assuming rationality on the part of people who run around dressed as plague doctors while crippling society is our best bet. Also, I'm not sure the fact we may be more acceptable to anarchists is something to brag about."

"I agree," Logan said. "I do think we can point out to analysts in one-on-one discussions that there are real differences between BankCoin and the networks NASLA has hit. Other than that, though I think the lower the profile we maintain, the better."

Nukem nodded, disappointed but convinced. "Yeah. Probably so." He glanced at his watch. "Anyway, good meeting. Dirk, I think most of what you said was crazy. But what the heck, these people obviously *are* nuts, so maybe you're right.

That would be great news, at least for us. So, thanks for the interesting thoughts, and see you all next week."

Frank followed Dirk and the others out of the room. The anarchist mindset didn't make a lot more sense to him than it did to Nukem. But it did seem to match well with the facts. And he'd always been partial to facts.

Chapter 28

You Sexist Pig!

N O ONE AT the bank had ever told Audrey Addams she was beautiful. Not because she was unattractive, but because she was unapproachable. Even after hours, her colleagues agreed, her severe expression, hairstyle, and wardrobe sent an unmistakable message that read "stay away." Audrey was okay with that.

Her friends wouldn't have called her severe when she was growing up in a small town in upstate New York. True, she was shy and bookish, overshadowed by her big, football playing brothers and ignored socially at school because she was a straight-A student. Her father, a dairy farmer, doted on her because she was his only little girl. But he never took seriously her ambition to be the first Addams to attend college. That is, until the day she packed up and left with a full room, board, and tuition scholarship to a state school in Buffalo. Her mother knew her better and cried. Wherever Audrey would be after college, it wouldn't be farm country.

During her sophomore year, Audrey decided Buffalo would be a stepping stone to something bigger. During her junior year, she set her sights on the biggest city of all – New York. Scholarship money didn't pay for sorority fees, but that was okay. She was happy to hunker down in her dorm room and study harder to be sure she not only got a job in the city, but a good one.

Her determination paid off. She graduated close to the top of her class and accepted an offer from a bank with a management training program. The pay was generous, too. She'd be able to save up to go to business school – the next stage in the life she'd mapped out for herself. For the first few years, things at the bank went even better than she hoped. She advanced so rapidly that the need to add a business school degree to her resume faded and then disappeared.

But then things changed, and her promotions stopped. Although he would have been amazed to hear it, the reason was the CEO.

The bank wasn't a big, prestigious Wall Street institution, but a smaller one called Bowery Savings & Loan, a solid, modest business with no ambition to become a player on the New York financial stage. Until Willie Bigelow became CEO.

It took Willie only eighteen years to make it from the mail room to the top spot. He was intelligent, to be sure, and had a great aptitude for banking. But his real skills were personal – all agreed that no one could hold a candle to him when it came to morale and team building. He wanted everyone to think Bowery S&L was the only place they would ever want to work. And he backed that ambition up in every way he could, including by taking the bank on a daring and exhilarating expansion campaign that often scared the board of directors out of its wits but always worked out in the end. Almost every employee, from the receptionist to the executive VP, loved Willie Bigelow.

One of the few exceptions was Audrey Addams. Where others saw a fantastic boss and a brilliant deal maker, she saw a portly man with perpetually disheveled hair and a taste for inappropriately flamboyant ties. The more successful the bank became, the less worthy she thought he was to lead it. Of course, she never criticized him directly. But she didn't need to; a sniff and a look at the right time could speak volumes. The more out of sync she became with her peers, the more she compensated with aloofness. And the more aloof she became, the more the word got around: Audrey Addams was not a team player. And that was that.

Like many surprising success stories in the world of big business, Willie Bigelow's eventually ended. He pulled off the biggest coup of his career by acquiring a storied bank, First Manhattan, after it made a series of large and disastrous loans that left it with insufficient cash reserves to meet regulatory requirements. But even in that weakened state, its assets were almost three times those of Bowery S&L. It was a complicated deal, too, because Willie's bank needed to convert from a savings and loan institution into a commercial bank before it could merge. But Willie was convinced this was the transaction of a lifetime, and he stuck with it doggedly, huddling with the lawyers and bucking up the courage of his board. As a last concession to seal the deal, he agreed that he and Benson Cronin, the suave head of First Manhattan, would be co-CEOs of the combined enterprise. It seemed like a safe bet. The chairman would come from Bowery, and he and Willie were tight.

All seemed to go well, and the bank's stock rose encouragingly.

Behind the scenes, though, Cronin was only biding his time, waiting for the right time to bump the bumpkin in the office next door. The opportunity to make his move came when the chairman, suffering from health problems, unexpectedly retired a year after the merger. The board was still split fifty-fifty between the directors of the two banks that had merged, but Cronin began meeting privately with those who had come from Bowery S&L. He showed them a skewed industry survey that suggested they'd been severely under-compensated for years under Bigelow's leadership. He didn't mention that his own directors had been paid about the same.

Cronin sprung his trap at a board meeting under the "other business" topic at the end of the agenda. Without warning Bigelow in advance, he proposed a dramatic increase in director pay. Willie was shocked at the numbers Cronin proposed, predicting analysts and stockholders alike would object. He suggested the board should instead hire a compensation consultant to recommend any adjustments that might be in order. Instead, the board asked him to step out of the room. When he was invited back in, he learned they'd voted to adopt Cronin's recommendation instead of his own. And also, to demote him to chief operating officer.

Cronin moved quickly to consolidate his new power by reorganizing management, demoting or letting go former Bowery S&L staff wherever possible. And he made Audrey Addams his chief of staff. Her file showed she had the qualifications and had never been part of Bigelow's team. Best of all, placing someone with her imperious manner in such a visible and influential role would send a message that the free and easy Bigelow days were over. When he invited her to join his team, Cronin assured her that further advancement would follow in due course.

Of course, she took the job. She'd been in Cronin's corner since the first time she heard him speak. At last, the bank – her bank – had a leader who looked and acted the part instead of an ill-groomed ruffian with a Brooklyn accent.

For a year, Addams felt she'd died and ascended to career heaven. Cronin was as respectful and courteous to her as he was to the board. Within a few months, it was clear he trusted her completely and relied on her absolutely to make his job as efficient and painless as possible.

Bigelow, naturally, didn't stick around. He stayed just long enough for his most recently awarded stock options to vest and then left to become CEO of another up and coming bank. Cronin replaced him with Larry Bragg, someone he'd known since college, sharing a dorm room with him there, an apartment while in business school, and vacations after that with their families.

That was when things on the sixty-fifth floor really changed. Whenever anyone left or a new job was created, Bragg gave preference to cronies from his and Cronin's past. Within a year, he went further, filling spots with former colleagues without engaging a search firm at all. And the hires were always men.

Once the new order of things became clear, some of the best female managers quit to pursue better opportunities elsewhere. That trend snowballed as those who remained felt more and more isolated. By the time Bragg's second anniversary at the bank came around, the only women left in management were those who refused to be edged out as a matter of principle or were so close to retirement that making one last move made no sense.

That would have been bad enough. But junior staff changes on the sixty-fifth floor were equally disturbing. It seemed that whenever a new manager came on board – male, naturally – the only thing he paid attention to when interviewing an administrative assistant candidate – always a woman – was her appearance. After a while, the vice presidents began firing and hiring their admins in a blatant race to see who could hire the best looker.

Audrey ignored the disgraceful process for as long as she could. Cronin, she was sure, was above what was going on. He was on the road a great deal, after all, and relied on Bragg as much as he relied on her to keep the place running smoothly. But turning a blind eye grew more difficult as the number of Bragg hires increasingly outnumbered the managers from the old Bowery S&L days.

And then there was this: some new employees not only had the biases of sexist pigs but were perfectly happy to act like them, too.

The change wasn't immediately obvious. Some female employees shut down their bosses if they made an unwelcome move. But others were afraid of losing their jobs, opting instead to put up with as much as they could and avoiding non-public places as much as possible when their predator was around.

That approach became increasingly necessary as word spread that anyone who complained to the human resources department – now also headed by a Bragg hire – was met with skepticism and endless forms to complete. And no corrective action was ever taken.

Word also got around that if a woman persisted in her accusations, the director of HR would suggest that perhaps she would be happier working somewhere else. If so, she would receive a glowing recommendation plus twelve extra weeks paid vacation while she looked for a new job. Of course, there would be paperwork to sign – the confidentiality agreement and release of all claims of any kind against the bank, for instance. Just the usual forms.

If the accuser didn't take the bait, the director of HR would flip through the papers in her employee file, shake his head, and observe that there didn't seem to be any room for advancement for her there. As a matter of fact, now that he examined her file more carefully, her performance of late had really been quite poor ... Was she sure she couldn't use a nice vacation?

And still Cronin looked the other way, either not aware or not caring what was going on outside his corner office door.

It took a while for Addams to catch on because she was so unapproachable. She never engaged in chitchat with anyone, including the few female senior managers who were left. They might be colleagues, but they were also competitors for advancement.

Still, reality had a habit of barging into people's lives – even the Audrey Addamses of the world. For her, not one but two rude shocks arrived in a way she couldn't ignore. Both took place at a typically boozy going away party open to everyone who worked on the management floor – the kind of event that women who feared unwanted advances found excuses to miss or left as quickly as possible. Audrey rarely tarried either, but that was due to her lack of interest in socializing.

This time, though, she was taken by surprise. Soon after the party began, Ben Cronin tapped on a glass. So far, so good. Audrey expected him to say a few kind words about the departing employee. But when Cronin sat down, Larry Bragg rose to announce and congratulate the person who would take over the newly open job, one she'd applied for and thought she should get. But Bragg wasn't congratulating Audrey Addams. Worse, the person being promoted into the position was junior to her. Someone Bragg had hired just six months before. Someone, of course, who was a man.

Audrey was forced to stay for a full half hour before she could confront Cronin without being overheard. When she did, he made what she heard as a game, but lame, effort to explain. The job wasn't a big enough step up for her, he said. Be patient. He had his eye on a better, more appropriate position he expected would open up – maybe as soon as next year. Give him time.

She didn't buy it. Furious and humiliated, she retreated to the back of the room, wanting to leave but determined not to let anyone notice and think she cared.

She didn't fool everyone, however. Glen Olson, one of Bragg's latest hires, noticed her sitting alone, checking her email. He'd happened to be watching her when Bragg made his announcement and saw her face change from anticipation to anger.

People were leaving by now. Only the hard-core party types remained, clustered in the front of the room, laughing loudly. He detached himself from them and strolled over to Audrey.

"Hi," he said. "You were out of the office the day I came on board, and I've been waiting for an opportunity to thank you ever since. I really appreciate how helpful and professional you were when I was interviewing."

She examined his face cautiously. He'd been perfectly proper during the hiring cycle – very respectful. But that could have been an act. She was, after all, Cronin's chief of staff and might have some influence over her boss's hiring decision. No need for an act now, though. He could walk into the CEO's office any time he wanted without her say so.

And he was speaking just as respectfully as before. Indeed, he was offering a sympathetic ear without suggesting he knew of any reason why she might need it even though she guessed he'd caught on. He listened carefully to everything she said, frowning or nodding appropriately as the moment required and exactly on cue. He also filled her glass whenever it was empty.

It became empty several times. That was unusual, because Audrey Addams rarely allowed herself more than a single glass of wine, regardless of the site or circumstances. By the time she was finishing her third, she was venting her frustration and revealing her hurt at being passed over. They were sitting down now on a couch.

She didn't notice when the last of the partiers left the room, but he did. He put his arm consolingly around her shoulder, and the unexpected and rare experience of being touched sympathetically put her over the edge. She began to cry, leaning her head on his shoulder.

"I just can't believe it," she sobbed, "I've given my heart and soul to this place. I'm here till all hours every night. All I've ever wanted was a fair shake, and now this happens."

"I'm so sorry," he said, taking her hand. "That sounds terribly unfair. I can tell how bad this is hitting you." He was stroking her hair now.

But his efforts to console her only made her cry harder; she'd been bottling everything up for so long with no one to confide in. It was beyond unfair.

Through her tears, she dimly became aware that the hand that had been touching her hair was moving downward. He continued to make soothing sounds, but now both hands were in places they had no right to be.

The reality of what was happening hit her like a thunderbolt. She jumped to her feet. Looking around, she realized for the first time they were alone and threw the drink he'd just refilled in his face. Her own was burning as much with humiliation at being taken in by his act as with rage and alcohol.

But his reaction was infuriatingly cool. He stood up and, without touching her, slowly backed her up, quivering, against the wall. Then he slowly pulled her scarf from around her neck.

"Very pretty," he whispered, his face just inches from hers. "Silk, isn't it? Must have cost a lot." He used it to mop his face and then dropped it on the floor where he pushed it around with his foot, wiping up the rest of the wine.

"Well then," he said, "have it your way – which is to say, at home, by yourself. I can't imagine an ice queen like you getting some any other way."

He started to walk away and then turned around, now with the same pleasant smile she remembered from when he was interviewing. "Oh," he said, "one more thing. Don't count on Ben keeping his word about setting you up for the job he just promised you. I've known him for years, and he knows he's got it made with you as his chief of staff. With Medusa guarding his door, he never has to play the bad guy. You're there for good."

Chapter 29

Home, James!

AS USUAL, THE first topic on the agenda of the National Security Council meeting was the one President Yazzi had grown to dislike the most: "Update on Rising Tensions with the Russian Federation."

As the other attendees settled in, Yazzi wondered whether he'd been more naïve than most other presidents. Surely, each of his predecessors had been as focused as he was on grand domestic objectives. From that perspective, foreign affairs, and international crises in particular, were unwanted distractions from a president's real work. Such matters demanded attention, to be sure, but shouldn't be allowed to stand in the way of achieving real accomplishments. And yet inevitably they did, sometimes swallowing entire presidencies. Look at poor Lyndon Johnson, who's tremendous progress on social and civil rights issues had been tragically overshadowed by the Vietnam War. Was Yazzi's presidency, too, on the verge of falling into an international abyss? His earlier decision to return Johnson's desk to the Oval Office suddenly seemed less auspicious.

It was time to get going.

"Ladies and gentlemen," Yazzi said. "Let's begin. Jim, I see you're first up – again."

Jim Wakeman, the national security adviser, stood up, looking weary as he smoothed back his thinning grey hair. "I'm afraid so, Mr. President. As you know, the Russians never withdrew from Belarus after their recent military exercises. We've been monitoring the situation closely, of course, and over the past week, we've detected more Russian forces crossing the border. Judging by the activity we see in satellite photos of western Russia, it looks like they intend to at least double the number of troops already there."

"Just troops?" Yazzi asked.

"Unfortunately, no, sir," Wakeman said. "They're also moving in missile batteries, tank units, and field artillery. That's bad enough, but what's really turning the strategic situation upside down is the military-economic treaty Belarus just signed with Russia. We hadn't expected the pro-Russian presidential candidate to win in Belarus and certainly didn't see a treaty following so quickly, so frankly this is catching us off guard. Clearly, it must have been negotiated behind the scenes before the election, perhaps in exchange for substantial Russian assistance with vote-tampering. So, almost overnight, Belarus has shifted from making membership overtures to NATO to pledging allegiance once again to the Kremlin."

"What's Denikin's objective?" Yazzi asked.

"That's hard to tell, sir," Wakeman said. "Instead of concentrating his forces in a single location, he's spreading them more or less evenly along Belarus's borders with Lithuania, Poland, and Ukraine. And the situation on the ground is different in each case.

"Let's start with Ukraine, where he's stirring the pot on multiple public fronts. He's claiming the Ukrainian government is mistreating ethnic Russians in the western part of the country, and channeling even more economic and military aid than before to the separatists in Eastern Ukraine.

"So, what about Lithuania?" Wakeman said. "Denikin is suddenly claiming the government is mistreating Russians there, too. There's about a hundred forty thousand ethnic Russians there – about five percent of the total population overall and a much higher percentage in Vilnius, the Lithuanian capital.

"Next, let's take a look at Lithuania and Poland together. Denikin is contesting, 'on behalf of the people of Belarus,' if you can believe that, the boundary between Lithuania and Poland established at the end of World War II."

"That's quite a juggling performance," Yazzi said. "But what about the military forces? It doesn't make sense for Denikin to take on Ukraine, Poland and Lithuania all at once." Yazzi said. "What's he really up to? And which country is his real target?"

"Well, there's a chance this is all just for domestic consumption," Wakeman said. "As you know, Denikin has a history of manufacturing crises and incidents abroad to show how tough he is. But, if he does have a territorial objective, here's what we're thinking. During the Cold War, the location of the border between Poland and Lithuania didn't matter that much to Russia, because the Byelorussian Soviet Socialist Republic, as Belarus was called back then, as well as Poland and Lithuania were all part of the Soviet bloc. When the Soviet Union broke up, it lost most of its year-round access to the Atlantic. The only major warm-water ports Russia has on the Baltic now are St. Petersburg and Kaliningrad – but Kaliningrad is an isolated bit of territory surrounded by Poland and Lithuania."

"I'm sure Denikin would love to get unhindered access to Kaliningrad, for domestic bragging rights if nothing else. He's made some speeches in the past where he's spoken of direct access to Kaliningrad as something Russia should be entitled to. With Belarus back under his thumb, he's halfway to achieving that objective. So, our best guess is he wants to force Lithuania to grant Belarus a land corridor between Lithuania and Poland to Kaliningrad. This is playing very well with his base in Russia and, as you'd expect, in Belarus. The Lithuanians and Poles, of course, are livid. If that's his game plan, the rest is just camouflage to keep us guessing until he's ready to act."

"Remind me how Russia ended up holding on to Kaliningrad." Yazzi said.

"It's actually more than just the port, although not much – the territory is only eight-six square miles in all, and its full name is the Kaliningrad Oblast. Roosevelt and Churchill let Stalin have it at the end of World War II, and Russia managed to hang on to it when the USSR collapsed. It has a well-developed deep-water port, but to use it today, Russia has to ship goods across either Lithuania or Poland. Both of those, of course, are members of NATO, so in times of rising tension they could stop anything from going into or out of Kaliningrad. If Denikin can seize a land corridor for Belarus through to Kaliningrad – or more likely bully Lithuania into granting one – he'd solve that problem."

"It's obvious why Belarus would play ball. But why should Lithuania knuckle under to Russia?" Yazzi asked. "There's no love lost between them."

"True, sir. But one could imagine a treaty between them under which Russia once and for all recognizes the sovereignty of an independent Lithuania. It's a tiny country, and one power or another has occupied it for most of the last five hundred years – first Sweden, then the Russians, and finally the Soviets. Twenty square miles of territory, more or less, might seem like a small price to pay to get Russia to sign on to a non-aggression pact."

"Unless you consider who's giving the guarantee," Yazzi snorted.

"Point taken, sir. Anyway, that's our best guess."

Yazzi scanned the circle of intent faces surrounding the table. Yes, he'd have to act. This time Denikin was going too far. Better to make a decision here and now rather than delay.

"Thank you for your update, Jim. I'd like to clear today's agenda and spend the rest of the morning discussing whether it's time to launch an attack against the Russ. We've got to get Russia to back off from this senseless, ongoing campaign of aggression."

* * *

Shukov finished reading the field report he'd requested and smiled. He was pleased at how well his new "out of the box" model of thinking was working out. Not only pleased, but refreshed. He hadn't put in a late night yet this week.

The BankCoin network, it seemed, employed a clever approach to keep issues secret until patches were installed throughout the system. His agents had learned that a special department of the BankCoin administrator, First Manhattan Bank, was charged with maintaining security in a centralized manner. All flaws identified by any bank network member were sent in secret to the security administrator, which developed and distributed patches directly to the network members, bypassing GitHub. Only after all banks confirmed installation of the patches was the new code incorporated into the public version of BankCoin at GitHub.

So, the way was clear: to engage in some old-fashioned spycraft. He'd need to infiltrate First Manhattan Bank and to direct additional agents to work their way up through the ranks of the BankCoin Foundation. Once he had people in the right positions in both organizations, he could report with confidence to the JCSC that there would soon be a way to destroy the BankCoin system.

He went back to what he had been doing before the field report had arrived: studying the FSS organizational chart. It looked as if several positions might be opening up soon. He wondered which promotion would be his?

* * *

"And how are you today, Mr. Adversego?"

"I guess I'm okay, Jim. How about you?" At first, Frank had been uncomfortable having an assigned driver in New York. Surely the chauffeur would become chatty sooner or later. Then Frank would never get any work done during the drive to and from the airport. Worse, he'd be trapped into trying to sound intelligent discussing topics he knew nothing about, like sports and reality television.

But Jim was the soul of discretion. Polite, respectful, and quiet, yet ready to answer every question as briefly as possible. It was like having Alexa as a chauffeur. Frank had decided early on he could definitely get used to this town car business.

"I'm good, sir. To the airport?"

"Yes, please."

Frank felt uneasy about no longer looking forward to returning to Washington. True, his DC apartment seemed small and tawdry now, like the divorced male, Ikea-dominated flat it was. But he'd never been ashamed of it before. After all, virtually no one except Marla and Tim ever saw it. Still, it bothered him now. Enough that he'd finally broken down and bought some new furnishings, something he hadn't done in years. Okay, decades.

His old wardrobe – if that wasn't too grand a word – embarrassed him, too. So, the new suitcase he was carrying today – instead of his venerable, beat-up, old backpack – was transferring some sports shirts, slacks, and shoes to Washington. Someone must be monitoring his closet in New York because anything that relocated to Washington was immediately replaced. That was spooky but also convenient.

He was glad to be returning this time, though. Marla and Tim were coming over for dinner. His daughter was very visibly pregnant now, and seeing her looking healthy and happy would make him smile. He wondered whether she would notice the snappy jacket he was wearing?

The answer he got the next evening was yes. She also noticed his new shirt, shoes, belt, and slacks. When he met Marla and Tim at the door, she took him by the shoulders and turned him around, whistling softly as she did.

"Well, will you look at that!" she said. "He can be taught! Scratch that – what am I saying? He can be dressed up."

"Don't expect a 'thanks' for that," Frank said, tilting his nose upward. "I'll have you know I've actually bought a few things myself."

"Really?" Marla said, marveling. "Like what?"

"Like a new dining room table and chairs. And a few other things, too." He pulled his phone out of his pocket to show her pictures. "If you start treating your father with a little more respect, I might even ask you over to see them after they're delivered."

Clearly, he couldn't wait for her to see what he'd ordered. "Okay, point taken," she said. "I'll see if I can behave."

When he handed her the phone, she saw an expensive antique-style dining room set in a showroom. On the wall behind it was an oval mirror in an ornate gilt frame, flanked by candle sconces. Next to those, she saw a pair of pictures of an English hunt club pursuing a fox. Everything was distinctly tasteful and would look utterly ridiculous once it was surrounded by everything her father wasn't replacing.

Frank frowned. "You don't look impressed. I'll have you know that furniture cost —"

"Five times as much as the rest of what's in your apartment combined," she said.

Frank frowned more deeply. He'd bought the furniture in New York City, and the multiple was closer to ten.

"Well, what's wrong with that? You've always told me I should quit living like someone in a college dorm."

"Well, I guess," she said. "That's a fair point."

After they said goodnight, Marla turned to Tim. "So, what do you think of my new dad? The one in the pressed pants with the furniture from the English country house about to be shoe-horned into his eight-hundred-square-foot condo? Will he be wearing an ascot in front of a fake fireplace the next time we visit him?"

"No." Tim laughed. "I think he's just getting used to having some money for a change. And he's right — for as long as I can remember you've been pushing him to get some real adult furniture."

"Okay," she said, looking out the window of the car. "But I don't want him to make a fool of himself either. Or try to change who he really is."

"Don't you think you're selling him a bit short?" Tim asked.

"Am I? Don't get me wrong — I love my father dearly. But he's a really unsophisticated guy. He'd like you to think otherwise, but he's not."

"What do you mean?"

"Oh, come on. You know him better than that by now. How about this — I'm sure you can recall a situation where he was the butt of a joke and didn't even realize it. And it can go deeper. If someone said something mean to him, it might go right over his head. I've seen that happen. When I asked him later if it had made him angry, he just looked puzzled. When I explained it, he was amazed anyone would do that."

"Well," Tim said, "I think we just have to wait and see."

Chapter 30

Knock, Knock

FRANK HAD RETURNED to New York, where he was confronted by more new clothes in his closet and the old challenge of justifying his existence at First Manhattan. He had found nothing of interest in his review of BankCoin on his air-gapped system, meaning he was once more back where he started. Which was to say, nowhere. Now what? He turned to a list he kept of things to worry about and decided to do a thorough review of an even earlier version of BankCoin – the earliest one that existed, instead of the first version First Manhattan had adopted. That program would contain all the essentials needed to make the platform work, but none of the bells and whistles that were added later to optimize its operation. In theory, at least, understanding the starting point better might make it easier to spot malware added later.

But when he went online, he found that the GitHub repository didn't include any earlier versions of BankCoin. *Hmm.* Schwert must have been working on BankCoin somewhere else then, maybe at one of the other "forges" that hosted open source software. But Frank couldn't find an earlier version anywhere, at least under Schwert's name. So where was it?

He went back and looked for clues in the source code for the version of

Blockchain he already had. Huh! He hadn't ever noticed it before, but it didn't include any of the historical information you'd normally expect to find there – no listing of prior versions and no record of what changes had been in earlier releases or who had made them. Schwert must have cleaned all that out before he launched BankCoin into the world. That was odd.

So where were the original versions? Magnus would know. Frank got up and walked to his cubicle.

"Hey, Dirk."

The programmer turned and peered at Frank over his spectacles. He blinked several times but said nothing.

"Do you mind if I ask you a question?" Frank asked.

"That is a question. Another question, I suppose you mean?"

Frank laughed; Magnus didn't.

"Sure," Frank said. "And maybe more than one. Do you have a few minutes?"

"Actually, it looks like I am about to lose them. What can I tell you?"

"I was looking at the BankCoin logs at GitHub and noticed the first version is very mature. Can you help me find the earlier ones?"

"No," Magnus said.

"No, as in 'No, you won't,' or no, as in 'No, you can't.'"

"The latter."

"So, who could?"

"Only Schwert."

"Are you saying he did all the early work on BankCoin by himself?" Frank asked.

"That is apparently the case. Schwert, it seems, developed BankCoin on his own system and then revealed it to the world. Rather like Satoshi Nakamoto, so it is not so strange."

"Well, it's strange to me," Frank said, "given that the banks adopted it so quickly. It took a long time for bitcoin to be taken seriously. And the version Nakamoto first put up on the internet still needed a lot of work before anyone used it to even buy a pizza."

"This is true, but your point is what? Blockchain is now widely accepted. And there are very many other blockchains. The general approach is well-known and documented. Why should not Schwert build a blockchain on his own?"

"Well, okay," Frank said. "But why should First Manhattan have bought into it so fast?"

"Why do you say it did?"

"Didn't it?"

Magnus gave Frank an appropriately pitying glance.

"So. Schwert posts a message at a popular blockchain site to announce his new creation. Along with the message is a white paper – just as so many others have done. And there is an address at GitHub. 'Come look at my blockchain,' he writes. So, some do. And they like what they see and tell others. They, too, tell others. Soon, many people are talking about his blockchain. The word gets around. Is this so strange?"

No, actually it wasn't, Frank had to admit. "Okay," he said. "I understand."

"Enough questions for today?" Magnus asked.

"Sure – thanks." As usual, everything Magnus said made perfect sense but failed to satisfy. Frank couldn't decide whether that was helpful or maddening. What he could decide was that he was yet again back where he was before: staring at his worry list, trying to decide what to do next.

In the end, he decided to try using his air-gapped copy of BankCoin instead of just studying it. Perhaps if he reviewed it from that perspective he might stumble on – he wasn't proud – something he'd missed when examining it as a static piece of software. And where better to begin than by adding a block of his own to the Genesis Block – the very first block of transactions created by the great Günter Schwert? But first he wanted to understand better how BankCoin made that possible.

He scrolled through the code that had created the Genesis Block, taking notes as he went along. Then he went through it again and leaned back. He was left with two somewhat contradictory impressions.

The first was a reaffirmation that Schwert was a brilliant computer architect. The structure of the code was impeccable. Economical, robust, and – to a programmer at least – beautiful.

The second was that, for all his brilliance, Schwert could be sloppy. This little bit of source code here, for example – it was supposed to lead the program on to its next task, but instead, it was followed by some unrelated code. He was surprised the extra "call" to nowhere didn't hang up the whole program. There were a couple other examples just like that. He expected Schwert or someone else must have cleaned those bits of coding cruft in a later release. Well, what the heck. He'd seen sloppy programmers before who were otherwise masters of their craft – so good at the big picture they didn't have the patience to go back and double-check everything so long as the code ran.

So, he was back where he started. Or even behind that point, because Schwert's coding skills were so elegant that Frank wasn't sure he'd yet grasped all the subtleties of the program elements that created the Genesis Block and would create every block thereafter. Most programmers were like bricklayers: you put this on top of that and then another one of these on those and so on until you had a wall of code modules that did what you wanted them to. These days, a lot of those bricks were open source code someone else had written and posted to GitHub so that anyone, like you, could include them in their own wall.

In contrast, Frank was sure every line of code he'd just reviewed had been written by Schwert himself. And not as an assemblage of bricks. There were continuous threads of logic that flowed through the block generation code from beginning to end. That was how the most brilliant programmers Frank had known so long ago at MIT had structured code. In those days, even a powerful computer had a tiny fraction of the power a cheap flip phone from a decade ago commanded. It would take a hundred of those early computers to run the kinds of programs developers wrote now to run on an entry-level laptop. But a real code master would still design an algorithm that was elegant in its simplicity, able to achieve great things with meager resources.

Schwert was clearly such an artist. But why bother? BankCoin was a complex piece of software, to be sure. But it hardly challenged the powerful computers the member banks were using. Was it art for art's sake? Perhaps it just came naturally to Schwert. Either way, it continued to make Frank's job difficult.

Knowing that Schwert was a better programmer than he was left Frank feeling both frustrated and mildly intimidated. He hated to admit his own limitations. But after banging his head against the BankCoin architect's coding wall for a while he decided perhaps it was time to swallow his pride and ask Schwert to walk him through the security precautions he'd presumably taken in creating BankCoin.

Why not? Frank emailed him to make the request.

* * *

When two days passed without a response, Frank presented himself once again at Dirk Magnus's cubicle. As usual, the truculent coder either didn't, or wouldn't, acknowledge Frank's presence until he spoke.

"Knock, knock," Frank said.

Magnus's goggle eyes swiveled around and fixed themselves on Frank.

"'Knock, knock,' I believe, is perhaps one of your American jokes?" Magnus asked.

"Well, yes, but not this time. It's just slang. Anyway, can you tell me how to get in touch with Schwert? I emailed him, but he didn't respond."

"I can give him a message, yes." Magnus said. "Or, also, another maintainer could."

"You mean the Cabots talk only to the Lodges, and the Lodges talk only to God?"

"Excuse me, please?" Magnus asked.

"Sorry. It's an old Boston saying. You see, the Cabots and Lodges were the highest of society and – never mind. So, you have to be next in line to Schwert before he'll waste his time answering a question. Is that it?"

"I would not say it that way, no. He works very hard and relies on us to support him in his efforts. It is a very large and busy project as you know."

"So, what if I was the executive chairman of First Manhattan? Would he answer me then?" Frank asked.

"And what precisely does the bank pay Mr. Schwert?" Magnus asked.

"Okay. Nothing. I get your point. So, could I ask you to pose a question to his highness for me?"

Magnus snorted.

"Ask him," Frank continued, "if he could send me a brief overview of how he designed security into BankCoin. That assumes that he did, instead of relying on the banks to prevent their systems from being breached."

"So that someone can someday hack into our network and find his description? That would be a nice roadmap for a black hat to have, yes?"

"Okay, then ask him to give me a call."

"Schwert does not ever use a phone. I would be surprised to learn he owns one." A twinkle appeared in Magnus's eye. "Not even so he could speak to one of your Cabots."

Magnus turned back to his computer screen, leaving Frank frowning at the back of his head. It also left him with no choice but to return to his office in frustration.

What was going on with this world? First Manhattan had turned the global financial system over to someone no one had ever met who couldn't even be called on a phone. But to be fair, they weren't the only adults acting like children. The most revered and aggressive investment bank on Wall Street had opened a bitcoin exchange. And not only had Satoshi Nakamoto never been seen or heard, but it had been years since he vanished from the virtual earth he'd once – maybe – inhabited. Why should BankCoin be any different?

Perhaps because this whole circus was stark raving, barking mad.

* * *

It was a Monday morning, so Frank was in New York City. Not because there was something productive to be done, but because it was the day he was required to present himself before Horace Nukem and assure the executive chairman that all of First Manhattan's assets, as well as its stock price, were safe and sound, not necessarily in that order. Privately, Frank and Ruth had begun referring to the weekly gatherings as Nukem's EHPPOS therapy sessions. The acronym stood for Everything Humanly Possible is being done to Protect Our Stock.

It was a bleak way to begin the week, Frank reflected as he stepped into the elevator. There was never anything new or interesting to report. Once you built a state-of-the-art cyber castle, maintaining it was as dull as keeping a real fortress in proper shape – the equivalent of repointing the stone work if you noticed any bits of mortar coming loose. At the same time, you'd have no way of knowing it if someone was tunneling underneath your feet, preparing to set off enough explosives to bring the whole castle down in ruins. Unfortunately, even the technically-challenged Nukem knew that.

So, what was the point? Maybe the former general still enjoyed reviewing his troops. Or perhaps he figured giving his staff a weekly dose of his dour countenance would focus their minds on the risk at hand. If so, Frank had to grant him that much. But it wasn't as if it opened any opportunities to do more than they already were.

Frank picked up a cup of coffee and walked to the glass-walled conference room. Yup. There the executive chairman sat, enthroned at the head of the table like a great stone Buddha with indigestion. Or maybe hemorrhoids.

Oh well. Nothing to be done but get down to the non-business of the day.

Chapter 31

Frank Gets Called on the (Red) Carpet

TED MILLER STARED at the phone message. Why would a talent agent be calling him? And about Frank Adversego, of all people? Well, there was only one way to find out.

"This is Lou," the voice at the other end answered.

"Hi, Lou. Ted Miller returning your call. You wanted to talk about Frank Adversego."

"Right! Thanks for the call-back. Here's the story. I'm Donna Shawn's agent. She's up for best supporting actress in *The Lafayette Campaign*. Fantastic cybersecurity thriller! Have you seen it?"

"No, sorry. Afraid I don't get to as many movies as I'd like to," Miller said. Where the heck was this going?

"Yeah, well, you should make an exception for this one. Anyway, Donna's date has come down with the flu, and she needs a stand-in escort for the Academy Awards ceremony this Sunday night, so I got to thinking, and it hit me – who could be a better escort than Frank Adversego? The real-life one, instead of her co-star! So how about it? Can we have him for a few hours on Sunday? It'll be terrific publicity for your bank."

Miller stared at the phone. Frank Adversego hovering on the edge of the red carpet? Really? Still, it might make for some nice press.

"Ah, I'm afraid I'll have to get back to you," Miller said.

"Okay, but I can only give you two hours. If your boy can't make it, I've got to move to the next name on my list."

"Got it," Miller said, shaking his head. Then he punched in Lola Logan's number.

"Lola," he said when she answered, "you're not going to believe this."

* * *

Frank was feeling great. He was sitting in the bank's corporate jet on the runway of a private airport outside New York City, and he and Lola would be the only passengers. Wherever he was off to must be really important! The flight attendant handed him a drink, and he looked out the window. There was a town car now, gliding across the tarmac toward the plane. That would be Lola.

Minutes later, they were in the air, and she swiveled her seat around to face him.

"So, are you all set for your big evening?" she said.

"Well, I hope so. What is it?" he said, raising his glass.

"Didn't Ted Miller tell you?" she said, feigning ignorance. "You're escorting Donna Shawn to the Academy Awards ceremony tonight."

"What?" Most of the scotch spraying out of Frank's mouth landed on Lola. *Okay*, she thought, *maybe I deserved that.*

Frank jumped out of his seat. "Oh, hey, I'm sorry about that! Let me get something you can dry off with – but *what?*"

"Well, we got a call from her agent. Apparently, she plays somebody named Josette in *The Lafayette Campaign*, and her date came down with a nasty case of stomach flu. Her agent thought you'd be a great escort for her since the movie is based on one of your cases. Wasn't that a great idea?"

"No!" Frank said. "Not at all! I've never even watched the Academy Awards on TV. All I know is everyone will be famous and fashionable and photogenic, and then there'll be me! I won't have a clue what to do, or what to say, or which way to look! Let's get the pilot to turn around right now!"

The plane was over Kansas by the time Frank had mostly calmed down and then only after spending a half hour on the phone with his daughter. Although outwardly sympathetic, she was as inwardly thrilled as he was terrified. Boy, would her dad look great next to Donna Shawn on Marla's Instagram page!

* * *

"How long is this going to take?" Tim asked. A little known but expensively-draped actress was smiling, posing and waving on the television screen, stretching out her moment of red-carpet fame for as long as possible. "This is excruciating."

"Hang in there. It can't be too much longer," Marla said. But she was bored, too.

"Yeah, well," Tim said, "give me a holler when you see Frank. I'll be in the bedroom getting some work done."

Five minutes later she called out. "Tim! Now!"

Marla watched the screen anxiously as her father stopped a few steps before Donna Shawn did, doubtless as he'd been coached to, allowing her to dominate the video stream. There she pirouetted for the cameras, flashing the expected thousand-watt-smile as the disembodied voices of the broadcast hosts made their predictable comments.

"Well, doesn't she just look great!" one of the commentators cooed in a cloyingly delighted voice, "That dress is certainly going to put the designer on the map! I've never heard of him before, be I'm sure we all will now."

But Marla wasn't really listening. Instead, she was focused on her father, just visible at the edge of the screen, standing stiffly and obviously wondering what to do with his hands. Thankfully, it was only another minute before Shawn towed him off camera.

* * *

Frank was feeling jittery but relieved the next morning as the private jet left Bob Hope Airport. He'd taken no chances the day before, drinking nothing but sparkling water after Lola broke the news of their destination to him. He thought he'd comported himself with dignity, or anyway, at least avoided disaster, and hoped any pictures or video clips that made their way online would confirm his belief.

Blessedly, escorting Donna Shawn had proven to be a far smaller challenge than he'd feared. It was clear from the first he was just another accessory to her, something like a two-legged handbag to be carefully positioned to accentuate her appearance for the benefit of the photographers – complementary but not distracting. As long as he kept smiling as he was swept, pushed, or poked along, Donna seemed happy enough.

He'd grown more nervous as the time to announce the best supporting actress approached, though. It was unnerving not knowing when, and from where, the video cameras might zoom in to capture Shawn's anticipation and then jubilation or desolation, doubtless capturing a slice of his own face in the process.

And then she won. Whatever slight attention she'd paid to him up to that point was history. The rest of the event and the party thereafter were blurs of faces familiar and otherwise, limousines, noise, laughter – she taking part and he watching from a safe distance in the background. He was relieved when he found a couch in a corner of the party, its black leather providing the perfect background for him and his tuxedo to blend into.

That part had been hard. There was no pretending he belonged there in a tuxedo, or really anywhere in such a monkey suit. How had accepting a job to earn tuition for his grandchildren led to being assigned a gig as arm candy for an actress? And not just any actress. He was being taken advantage of by a young woman playing the part of another young woman who had taken advantage of him in real life.

It wasn't until almost three a.m. that Shawn collected him from the couch so they could be seen leaving together.

Chapter 32

Lights! Action!

F RANK SUDDENLY FOUND himself sitting in the dark. The question was why? Just a moment before, he'd been typing away. Now the only light in his apartment was coming from the screen of his laptop. He felt his way to the window and looked outside – everything was black across the street, too. The scene was extraordinary – pitch-black, with no glow of city light reflected by the sky, either. Was the power off all over Washington?

He made his way to his front door and looked out; *good;* the battery-powered exit light in the hall was still on, casting a dim, reddish light. He entered the stairwell under the sign and started up. When he stepped out onto the roof, the stars overhead startled him – in the city he'd never been able to see any but the brightest ones before. Now the milky way arched majestically across the moonless sky.

He was surprised he could see so much in the ghostly light it cast; faint forms stretched off in every direction. Here and there, the windows of a building with emergency generators glowed. The only other lights visible were the headlights of the few cars still moving so late at night.

Back in his apartment, he scanned his laptop for news, but it was too soon. He tried typing "#blackout" on Twitter, and that was a different story. Holy cow – it wasn't just Washington! He scrolled downward – there were people tweeting in Denver; Seattle, too. But not Chicago, New York, or Los Angeles. He scanned farther down; *hmm*. That was strange. The lights were out in Denver, but not Boulder. And though Seattle and the nation's capital were down, Portland and Baltimore weren't. That's not how blackouts worked; they started in one place and spread out to surrounding areas from there. How could the outages be so widespread and so local at the same time?

The answer was obvious: someone had hit the United States with a massive, targeted cyberattack. But not an assault launched by NASLA, because so far as he knew, none of the power grids used a blockchain.

So, who would it be? Was it one of the state actors he'd been obsessing about for so long? North Korea? Iran? Russia? Russia, probably, given the news lately, but it was always a bad idea to jump to a conclusion, no matter how obvious it might seem.

* * *

"Okay," Yazzi said. "Let's go. Jim?"

There were a few empty chairs at the hastily called meeting of the National Security Council, but the members most crucial to the issue at hand were all present.

"Thank you, Mr. President," Jim Wakeman, the national security adviser said. "What you see on the screen over there is the list of cities hit by the outage – eight in all. What's not on the list is as notable as what is. If the blackout resulted from an accident or system failure, the impact would look very different. The way a normal outage unfolds is predictable – it's like watching a string of dominoes falling over. Something goes down, and that overtaxes something nearby, and that goes down, and so on, until enough backup power sources kick in to shore things up or automatic controls take over and contain it. But there's no discernible rhyme or reason to last night's outages. Some cities stayed online while others close by didn't.

"Also, everything that went down did so almost simultaneously – that couldn't happen except as a result of a cyberattack. Everything came back up in sync, too."

"So, what do you make of that?" Yazzi said, "I mean, the fact that power was restored after only a few hours? And what about this: why would someone do this at night? It's more like a warning than an attack."

"Exactly, sir. I think you've come to precisely the right conclusion. Someone wanted to show us what they were capable of without doing enough damage to compel us to retaliate with force."

"So, who would that be? Russia? Iran? North Korea? A terrorist organization?"

"You could make a case for any of those, sir. Unfortunately, it will likely take a while for our cybersecurity folks to uncover any details that point to one suspect over another. But let's assume it was the Russians, since that's where tensions are greatest right now. They could be firing a warning shot across our bow, showing what they intend to do if we stick to our guns with oil prices."

"How bad could the next attack be?" Yazzi asked.

"That's the big question, sir. Did they hit these particular cities because they're the only ones they've been able to compromise, or are there lots more? Could they take down the entire power grid or major parts of it? We don't know, at least not yet, and we may never."

"How long would it take to recover if they took down the grid everywhere?" Yazzi asked.

"That would depend," Wakeman said, "on whether the attack was reversible, like this one, or instead was designed to cause real damage to infrastructure. There's also the question of keeping the power on after we restored it. Until we found and eliminated the vulnerability they exploited, they could shut us down again."

"So, to summarize, we don't know whether we're teetering on the edge of a national disaster or if we just witnessed an epic bluff," Yazzi said.

"That's pretty much it, yes, sir." Wakeman admitted. "But if Russia was behind last night's attack, we'll probably find out soon unless we ease off on the embargo."

"That's not going to happen," Yazzi said. "Still, this is like the Cold War all over again, isn't it? The more we drive Russia toward bankruptcy, the higher the risk they retaliate by attacking us while they still can. If they do, we can't stand by without retaliating. I don't like the escalation risk here."

"No, sir. Neither do I."

Yazzi turned back from the list. "I think," he said, "the best way to avoid that risk is by making sure the Russians have nothing to retaliate for."

"How, sir?"

"By calling the Russians' bluff."

* * *

"The Russian ambassador is here, Mr. President."

Carson Bekin stood up to go.

"No – stay." And then, into his telephone, Yazzi said, "Thanks. Don't tell him, but he'll be waiting for a while."

Bekin smiled as he sat back down. "How long will you keep him twiddling his thumbs?"

Yazzi took a quarter out of his pocket. "Let's find out," he said. "Heads, it's fifteen minutes, and tails, a half an hour." The president flipped the coin, slapped it on the back of his other hand, and held it out for his old friend to see.

"Tails," Carson said. "He's not going to be happy."

"Good," Yazzi said. "I don't want him to leave with any doubt what the message was."

"Hah! I'm sure there's not much danger of that," Bekin said. "You've rarely been accused of subtlety. But how do you plan to play this? You don't have proof the Russians were behind the power grid attack."

"You're right, I don't. But I'll bet you this quarter they were."

* * *

The Russian ambassador – tall, red-faced and overweight – was at his most imperious when he was ushered at last into the Oval Office. Yazzi's rising to greet him did not lessen his annoyance; it would have been quite a snub for Yazzi to stay seated. But then Yazzi did the next best thing by returning to his desk instead of inviting Gorsky to sit across the coffee table from him on the sofas nearby, as he had during past visits.

"So sorry to keep you waiting, Mr. Ambassador," Yazzi said. "Unexpected affairs of state. I'm sure you understand."

Gorsky did not directly respond to Yazzi's excuse as he lowered his substantial weight into the chair facing the president's desk. Instead, he said, "Perhaps you will now share the reason for this sudden and unexpected summons," he said.

"Sudden, yes. But unexpected? Please, Mr. Ambassador. I'm sure you have an excellent idea why you're here."

"I have many excellent ideas, thank you very much," Gorsky sniffed. "But not on this subject. You will please respond to my question. Russia does not expect its senior representative in your country to be treated in this fashion."

"Very well," Yazzi said, leaning forward. "The reason is that I would like you to convey a message for me to your esteemed president, Mr. Denikin. Are you ready?"

"I am all ears, as I believe you say," said Gorsky, his florid features reddening further.

"Excellent. Please tell Mr. Denikin we have found the calling card of one of his friends tucked into the control systems of each of the cities that recently went dark across our country."

"How interesting," Gorsky said. "And whose card might that have been?"

"Another of your 'Fancy Bear' type units."

Gorsky gave the president a thin smile. "Such an odd name! What does it refer to?"

"Yes," Yazzi said. "And it would be more exact to say the GRU, your main intelligence directorate, hacked into our power grid and deprived millions of American citizens of access to electricity. The actual unit behind the attack was just the tool in their hands."

"I'm afraid that you will have to help me with this, Mr. President," Gorsky said. "My country has repeatedly rejected the fantasy that such a quaintly named unit, or any similar group, exists within or under the control of the directorate. We have been quite explicit in this regard. If indeed you have attributed the unfortunate blackouts to such a cyber weaponry group, we could by definition then not be responsible."

"Your repetition of false denials does not change my message," Yazzi said. "Please inform your president that if the United States suffers another blackout, our response will be immediate and of equal, or greater, impact. And I can assure you, things will not return to normal after a few hours."

Gorsky raised his eyebrows. "Indeed! But against what would you respond, Mr. President?"

"I'm sure you don't expect me to answer that question. Good day, Mr. Ambassador."

* * *

Crypto felt an enormous sense of relief when the hand on his countdown clock reached the nine o'clock position. Within eight weeks, at most, it would reach the midnight hour. To be assured of success he must wait to strike until then. But if he had to launch his attack even now, he believed there would be a good chance of victory. With every day that passed, the odds for success would increase. When he dared to be optimistic, Crypto believed BankCoin's event horizon had already been crossed.

And yet it brought him little relief because the Bees had seized upon the same realization to rachet up their attack. At any moment, they screamed, he could be discovered. What then? There could be no guarantee he would not. Waiting was reckless, not acting too soon.

Of course, they could be right. But how could he know for sure? His countdown algorithm had no basis in science. It was no more than the product of a series of educated guesses. And in any event, the real world, and the actions of those in it, were far too unpredictable to capture in such a simple mechanism. It might be that true midnight had passed months ago, or instead that it would not arrive until later than his little program predicted. But how could he live with himself if he struck too soon, and societies recovered before governments fell?

It did not help that he had little left to prepare until the last few days before the attack itself. Evenings, he found himself roaming aimlessly on the internet, looking for distraction. One night he stumbled on a stanza of a poem by Swinburne that spoke to his condition:

I am tired of tears and laughter,
And men that laugh and weep;
Of what may come hereafter
For men that sow to reap:
I am weary of days and hours,
Blown buds of barren flowers,
Desires and dreams and powers
And everything but sleep.

But he also stumbled on a snippet written by an advertising executive, of all people, and A Bee added that to her daily litany of woe. It read:

On the Plains of Hesitation bleach the bones of countless millions
who, at the Dawn of Victory, sat down to wait, and waiting—died!

B Bee took a more literary approach, credibly rendering in his booming voice Brutus's famous caution in the play *Julius Caesar:*

There is a tide in the affairs of men.
Which, taken at the flood, leads on to fortune;
Omitted, all the voyage of their life
Is bound in shallows and in miseries.
On such a full sea are we now afloat,
And we must take the current when it serves,
Or lose our ventures.

But still, Crypto forced himself to wait, in defiance of Bees and Bard alike.

Chapter 33

No Pain, No Gain

F RANK WAS STILL annoyed at being ignored by Schwert. So, he took a break to see if anything new had popped up about him online.

Rumors continued to abound, but that was all. At one site, people claimed Schwert was really Giles Campbell, a brilliant but eccentric Cambridge-educated mathematician. Before dropping out of public view several years before, he'd made a bundle designing sophisticated investment algorithms for a huge hedge fund. No, others said, he was the alter-ego of Barry Lemuelson, the rich heir to a German chemical fortune who designed dazzling virtual reality games. Ridiculous! insisted a third story. Schwert was really a team of venture capital-backed entrepreneurs providing BankCoin-related consulting services using their intimate knowledge of its workings.

But no one really knew. Maybe George Marchand could find out?

* * *

"If we were investigating Schwert, I couldn't tell you, or give you, any details," George Marchand told Frank over coffee at their usual rendezvous. "But we aren't, so I guess I can tell you that much."

"Well, I think you should check him out," Frank replied. "And don't say it's a domestic matter, so the CIA can't touch it. The global financial system is using BankCoin, and there's no more reason to decide Schwert's American over any other nationality."

"So, you're telling me the CIA should drop all the other important work we're doing and investigate every hotshot coder that works for free on an open source project?"

"This isn't just any project."

"True. But there are lots of other significant projects. Also, true?"

"Well, sure. But there wouldn't be as much chaos if any of those systems failed."

"Really?" Marchand asked, his eyebrows rising as he looked at Frank over the rim of his coffee cup. "You don't think it might be just a tad disruptive if the telecommunications system went down? Which, by the way, BankCoin relies on. Or all the cloud services providers? I doubt there'd be much banking – or anything else – going on if an enemy took them down. Major parts of all those systems are based on open source software. Anyway, even if we wanted to do what you're asking, we don't have enough people with the right skills to tackle that type and scale of investigation."

"Then how about the FBI?"

"I think I'd know if they were monitoring Schwert, and the answer is no."

"For Pete's sake, why not?"

"Well, there's the fact that to the best of your knowledge, your boy hasn't broken any laws yet. Right?"

"Yes, but would I know it if he had? And anyway, don't you and the FBI infiltrate organizations and follow individual suspects all the time to see if someone is planning a terrorist attack?"

"Of course. But only if we have reliable information there's a real risk. And so far, all you've told me about Schwert is that he's fanatical about his privacy."

Frank was getting frustrated. "Okay, but you'd have to agree that the banking system is 'critical infrastructure,' yes? And the CIA is charged with protecting that against external threats? Right?" Frank gave the last word a distinct "Gotcha!" inflection.

"In normal times, yes. But these aren't normal times," George said.

"Nice try," Frank said. "The last times I can recall that anyone called 'normal' were maybe the 1980s. And anyway, if times aren't normal, you have to adapt to the abnormalities."

"Okay," Marchand replied. "Fair point. So indirectly, it's Yazzi's fault. He appointed a lot of cabinet secretaries who are too turf conscious. Security is a big deal these days, so everyone wants to have cyber specialists on their own staff. It's a way to make your agency more important even if it's at the expense of someone else – like the FBI."

"That's crazy," Frank said. "What about the Department of Homeland Security? Weren't they created to stop that kind of nonsense? Coordinate communications so another 9/11 couldn't happen?"

"In principle, yes. But in case you haven't noticed, ever since things became 'abnormal,' as soon as an administration or the legislature creates something, the special interests, the next president, or the next Congress try to tear it down again. Look at Obamacare. Heck, even social security, and that's been around for going on a hundred years. A lot of congressmen are trying to cut back on that. Or Glass-Steagall – Congress passed that act back in 1933 to prevent another Great Depression. It took sixty-six years for Congress to kill important parts of that, but when they did, even a lot of Democrats got on board – and it was Bill Clinton that signed the repeal bill. Oops!

"So, then the Great Recession follows," George continued, "and once again, it's the banks that pull down the house of cards. What a coincidence! So, Congress passes the Dodd-Frank Bill to stop a housing finance disaster from ever happening again. And what happens? This time around, it doesn't even take ten years for Wall Street to get Washington to cut those reforms back. I tell you, these days, nothing's off the table if someone can make a buck by undermining it or improve their chance of getting reelected by killing it outright."

"So that's it?"

"Afraid so. But I'll let you know if I hear anything different."

* * *

Josh Peabody swallowed the last bite of his forty-eight-dollar steak and poured another glass of ninety-six-dollar cabernet. Time to talk a few minutes' worth of business so he could use his CryptoBoom! credit card to pay for lunch.

"We're down fifteen percent so far this year. We've got to do better than that," he said.

"Agreed. The question is how," Vance Morganthau, his chief trader said. "It's been crazy out there lately."

"So what? Crazy times are when you make crazy-big money!" Peabody said. "When everything's stable there's no way to make a killing."

"Well, sure," Morganthau said. "but don't forget we were up by twenty percent back in February. Who cares where we are today so long as we do well over the life of the fund?"

"The institutions we're expecting to put two billion dollars in our second fund, that's who! I want all our existing investors to double their investment in that one, and they won't be in a buying mood if CryptoBoom! is down fifteen percent!"

"I understand," Morganthau said. "But still, none of us has a crystal ball. We've just had a run of bad luck the last few months. Every time we've bet big, we've been burned by another cyberattack. And don't forget, this isn't like the stock market. There's no history to look at. And there aren't any analyst calls or earnings announcements on a neat schedule we can anticipate and bet on to make a nice profit. So, what do you expect me to do? The only coin you can rely on to go up all the time is the Russ."

"So, let's bulk up on Russ," Peabody said.

Morganthou almost choked on his cabernet. "What are you talking about? We can't touch it. It's on the sanctions list just about everywhere."

"Not quite everywhere. We could buy and hold a position in, say, Malaysia."

Morganthau looked around the dining room before answering. "Come on, Josh," he said quietly. "Don't even say that. That's jail time talk."

Peabody smiled and shrugged. "No harm in thinking, is there? Maybe there's a way to work the Russ back into our portfolio without going over the line."

"I can't imagine how. I don't even want to imagine."

"Okay," Peabody said. "It was just a thought."

Morganthau frowned. Just a thought, indeed. He'd seen that look on Peabody's face before.

* * *

Frank was enjoying his flight on the First Manhattan corporate jet far more than his last trip; this time, it didn't involve a cameo appearance at the Academy Awards.

The opulent swiveling seats, one to each side of the aisle, were large and comfortable, and the attention of the two attendants was unrelenting. They were spending as much time with him as with the president and executive chairman of the bank, too.

Frank was impressed with how easy it was to fly privately. No TSA inspections to slow you down – the limousine took you right out to the jet on the runway at the private airport! He'd always known the ultra-rich traveled this way, but he hadn't realized how luxurious and convenient it was. The cost must be absurd, but it sure beat standing in an endless security line before squeezing into a seat in coach.

For the first time, it occurred to him that all this might be hard to give up when his bank gig ran its course. Maybe they'd keep him on staff after BankCoin was thoroughly debugged and trustworthy?

Or perhaps they wouldn't. How would he feel about going back to working day in and day out in his little condo in Washington?

How indeed?

He thought he knew the answer to that, and it made him uncomfortable.

* * *

"So, you're telling me my idea is no good, is that it?" Doogie Petrie said, pushing back from the conference room table. "Do you know how long it took me to code that proof-of-concept program?"

This should be interesting, Frank thought. The first time Doogie contributes anything beyond snide remarks he gets shot down.

"I'm sorry about that," Colonel Dix said. "But I've made it clear from the outset we need to design an attack that isn't traceable to the United States. And it also can't result in an actual loss of money. Your proposal fails on both fronts."

"Geez!" Petrie said, snapping his laptop open. "Do you guys know anything about cracking at all?"

Colonel Dix frowned. "You seem to be a bit confused, Doogie. This isn't typical criminal activity. This is achieving vital national goals through cyber weaponry."

"Well, *excuse* me," Petrie said, drawing the second word out. "Thanks for clarifying that for me. Somehow, I imagined taking down a multi-billion-dollar global trade network might be illegal."

"Be that as it may," Colonel Dix said, "Those are the rules. Now, has anyone else come up with a new exploit that shows promise?"

As it happened, Frank had been mulling over an idea for the last several days. "Yes, I've got one to suggest," he said.

"Great," Colonel Dix said. "Let's hear it."

"Okay," Frank replied. "It's based on the fact that the Russ network, like every cryptocurrency system, relies on wallets to hold the alt coins. The blockchain holds the master record of all the transactions that have come before, but as a practical matter, all anyone who's buying and selling products using Russ cares about is the balance in his wallet."

"So, you want to target the wallets, rather than the blockchain." Colonel Dix asked.

"That's right. As we've seen from the real world, lots of criminals have successfully stolen cryptocurrencies from individual accounts. I believe I've found a way to change the balances of Russ wallets, and if we code it right, it won't be traceable. Russia might suspect us, but they wouldn't be able to prove it. Once we had the malware in place, we could use it to change the balance of only some wallets, or of every single one."

"Huh!" Petrie interrupted. "And somehow, I got the idea we weren't allowed to make anyone lose a pile of dough!"

"That's true," Frank agreed, "but that's what makes accounts a good target

– the blockchain remains untouched, so the accurate balances can be restored. But that would take a lot of time and effort because the Russ blockchain wasn't designed with that in mind. If we set the attack up so it hits a bunch of wallets here, and then a week later another bunch there, and so on, we'll undermine the credibility of the Russ as a payment vehicle. Or, if the president wants to, we could hit all the accounts at once and bring the whole network to a screeching halt. It would take them months to find the issue, fix it, and then work all that data back through the system to restore the balances. So, we can get two different attack profiles out of the same virus."

"Huh," Petrie said and slumped back in his chair.

"That sounds like it has potential," Colonel Dix said, looking around the table. "What do others think about Frank's idea?"

The rest thought it sounded promising. Only Dirk, as usual, looked unimpressed.

* * *

Josh Peabody settled in and read the headline that had just popped up. Crap! There'd been another big theft of a coin CryptoBoom! owned. He clicked the story open and then pounded his desk with both fists. The exchange the criminals had hit was the one his fund used. He did a few quick calculations and decided the loss would amount to more than four percent of the fund's entire value. If he couldn't figure out a way to offset these losses he'd have to postpone, or even abandon, his plans to launch a second fund.

And there was only one way to do that, right?

He'd been thinking a lot about the Russ and believed he'd found a way to go big on it. Not necessarily legally but without getting caught, which after all was the only thing that really mattered. Now where was the address of that Russian financier he knew?

* * *

Crypto gazed at his countdown clock, trying to block out the fury of the Bees. They were more determined than ever in their demand that he either launch his attack or terminate the existence of Frank Adversego.

If only they could be patient – it was at most a matter of weeks until he could plunge the world into financial panic and then social chaos. As Alfred Henry Lewis, an American journalist, had observed in 1906, "There are only nine meals between mankind and anarchy."

And, indeed, it was an observation that was hard to dispute. What would happen if the only money that still existed was the cash in physical wallets and piggy banks? When nothing could be bought and nothing sold, at any price?

How would people act when they had no electricity? No heat? No food?

For how long would police show up for duty without any prospect of pay? And how could they arrive at all with no gas in their cars?

How would people react when starving neighbors arrived at their doors, demanding food? What if those neighbors were armed?

The answers to those questions were easy enough to predict. He just needed a bit more time.

Chapter 34

Keep on Pump'n

CRYPTO WAS PEDALING furiously on his stationary bicycle, intent on devising a strategy to convince the voices to withdraw their demand that he kill Frank Adversego. For all his willingness to bring down global society, Crypto was incapable of committing an act of violence or ordering anyone else to do so. But the voices were making him frantic. Unless he could find a way to appease them, he was afraid of what they might drive him to do.

Lately, the Bees had become obsessed with Frank's participation in the Russ Task Force; they found his recent attack concept particularly alarming. If he could devise a way to take down the Russ, did that not prove that he might imagine, and then discover, Crypto's plan to destroy BankCoin? Adversego was just one member of the group, Crypto had pointed out. With or without Adversego, the task force would represent a risk. But that only made things worse; now the Bees wanted him to wipe out the entire group. *Wait and see,* he'd begged them. There's no need to act now, because we can monitor what he and they do, and that's a good thing. Crypto hadn't expected that rationale to help for long, and it hadn't.

Well into his second hour of exertion, a way to deflect the Bees came to him. It worried him that their incessant nagging was distracting him to the point he hadn't come up with a solution weeks ago. If that was any indication, he'd have to spend more time on this wretched bicycle.

He was still showering after his exercise when the Bees renewed their attack. This time, he was happy to have them bring up the Russ Task Force.

You must stop him! A Bee screamed.

Now! B Bee boomed.

Really? Crypto thought. *Are you so sure?*

He smiled at the silence that followed. *Ha!*

Aren't we? A Bee whispered at last.

Well, I don't think so, Crypto thought. *Have you forgotten that the Russ is our target as much as BankCoin?*

There was another long pause.

Continue, A Bee said.

I expected as much, Crypto thought. *Will we not be better off when Adversego or someone else on the task force comes up with a promising attack of their own? Then there will be two paths to the destruction of the Russ instead of one. Their plan could be better than ours. We might even abandon our method and use the American's plan instead.*

It was as brilliant an idea as it was simple. It was several days before the Bees bothered him again.

* * *

"Got a minute?"

"Sure, Vance. Come on in." Josh Peabody had been expecting his chief trader all morning.

"So," Morganthau said carefully, "I think it's great you've decided to get back in the trading saddle again. But I was curious about this new fund you just bought into. I'm not familiar with it."

"That's right – it's brand-new. That's why it offers such a wonderful opportunity. I'm expecting a really big run up in value. And it will be a great risk hedge for us, too."

"Cool," Morganthau said. "How come?"

"Because it has a different investment focus from ours. It invests in coins we don't, so we'll get exposure to opportunities we wouldn't otherwise."

"Really? Like what?"

"I don't know specifically. They're very private. But the guy making the decisions is supposed to be a real magician. I figured we'd start with a small position and see how we do."

"You call ten percent of our fund small?"

"Okay, 'smallish' then. I'm just feeling pretty good about this one. Let's wait and see."

"Okay. I guess you know best," Morganthau said. But he doubted it.

* * *

Frank's strategic thinking on the Fang front had evolved. On the one hand, he hated to admit failure in the defense of his feeder. But on the other, he reminded himself, a foolish consistency was supposed to be the hobgoblin of small minds. He decided the rational thing to do was change his strategy entirely. Instead, he would trap and transport Fang to a suburb with a much higher per capita percentage of bird feeders. The ever-helpful internet introduced him to several alternatives. Fang could hardly object to that.

But predictably, the humane traps he purchased all failed abysmally. Every morning he would find the latest version tripped, the bait gone and the inside Fang-free.

Now what? Clearly, he needed to come up with his own squirrel entrapment device. But how? Mankind had been devising traps for millennia, powerfully motivated by hunger in the ages-old struggle between man and rodent. What could Frank invent that had not already been conceived?

Who knew? But his new challenge provided a welcome distraction from the lack of fulfillment he was experiencing at his day job. If he couldn't save the global banking system from disaster and destruction, perhaps he could at least bestow a successful squirrel trap on humanity.

And so, he persevered. It was good he was well paid because his accumulated investment in defensive and offensive rodent weaponry was becoming substantial. No longer was he constructing his inventions from materials he scrounged from his apartment or purchased from the local hardware store. Only the highest grade, gnaw-proof materials would now suffice. Lately, he'd grown inordinately fond of titanium.

Chapter 35

Message Time

SERGEI DENIKIN WAS meeting with Yevgeny Manturov, his minister of foreign affairs, and Maxim Noskov, the Russian minister of defense.

"What do you make of Yazzi's warning?" Denikin asked.

"In one sense, it's hardly surprising," Manturov replied. "We sent a message. He could scarcely ignore it, so he sends a message he thinks we cannot ignore. The question is whether he is bluffing. After all, our message was an attack that put millions of his countrymen in darkness, and his is merely words. Why did he not first respond in kind and then summon our ambassador to underline his intentions?"

"Perhaps we are not as vulnerable to their cyber weapons as we have assumed," Denikin said. "Or maybe he does not want us to know how great his cyberattack capacity is. After all, we hesitated to launch our attack for the same reason."

"All quite possible, sir," Manturov said. "I'm afraid we can only guess at what he will do until he does it. Added to this, Yazzi has not yet been tested in office, and his prior career gives us no clues how determined he may be, and how much risk of escalation he will accept."

"What of his defense and cybersecurity officers?" Denikin asked.

"As you know, Mr. President, the American military is subject to strict civilian control. The heads of their armed forces can only make recommendations; the president has the final word. But I can say that Yazzi has surrounded himself with progressives and advocates for the exercise of soft power rather than military force."

"What would you advise?" Denikin asked, turning to Noskov, the minister of defense.

"At this time," Noskov replied, "I have grave concerns over the possible consequences of an escalating cyber war – what if the Americans were to cripple our productive capacity? True, we are not as dependent on internet-based systems as the West and therefore not as vulnerable. But we are also in a position of great economic vulnerability. Nor would we wish to engage in a costly and protracted military confrontation."

"Absolutely not. The elections are only three months away. Anything new we put in motion we must successfully complete well before then."

"If I may, sir?" Manturov said.

"Yes?"

"We have opened one front and the American president has – perhaps – called our bluff. We have not acknowledged his accusation, and should not. We should leave him guessing and instead open a second front – one that will allow us to apply pressure in a manner he cannot afford to respond to militarily. At the same time, he has run out of new economic sanctions, so our trade risk is low. With the Russ blockchain now fully deployed, our ability to survive has been extended. Let us take this opportunity to decisively and dramatically turn the tables on the Americans, and yet do so in a way that does not confront them directly."

"And you have a plan in mind that can accomplish this?"

"I do, sir."

"Then I am listening," Denikin said. "Tell me more."

* * *

Davit Nozadze leaned just far enough to the right to scan the forest on the other side of the tree, hopefully without being seen from that direction. But there was nothing to see. All that stirred were the leaves, fluttering in the light breeze. Yet he knew those he was on the alert to detect might be out there somewhere.

He turned and caught the eye of his compatriot, Tamaz Gelashvili, also hiding behind a tree. Like Nozadze, he wore camouflage. Gelashvili moved his head from side to side. Nothing to be seen from his vantage point, either.

A decade before, the Russians had seized South Ossetia from his country. One had to be ever vigilant lest the enemy go on the move again, perhaps sending troops across the border from South Ossetia to seize his own town of Tsilkani, Georgia.

He and his comrades spent much of their free time in the woods, protecting their homeland from the would-be invaders.

He leaned to the side again. There! Was that someone moving in the distance? Yes! He eased back and jerked his head in the direction of what he'd just seen. Gelashvili acknowledged his signal with a nod and they both dropped to their knees before peering around their trees once more.

Now he could see them clearly: a file of men in unmarked uniforms marching through the forest, as methodical as an army of ants.

But something was terribly wrong. These were not his school boy friends, playing Georgian patriots and Russian invaders in the forest. These were fully-grown men, hundreds of them, wearing balaclava masks. Their packs were enormous and they were carrying rifles. And there was something behind them. Something too large for the dirt woods road the men were filing along – Davit could see small trees thrashing down to the ground as it neared.

It was a tank! For a moment he thought the gun in its turret was pointed at him.

He cast a terrified look at his friend and then slid down until he was lying flat on the ground, trembling uncontrollably as he pressed his face into the stench of the moist leaves to avoid detection.

It was five minutes before either of the young boys was brave enough to look up. When they did, they held their breath for what seemed like an eternity, and saw nothing. They exchanged the briefest of looks before jumping to their feet and tearing off for home faster than either had known he could run.

* * *

"Little green men? Again?" Yazzi said, shaking his head. It was the first topic in his daily brief today and a staffer was setting up an easel. That wasn't a good sign.

"I'm afraid so, sir," Jim Wakeman said. "But this time it's substantially more serious. Not only is Denikin opening up a new front, but he's enlisted the aid of Iran as well."

The staffer placed a large map on the easel, and Wakeman picked up a pointer. "On this map we're looking at two former Soviet Socialist Republics that share a common border: Georgia and Azerbaijan."

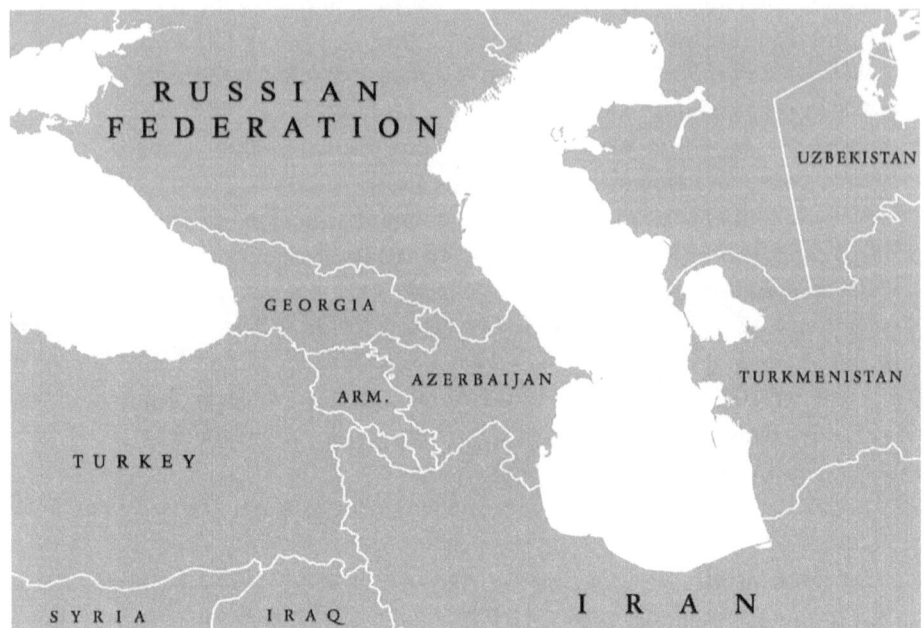

"Tactically, it looks like Ukraine all over again, with multiple sightings of masked commandos in anonymous green military uniforms carrying Russian weapons. We're receiving reports of units crossing into Georgia in multiple locations from Russian-occupied South Ossetia. They're following the same social media script as in Ukraine, too. It started two days ago when a bunch of posts popped up in Georgia, each one reporting a different made-up incident. Most claimed the police were mistreating ethnic Russians. Another set of posts immediately followed, calling for people to form militias to defend Russians and Russian rights. This morning, the little green men surfaced and seized four police stations. They're still holding them with Russian flags flying overhead. We're getting reports the Kremlin is preparing to play the same game next door in Azerbaijan."

"What's going on there?"

"Our best guess is its still just Denikin trying to divert domestic attention from the impact of depressed oil revenues. The Russ income has been a huge help, but it hasn't covered the full revenue loss, so to outlast us, he's had to belt-tighten with a vengeance. Public services are suffering, people are getting laid off, and even the oligarchs are restless. Denikin will deny it, but everyone at home and abroad will know the militiamen come from Russia. That makes it a perfect way for him to tuck it to the West without admitting responsibility."

"How serious is this?" Yazzi asked.

"There's no way to tell yet. If it's just a diversion, it could stay fairly low level and then peter out after a few weeks or months. As you know, that's what happened in Belarus, where instead of demanding a land corridor from Lithuania, as we feared he might, things just died down. After a couple of weeks Denikin quietly moved his forces back out again and that was it. Or this could be the real thing, like the Crimean and South Ossetian takeovers. We'll just have to wait and see."

* * *

President Yazzie didn't have to wait long. Two days later the situation had become serious enough to merit an emergency meeting of the National Security Council. Which was where he was sitting now, reflecting on the situation as an army colonel droned on with an update on the massing of Russian forces. The problem with diplomacy, Yazzi reflected, was that there were two sides to every interaction, and the other guy always had a mind of his own.

But he should pay closer attention. He focused again on the map of the Near East spread across the wall of the Situation Room, centered on Georgia and Azerbaijan. On either side of those two countries, Yazzi could see dozens of symbols and arrows.

"Last of all, sir," the colonel intoned, "the squares you see on the Georgian border identify Russian armored brigades, made up of T-90A main battle tanks – that's the heaviest armor they have. Satellite photos show as many as sixty tanks already deployed along the Georgian border with at least another eighty-two likely in transit.

"You say 'as many as.' How do you miss a tank?" Yazzi asked.

"It's not as easy to track tanks as you might expect, sir. The Russian's largest air transport, the An-124, can carry several at a time. If they're loaded, unloaded, and then positioned at night, we could miss that. The Russians – like us – use camouflage nets and other tricks to make military vehicles hard to spot, too. They also have very realistic, full-size tank mock-ups they can set up quickly when they move the real ones away. So, we might actually be looking at mock-ups on the Georgian border, if they want us to over-estimate how large a force they're bringing to bear."

"Okay," Yazzi said. "Please go on."

"Thank you, sir. This is the largest deployment of An-124s we've seen since the Soviet Union collapsed – more than a third of all they have in active service. We've also seen indications they're activating some of the two hundred armored units they normally hold in reserve. Those are being brought in to fill in the voids left by the active units and tank crews moving to the Georgian border. Taken together with the artillery and missile batteries, air wings and ground troops already in place and on the way, this is a very substantial and credible force – much larger than the one the Kremlin assembled back in 2008 when its objective was to seize just South Ossetia and Abkhazia."

"How about the Georgians? What do they have?"

"They lost a large percentage of their tanks and other weaponry to the Russians in 2008, but they've more than recovered since then. Still, the Russian forces we're seeing are greater in every category. The Georgians only have about thirty-seven thousand personnel in active service, and their entire annual military budget is less than three hundred million dollars."

"But enough of a force to put up a stiff resistance?" Yazzi asked.

"Only on a suicidal basis, I'm afraid, sir. Our assumption is that if the Russians throw everything we're looking at now across the border, the Georgians will have to surrender."

"Very well," Yazzi said. "Let's move over to Iran then. What do they have on the Azerbaijani border?"

"A force similar in size to the Russians, sir, but different in some respects. The Iranians have always loved big armor. They have as many as two thousand main battle tanks, and over a quarter of them are either in transit or already in position. They've got over a half million personnel in active service, and about twenty percent of them – mostly career troops, as compared to conscripts – are being deployed to the border."

"And the Azerbaijani forces?" Yazzi asked.

"More substantial than the Georgians, sir," the colonel said. "They've got over eighty thousand ground personnel, and some of their equipment is impressive. They might take down a few enemy aircraft, if they're lucky. But, given the size of the Iranian force and the risk of Russia rolling over Georgia in a matter of days, we assume the Azerbaijanis would surrender as well, especially if given a joint ultimatum from Russia and Iran. Likely, both the Georgians and the Azerbaijanis would decide they'd get better terms negotiating a settlement before hostilities break out than after their armed forces have been crushed."

"Thank you, Colonel," Yazzi said, turning to Secretary of State Calhoun. "So, tell me, Hugh, what are the Russians up to? And what do they want?"

"Mr. President, I don't think a permanent takeover of Georgia and Azerbaijan is what Denikin has in mind."

"Why do you say that?" Yazzi asked.

"For starters, because there are other former Soviet Socialist States we expect would rank higher on their wish list. Also, they already took the territory they most wanted – South Ossetia – from Georgia back in 2008. Next, there's nothing uniquely appealing about Azerbaijan. It's not a very large economy, and most of its wealth comes from oil and gas, something neither the Russians nor the Iranians need more of."

"So, what's special about Georgia and Azerbaijan then?"

"Location, sir, from two perspectives. First, between them, Georgia and Azerbaijan own all the territory between the Black and Caspian Seas. That's been a vital transportation route since Marco Polo opened the Silk Road between Europe and Asia seven hundred years ago. The second reason is if Denikin can make Georgia and Azerbaijan follow his orders, he'll control the ground all the way from the Indian to the Arctic Oceans. That means he could blockade all land and air traffic between Asia and Europe – all oil and gas pipelines, rail and truck routes, air cargo routes – everything. Then all cargo would have to go on ships, traveling thousands of miles out of its way and far more slowly. The trade disruptions and additional costs would be enormous."

"What would the impact be on the US?" Yazzi asked.

"Substantial, because our trade, transportation, and supply chains are so intertwined with those of the Europeans."

"So, let's assume that's what the Russians are thinking. How about the Iranians?"

"I think it's mostly opportunistic on their part. If Russia wants to muscle Azerbaijan, the Iranians will be happy to join the party. There are a few concessions we expect Teheran would be happy to extract, like building its own oil pipeline direct to Europe, and more leverage to use against us and NATO."

"So, what specifically does Denikin want?"

"Getting rid of the sanctions for sure, sir. After that, undermining NATO unity. Europeans would likely be a lot more worried about heating their homes this winter than curbing Russian military actions hundreds of miles from their borders. It's a perfect way to drive a wedge between us and our allies."

"You don't think our NATO allies will stick with us to get the Russians to back down?"

"I'm afraid not, sir. We've already imposed all the embargoes on Russia we could come up with, so that only leaves force, and I don't see anybody in Europe stepping up to that plate. So that would leave only us."

"The Russians can't assume we won't act alone, though," Yazzi said.

"True, sir. But I expect they're pretty confident we won't go to war over two countries most Americans have never heard of and couldn't find on a map if they have. And they're right. After Iraq and Afghanistan, we could never persuade Congress, let alone the American people, to support another war in the Near East, and against a nuclear-armed adversary at that."

Yazzi looked around the table. "Is there anyone who thinks differently?"

No one spoke up.

"I'm having a hard time accepting," Yazzi said, "that the largest and most powerful country in the world's history has to stand by and watch as two of its greatest enemies may be preparing to snatch two sovereign nations – it's like Hitler taking Austria and Czechoslovakia without anyone raising a finger all over again. Thank goodness, we have one weapon Chamberlin didn't."

"Agreed," Calhoun said. "Much as I wish it were otherwise, I think it's time to take down the Russ."

"Where do we stand on that?" Yazzi asked Jim Wakeman, the national security adviser.

"We're close, sir. I don't have an exact date for you at the moment, but I will by the end of the day."

"And the Russians and the Iranians? What's the timeline there, John?" Yazzi asked.

"We estimate it'll be at least ten days before all the forces we see in motion arrive. After that, we expect they'll need at least another week to get their logistics taken care of – beefing up air control systems, positioning and coordinating missile defense units, and so on."

Yazzi paused to think. Once again, all the information had been delivered, all his questions had been answered, and all eyes were upon him. In one sense, the decision was easier. It wasn't that every alternative was were equally bad. This time, there appeared to be only one workable option at all. Intervening militarily was out of the question. Even if he was willing to go to war – even if Congress, for once, had the guts to approve going to war – there was no time. It would take weeks to move enough carrier-based planes, in-flight refueling air tankers, and logistical support within range and months more to deploy sufficient ground forces to prevail. And his advisers were telling him the game would be over within a few weeks, ending with concessions by Georgia and Azerbaijan, and not with a territorial acquisition, like Iraq's attack on Kuwait, that the US could reverse through force.

Nor could he bring the Russians or the Iranians to heel through non-military action, because they were already subject to every kind of sanction imaginable. No, there really was only one alternative this time, good, bad, or otherwise. He made his decision.

"In that case, we'd better get started. I'd like a full report first thing in the morning spelling out in detail how the attack on the Russ will take place within a week. We've got to put an end to Denikin's aggressions once and for all."

Chapter 36

The Old Switcheroo

F RANK WAS IN his office five days a week now, but he was rarely on the system Crypto could monitor. And when he was, he was spending most of his time indulging a bizarre fixation on the habits of squirrels. That could only mean one thing: the rest of the time he was working away diligently on his air-gapped system. Yes, Crypto could have someone hack that computer, too, but Frank would likely notice it if his air-gapped server suddenly gained wireless capability.

Crypto was less worried than the Bees by Frank's presence on the air-gapped system. Crypto was a firm believer in the "keep it simple" principle and was confident his faithfulness to that rule would keep Frank at bay. Not only were minimally complex programs less likely to go awry, but their very simplicity often allowed them to escape detection. Presumably Frank would be looking for trapdoors, Trojans, and the like. Good for him. If that's what he was up to, he'd never catch on. He wasn't even searching in the right place.

Another reason Crypto was less concerned was that he could launch his attack any time he wished. But he did not wish to, not yet, because the longer he waited, the more destructive the result would be. That's what his countdown clock was all about. Every bank had records of the account balances of its customers before they were transferred into BankCoin wallets six months ago. Had he struck soon after the network went live, the banks could have rebooted their old systems and software, picking up where things were before. Launching the attack then would have been highly disruptive, to be sure, but hardly devastating. After a few days or weeks of scurrying around, financial life would have gone on as before.

The longer he waited, the more impossible that task had become. Billions of people had made money, and others had lost it. Many had made deposits and others withdrawals; most had done both. Untold numbers had sold things and the rest had bought them. Exchange rates had risen and fallen again in unending pulses of reaction to global events. In short, everyone's wallet balances had been changing constantly since the system went live. The only records of the transactions resulting in all those changes would be in the blockchain itself.

It would be a hopeless challenge to recreate the record of what had happened without access to the BankCoin blockchain. As importantly, it would also be impossible to tell how much money anyone now had, because Crypto's attack would destroy all the wallets as well. If he waited long enough, the pre-BankCoin records would be so hopelessly out of date that they would be effectively useless.

There had been a time, before the agitation of the Bees began to rise, when Crypto would often lie awake at night, imagining that he could peer down from some magical point in space that permitted him to see everyone in the Western world, all enjoying a day on a perfectly sunlit beach. Each individual was diligently building his or her financial sand castle, unaware that someday very soon Crypto would send a mighty wave against that beach, a wave that would forever sweep it clean. It would be easier to recreate those billions of sand castles than it would be to restore the balances of the BankCoin wallets of the world.

Nor would there be enough time, because the world would immediately be plunged into economic and social chaos. No one would know what they were worth, nor could they prove it. No one, therefore, could buy anything, because no one would be willing to sell something to someone who could not prove they could pay for it. There would be no way to calculate taxes and no way to pay them. Shipments of goods in transit would be halted in limbo because there was no way for payment to be made on delivery.

With BankCoin now globally adopted, the economy of virtually every country would collapse with no feasible path to recovery. Governments would be caught flat-footed, because no one had believed such a thing could happen. Thefts from BankCoin wallets? Yes. But the obliteration of every copy of the BankCoin blockchain and every wallet balance? Never. And yet, so it would be. No one would want to recreate BankCoin, and the challenge of taking the mothballed, traditional financial system out of storage would be Herculean – far too difficult to accomplish in the midst of so much chaos. Let BankCoin run long enough, Crypto was convinced, and society could not fail to collapse.

But the days when Crypto could indulge himself in such theoretical ruminations were now over – his countdown clock was ticking down, and the fury of the Bees was ratcheting up. Now the need to accurately answer the question was urgent: how long was long enough to guarantee a sufficient depth and duration of chaos? Crypto wanted more time. But the Bees would have none of it. Six months was enough, they insisted. The risk of discovery was too great.

Take it or leave it: launch now or eliminate Adversego. Pick one. B Bee's ultimatum was thunderous.

Crypto was crumpling under the pressure of the escalating anger of the Bees; he hadn't endured an onslaught like this since his university days. *Pick one! Pick one!* A Bee repeated the litany incessantly until B Bee would suddenly take over, thundering the same words. They continued endlessly in this alternation except when they both abused him at once, supported by a chorus more overwhelmingly ominous and intimidating than ever before. Crypto felt the combined aggression was driving him mad.

Once again, he retreated to his stationary bicycle, and after an unusually long and exhausting stint, he thought of a way to pick neither of the alternatives the Bees were forcing upon him. He hated his new plan because it would once again require him to call on assistants. Even if he took every precaution possible to mask his identity and the payments he would have to make, there was always the possibility he could be traced.

But he had no choice. He had already raised his medications as far as he dared, and the extra dosages were dulling his ability to think. That also added danger: what if his judgment failed him and he made a foolish mistake? Better to risk exposure after the attacks were successful than to bungle the entire enterprise due to foggy thinking.

I have been considering, he informed the Bees. *We cannot kill Adversego, because to do so would bring the police, the FBI, who knows who else to the case. If we are caught, all our plans will have been for naught. But if we can get Adversego to quit of his own volition, we will achieve the result you wish. Do you follow me?*

There was silence; he had caught the Bees' attention. He continued.

So, I have come up with a plan to achieve that end. It involves a set of psychological techniques that will frighten Adversego into resigning. The key to its success is to increase the stress and uncertainty gradually to break his nerve. These methods were perfected by the Stasi in the former German Democratic Republic and were proven to be extremely effective – there are ample records that demonstrate their success. It will work with Adversego as well. Let me explain how ...

It wasn't easy, but he succeeded. The Bees agreed to back off while he gave his plan a try. Another idea had occurred to him on his bike as well – a Plan B he could hold in reserve if there was no other way to avoid giving in to the demands of the Bees to kill Adversego. He set to work to prepare for that contingency as well.

* * *

Frank was tired when he returned to his suite in Manhattan. He wanted nothing more than to clear his head of the day's frustrations and engage in some mindless pursuit, like reading a far-fetched, satirical, political, cybersecurity technothriller. He reached into the credenza for his bottle of expensive scotch, but there was nothing there. That was odd; he always put things back in the same place. Perhaps he'd pushed it in farther than usual.

He got down on his knees to look, but no bottle. There was a small card, though, folded in half so that it stood upright, like a miniature tent. He pulled it out and saw that there were two words on it. The card read:

Not Here

Well. That was darn peculiar. He wondered what it was all about. If a member of the housekeeping staff or a maintenance person had stolen his hooch, they'd scarcely leave a cryptic note to underline the fact. And it wasn't as if the card was telling him something he didn't already know.

He stared at it. What should he do? Report the theft to building management?

If he did, what would they make of the little note? Would they believe him or suspect he was spoofing them for some bizarre reason? Maybe he should think about this for a while.

When he went into his bedroom later that evening, he saw the bottle of scotch sitting on his chest of drawers. In front of it was another small, folded card. On it was a single word:

Here

* * *

Every day thereafter, Frank found more evidence that someone was tampering with his belongings. Things were moved around his suite but never disappeared, so the motive wasn't theft. What was it, then? If it was to make him uneasy, it was succeeding. But to what purpose?

After four days of unwanted surprises he hid a web camera as best he could to see who was behind the strange activity. Then he could record the culprit, and building management would have to believe a video. The next day, he set up his tablet on his desk at work so he could monitor the feed from the camera. Nothing appeared until late morning, when he caught a flash of motion out of the corner of his eye just before the video feed on his tablet went dark. When he returned to his suite, he found the camera smashed on the floor.

He cleaned up the pieces and sat down on his couch, staring out at Central Park. He decided that the destruction of the camera was meant to make him more uneasy. Whoever had killed it wanted Frank to know he wouldn't hesitate to use violence if Frank didn't do whatever it was he was supposed to do. But – what was that?

He concluded there were only two possible motives. Someone was either unhappy that he was working for First Manhattan or that he was part of the RussCoin Task Force. Of the two, the former seemed more likely, as his role there was public, and it was his bank digs that were affected. So now what? Should he go to the police? He could, but he couldn't imagine they'd do much. Nothing had been stolen, and no one had been hurt. The authorities had more important things to worry about.

How about the bank? Assuming they took him seriously, they should be concerned. Colonel Dix, at the RussCoin Task Force, would certainly pay attention. But would he agree someone was trying to scare Frank into resigning? Or would he suspect the threatening behavior related to something in Frank's private life he wasn't owning up to? Maybe instead of having his Manhattan apartment watched, Colonel Dix would have someone watch Frank instead, as a potential security risk. Nothing personal, of course.

Either way, the most logical thing for Dix to do would be to drop Frank from the task force. That would be understandable, but Frank didn't like the idea of being let go when he was blameless, especially when he felt he was providing real value. And anyway, the odds seemed higher it was his BankCoin work that was at issue.

He decided to go to the bank and ask them to hire a private investigator and leave the colonel in the dark for now. That made sense.

* * *

Frank was leaning forward, his hands clasped together on his knees. Audrey Addams was staring at him across her pristine desk. In between them, like toy soldiers arrayed on a pretend battle field, was Frank's collection of miniature paper tents.

"So, let me get this straight," Addams said. "Every day when you go back to your apartment, something's different, and you find one of these messages. You don't know who's leaving them, and you haven't mentioned it to building management."

"That's right," he replied.

She frowned. "Have you given an apartment key to anyone?"

"Nobody."

"And you've got no idea who might be behind this?"

"Not specifically. But my theory is someone's trying to get me to quit working on the BankCoin project."

"Why in the world would you think that?"

Frank hunched down in his chair. "Well," he said, "Let's assume someone's hacked BankCoin. Wouldn't they be afraid I'd figure that out? Anyway, what else could it be?"

Addams frowned more deeply. In fact, she was more suspicious about what Frank might be up to than she was inclined to believe his strange story and gnomic cards. Her bank was already paying him an outrageous amount, and in her opinion, he'd done precious little to earn it. She'd been at the bank for fourteen years, three as Cronin's chief of staff, and she hadn't received a tenth as many stock options as Frank, let alone anything close to his salary.

"Well," she said, "it seems like quite a leap to me to assume whoever is playing tricks on you is thinking about First Manhattan. If their goal is to make you quit, why don't they just say that on one of these silly cards?"

Frank shifted uneasily in his chair. He was troubled by the same question and hadn't come up with a good answer.

"So," Addams said, "why should the bank hire a private investigator for you? I don't see a single word on any of these cards that's the least bit threatening. For all I know, some oddball friend of yours is pranking you." The look on Addams's face suggested that in Frank's case, adding "oddball" to "friend" was likely the waste of an extra word.

Pointing out he had no friends, oddball or otherwise, would be too humiliating, so Frank shrugged instead.

"Well, Frank," Audrey summed up. "I'm afraid I can't see my way clear to authorize spending bank funds to hire a private investigator. However, you should feel free to do so yourself, and," she added, raising one eyebrow as she pushed Frank's notes into a pile in front of him, "I believe we're paying you more than enough to do that."

Addams stood up, and Frank reluctantly did the same.

As soon as he left, Addams picked up her phone and called bank security.

"Henry, Audrey Addams here. We've got an employee named Frank Adversego who's acting a little strange. He's a systems security guy and has access to everything. I'd like you to have your people keep an eye on him. Yes, he's signed the usual agreement, so we have the right to access his email and his phone records. Let me know if you see anything unusual. Also, I want a daily log of who he speaks to by phone outside the bank and a copy of every email he sends inside or outside the bank. Thanks."

Then she had another thought. What was the name of that FBI investigator? She opened her contact management program. Right: Ryan Clancy. She should let him know, too. She put in a call to him and left a message that she might have some important information.

Then Audrey Addams indulged herself in something she rarely did. She smiled.

* * *

Ryan Clancy looked at the notes from his call with Audrey Addams. He was significantly more concerned about what Frank had reported than she was. Word had come over from the CIA that the Russian Federal Security Service was starting to take an interest in BankCoin. Well, why wouldn't they? It was an obvious target and a spectacularly attractive one, too. Find one flaw in that technology, and you could bring the whole global financial system house of cards down. What were the banks thinking? Crazy.

Anyway. If the CIA was right, the Russians would be highly likely to try to turn an employee at First Manhattan. Clancy would need to ask his contact there to keep a closer eye on Adversego. Maybe the Russians had dug up something from his past they could use to blackmail him. And there was always money. That had a long history of working.

It was rare good luck this Addams person would be sending so much information to him. He wouldn't even need a warrant to directly monitor what Adversego was doing.

* * *

Frank was feeling discouraged as he headed home to Washington. He was convinced Audrey Addams thought he was a little crazy. And for the first time, he realized she looked at him as a useless drain on bank resources. After all, what had he come up with so far? Is that what everyone at the bank thought? That possibility bothered him a lot.

There was a cold drizzle waiting for him when he landed at National Airport but no driver holding an umbrella the way there would have been in New York, waiting to escort him into a fancy town car. Instead, he stuffed himself into a beat-up Uber that must have been within a hair of failing to make the grade. Also, the driver's taste in music sucked.

At least Frank hadn't deployed his first homemade trap yet. He didn't think he could face returning home to still another defeat in his war with a beast with less than one percent of his own cranial capacity. And there would be no fancy bottle of scotch waiting for him in his cupboard.

What a day. And now his Uber driver had the cold-tolerance of an Eskimo. Or maybe his car heat wasn't working. Either way, Frank was chilled to the bone. When he got home, he'd make a pot of coffee right away.

Which is what he did. Plopping down in his living room to wait for it to be ready, he stared blankly at the water dripping onto his balcony. Now what?

A bit of motion caught his eye. Huh. Fang was perched on the railing outside. Just what Frank needed. A gloating squirrel.

But then the animal dropped to the balcony floor and hopped hesitantly forward. The drizzle had turned to sleet now. When Fang rose on his hind legs and placed his front paws on the glass, Frank could see how soaked and pathetic the tiny animal was. It stared at him for a while. Then it disappeared.

Frank looked out into the now-empty darkness and felt his face begin to burn with a sudden and obvious realization. What was the matter with him? Was a blue jay or a cardinal more entitled to be fed just because it was colorful? Every living creature needed to eat. What kind of species bigot was he? And how had he allowed himself to become so ridiculously obsessed with a squirrel? Maybe the pressure of his bank job was affecting him more than he'd realized.

He filled a bowl with seeds and placed it on his balcony. Then he waited, wondering whether Fang could find it in his tiny heart to forgive him.

Chapter 37

Girls Just Want to Have Fun

AUDREY ADDAMS HAD felt unnerved ever since the office party where Glen Olson had made his advances. She felt as if all eyes were on her – and perhaps they were. What if Olson was gossiping right now, talking to someone nearby? Who knew how he would describe their encounter? Eventually, she broke and called Sylvia Bunsen, the only person in the bank she could think of with whom she could share what had happened.

Sylvia had been playing cat to Audrey's mouse for months, thus far with no success or any apparent realization by Audrey of what Sylvia had in mind. But Sylvia was persistent. Audrey's exquisite aloofness appealed to her; she loved an amorous challenge now and then. She had no idea whether Audrey was gay or straight, but she was betting the odds were in her favor, assuming Audrey had any interest in playing on either team at all. If so, Sylvia looked forward to the day she could whisper softly in Audrey's ear that she was beautiful.

Audrey had first caught Sylvia's eye at a bank off-site retreat. She maneuvered herself on to Audrey's group during one of those silly games intended to build team spirit. She followed up a few days later with an invitation to grab lunch, and then another; Sylvia was nothing if not persistent. Eventually, Audrey said yes. Fishing around over their salads, she found out Cronin never shared budget details with Audrey. From the way she admitted it, Sylvia could tell Audrey couldn't stand being excluded from anything on the management front.

Conveniently, Bunsen worked for the bank's chief financial officer. From then on, she baited her lunch invitations with suggestions that she had interesting budget information to share. Audrey always took the bait but never reciprocated with an invitation of her own. That made Audrey's unexpected call a welcome surprise.

The restaurant they met in was quiet, discreet, and almost empty. Sylvia was understanding and patient, offering Audrey all the time she needed to describe what had happened and work through it out loud. For the first time, Sylvia felt she was establishing a bond and wondered how far she could take it. Should she reach across and take Audrey's hand? No; not yet. Too risky. And anyway, best to hedge her bets; Audrey wasn't the only woman who appealed to Sylvia, and she had a second agenda to pursue as well.

"I don't want to interrupt," Sylvia said, "but I should ask. Are you planning to go back to the office this afternoon?"

"Yes," Audrey replied, with a look that managed to mix determination with revulsion.

"Okay, then we've got to buck you up first. Time to get you back on an even keel. Right?"

"Right."

"Okay. Let's talk some shop so you can pull yourself together. What's new on the blockchain project?"

Why that? Audrey thought. She found it deadly boring. But lately, Sylvia always asked about it.

"BankCoin? Not much. Well, I guess one thing. There's this guy named Frank Adversego we brought in to be the senior cybersecurity risk manager a while back. As completely clueless a wonk as you could ever imagine. I think he's starting to go over the edge."

"Over the edge? How?"

"He's convinced someone's, I don't know, stalking him. Moving things around in his apartment – trying to intimidate him or something. He thinks the bank should hire a private investigator to stake out his place."

"And you told him what?"

"I told him no way. We're paying him a ton of money. If he wants an investigator, he can jolly well pay for one himself. And then I called up bank security and told them to send me a daily log of his external phone calls and copies of all his email."

This time, Sylvia did reach across the table but only to give Audrey's hand a friendly squeeze.

"You go, girl! That's the spirit! Now let's go back to the bank and give those men hell."

* * *

Sylvia Bunsen loved to dance. She also loved women who loved to dance. That's what the clubbing scene was for. On the dance floor, she introduced herself as "Jinx" Bunsen. It was a made-up nickname she thought would appeal to the kind of person who appealed to her. In any event, it seemed to charm the lovely Svetlana, and she was very appealing indeed. They'd met at a club three weeks ago.

Sylvia wasn't sure what Svetlana did for a living but figured it must have something to do with technology, because she was always asking about the BankCoin project. Sylvia didn't mind. Sometimes, it was fun to play at being the mouse instead of the cat. How much she decided to share was up to her, and she loved teasing Svetlana, giving up little but looking into her eyes a lot over a glass of wine in a way that promised more if the price was right. As it always was when at last Sylvia gave her the information she wanted.

Audrey's little story about Frank therefore made Sylvia's day. She could go dancing tonight!

* * *

Marko Andropov was sitting at his terminal at the Russian Federation embassy in Washington, DC. On the embassy directory, he was identified as its chief of protocol, which indeed he was. But his more important role was to serve as the senior FSS agent for the northeastern United States.

Periodically, he toggled back to the screen he'd left open since emailing Audrey Addams earlier that morning. Of course, the email would not appear to have been sent by him. Instead, he had spoofed Frank's email address as the sender. The message was short and read as follows:

Audrey,
I think this article on alt coin security is important: [link]
Frank

The link looked exactly the way it should, and if clicked, it would lead – although not immediately – to the web address displayed in the email. Before it took Addams to that destination, it would skip through a Dark Web site Andropov had prepared for that purpose. The delay would be almost imperceptible but more than adequate to allow the malware on Andropov's site to begin uploading to the First Manhattan system.

There – Addams had just clicked on the link. *Good.* Andropov was now inside the First Manhattan Bank's network and able to shadow the email and activities of both Audrey and Frank.

* * *

Da!

Shukov closed the decoded version of the message from Andropov. It included welcome news: not only had Andropov penetrated First Manhattan's network, but he would be sending Shukov a daily summary of the activities of the most important cybersecurity investigator on the First Manhattan staff, together with copies of all of his email and external telephone logs.

Shukov was pleased with the progress his malware team was making, too. At the next JCSC meeting he would report that it was only a matter of time before the Russian Federation would be in a position to take down the Western world's banking infrastructure.

That was a great relief.

Chapter 38

Time to Get With the Program

FRANK HAD AN idea. He tapped his fingers and stared at the screen. *Hmm.* It might be worth the effort.

There was a knock at the door. It was Ruth.

"Good timing!" he said. "Come on in!"

"What's up?" she said, taking a seat.

"A new idea. Can I bounce it off you?"

"Of course," she said, sitting up straighter.

"I've been struggling with how to scan the whole codebase to find any malware that might already be there. I've gone through BankCoin more times now than I'd care to admit, each time trying to come at it from a new perspective – and so far, no luck. Maybe there's no big vulnerability or malware to be found – but what if there is and I've just missed it? The problem is how to recognize the bad code in the middle of hundreds of thousands of lines of good stuff. It might seem innocuous until you really understood how it would act. So, what I'm thinking is that the best way to find it would be to write code for the most likely attack scenarios and then look for something similar. Not exactly the first thing anyone would try, but I'm running out of ideas. What do you think?"

"I take your point," she said, "but what are the odds you'd come up with the same approach?"

Given Frank's participation in the Russ Task Force, much better than Ruth might guess. But he obviously couldn't share that.

"Well, not a hundred percent, of course. But there's an attack I've always thought was improbable that maybe I've been underestimating. Let's say the Russians or North Koreans want to take down the whole BankCoin network. How would they go about that? One approach would be to penetrate the system of a participating bank and then somehow get inside BankCoin, too. Next, they'd create a smart contract that contained malware instead of transaction details and submit it for inclusion in a block the same bank created. Are you with me so far?"

"Yes, and I think I see where you're going. But remember that if a block has too much data, it triggers an alarm."

"Right!" Frank said. "Good. But now let's say the enemy hacker can somehow prevent any other smart contracts from being included in the same block. I checked in this morning to see how big the blocks are getting these days, and it looks like the volume and complexity of smart contracts have really taken off. That means if the bad guy can keep them out of a block, he might have several thousand lines to work with and not worry about triggering an alarm. So, the question is, would it be possible to create a piece of malware that was small enough to get past the malware alert and infect the whole BankCoin network? If so, Schwert's original mechanism doesn't work anymore, and an attack against one bank could threaten all."

Ruth nodded. "Wow," she said. "That might work!"

"Right," Frank said, "So, what types of malware could take down BankCoin, and which would require just a few thousand lines of code?"

"Well," Ruth said, "I guess if we're talking about taking it down temporarily, it could encrypt every copy of the blockchain. And if someone wanted to destroy the system, it would erase them."

"Right!" Frank said. "That's what I think, too. Right now, there aren't any air-gapped, archived backup copies of BankCoin in the traditional sense, because every live copy is a backup of every other live copy."

"Well, then the first thing we should do is create backups and then air gap them so we'll always have ..." She paused. "No, that wouldn't work, either."

Frank smiled. He already knew that, but he was pleased Ruth had spotted the drawback so quickly. "How so?" he asked.

"Because the malware might have already been added to the BankCoin copy we archived. It may be the hacker didn't want to activate the malware immediately. If that was the case, we couldn't ever reboot from our archival copy after an attack and know we were home free, because the same enemy could just trigger the same malware again."

"Exactly!" Frank said.

Then Ruth's eyebrows shot up. "And what about this – a smart contract by definition is a program that's supposed to trigger a payment at a later date. So, if the malware is already planted somewhere in the blockchain disguised as a smart contract, you'd never be able to spot the block carrying the attack trigger, because it would look just like any other block that updated a smart contract. And millions of those updates are added to BankCoin every day."

"Bingo!" Frank said, pleased. "So, I think we agree we should assume, for safety's sake, that some kind of malware might already be in the BankCoin blockchain. That's the easy part. The hard one would be finding it if it's there – and by 'there' we're talking about somewhere in a blockchain that now contains billions of transactions. How do we spot it? That's why I'm thinking of going through the exercise of designing the same sort of attack. If we're successful, we'll have a better idea what to look for in the existing blocks, and what to scan for in the ones ahead."

"That makes sense. I'm a pretty good coder, and Dirk doesn't keep me very busy. Mostly, he keeps me on standby to cover meetings for him when he can get away with it. Would you like some help?"

Frank paused. He didn't normally enjoy collaborating on code. But Ruth seemed to think a lot like him. It could be a big help. "Sure. That would be great. Why don't you pull your chair around to this side of my desk?"

She did, and soon, they were deep in techno-speak, discussing possible approaches and pointing by turns at things the other was typing into the keyboard of Frank's air-gapped system. When they were finished with an outline of their next steps, Frank emailed Hank Taylor to let him know about the new project.

That email was duly collected and forwarded by Audrey Addams directly to Ryan Clancy at the FBI. And indirectly to Aleksandr Shukov.

* * *

Shukov finished reading Frank's email. It was almost too good to be true. This Adversego person had decided to design the very same type of malware the FSS was charged with developing. When Adversego was through, what he created would even be on a system inside First Manhattan Bank itself. All Shukov needed to do was wait until it was complete and then devise a way to move it over to First Manhattan's live version of BankCoin. Or he could transfer it onto the copy maintained by another bank, some of which were in countries friendly to Russia.

Best of all, if the Kremlin decided to launch an attack and used that malware to carry it out, the FSS could anonymously tip the Western authorities and all eyes would be on Adversego and not on the Kremlin.

What fools these Americans were! Still, he should not rely solely on this potential good news. He must continue to drive his team to create his own means to destroy BankCoin. Better two potential avenues to the promotion he knew he so richly deserved than just one.

Yesterday he had come up with a new idea on that front. Who should know better where to find a fatal vulnerability in a financial blockchain than someone who had devised such a network himself? Conveniently, such an individual existed, and the blockchain he had designed was supported by the Russian Federation. Shukov looked forward to drawing on the expertise of Oleg Lupanov.

* * *

Clancy was less enthused when he read the same email. So, Adversego was hard at work developing software that could take down the entire BankCoin network.

He crossed his arms and massaged his biceps. Did that mean Adversego was just doing his job or that whoever was playing games with his apartment had blackmailed him into action? If the latter, Adversego was being very clever, reporting his idea to a coworker to make his actions look innocent. Of course, that wouldn't save him from being a prime suspect if an attack did take down BankCoin. If he was the culprit, he'd likely disappear just before it occurred. Defect to whatever country he was working for or perhaps be set up with a new identity and a fat bank account in some other place. That could happen.

Clancy looked up at the ceiling. Should he ask a judge to approve taking Adversego's passport away?

No. If he did that, whoever Adversego's handler was would drop him immediately. Then they'd move on to someone else, and Clancy would be worse off than he was now. Better to keep a close eye on Frank instead.

Chapter 39

Here's Russ in Your Eye!

DIMITRI USTINOV TOLD himself he had no reason to feel tense. He was a respected civil servant, and a recently promoted one at that. Following on the heels of the runaway success of the Russ he was now the Superintendent of Digital Finances for the Department of Information Technology in the Sphere of Budgeting and State and Local Finance Management.

Yet here he was, sitting in the reception area of the central offices of the Federal Security Service, waiting to see a senior investigator of the FSS, and he did not know why. That did not bode well. Ustinov could only hope he would not be asked to provide any of the information he had so consistently failed to obtain from Mikhail Filitov.

Precisely at the top of the hour, he was summoned by an aide who ushered him down endless hallways and through many turns before depositing him in an empty meeting room. And there he waited. For a long time.

When at last the door opened, not one but two men entered. One was short and stocky with a bald dome that shone to the point of suggesting a liberal application of furniture polish. He wore a more cheerful expression than Ustinov would have expected to find within the bowels of the FSS. The second entrant was tall and thin, with close-cropped hair graying at the temples and a face that gave away nothing. It was also disconcerting: his almost lipless mouth divided his chin from the rest of his head like a long, puckered scar. Ustinov wondered which one was Aleksandr Shukov.

"Ah, Dimitri Fedorovich," the short man said. "I am Sergei Ovechkin. A pleasure to meet you. I am so sorry to keep you waiting. Please forgive me." He gripped Dimitri by both shoulders as he spoke as if he was a long-lost brother. "And this is Aleksandr Shukov." Shukov smiled slightly and shook Ustinov's hand. "Now sit," Ovechkin said. "Sit – and we shall talk."

Ustinov took a seat across the conference room table from Ovechkin. Shukov chose one several places away at the head of the table behind a pad of paper and pen that had been there when Ustinov entered the room. "So!" Ovechkin said. "Now you will tell me about the Russ."

"Of course, I would be happy to do so," Ustinov said. "Are there specific aspects that are of particular interest? Current transactional volumes? Its technical status, perhaps?"

"Everything," Ovechkin said, slapping one hand lightly on the table. "Assume I know nothing and wish to know everything."

"All right then," Ustinov said uncertainly. "Would it be appropriate for me to begin by describing what a blockchain is? Yes? Well –" he embarked on that topic, but it was awkward trying to speak to both men at the same time. Ovechkin was smiling and engaged while Shukov's face remained expressionless. And he was sitting so far to the side that after a while, Ustinov unconsciously spoke only to Ovechkin.

Ustinov waited to be prompted after he exhausted his shallow technical knowledge about the blockchain. But Ovechkin only smiled and nodded, so Ustinov launched into a description of how international transactions in Russ were conducted. He glanced at Shukov and noticed that he had not taken a single note. Was he even listening?

Halfway through that topic, Shukov interrupted him.

"This is all very interesting," Ovechkin said. "But you have not yet told us about the leader of the Russ Project, Oleg Lupanov."

Ah. So that was why he was here. Ustinov began to perspire.

"No, sir, I have not."

"And why is that?"

What could he say? If the FSS was interested in Lupanov, it likely knew volumes more about him than Ustinov did. Was it possible this was not true?

"Uh, he works remotely, you see, which..."

"Exactly," Shukov said. "I am sure you will not be surprised to learn we would like to know whether the Western BankCoin blockchain has vulnerabilities. As an expert in such technologies, we believe Lupanov could provide useful insights to us. We wish to speak with him, and you must arrange this."

Ustinov's mind was racing. The less he committed to in this room, the better. "I would be pleased to convey that request on your behalf," he said.

"Excellent!" Ovechkin interrupted, standing up. "I'm sure we can rely on you." Ustinov was not, but he gratefully rose as well. Shukov remained seated.

As an aide escorted him down one corridor after another on his way back to the real world, Ovechkin had a hard time thinking past the reality that he knew nothing about Lupanov beyond his email address. Thank goodness he at least had that.

* * *

Frank and Ruth decided that if a state actor wanted to take down BankCoin for good, the best approach would be to erase every copy of its blockchain. Off-the-shelf software already existed to perform such a task. But that's not what an attacker would use. It would be easy to scan BankCoin to see if those specific lines of code appeared anywhere. A real enemy would therefore design a program from the ground up that was the most innocent looking, smallest package of code capable of doing the job. They spent hours in a conference room with a whiteboard thinking that through and eventually ended up with an approach they thought was worth coding. Then they set to work at their keyboards.

Ruth was spending most of her time in Frank's office now when he was in New York. To his surprise, Frank found he enjoyed the company. Either of them could look up from their keyboard, ask a question, get an answer, and then pick up where they had been without missing a beat. Their simultaneous coding on the same program worked just as seamlessly.

At the end of the day, Frank would glance at his watch, suggest they call it a day, shut down his computer, and stand up. Ruth would follow him out on to the floor, hoping that this time, for a change, he might suggest they continue to talk shop over a drink or dinner. But he never did.

* * *

The weather had improved since Ustinov last stood waiting outside the anonymous, locked lobby of the building at number fifty-two Savushkina Street. This time, Filitov ushered him immediately into the world headquarters of RussCoin.

"It is good to see you, my friend," Filitov said. "How are things in Moscow? With your family?"

"All fine. And with you?"

Filitov laughed. "I sit alone here in this little room for a few hours a day. I have been divorced for years. My daughter has not yet given me grandchildren. What is there to tell?"

Ustinov decided not to waste further time on pleasantries; better to emphasize the seriousness of the topic that had brought him there. "Ah – that's the question, isn't it?" he said. "During my last visit, you told me almost nothing about Oleg Lupanov. I asked for a comprehensive update on RussCoin then, including full details regarding all programmers and staff. I will say your report was quite satisfactory in most respects. But still you gave no telephone number or physical address for Lupanov. This data must now be provided."

Filitov stroked his chin. "Your concern is understandable," Filitov said. Then he held up one finger. "But first, a toast to your promotion!" He trundled over to the small table in the corner and returned with a bottle of vodka and two small tumblers, the cleanliness of which looked suspect at best. "I am delighted," he said, uncorking the bottle and filling the glasses, "that your able leadership of the Russ Project has been recognized. To your health!"

Ustinov did not enjoy the Russian custom of drinking over business, especially in the morning. But he could hardly refuse such a toast. "*Nostrovia*!" he responded, lifting his glass, and drank the minimum amount possible without seeming to be rude. Filitov avoided giving offense by draining his own and immediately refilling both their glasses.

"So!" Filitov said. "Now we talk business. May I know the reason for this sudden need for information about Oleg Lupanov?"

"Unfortunately, no – I am not at liberty to say. And my need is not for more information, as such, but to speak with him."

"Ah!" Filitov said. "As I have stated previously, this may be difficult. I have never spoken with Lupanov, nor do I have a number to call if I wished to. I believe that I gave you his email address. I am afraid that I can do no more."

"But you could introduce me by email," Ustinov said, leaning forward and taking a bigger drink from his glass this time.

"I could do this, yes." Filitov said, and then added with a smile, "For what it would be worth."

Ustinov stared for a while at Ustinov, and found it necessary to finish his vodka before responding. "And you could emphasize how important it is that we speak!"

Filitov laughed. "I could emphasize, also, how important it is for him to brush his teeth. I expect he would give equal attention to both observations."

Ustinov's thinking was becoming a bit fuzzy. He had no leverage to use on Filitov, and Filitov knew it. But the bearded Russian was Ustinov's sole link to the developer upon whose good graces and performance Ustinov's career currently rested.

"I'm sure you will do all you can," was all Ustinov could think to say. "And I will be grateful to you for doing so," he added earnestly.

Filitov smiled and refilled Ustinov's glass. "In that case, let us drink to your further success. Come – and you must do better this time!"

Ustinov did do better and then left, his head spinning as it hoped for the best.

* * *

Josh Peabody was feeling much better these days. The value of his CryptoBoom! fund was moving up nicely into positive territory. That was because more than half of its funds were now invested in a new cryptocurrency fund called No Pain No Gain, Ltd.

And just in time, too. The plan was to begin pitching his second cybersecurity investment fund to existing and potential investors in two weeks. He wanted CryptoBoom! to be showing strong double-digit returns by then. Would he make it?

What the heck. He typed in the instructions that would move the rest of the CryptoBoom! funds into No Pain No Gain. CryptoBoom! was a venture fund, and nothing ventured, nothing gained, right? And anyway, it would only be for a month or two. Then he could shift most of the money back.

Besides, he was just moving money from one pocket to another, since he was the sole owner of JP Ltd., a shell company in Bermuda, the sole asset of which was all the stock of a shell company incorporated under Grand Caymans law, and so on down through a Panamanian company and a Venezuelan company until, at last, you got to No Pain No Gain, a Myanmar investment company.

During the next two weeks, he was sure to profit handsomely – the Kremlin had been boosting the value of the Russ heavily ever since the US and its allies added it to the sanctions list.

And the only thing the No Pain No Gain fund invested in was Russ.

Chapter 40

New Pen Pals

T HE MAN KNOWN to Filitov as Oleg Borisovich Lupanov opened the two emails and smiled. The first, from Filitov, read:

Dear Oleg,

It gives me great pleasure to introduce you to Dimitri Fedorovich Ustinov, Superintendent of Digital Finances for the Department of Information Technology in the Sphere of Budgeting and State and Local Finance Management (copied in above). As you know, the Department is the financial sponsor of the Russ Project, and it has been very generous.

While you have been most gracious in contributing your own time without compensation, this has not been so with all the programmers whose assistance has been essential to our success. And, of course, it has been necessary to incur many other expenses to ensure the acceptance of the Russ in the marketplace.

Now, about Dimitri Fedorovich. He has been a constant supporter of the Russ Project, and I could scarcely be accused of exaggeration if I say his support has been instrumental in retaining the Department's confidence and financial backing. This was particularly so in the early days when we had only promises to show for our efforts.

So, to the point. Dimitri has a matter of importance he needs to discuss with you. He has asked me to provide this introduction so that you understand how significant the Department remains to the success of the Russ, and now I have done so. I am sure that you will give him every assistance he may request.

With kindest regards,

Mikhail

He looked up from the email and smiled – he could not remember when he had last read such a fawning message.

But it was no joke, because the second email began as follows:

Dear Mr. Lupanov,

It is with great pleasure that I make this acquaintance, following on the kind introduction of Mikhail Filitov. Let me begin by thanking you for the exemplary leadership and technical brilliance you have brought to the Russ blockchain project. The Russian people, as well as myself, are in your debt.

And yet I find myself in the position of needing to ask you a favor on behalf of Aleksandr Shukov, Superintendent of Cyber Activities for the Federal Securities Service.

Mr. Shukov has informed me, in the highest confidence (which I am sure you will respect), that he and his colleagues wish to consult with you regarding the BankCoin technology of which I expect you are aware...

It was a deliciously ironic message. But, also a troubling one, because certainly Lupanov would have to respond to avoid suspicion, and that was impossible. Clearly, a face-to-face meeting was out of the question; he could think of no circumstance that would justify putting Lupanov's cherished anonymity at risk. A telephone conversation would be almost as bad. Surely, the caller would be capable of tracing the call before its completion. And just as assuredly, he would.

That left only email or some other kind of online exchange, such as setting up a page on the Dark Net where the FSS could post questions and Lupanov could type in his answers. At the least, insisting on that mode of communication would raise serious concerns.

But neither could he ignore the request. At most, Lupanov could wait a few days before responding or give an ambivalent response or both. But then what? All too soon, he would have to refuse to meet or speak or quit replying. In either case, he had to believe the result would be a concerted effort by the FSS to find Lupanov; perhaps he might even be locked out of the Russ system.

No, this was not good at all, and it would be Crypto who would have to find a solution. Because, of course, that was who Lupanov really was.

* * *

The solution was obvious to the Bees, of course.

You must launch the attack! A Bee shrilled.

Now! Without delay! B Bee echoed in his booming bass.

Crypto jumped; even after all these years, such sudden interruptions still sometimes took him by surprise. In this case, he was doubly shocked, because the Bees might be right.

Indeed, the situation was becoming too complicated – Adversego was doing who knew what on his air-gapped system; the Russ Task Force was beavering away and might discover a vulnerability in the Russ blockchain – perhaps had even stumbled on the flaw Crypto had built into it. What if the FSS had infiltrated the task force? They would then know of the flaw as well, and could patch the Russ blockchain before Crypto launched his attack. What then? All his plans would lie in ruins.

But it was still too early to launch the attack – even another few weeks would make an enormous –

Idiot! B Bee boomed. *Idiot! Idiot! IDIOT! Later will always seem better! But later will be too late when suddenly you have handcuffs on your wrists!*

Crypto could not argue with that. But he also needed to think, and the Bees were making that impossible. What was the balance between opportunity and risk? And if the time was now, how would his detailed plans for the attack need to be adjusted? With the Bees in hot pursuit, he stumbled off to his exercise bike.

* * *

Crypto was beyond exhausted; he had never ridden so long and so hard. But the effort had produced a solution and, with that result, great relief.

He must assume the Bees were right: it was time to launch the simultaneous attacks on BankCoin and the Russ he had been planning for so many years. Later would be incrementally better but not crucially so. Suddenly, the culmination of his ten-year quest was before him. Now that he had overruled his natural caution, he found himself elated. Just a few final actions, and then he could at last rest and watch – simply observe as multiple waves of financial catastrophe circled the world, governments collapsing in their wake. The sense of relief that enveloped him was so enormous that even the Bees left him alone for a few hours.

Later that day, he had the chance to share his good news; it was time for the weekly meeting of his general staff. He looked forward to the joy it would bring to those who had followed him so faithfully and for so long.

Crypto browsed on to the Tor site where their meetings were held. As always, there would be no video and each participant's messages would be encrypted on transmission and decrypted on receipt. As well they must since he and his lieutenants were plotting nothing less than the takeover of the developed world.

Comrades, he typed. *It is my pleasure to inform you that the day we have awaited for so long grows very near. I cannot yet share the details, but be assured that you will know them very soon.*

There was an explosion of enthusiastic responses; Crypto waited until the last had scrolled across his screen.

Indeed, Comrades, he typed, *the day grows nigh. But we must not let that distract us from our normal preparations. So, I now ask you to make your status reports. Comrade Cronkite, will you begin please?*

With pleasure, Comrade Chairman, the director of communications responded. *I am pleased to report the systems of every news agency on our target list have been penetrated. When you give the word, your announcement will be broadcast to billions of people across the world.*

Excellent. And now from General Guderian.

Comrade Chairman, the troops are ready and awaiting your call. In the United States, the militias are well armed and eager to overthrow a government they hate and distrust. Throughout Europe, most recently, we have harnessed the zeal of anti-immigrant groups to our cause. In the Russian Federation, the old-line communist guard chafes under the trappings of pseudo-democracy as the economy collapses. Meanwhile, the mad dictator, Denikin, can only think of playing with his toy soldiers abroad. The timing could not be better.

And so, the reports continued. Crypto was pleased. His forces were as ready as they would ever be.

* * *

Crypto was exhausted after the emotional rollercoaster of a day. Time for bed. But first, a final glance at his countdown clock. He tapped a few keys and a tired but triumphant smile spread across his face. The hand on his countdown clock now stood at the eleven o'clock position. Even the Bees were silent. For once, he could say without reservation that life was good.

He turned away from his laptop, but then a soft *ding!* called him back. He looked at the time – *right.* That would be his evening BankCoin Google alert. Reviewing it could wait till morning. But habit won out, and he opened the alert instead.

With a lurch, he jolted into full awareness, shocked not only by the title of the story that confronted him but by the sudden, furious return of the Bees and their full-throated chorus, all in full cry.

He clicked on the story title that had grabbed him by the throat and saw a picture of a familiar face – one with a moustache and goatee and framed with long, stringy, black hair. He looked something like an overweight Frank Zappa holding a laptop.

The horrifying title of the story read, "Head Mutha Forks BankCoin."

Chapter 41

Muthas of Invention

I T TOOK THE better part of a day for Crypto to understand exactly what had happened. Shame on him – as the Bees were quick to note – he'd been paying too little attention to the BankCoin software development community of late. That had seemed reasonable. There wasn't – or shouldn't have been – much going on there. The last thing the banks wanted after switching over to the blockchain was for anyone to tinker with it unnecessarily. Maintain it, yes. Fix bugs, certainly. But otherwise, please! Just leave it alone!

But that meant there was nothing new and cool for the developers to do. With the long, high-pressure sprint to the launch date months past, camaraderie within the community had broken down. Everybody was bored, and flame wars over minutia were becoming common. All of which, Crypto now realized, had provided the perfect opening for a group of BankCoin competitors to make its move.

Shame on him, too, for not paying enough attention to the business landscape. He'd been dimly aware that the big investment banks – IBs as they were sometimes called – were furious at being shut out of the BankCoin system. It was, of course, entirely their own fault. Back when BankCoin was still just a proposal, First Manhattan Bank had courted the IBs energetically, inviting them to participate as equals. But the IBs were working on their own alt coin network and took a pass. They believed their approach was superior and would be finished sooner. It ended up being neither, allowing BankCoin to sweep the field. It also allowed the banks, now victorious, to withdraw their invitation to the IBs to join the BankCoin network. That left the IBs licking their wounds and trying to figure out how to get back in the game.

The reason it mattered, of course, was money. With trillions of dollars now changing hands on BankCoin, big banks were making good money on transaction fees. True, the IBs weren't barred from the marketplace entirely. They could present transactions to the banks, who would then process them on the IBs' behalf. The banks would even share a piece of their fee – an insultingly small amount: just five percent.

Clearly, at least to the IBs, this situation could not stand. After BankCoin became successful, they formed an alliance with the goal of devising a strategy to turn the tables on the banks. One approach they considered was to cry foul to the regulators, saying the banks were violating the antitrust laws by denying the IBs the ability to become equal participants in the BankCoin network. But following that route would take years, and the IBs would miss out on enormous profits in the meantime. And besides, they had no desire to see the feds adopt regulations that might restrict their own activities if they succeeded in defeating the banks.

Having failed once to develop a blockchain-based system at great expense, the IBs had no appetite for starting all over again. But wait – one of them suggested – why not simply fork BankCoin? In other words, copy the BankCoin software line for line and use it to create an IB blockchain network that was identical to BankCoin in every respect except one: the IBs would control it.

It was a brilliant idea. Anyone, anytime, anywhere, had the legal right to download and use the BankCoin platform and related tools for free, because they were open source software. And BankCoin customers could move their accounts without having to get used to anything new. *Come to us!* the investment bankers could say to the entire world. *Use our network instead – for less!*

That was the clincher. The IBs enjoyed much higher profit margins, so they could afford to undercut the banks – even run at a loss for a while. Eventually, the banks would have to either beg their way into the IB network, welcome the IBs into theirs as equal partners, or agree to merge the two networks. Then transaction fees could go back up, and life would go on.

Carrying out the first stage of the plan was easy enough. You didn't need to be a BankCoin genius to copy the banks' blockchain and wallet system software. After that, though, things would be different. The software might be free, but it was complex. Each of the IBs would need a team of experienced BankCoin developers to keep its new system running smoothly once billions of dollars a day was changing hands.

That would be a challenge. The BankCoin software development community was loyal and tight. Anyone helping a bunch of filthy rich Wall Street investment bankers stab the BankCoin project in the back would become an instant pariah in the open source world.

Leaving a community based on a disagreement over a technical issue, though, would be entirely different. That would be a matter of programming principle! And that's where Head Mutha came in.

Mutha was instantly recognizable anywhere he went because at the onset of puberty he became infatuated with the music of Frank Zappa and The Mothers of Invention. Ever since he first heard "Peaches en Regalia" on his headphones, he'd done everything he could to emulate the famed composer/musician in facial hair and clothing. He achieved considerable success in that ambition. When he turned eighteen, he legally changed his name to Head Mutha.

Head Mutha had other distinctive traits. They included a fanatical belief that most technical things should be performed in one way – his – and no other, as well as a willingness to engage in the most spectacularly abusive online arguments with anyone who disagreed. Those traits were not unique in the programming community.

Milton Blefescu, the chief information officer of Silvermensch Sax, the most powerful IB of them all, had never heard of Head Mutha. But he knew programmers and their idiosyncrasies and believed he could use that knowledge to solve the IB's hiring problem. All he needed was a suitable point of contention to exploit. He deployed several members of his staff to scan the BankCoin discussion logs looking for a possible division to work with. With Head Mutha, they hit pay dirt.

The technical matter at issue was beautifully arbitrary and utterly insignificant. The BankCoin software needed to be tweaked to reflect a minor change in regulatory compliance requirements. There were two obvious ways to alter the code. To any objective observer, either approach would work equally well, and there was no technical advantage to using A instead of B. But it *was* necessary to choose only one of the two. The Silvermensch Sax employee reviewing the BankCoin change logs noticed that Head Mutha had put in a "pull request" to upload a piece of code based on alternative A into the BankCoin blockchain. In an accompanying note, Mutha stated that if anyone thought alternative B was a better choice, they were too big an idiot to have anything to do with BankCoin.

These facts were duly reported to Blefescu, who recognized in them the perfect opportunity. Now, on to tactics.

Blefescu happened to be a fan of the satirist Jonathan Swift as well as the history of computer programming. Both reminded him of the section of *Gulliver's Travels* in which Lemuel Gulliver reported on the endless, bloody rebellion launched by those Lilliputians who believed that hard-boiled eggs must only be opened at the large end rather than at the royally mandated smaller end. For generations, the Big Endians and the Small Endians had fought and died over this sacred principle. Real-life engineers would later fight as passionately over the otherwise arbitrary decision whether bits and bytes should be ordered from the greatest or the least significant number. The latter adopted the name Big Endians, and their opponents perforce became the Small Endians.

Blefescu designated proponents of Head Mutha's alternative as the Big Endians. He ordered half his staff to go online to stoke the flames in favor of the Small Endian cause, calling Head Mutha the most clueless coder the world had ever seen. The other half was assigned to defend the technical elegance and moral superiority of the Big Endian approach, using equally abusive language. And everyone was tasked with piling on any BankCoin developer foolish enough to weigh in.

Within twenty-four hours, the BankCoin community was hopelessly divided, and within forty-eight, Silvermensch Sax and the other IBs had recruited Head Mutha and enough other top BankCoin programmers away with eye-popping salary offers to announce their new Big Endian blockchain-based payment network.

The bond traders on the IB strategy team wanted to call the new network GreedCoin, but saner heads prevailed. iBetterBankCoin would play much better, the marketing guys argued, and besides, the similarity in name would really piss off the banks. The second point won over the bond traders.

The part of the press release the IBs issued that drove the banks truly berserk was the announcement that BankCoin holders who signed up to the new network within sixty days would pay no transaction fees for the first six months. They signed up in droves. By the end of the day, the BankCoin system was losing market share at the rate of more than one percent an hour and rising.

Reading the accounts online left Crypto rocking slowly back and forth, moaning and clutching his head in pain as if he was being swarmed by a cloud of attacking, shrieking banshees. Which was not far from the truth.

* * *

The pressure on Crypto was now intense. To the good, the Wall Street pundits predicted the BankCoin and iBetterBankCoin networks would merge within weeks and perhaps days. But on the technical side, he had no way of knowing whether the IBs had made changes that would prevent him from taking the iBetterBankCoin network down, because only IB employees had access to the forked software. His strategy depended not only on taking down the entire Western financial infrastructure but also on the absence of another system capable of immediately replacing it. Until the two networks merged – assuming they did – he could not strike. And the Bees were driving him insane.

* * *

It took all of Crypto's powers of persuasion and persistence, but at last he brought the Bees back under some degree of control. But their terms were harsh: Frank Adversego must be stopped before he discovered Crypto's plan. And just in case, Crypto must acquire a gun. As part of his truce with the Bees, he agreed to order a 3D printer and download the plans for a disposable gun from the Dark Web. Anything to buy more time.

Crypto was also being plagued by a strange dream, one he could not understand. Every night, he was forced to watch an invisible magician doing card tricks. He knew the magician was there, because he could see a top hat, magic wand, and a pair of white gloves. At the end of the dream, the gloves would shuffle the deck one last time and then spread it fan-wise across a table. Finally, they would select two cards and place them side by side, face up, on the table. Just before the dream ended, three elegantly handwritten words would appear below them. Those words were always the same: *Pick a card*. The cards, too, were always the same: the king of spades and the queen of hearts.

It made no sense.

Chapter 42

Squirrel!

FRANK FELT UNEASY after his weekly Russ task force meeting. Several weeks before, the president had ordered NSA developers to work non-stop to develop malware to conduct the attack conceived by Frank. Today, Dix had told the team the software had been completed, and that the president had authorized final preparations to conduct the attack.

What was troubling Frank was the prospect of retaliation. If the Russians decided the Russ was the victim of a cyberattack, as they eventually would, they would suspect the United States, no matter how hard it was to trace the hack back to its source. What could be a better way to retaliate than by launching an attack on BankCoin? The Kremlin had access to some of the best black hats in the world. It would be absurd vanity to assume they would not succeed where he had failed, finding a fatal flaw in the blockchain most of the financial world now relied on.

So far, he hadn't raised his concern during a task force meeting. Counterattacks weren't part of the group's remit. Now that a strike on the Russ might be imminent, though, he felt he needed to make his concerns known to someone. He typed them up and sent them off to Colonel Dix.

* * *

Whoever was messing with Frank's mind in New York had broadened his attack. The same odd events were now occurring at his condo in Washington. And in both places, they were becoming more disturbing.

Last week, he'd reached into his closet in New York for a blue blazer and found it slashed to ribbons. When he returned to Washington, his new loafers were right where they should be. But they were charred beyond recognition. This was getting hard to ignore. But he was uncertain what to do to make it stop – quit the bank? Resign from the task force? Maybe it had nothing to do with either – why didn't whoever it was tell him what they wanted him to do or stop doing?

Things at work were strange as well. He'd clearly made a big mistake going to Audrey Addams; he was sure she looked at him differently now. And Dirk Magnus seemed to be avoiding him. Perhaps the rest of the IT staff was, too, except for Ruth. Or maybe it was just that everyone was on edge, wondering how the bombshell dropped by the investment bankers would play out. Should he just resign? No, there was no point reacting until he knew what reaction would be meaningful. Even then, though it might be more stubborn than smart, he wasn't willing to quit for anyone's reasons other than his own.

Instead, he doubled down in his office, pursuing a new angle. Perhaps he'd been wearing self-generated blinders all along, studying only his air-gapped copy of BankCoin. A real enemy trying to hack a live copy maintained by a bank would have additional targets and points of potential weakness to work with, like customer wallets, analytics software, and much more. Each of those programs could have vulnerabilities or be configured in a way that might allow a black hat to get to the BankCoin blockchain itself. That was an interesting observation.

So, he set up a new system, this time connected to the internet and as close as possible to the kind of real-world environment an enemy agent or terrorist would encounter. He also added a lock to his office door – what if the person doing strange things in his apartment was also a bank employee?

When he had the servers properly configured, he downloaded a full copy of the BankCoin blockchain, right back to the Genesis Block, together with all of the billions of transactions recorded to date, and linked it to the First Manhattan copy so it had access to new blocks as they were created. Then he added the other programs that First Manhattan ran inside the BankCoin firewall that interacted with BankCoin. That meant warehousing an enormous amount of data and software. So, fifteen new high-capacity servers were now humming away in his office in floor-to-ceiling racks, together with a portable air conditioning unit that struggled bravely and not completely successfully to counteract the heat the computers threw off. He could barely move. Or breathe.

Every few hours, he needed to turn everything off except the AC unit so he and the servers could cool off. Powering down the servers was fine. When he restored power, the system automatically updated itself, downloading all the transaction blocks that had been created while it was off line.

When everything was up and running, he tried every way he could think of to mess with the software. For starters, he looked for a way to interfere with the verification of new transaction blocks; if a hacker could penetrate as few as a couple dozen banks and block the confirmation of new blocks, the whole global network would grind to a halt. But his new copy of BankCoin performed that function flawlessly, no matter what he attempted, so he went on to the next approach on his list.

After several days, he ran out of ideas. That sucked, because the worst thing about life in his gilded cage at First Manhattan was that he had so few assigned duties to keep him busy. Now what? He decided to go back to his air-gapped system and the early version of BankCoin to look for inspiration.

For what felt like the hundredth time and might in fact have been not far short of that mark, he studied the BankCoin source code that created the Genesis Block. As always, the occasional bits of sloppy code annoyed him. He wondered whether Schwert later cleaned that code up. Without any more productive ideas to pursue, he logged on to GitHub to find out. To his surprise, all the lines of what he considered to be junk code were still there. Talk about lazy! Schwert might be the top dog on the BankCoin project, but that didn't mean he was perfect. Did no one dare to submit fixes for code Schwert wrote? Maybe not.

Well, maybe Frank would be the first. At the beginning, he'd loaded a series of developer tools on his air-gapped system, and he turned to them now to clean up the source code. Then he used a compiler – a software program that turned human-readable source code into machine-readable object code – to add the edited code back into the copy of BankCoin on his air-gapped system. To be sure the software would still run, he created a new block of test transactions and gave the command to add it to the blockchain.

It didn't work. Specifically, the new block failed to link up to the block before it.

Okay. That was humiliating. Had he made a mistake? Then he remembered that Schwert had built his own compiler for BankCoin development. All the banks used it, and Frank had dutifully loaded a copy on his air-gapped system, too. He'd always thought the need for a special compiler was odd – source code was source code, after all. He couldn't imagine what could be so different about BankCoin as to require the use of a customized compiler whenever a developer needed to turn new BankCoin source code into object code.

He went back over the changes he'd made to the source code and couldn't see anything that should have caused a problem, so he opened the Schwert-approved compiler and repeated his actions – compiled the source code, updated his air-gapped system, created a block of pretend transactions, and tried to add it.

The Schwert compiler didn't work either. So, he must have screwed up. But how? The changes were so minor …

He decided to run each of the two compilers using the original BankCoin code instead of his cleaned-up code and see if that told him anything. It did. The Schwert compiler took longer to do the job. Not just a little but twice as long. That was really odd. He sent off an email to Dirk Magnus, asking if he knew what was so different about the Schwert compiler.

He drummed his fingers on his desk. What could make one compiler run at the same speed as another when converting one set of source code and so much longer when running the same code with such minor changes? Wasn't a compiler just a …

He slapped his head. Idiot! Of course! A compiler was only a compiler until you turned it into something else, and Schwert had created his own compiler! What Frank had thought was junk code must not be junk at all – it must be commands that triggered Schwert's compiler to add in a lot of extra code not reflected in the source code at all! When Frank deleted what he thought was junk code from his copy of BankCoin, it was no longer capable of creating a viable block of transactions no matter which compiler he used.

Frank ran the two compilers again using Schwert's original source code and watched the object code as it was compiled. Sure enough, as soon as Schwert's compiler got to the first bit of code Frank had thought was an error, it started churning out lots of object code that his compiler didn't.

That meant the source code every bank in the BankCoin network was relying on was incomplete. With a lurch, he realized that also meant every block in the BankCoin blockchain contained mystery code with a purpose Frank was sure would prove to be malevolent.

Frank stood up and started pacing a circuitous route between the server racks crammed into his office. All the pieces were falling into place now. The malware he'd been seeking for so long had been there all the time, built into the blockchain itself but invisible. That meant the virus scanner he'd admired so much was only there to mislead security professionals like him. No! That wasn't entirely true – it would also protect BankCoin from any other attacker, making sure no one else could interfere with the master plan of its designer, whatever that might be. And with the malware already in place, it would take only a few lines of code in a new block to trigger the malware – far less code than the two hundred lines of extra software needed to set off an alarm from the virus scanner.

That had to be it, in part because it was so simple. Once the block containing the triggering code was distributed throughout the BankCoin network, it would transmit the order to the block before it, which would then do the same, and so on, all the way back to the Genesis Block, triggering whatever mayhem the malware had been designed to unleash.

He was pacing faster now, dodging his way between the server racks and changing direction every few seconds, his mind moving on unimpeded. He'd finally discovered the fatal vulnerability he'd always feared might lurk in BankCoin.

And also identified his enemy – it could only be Schwert himself. Schwert had indeed been careless, but not in the way Frank had first assumed.

The mysterious programmer's slip had been to save a bit of time by not hiding the bits of code that would instruct his compiler to add the mystery code. Perhaps he thought no one would notice. Or maybe Schwert intended them as temporary shortcuts he would return to fix later on, but then forgot about. That was probably it. BankCoin was a massive and complex program; it was incredible that any single developer had come so close to perfection.

So, what did the additional code do? The tools on Frank's air-gapped system also included a decompiler. As its name suggested, a decompiler did the opposite of what a compiler accomplished. He could use one to turn the object code Schwert's compiler had created back into source code that he could read and understand. Then the answer to the question would be clear.

But no such luck. When he ran the code through the decompiler, he found that Schwert's compiler had done something else unexpected: in addition to converting the source code into object code it had "obfuscated" it, meaning it stripped out the information that made source code easy to understand. Then, it went a step further, scrambling the code in ways that wouldn't stop it from running but would make it impossible for Frank's decompiler to turn it back into understandable source code.

That cinched it; the camouflaged code must be malware. Otherwise, why prevent it from being usefully decompiled? But figuring out what it was intended to do would be a tedious and challenging process. He would need to analyze the object code line by line, parsing out what it meant with none of the plain English – plain English to a programmer, that is – labels and guidance that source code provided. Instead of reading, for example "</search:config>" he'd be looking at nothing but ones and zeros and trying to figure out what that was telling the computer to do.

Clearly, this would take a while. He had a lot of code to go through. He looked at his watch and realized he'd need to hurry if he was going to catch his plane. Just as well; he'd rather tackle the job at home. He copied the extra object code onto a thumb drive and dropped it in his pocket. Then he locked his office door and headed for the airport.

* * *

The days had turned into a blur of late for Crypto; everything seemed to be confusion and danger now. And his nights were troubled. Almost immediately after falling asleep, what he now referred to as The Dream would come to him, always ending in The Question. It was repeating endlessly now, leaving him as exhausted in the morning as he had been the night before. The Dream had changed subtly, too. The visage of the king of spades had morphed into the sour, frowning face of his father and that of the queen of hearts into the sad features of his mother.

What did The Dream and The Question mean? What *could* they mean? He had no idea.

So very much had changed. In the early days of his quest, he had felt like a classical composer, summoning grand, creative visions from his heart and brain to create a majestic melody. Those had been wonderful days, working out the concept of the blockchain. Then came the equally pleasurable, but more structured, steps. Just as a composer transformed his melody into the complex score of a symphony, Crypto mapped out the detailed architecture for the blockchain. As time passed, his work changed yet again. To extend his musical metaphor, like the composer who must next laboriously create the score for each section of the orchestra – strings, woodwinds, and so on – Crypto nurtured the evolution of his creation by translating his architecture into an assemblage of software modules, each making its own contribution to the harmony that was the sum of the blockchain's creative parts.

Then the truly hard and unforgiving part began. Once his full symphony score was complete and revealed at GitHub, he had to deal with the developer musicians, as it were, with all their tedious quirks and passions. And then the outside world as well. Just as a composer was vulnerable to the whims and business concerns of the management of the grand concert house where his magnum opus would premiere, Crypto was subject to the caprices of banks and bureaucrats and regulators. All the nonsense and idiocy that dragged true genius into the gutter.

Not a perfect metaphor, Crypto thought. *But also, not bad.* With opening night now fast approaching, he was increasingly a spectator, waiting to see whether his true creation – the long-planned attacks – would collapse before the curtain went up or open to resounding applause and standing ovations. The latter, of course, from a very select audience of anarchists. He wasn't expecting good reviews from the critics.

The emergence of the investment banker's blockchain was a cruel development, now that he was so close. Whatever it took to save his decade of creativity and sacrifice he would have to do. He was in agreement with the Bees about that, with the sole exception of murder, no matter what he had told them. There were some lines he would not agree to cross.

Ding!

He glanced at his computer screen; the tone had signaled the arrival of the daily download of Frank's activity sent by Crypto's spyware. He scanned his way downward and then almost screamed, reflexively clutching his desk with both hands as a gut-wrenching attack of vertigo seized him. There, on the screen, was a short email Frank had sent to Dirk Magnus. It read:

Dirk, can you tell me what's so special about Schwert's compiler?

It was time for Crypto to go to Plan B.

* * *

With the change of atmosphere in New York, Frank was once again looking forward to returning to Washington each week. When he arrived home this time, it was a dark and windy night. He dumped his things in his kitchen, poured himself a scotch and settled down in his living room with his laptop. Something moving outside the sliding door caught his eye. He couldn't make it out, though; it was only when the headlights of a passing car cast light in his direction that he caught the shadowy movement. Whatever.

He took a bigger pull than usual on his drink. His initial elation at discovering what he was sure was malware in BankCoin had yielded quickly to frustration and anxiety. The extra code Schwert's compiler generated ran to over nine thousand lines. How long would it take him to slog through all that? What if Schwert launched an attack before he was done? He'd better alert the bank. Better to sound a false alarm if he was wrong than fail to alert others if he was right.

What *was* that outside? It looked like something flapping back and forth where the feeder used to hang. Whatever it was, it was very distracting.

He got up, turned on the light on the balcony, and immediately stepped back, fighting a surge of nausea.

There, hanging from the balcony above, tossing in the embrace of the gusty wind, was the eviscerated carcass of Fang.

He turned and looked wildly around. There it was! On the dining room table! He ran over and picked up a small, folded piece of cardboard. On it, he read:

BankCoin – Russ Task Force – or Marla

Choose one

"Due to an unexpected family emergency I've had to leave town and will be out of touch for at least a week."

With trembling fingers, he typed the message into emails to Audrey Addams and Colonel Dix. Then he dashed out of his apartment, keying an Uber request into his phone as he ran.

Chapter 43

Fancy Meeting You Here

T HE UBER ARRIVED at last, and Frank jumped into the back seat.
"Here for Frank?" he barked.

"Check."

"Great – step on it. Get me there in fifteen minutes and it's a twenty-dollar tip."

"Great!" the driver said.

The sedan lurched away from the curb, as Frank's mind raced ahead to its destination. He'd sent the messages as instructed, but who knew whether that would make any difference. For all he knew, whoever was threatening him might have already kidnapped Marla to make sure Frank would obey whatever orders arrived next.

He pulled out his phone and called George Marchand. Thank God – he answered.

"George – Frank," he almost shouted. "The usual place. Half an hour. Don't let me down!" Then he hung up, his mind still in a whirl. What should he do next? No – don't call Marla. His phone or hers might be tapped. Just get there as fast as possible and hope to find her there. What would he do if he didn't? Better not to think of that.

If she was, they'd go straight to the coffee shop and wait for George. That was a public place; they should be safe there with so many witnesses. George would have to figure out where and how to keep Marla safe until whatever was going on was over.

And then what should he do? Did he already know too much? The answer to that was clear, now that he thought about it. He'd need to ask George to find a safe house for him and Marla both. And Tim, too.

And what could all this be about? Who was behind it?

The thoughts went around and around until finally he was outside Marla and Tim's small apartment building. He realized he'd forgotten to add a tip on the app and threw a twenty-dollar bill at the driver before bolting out of the car and up to the building. But after he threw the door open, he paused, his heart pounding; the light was out in the hallway. He could barely see.

He heard a sound behind him. Then he couldn't see – or think – anything at all.

* * *

George Marchand waited a half hour at the coffee shop before concluding that something had gone wrong. Damn Frank – why hadn't he said what was up when he called? Was it because someone was listening, or was he too agitated to think clearly?

He called the Frank's cell phone and then his number at the bank. No answer at either. He hung up without leaving a message.

Now what? Calling the police was no good, at least to start with; if he could persuade them to get involved at all, it would take far too long. Frank wasn't working with the CIA, and the Agency had nothing to do with BankCoin. So, he couldn't think of an excuse to contact them in his official CIA capacity. He knew Frank was working for CYBERCOM on the Russ Task Force because he'd made the introduction. What was the name of the person he'd introduced Frank to?

He found the name and number and called him up.

"Colonel Dix? This is George Marchand. You may recall I was the go-between who helped recruit Frank Adversego to your task force."

"Yes, I recall. Sorry to hear about whatever happened in Frank's family."

"Excuse me?"

"Family emergency, apparently. I just got an email from him, saying he'd be out of touch for at least a week."

Okay. *This was bad*, George thought.

"Still there?" Colonel Dix asked.

"Yes. But Frank isn't. Based on what you just told me, I'm concerned he may have been kidnapped – or worse."

"Whoa – because?"

"He called me an hour ago, agitated, and told me to meet him in half an hour. He said something like 'Don't let me down,' and then hung up. He never showed up."

"I see," Colonel Dix said and paused. "Is he also a friend of yours?"

"Yes. Can you keep me in the loop?"

"I'll do what I can. Better let me get moving on this."

"Thanks."

Was there anything else he should do? Well, there was Marla, his goddaughter. Should he wait or share his concern? That was a tough one. She'd probably panic if there was nothing more he could tell her.

Was there anything more he could say?

Not much. All he knew was Frank wanted to meet him in half an hour. Did that amount of time tell him anything?

If Frank was at home – where he almost always was when he was in Washington – it would only take him ten minutes to reach their meeting place, and given how worked up he was, he wouldn't have walked; probably he was already on the way when he placed the call. So, what was he using the extra twenty minutes for?

Right. He decided he better get to Marla. Fast.

Thankfully, she was there when he arrived, just getting out of her car, balancing a bag of groceries with one arm on her very pregnant stomach while she reached inside the car for another. Grim-faced, he slammed the door and strode quickly up to her. The sound caught her attention, and she straightened up. A look of concern, and then fear, spread across her face.

* * *

Frank woke up lying on something that felt like rough cloth. He reached around – was he on a couch? His head throbbed and his mouth felt foul, as if he'd been vomiting. He had dim memories of being roughly handled while drifting in and out of consciousness. He thought he'd been in multiple places, his hands tied behind him and a bag over his head, able to guess where he might be only from what he could hear when he was aware. Maybe in the trunk of a car. Maybe being carried somewhere. Maybe the sound of a plane. He was reasonably sure he remembered being given injections that were followed by immediate blackness and later made him ill.

How much time had gone by? He had no way of telling. Where was he? Same answer. He had no idea even what continent he might be on.

Maybe he should be less ambitious to start with. What kind of room was he in?

He struggled to his feet and immediately sat down again as he felt consciousness ebbing away once more.

* * *

Ryan Clancy frowned at the message he'd just received: Frank Adversego had unexpectedly left town to attend to a family emergency. He'd be unreachable for at least a week.

Or maybe forever, Clancy thought. He called his chief investigator and told him to come to his office ASAP. It was time to take seriously the possibility that Frank Adversego was a foreign agent. And that a catastrophic attack on BankCoin might be launched at any moment.

Chapter 44

Wakey, Wakey, Rise and Shine

F RANK'S EYES FLUTTERED open. Where was he? It was lighter, but his head was spinning. He was someplace he didn't recognize and, yes, lying on a couch. Was Marla safe? There was no way to know. He tried to sit up and decided that was a very bad idea. Lying back down, he drifted in and out of sleep for a few more hours before deciding it was time to make himself stay awake and face up to whatever had happened to him. He was also ravenously hungry.

After a while he felt a bit steadier. Now what? A set of floor-to-ceiling drapes allowed a few streaks of light to enter the room. He made his way to his feet this time without feeling too faint and wobbled across the room. He would have been dazzled by the sunlight when he drew the drapes open except there was some sort of coating on the glass to block the glare. But the view was still enough to make him back up involuntarily. He must be close to a hundred stories up in the air. Time to sit down again.

He did, his head pounding, and examined the room he was in. It was spacious and well, if somewhat eccentrically, furnished. It looked like a hotel room, but it lacked some of the amenities he'd expect to find if that was the case. Like a telephone or any other means of connecting with the outside world, except for a large TV. He looked for a remote but found none. He walked up to it and tried the power button, but the screen remained dark. He was more fortunate when he explored the piece of furniture it stood on. Behind one door was a half-size refrigerator filled with food.

The room contained a few objects he wouldn't expect to find in a hotel. That modern art coffee-table book over there, for instance, and the speakers on the bookshelves, which were in the same useless state as the TV. There were also two doors. One led to a bedroom and a bathroom, and the other was locked.

That covered his immediate vicinity. But where was that vicinity located?

He stared out the window; he could see a lot of tall buildings, a harbor with a single, tiny ship in the distance either coming or going, and maybe hazy mountains in the distance. He put that information together and tried to figure out what it added up to. San Diego? No. Too many tall buildings. Vancouver? No sea planes. Manhattan? It didn't look like New York at all. Abu Dhabi? Too much greenery. He tried to think of other large cities with harbors, but he didn't know enough about any to decide whether one might be a match.

Then a thought struck him – could this be a guest room in one of the rumored penthouses of the mysterious Günter Schwert? Assuming those rumors were true, that seemed both possible and likely. If so, what did that imply about his immediate, and hopefully long-term, future? There was no way he could think of to tell.

What next? His stomach prompted him with an answer. He wolfed down two sandwiches from the refrigerator, registering with regret that there was no beer.

He spent the next hour reviewing everything he could recall since he lost consciousness outside Marla's apartment, searching for anything that could be useful or might give him an inkling of his location. But he had precious little to go on, and he'd hardly been in a very observant state. So, he went back over anything that seemed out of the ordinary since the gnomic table tents began appearing in his New York flat. Another blank; he'd already plowed that field down to the bedrock days ago. Why the heck hadn't he just hired a private investigator when things first started getting weird?

After that, he confronted the dire reality that he had absolutely nothing more to occupy his mind or anything at all to do except flip through the coffee-table book, which didn't take long since he wasn't much interested in modern art. When he'd milked that distraction for all it was worth, he stared out the window. He wondered where that ship was headed, wishing he was on it, regardless of its destination.

It grew dark, and he got up to flip the light switch. Nothing happened. Or when he tried the switches of the floor and table lamps.

It was going to be a long, dark evening.

He tried not to think about Marla.

* * *

The same cycle of day to night repeated itself two more times. During that endless stretch of boredom, he came up with a few escape strategies, each of which failed. Smashing furniture against the locked door neither caused it to break nor inspired anyone to open it. It did mean that he no longer had anything to sit on except the couch, which he'd determined was too heavy to serve as a battering ram.

The presence of a working refrigerator meant there was at least one live outlet in his prison. That suggested another plan. Using a dull fruit knife from the cheese plate in the fridge, he stripped the insulation from one end of the cord he yanked out of a non-working lamp. Then he inserted the other end into the wall socket powering the refrigerator and tried to coax a strong enough spark from the bare wires to set any of the following objects on fire: (a) toilet paper, (b) a page torn from the coffee-table book, (c) stuffing removed from the sofa through a hole he hacked in a cushion, and (d) dust and other crud scooped from under the couch cushions. But he couldn't persuade anything to smoke, much less ignite, and therefore failed to trigger the fire alarm.

After those efforts fizzled, he gave up trying to force someone to open the door. And anyway, the most he was likely to gain would be a second lump on the back of his head. His captor, whoever that might be, had provided food, so the plan couldn't be to starve him to death. That was good news. Unless you considered that he had plenty to eat for another week. Surely, he'd go crazy from mental inactivity before that ran out. He wished he had a pen or pencil so he could try to break the Guinness record for calculating pi without a computer.

* * *

Unbeknownst to Frank, events relating to BankCoin were racing ahead. The banks and the IBs were getting close to agreement on a merger of their networks. The financial press was monitoring the situation closely with multiple news services striving to be the first to spot the virtual puff of white smoke that would signal the standoff was over.

Meanwhile, Crypto was feverishly making final preparations for his attack. During an exhausting assault on his exercise bicycle the week before, he'd devised a plan to save both the remnants of his sanity and Frank Adversego's life.

And thank goodness. The Bees had grown hysterical over Adversego's fate when they learned of his email asking about Magnus's compiler. If Crypto didn't surrender to their demands, the Bees assured Crypto that his torment would never end – not for a day, an hour, a minute – even for a second until the moment he died, an event he would eagerly anticipate. The best he'd been able to negotiate was a standoff: they had agreed to Crypto's Plan B: kidnapping Frank and holding him for the time being. But then what?

Crypto's solution was to come up with a reason why Frank must live for the Bees' aims to be achieved.

His argument went like this: if the goal was to usher in an era of anarchy but not war, then humanity had to be convinced who had launched the attacks. Otherwise, the Americans would assuredly hold the Russians accountable, or the North Koreans, the Iranians – someone. And the Russians would blame the Americans, the Chechnyans, the Ukrainians – anyone. Every government would need an enemy to rally the patriotic citizenry against to preserve its own existence as the chaos spread.

That would never do. The goal of the attacks was to destroy world order, not entrench regimes and lead to destructive retaliation. He needed everyone to know they had been betrayed by their governments, their centralized institutions, their corporate masters. All must know the attacks were the work of a cadre of selfless idealists who had pledged their lives to rescuing humanity from the tyranny of oppressive regimes – capitalist, communist, and authoritarian alike.

Therefore: Someone with public credibility must watch the attacks as they occurred and then bear witness to the waiting world of what he had seen. That person would be Frank Adversego.

It was a brilliant inspiration. Even the Bees were impressed.

And it was just in time. Only a few hours later, the BankCoin and iBetterBankCoin networks released a joint press release, announcing that their respective blockchains had been merged. The last block of the iBetterBankCoin blockchain had been added to the BankCoin blockchain, every IB had opened a BankCoin node and a wallet for each of its customers, and the iBetterBankCoin blockchain had been shut down after less than a week in operation. There was once again only one global financial system.

Almost immediately, the TV screen in Frank's room winked into life.

Chapter 45

Fancy Meeting You Here

I F FRANK THOUGHT he was finally about to meet the foe he had imagined for so long, he was disappointed. Instead, all he saw on the screen was a cartoon avatar of a laughing dog, as if he was using some silly game app that requested, but did not require, you to upload a selfie before you could play. Nor was the voice that came out of the till-then dormant speakers recognizable. Some sort of device was being used to disguise it.

"And so, we meet," the odd voice intoned.

What to say, Frank wondered, taken aback by the strange, sudden presence. "I know who half of 'we' is," he settled on. "Would you care to introduce yourself?" He figured it had to to be Schwert, but who knew? Then he had an urgent thought. "And what about Marla? Is my daughter safe?"

"Who I am does not matter. What I am about to do does. You will pay close attention. And yes, your daughter was never touched."

"How do I know that?"

"Watch."

The dog avatar was replaced by what he guessed was a slightly askew video stream from the camera on Marla or Tim's laptop. It showed Marla sitting in her usual chair, holding a magazine in her lap but looking blankly into space, her face troubled. Without thinking, Frank jerked upright and took a step toward the screen. Thank goodness, she was safe! Assuming the stream was live and not recorded. He had to hope. And play his cards right, too. What next?

"Why should I do anything for you?" Frank asked and then added, "Günter." But if his guess was correct, the voice gave no indication.

"Because if you pay close attention and agree to tell the world what you are about to witness, your daughter will remain safe, and you will be released when I am finished."

"Why should I believe you?"

"Do you have anything better to do with your time for the next hour?"

Frank eased back down on to the sofa, his eyes still fixed on the image of Marla. "Point taken. Your show."

"Good. So. We shall start with the preliminaries."

The screen flashed to the headline of a story in the *Wall Street Journal*.

"As you see, since you became my guest, the banks and investment banks have merged their blockchain networks. Once again, BankCoin is carrying virtually all international financial traffic, excluding only transactions with the Russian Federation, China, and, to varying degrees, the least developed countries."

The screen switched to the headquarters of the National Security Agency in Maryland before reverting once again to the laughing dog. "I am aware of your work with the Russ Task Force and, therefore, that you know the extent of Russ-based trade between the Russian Federation and the scope of violations of current Western sanctions. The great majority of Russia's foreign commerce now flows through this channel, and the value of the ruble and the Russ are now inextricably intertwined.

"You are also aware your president has succeeded in pushing the price of oil to its lowest level in years. Yes, it recovered for a time when NASLA took down the GPN, but that respite is now over, leaving the Russian Federation once again dependent on the health of the Russ for its economic survival.

"Finally, I must mention that it has recently come to my attention that you have discovered that the BankCoin compiler incorporates some unexpected capabilities. Your awareness of that fact, of course, is one reason for the loss of your freedom. You will be interested to know that the Russ compiler also contains covert code. I will explain what the unique features of each program are shortly.

"And so, it is time to begin," the voice continued. "Which attack shall we launch first, Mr. Adversego? Should our target be the Russ or BankCoin?" The voice paused. "No preference? Then let me rephrase the question. Do you prefer pleasure first or pain? Still no answer? I am afraid you are not being very helpful.

Perhaps if I make it simpler. When you were a little boy, Mr. Adversego, did you eat the frosting on your birthday cake first or last?"

This was beyond bizarre. Frank felt as if he was in some sort of real-world James Bond movie except the evil genius taunting him was a cartoon dog with its tongue hanging out. Best to keep his own still.

"Well, never mind," the voice said. "In that case, it will be the Russ." Frank heard an odd, muffled clatter, and decided it was the sound of a computer keyboard, modified by the same software disguising the speaker's voice.

"So. I am just now adding a block of Russ transactions to the node I maintain in Kazakhstan. I prepared this addition many months ago expressly for this occasion."

Despite the gravity of what he was witnessing, Frank was fascinated. What would happen next?

"There. I have issued the block," the voice said. "Shall we see what happens now? I think yes."

The screen changed to display a variety of charts, numbers, and Cyrillic text. At first, Frank could make nothing of it.

"You will please observe the pie chart on the left. The red wedge, which already extends from the twelve to the three o'clock positions and continues to grow, shows the percentage of other Russ nodes that are verifying my block. Now, note the activity in the center of the display."

To Frank, it resembled a very flat sine wave on an oscilloscope or the horizon of a landscape with very low hills. The voice explained.

"This screen displays the changing value of the Russ. Indirectly, it also shows the level of price support the Russian government is giving to its cyber currency. When the line goes up, it means the value of the Russ is also rising because investors, or the Russian government, are buying it; when it falls, it means there are more Russ sellers than buyers or that the Kremlin is issuing more Russ to prevent it from advancing too quickly.

"Now, what we are about to witness promises to be most interesting. If you return to the first pie chart, you will see the red area has just passed the six o'clock position, meaning that more than fifty percent of the participating nodes have verified my block, which will now be added to every copy of the Russ blockchain and cannot be changed. Ah! And there we go!"

For the first time, Frank detected emotion in the speaker's voice, despite the software intended to disguise it, and that emotion was excitement. It was not hard to guess why: the value of the Russ had begun oscillating wildly; now it was falling. Frank watched, captivated, as the line dropped ever more steeply.

"What just happened?" he asked.

"The block I added was most unusual, you see. Instead of including random transactions, it contained a transfer of newly created Russ to every foreign wallet in the world – in all, more than one thousand times the number of Russ in existence until a few moments ago."

Frank struggled with all the implications of what he had just heard. But the plunge in the line of the chart in the middle of the screen conveyed the central message: the value of the Russ had been destroyed.

"How long will the effect last?" Frank asked.

"For my purposes, forever. Russia has no way to recover from this calamity. It can only restore the value of the Russ by buying back all the coins I have just issued, which it will never be able to afford to do.

"And so, the Kremlin's ability to transact trade has also been destroyed. None of its commercial partners will be willing to complete the delivery of goods now in transit or engage in new transactions, because the Russ now has no value. There can therefore be no further trade in goods subject to Western sanctions."

"And the next chart?" Frank asked. "What does that track?" Like the others, it displayed a plummeting value.

"The ruble," the voice informed him. "Without the support to the economy provided by the Russ, the Ruble will collapse as well. By tomorrow, hyperinflation will set in, destroying any value that remains."

"And the last?" Frank asked.

"Ah!" the voice replied. "My favorite. That shows the estimated cash assets of the Russian oligarchs, all of whom invested heavily in the Russ, knowing their friends in government would never let its value fall.

"So, Mr. Adversego, while you have watched over the last few moments, Russia and its elites have become completely, utterly, and irretrievably bankrupt. As has the Russian economy and, therefore, also the Russian people.

"This is a disaster from which the government cannot recover. The Russian people are on their own.

"You will bear witness that it was not the Americans or some other state actor that has achieved this end. This is the inevitable consequence of the actions of the Russian government itself, which staked its future on the Russ. The Russian people must seize this moment of opportunity to take control of their destiny. Do you understand me, Mr. Adversego?"

Frank understood perfectly. He could also guess well enough what was in store for BankCoin.

"You have not answered."

"Yes," Frank stuttered. "I understand very well. But why?"

"Why is for later," the voice responded. "First, we will attend to your BankCoin." Frank heard the obfuscated sound of clattering keys once more and looked wildly around the room. Had he missed some way to escape? He grabbed a heavy floor lamp and once again swung it like a sledgehammer against the locked door. But to no avail.

"Do not waste your time, Mr. Adversego. Your door is quite strong, and there is no one to hear you. Now, would you like to know what I have planned for BankCoin?"

Yes, he did. He dropped the lamp to the floor and slumped on to the sofa.

"Yes. Tell me."

"That is good, for I like this plan even better. But first, let us have some new information."

The screen cleared before showing a new set of charts, this time with captions Frank could read, except for the first chart, which bore no legend. The second chart showed the volume of BankCoin transactions – tens of millions of dollars' worth per minute. A half-dozen smaller charts below the first two displayed the value of the dollar, the Euro, the British pound, the Japanese yen, and the Chinese renminbi.

"And now, shall we begin?" There was another burst of muffled keystrokes.

Frank watched in dismay as a tiny red wedge appeared at the noon position on the first, unlabeled pie chart and rapidly swept full circle.

Within moments of the red area reaching the six o'clock position, the volume of BankCoin transactions shown on the second chart dropped to zero.

"What just happened? How did you do that?" Frank gasped.

"The validation of the block I just added to the BankCoin blockchain, of course," the voice replied. "And what was the unique feature of that block, you ask? For the West, I had a different idea – one you will surely appreciate. You see, the malware you have been seeking was not in the BankCoin software at all. Instead, it lay dormant in every block of the BankCoin blockchain, waiting for the signal contained in the block that was just validated. Having received that signal, the malware has gone to work. While we have been speaking, it has encrypted all the information on every BankCoin blockchain in existence. Then it encrypted that information again using a second encryption algorithm. And then yet a third. When this was complete, and for good measure, it erased every BankCoin blockchain copy in existence.

"Your BankCoin blockchain, and all the wealth it represented, no longer exists, Mr. Adversego. Nor can any existing technology resurrect it."

But that wasn't true! Frank told himself.

"No," the voice said, as if reading his mind, "you cannot begin again, using the current balances of BankCoin wallets as a starting point. This is because, most generously, in the same block, I also issued a one cent BankCoin payment to every wallet holder. Except in this case, that payment was accompanied by the same instructions to the same sort of malware, which also exists in each wallet: triple encrypt and then erase."

But still, Frank thought, *there were the original records to fall back on.*

"I see you are not yet convinced of the gravity of the situation, Mr. Adversego. But pause and consider: over the six months, trillions of dollars have been charged and paid, profits made and money lost, investments bought with BankCoin at one price and sold at another, and so on, endlessly. We are a grasping and litigious species, Mr. Adversego. A million courts in a thousand years could not settle the disputes over who is entitled to what. The values of everything have begun gyrating already. Look at the charts, Mr. Adversego."

Each chart, except the one for the renminbi, resembled the electrocardiogram of a patient in cardiac arrest, his life slipping rapidly away. Now the line on the renminbi chart was oscillating. Then, it, too, headed downward.

"So, Mr. Adversego, I have a message for your people, too. It is this: chaos is upon you! Your money is worthless. Your savings are vaporized. Your government cannot save you or support itself. Do not blame the Russians, the Chinese, the North Koreans, the Iranians – blame your leaders. Blame Wall Street. Blame your greedy corporate overlords. Blame yourselves! Take control of your lives, your communities, your future! From this disaster can come your salvation!"

This was insane, Frank thought. What could the real purpose be behind what had just happened? Assuming that anything had really happened at all. How could he know, trapped in this room?

He heard a click, and what until then he had assumed was a grill covering a ventilating duct fell open. The click was followed by a soft whir, and a camera emerged, training back and forth before it locked on Frank's face.

"And so, Mr. Adversego, it is time for you to perform your appointed role in the unfolding drama that will forever transform the world."

"Mine?"

"Yes – and a very important role, too. My followers have hacked into media networks around the globe and are about to seize control of their video streams. You will tell the world what you have just witnessed. You will tell both East and West that every record in existence of BankCoin and the Russ has been destroyed."

Frank was struck with two realizations in close succession. The first was that once he had gone on television, the person behind the voice would have no incentive to release him. And the second was that his copy of the BankCoin blockchain still existed, because he always turned his servers off to avoid overheating. From that copy, all but the last few days of activity on the BankCoin network could be resurrected. For both reasons, he had to escape.

But how? He looked out the window – if only he weren't so high in the air! Surely, he could smash his way through the glass. But as always, the placid view taunted him, the sun shining brightly as it had each day of his imprisonment, the sky cloudless as always, the tiny ship still in the distance …

Wait a minute!

He rushed up to the window: yes, though the tinted coating made things a bit blurry, he could see a wake behind the ship far out in the harbor – it wasn't anchored. And he was sure it was right where it had always been before!

"Time to go on the air, Mr. Adversego!"

"Later!" he yelled. Seizing the heavy floor lamp again, he swung it at the glass with all his might.

The false window dissolved into shards large and small, some shattering again on the floor, while others hung like enormous teeth in the window frame. Yes! Everything was dark on the other side!

He leaped though the gap, catching a sleeve on one of the glass stalactites, and groped his way forward as quickly as he could into the pitch-dark void. Behind him, the garbled voice shrieked in shock and rage.

Stumbling against objects he couldn't see, he found a wall and slid along it with one hand extended, hoping to find a window, a door, any way to escape. He felt something that might be a doorframe – Yes! He found a knob, but it wouldn't turn. He ran his fingers down both sides and found a light switch.

It worked. He was in a grimy basement filled with bins and bags of garbage. Against the far wall was a set of dirty wooden stairs that seemed to go nowhere. He ran to them and looked up, finding two doors held shut with a rusted hasp and padlock. What could he use to dislodge them? He saw a brick and smashed it against the lock. Nothing. He tried again. And again. The hasp and lock seemed to be pulling loose. His next blow sent them sailing across the room. He pushed the doors open and rushed upward.

He found himself on the sidewalk of a busy street, surrounded by people carrying cell phones, walking dogs, and hawking counterfeit goods. It looked like SoHo.

Someone eyed him strangely, and he realized he was holding his left elbow with his right hand. Both were covered in blood.

* * *

The cab did its best in the traffic, and the TV set on the back of the driver's seat confirmed Schwert had really done what he claimed. The talking heads on the screen were bewildered, just now receiving reports that something serious had happened but without a clue what to make of it.

It wasn't easy, but Frank persuaded the English-challenged cabby to lend his phone to the bloody passenger in the back seat. Thankfully, George Marchand's phone was on.

"George! Frank! How's Marla? Yes? Thank God for that. Now listen."

He gave as coherent a short explanation as he could; George agreed he would try to get through to someone at the Treasury Department to explain what had happened to BankCoin; Frank would return to the bank to be sure the last remaining copy of the global BankCoin blockchain was safe, driven by the realization that whoever had kidnapped him might also know of its existence.

Who else should he call? He dialed again, and Ruth answered.

"Ruth! Can you do me a quick favor?"

"Sure. Is everything okay with your family now?"

"Oh – yeah. Everything's fine. Would you go to my office and see if the door is locked?"

"Okay. Why?"

"I'll tell you when I get back. Just check – please!"

He held his breath until her voice returned.

"Yup. All locked up."

He expelled his breath loud enough for her to hear. "Are you okay?" she said.

"Yes – fine. I'll be there soon."

"Good. It's a madhouse here."

He spent the rest of the ride bandaging his arm as best he could with a piece of cloth ripped from the bottom of his shirt.

* * *

When he reached the bank, Frank dodged his way through the confused, milling crowd filling the lobby. He sweated in frustration as the elevator made its halting ascent; every time the doors *dinged!* open, he saw another scene of turmoil. But when he reached the IT floor, it was just about empty.

"You're going the wrong way," someone said as they hurried past him on to the elevator. "There's an emergency meeting of the security team in the auditorium."

He dashed through the cubicles, turned the last corner, and almost ran into someone standing outside his office.

And that someone was holding what looked like a gun.

Chapter 46

Bang!

"YOU'VE GOT TO put that down," Frank said, as steadily as he could. "If you shoot, people will hear it. You'll never get away."

"It is not so important I get away," the voice said, clear now.

Maybe someone was still on the floor, Frank thought. *Maybe someone will come around the corner and see us and yell; maybe that will distract the gunman. What should I do then? Run? Try to tackle him?*

* * *

The gunman, of course, was Crypto, or as much of Crypto as was capable of functioning in spite of the cacophony of screams exploding between his ears and his own existential anguish and despair. This was where all his plans would stand or fall, where the curtain would go up and the grand overture of a brave new world would begin or where everything would collapse – his hopes, the last decade of his life, the future of humanity.

Shoot! Shoot!

The roaring chorus in his head was like something out of Wagner – as if ten thousand Valkyries were assailing him. He half-closed his eyes and vainly waved his free hand in the air around his head.

Something strange was happening to Crypto now; Frank was dissolving into a swirling gray fog surrounded by a nimbus of light. Now something was taking form in that fog. Yes – it was the image at the end of The Dream. He saw the two cards hugely and clearly as if they were inches away – saw the sullen, angry face of his father as the king and the sad, forlorn image of his mother as the queen.

SHOOT! SHOOT!

The voices of the Bees rose above the din of the chorus, reverberated and echoed and still grew. The thundering inside his head was unbearable. It was *beyond* unbearable. He was barely able to stand.

SHOOT!

Yes – he would, at last, have to shoot. There was no other way. But could he do such a thing? Why did his parents not speak to him? Why did his mother not tell him what to do?

And then the queen extended her arms to him and the message of The Dream finally became clear.

Yes.

He pressed the 3D printer gun to his temple and pulled the trigger.

And then Crypto, Dirk Magnus, Günter Schwert, Oleg Lupanov, and the curtain on all their grand, heroic, hopeless dreams collapsed to the floor as one.

Epilogue

"YOU'RE LATE," GEORGE Marchand said, looking at his watch. "You were supposed to be here two weeks ago."

"Yeah," Frank said, "circumstances beyond my control and all that. Coffee's on me."

"No worries. I trust First Manhattan was grateful?"

"It took a little while. As you can imagine, there was the matter of just me, a 3D printer–generated gun, and a dead body to explain first. The police were a lot friendlier when it became clear the only prints on the weapon were Dirk's.

"And then, of course, everybody was preoccupied with reestablishing the global blockchain from my office system. It wasn't hard to push a copy out to all the banks, but there was that gap to fill in while I was staying at the Magnus Hilton. What a mess! But still, five days' worth of transactions was a heck of a lot easier to recreate than six months' worth.

"And don't forget about the wallets. My system didn't have that data, so the banks had to scan the blockchain from the very beginning through to the end to generate a report of what the balance of every BankCoin wallet in the world would have been when I turned my servers off. The Department of Defense made one of their most powerful supercomputers available to do that."

"Smart move," George said. "The markets took their biggest one-day loss since October 1987 the day after the attack, but they're coming back. Anyway, the bank must be grateful now, right?"

"I guess you could say yes and no. No, in that they let me go."

"Let you go? You're kidding?"

"It's kind of complicated. It looks like all the banks and IBs are going to stick with BankCoin, but that doesn't mean anybody's very happy about it. Individual and commercial customers were naturally shaken up by all the chaos, and the government's all over the BankCoin network now. A Senate committee and two separate House committees are slated to hold hearings, and Treasury and FBI investigative teams are camped out on the IT floor of the bank – I could go on. And that's just in the US. Who knows what regulations will come out the other end of the whole process?"

"But none of that was your fault," Marchand said.

"Sure," Frank replied, "but all in all, this was a huge black eye for First Manhattan. BankCoin was the CEO's big, shiny idea to begin with, and I was his big, shiny BankCoin security geek. So – big surprise – he was canned. So were most of the other employees most strongly identified with BankCoin. Including me, since I was so visible. You may recall they were trotting me around for months as the public face of BankCoin cybersecurity."

"Still, that seems harsh," George said. "You didn't design the system, and you were the one that pulled their chestnuts out of the fire – it would have been an unmitigated disaster without that."

"Yeah, well, there was also the fact I hadn't blended in much as a senior management executive, if you can imagine that. So, nobody had my back. I expect when you guys cracked the NASLA ring last week it left the bank feeling a lot safer, too, as backwards as that may sound given the Crypto attack. But that's all good and I can't complain. They bought out my contract, so I got paid for two years even though I only put in a little over six months of work. And who knows, maybe someday, First Manhattan's stock will come back, and my options will be worth a bundle. Frankly, I'm happy to be home again."

"Not going to miss the high life in the big city?"

"I guess it was kind of fun for a while – the town cars and fancy apartment and a couple times even a trip on a private jet – that was pretty cool. But it just wasn't me. I'm glad I sampled it, and I'm glad to be done with it." He was also relieved he'd been able to return the furniture that had looked so ridiculous in his Washington digs once it was delivered. What had he been thinking? And Fang was back! Whoever Dirk had hired to do his dirty work must have hung a road kill carcass outside Frank's condo.

"So, anyway, enough about me, as they say," Frank said. "What has anyone found out about Dirk?"

"Everything the résumé the bank had on file checked out as accurate, except for his name. Double Stanford graduate, lots of Silicon Valley experience, and so on. That was all legit. It's when you go deeper that things start to get interesting and a bit tragic. It turns out he grew up in East Germany, not Denmark. His father was pretty high up in the Stasi, the state security apparatus. When the wall crumbled, so did their fortunes. His father ended up ratting out Stasi and Soviet secrets to the CIA, got the family relocated to the US, and then promptly died, leaving Dirk and his mother – he was an only child of about fifteen then – alone in a strange country. His mother was a recluse for the rest of her life. She was Dirk's only relative in the States and died a while back."

"But how does that turn someone into an anarchist bent on sending the developed world back into the financial stone age?" Frank asked.

"I don't think we'll ever have the entire answer to that," Marchand said. "The most helpful thing the police found in his room was a diary he kept religiously over the years. It appears he was a high-functioning schizoaffective disorder sufferer since his college days – more delusional than crazy in the conventional sense. Or, to put it another way, the problem wasn't so much that his thinking was irrational. The big problem was that the foundations of his reasoning were unsound."

"I never would have guessed," Frank said. "He always seemed pretty normal to me, at least for a programmer."

"That part isn't surprising," Marchand said. "It looks like his meds worked pretty well for him most of the time. The forensic psychiatrist who reviewed the diary concluded he got too self-confident, though. It turns out he was managing his own dosages and probably never realized it when his grip on reality started sliding."

"That explains part of it," Frank said. "But not how he expected to pull off something so crazily ambitious. Are you sure he was acting alone? It must have cost a bundle just to put that fake penthouse apartment together."

"Oh, money wasn't a problem – it turns out he struck it rich on a startup he once worked at and had over ten million dollars salted away in index funds. And he never spent anything on himself. Did you know that the whole time he was working for the bank he was living in a rented room? Besides a lot of computer equipment, there was practically nothing in it except a bed, a dresser, a chair – and get this – an exercise bicycle."

"But still," Frank asked, "how did he imagine he was going to take over the world? Did he really think everyone would turn into an anarchist overnight and overthrow their government just because some wild-eyed geek appeared out of nowhere on their computer screen yammering about overthrowing the established order?"

"That part's a little pathetic," George said. "It turns out Dirk was the head of a secretive group of internet anarchists we've monitored for years but never took seriously. He'd enlisted eleven other true believers to become what he called his general staff. They were each responsible for an individual country or region, or a central duty, like communications."

"What's the pathetic part?" Frank asked.

"Dirk apparently believed his staff had signed up thousands of followers, spread out across the world, all of them waiting for the moment when Dirk would do something – he never shared with them exactly what – to take down the financial world order. He'd been marshalling his forces for almost ten years, or at least so he thought. In fact, all he'd recruited was a bunch of dreamers, fanatics, and fools. A couple of them pulled together a few other folks under them, but for most of his so-called general staff, it was more like an online game of *Dungeons and Dragons* than a real-world plan to bring about an anarchic Armageddon."

"That is kind of sad," Frank said, remembering Dirk's earnest, bulging eyes and complete confidence in whatever he said and did.

"And here's another interesting thing we learned from the diary," George continued. "After a while, Dirk started thinking he was Satoshi Nakamoto. It's clear he wasn't, because in earlier entries, he's wondering who Nakamoto might be, just like everyone else was back then. But it looks as if he really was Lupanov, the guy behind the Russ blockchain, as well as Schwert. Too bad for the Ruskies they didn't have someone like you working for them."

"So," Frank said, "when the dust settles, I guess the only country that got creamed was Russia, right?"

"You bet," George said. "We're still reading the tea leaves, but we figure over a trillion dollars' worth of Russ was in circulation before Dirk blew it up, and that's all gone. That sent the value of the ruble down by more than thirty-five percent in less than a week. Between that, the low price of oil, and the collapse of the Kremlin's global trade channel for embargoed goods, Russia is effectively bankrupt, just as Dirk predicted. It gives me the willies when I watch the news from over there, what with the food riots, martial law, and worse – that could have been us, too. The Russian foreign and finance ministers are meeting in secret with our folks and representatives of Germany, France, and England right now, basically begging for mercy."

"Really? I hadn't heard anything about that," Frank said.

"No, and you didn't hear it from me either, so keep it under your hat. Yazzi's no fool. He knows he'll get more out of the Russian president if he doesn't humiliate him publicly. But don't be surprised if a major nonaggression treaty between Russia and the West is announced within a few weeks. In return, all the sanctions will be lifted and the price of oil will be allowed to float again."

"How about the Russ?" Frank asked. "Will the Russians try to revive that?"

"From what I'm hearing, no, that's gone for good. The Kremlin figured out that when the roof caved in they owed vendors more in cash than vendors owed them in goods. They're abandoning the whole mess."

"Wow – it's good there was a ban on investing in the Russ. Otherwise investors would have lost a fortune."

"Some did, anyway," Marchand said, "A lot of people set up offshore shell companies to keep investing. It looks as if something like a hundred billion dollars in Russ was held that way when it crashed. And that's not the end of it. As a good faith gesture to kick-start the negotiations, the Russians turned over the names of everyone in the United States who directly or indirectly bought or held on to Russ after the sanctions went into effect. Anyone on that list should be looking forward to some significant jail time."

* * *

Josh Peabody stared at the dark screen of the Bloomberg terminal in his home office. There wasn't any point in turning it on, he reflected bitterly. The law firm representing the CryptoBoom! investors in their civil suit had placed a lien on everything he owned. And a judge had granted the injunction requested by the Securities and Exchange Commission to bar him from trading until his criminal trial was over.

There wasn't any point in looking at his phone, either. He hadn't received a text or email he wanted to read since his world blew up.

When you boiled it all down, the single piece of communications equipment still relevant to him was the ankle bracelet ensuring the only place he'd be leaving his house for was jail. The only question was when.

No wonder this country was in such a terrible state. If this was the reward for financial innovation, well, this country might as well just hang it up.

* * *

The meeting of the National Security Council was over, but President Yazzi lingered, alone, after shooing even Carson Bekin out the door. Sitting there in the room where so many other presidents had made fateful decisions always humbled him. Would he measure up the next time his turn came around?

Staring at the empty chairs, he replayed the events surrounding the Russian crisis as they had unfolded. He was profoundly grateful he'd been spared the need to launch his attack against the Russ. It wasn't often fate intervened to spare the Decider from his duty to make a choice. Magnus's successful attack against the Russian economy had been an unexpected stroke of luck, and Yazzi would choose luck over action every time.

* * *

Filitov lifted the kettle from the hotplate in RussCoin's former world headquarters and poured the steaming water over the tea leaves in the china pot. It was one of the few household possessions he'd insisted on keeping after the divorce. He did enjoy a good cup of tea.

His small office hadn't changed visibly, but everything else had. There was no longer any Russ Project, no RussCoin company, not even any Russ. It was regrettable. But the office lease was paid though the end of the year, and old habits die hard.

He wondered what poor Ustinov was up to. He had been such an earnest young fellow. The country needed more bureaucrats like him. Now it would need to manage with one fewer.

He'd heard that FSS superintendent was gone, too – Shukov – that was his name. Rumor had it the FSS director supervising the Russ Project had successfully laid the blame for the whole fiasco on him. Hopefully, the poor fellow had friends in high places to take care of him. If not, well, life in public service could be unjust.

Yes, it was all regrettable. But there would be other opportunities. The world was always adopting new technologies before it learned how to protect itself against them. It was good to be in a growth business.

He looked at his watch. Ah! Ten o'clock! Time to celebrate another day.

He set his cup down and returned to the table with a bottle and a spotty glass. Tea was all very nice, of course, but vodka was better.

* * *

Ruth Kim was one of the few bank employees on the BankCoin security team to come out of the incident well. She'd received a promotion. With Magnus gone, the IT department couldn't afford to lose someone who understood the system almost as well as he had. *And they didn't even know the whole story*, she thought. She had been under strict orders from Ryan Clancy, the person she'd been covertly reporting to at the FBI, to call him immediately if she heard from Frank after he disappeared. If she hadn't stood by Frank instead, the FBI would likely have seized him outside the bank. Then Dirk would have had time to destroy the last copy of BankCoin. She'd miss Frank. A lot.

Audrey Addams was also a beneficiary; although in her dour way of looking at the world, it was a case of good news and bad news. Like Kim, she'd gotten a fine promotion, because Benson Cronin wasn't the only executive who got the axe. Just before the attack, a female manager had filed a class-action lawsuit against the bank for sexual harassment, and dozens of employees had joined in. It was another public black eye for the bank at a time when it could least afford one. It didn't take the board long to confirm that the accusations were true and then fire the worst offenders named in the suit, including Glen Olson, the manager who had assaulted her at the office party.

That was all very good news indeed.

The bad news, for Audrey at least, was the board had brought Willie Bigelow back as CEO of her bank. And his taste in ties was still appalling.

* * *

Frank was fidgeting.

Fidgeting perhaps as he had never fidgeted before in his life. How much longer could this take? He was wiped out, too. He'd been sitting there for almost twelve hours.

Someone tapped him on the shoulder. He turned to see Tim.

Frank jumped to his feet.

"Everything's fine, Frank. Marla's great. And you're a grandfather!"

"Are you sure she's okay? Can I come see her?"

"Yup," Tim said with a tired smile. "The baby was born two hours ago. I came out then, and you were fast asleep. You looked so bushed I figured the news could wait a little while. Follow me."

Frank held back with great effort; he wanted to rush past his son-in-law, but he didn't know where to go. A few twists and turns later, Tim stopped in front of a door, putting one finger up to his lips. "I'm not sure whether Marla will be awake or not."

But awake she was. And in her arms was a small bundle with a pink face, wearing a knit cap.

Frank rushed in and crouched at the side of the bed. Marla was clearly exhausted but smiling nonetheless. "Isn't she beautiful?" she whispered.

Frank felt his heart leap – a little girl!

"The most beautiful little girl in the world," he said, and meant it. "And you? How are you doing?"

"I'm okay. I'm just very, very tired."

"Of course, you are!" he said. And then, hesitantly, "May I?"

"Yes," she said. "Stand up first." He did, and she handed the bundle to him; it weighed almost nothing at all. He backed up and sat down slowly in the chair beside the bed, staring at the tiny, wrinkled face. The eyes were shut tight.

In her whole life, Marla had never seen her father look so happy.

Then she smiled.

He wasn't even fidgeting.

* * *

Did you enjoy The Blockchain Revolution? Please consider recommending it to others and posting a brief review at your favorite online book site.

You can read the first two chapters of the first Frank Adversego thriller in the pages that follow.

The first four books in the Frank Adversego Thriller series are available as eBooks at Amazon and in paperback at your favorite online book site as well as at http://andrew-updegrove.com/books/

They can also be ordered in paperback through your favorite local book store.

The Alexandria Project, The Lafayette Campaign and *The Doodlebug War* are available as audiobooks published by Tantor Media. You can find them at Audible, Amazon, and wherever else audiobooks are sold.

Follow the further adventures of Frank at my author site, Tales of Adversego <Andrew-Updegrove.com>, and on Twitter @Adversego.

Acknowledgements

I'd like to express my sincere gratitude to those who generously assisted me in completing this book. For a variety of reasons, this was one of the most challenging books in the series to write, and I am greatly indebted to them for helping me to pull it all together and make it work.

First off, my very great thanks go to my daughter Nora. *The Blockchain Revolution* would not be the book it is without her many hours of reading, editing, suggestions and constant encouragement from beginning to end. By way of a single example, if there was a visual along the way that you especially liked, there's a good chance she suggested it.

I'd also like to give special thanks to several loyal Friends of Frank who read more than one draft of the book and offered special guidance. They include my brother Steve, who made many helpful plot suggestions (and to whom the book is dedicated); Rob van Son, who patiently guided me through the intricacies of the blockchain in an email exchange that extended over many months; fellow-author and former US Navy Captain Doug Norton, who provided many useful facts and corrections based on his military and diplomatic experience (be sure to check out his *Code Word* thriller series at Amazon). Thanks also to my brother-in-law

Grayson Holmbeck, a Loyola University psychology professor, who read an early draft of the book and provided much-needed insight into what the inner workings of Crypto's mind might be like.

My thanks also to the following beta readers who generously donated their time (in some cases reading more than one draft) and made many helpful suggestions: fellow authors Sylva Fae and Sarah Holmesley (be sure to check their work out at Amazon, too), William Lupton, Steve Oksala, Andrew Oliver, and Robert Minchen.

On the production side, I'd like to thank Glendon Haddix, of Streetlight Graphics, and acknowledge his excellent design skills. As with all of my previous books, his fantastic cover and clean interior designs make all the difference. I'd also like to thank Kelly Hartigan, who lent an eagle-eye and encyclopedic grammatical editing knowledge to the finalization of the text.

And finally, my thanks as always go to my wife Kathy. She put up with me through a gestation period that this time took longer to birth a book than it takes to produce a real-life human being, and we're still married. Thanks for that!

THE ALEXANDRIA PROJECT

Prologue

L ATE IN THE afternoon of a gray day in December, a panel truck pulled up to the gate of a warehouse complex in a run-down section of Richmond, Virginia. Rolling down his window, Jack Davis punched a code into the control box, and the gate clanked slowly out of the way. Once inside, he wheeled the truck around and backed it up against a loading dock as the gate closed behind him.

After unlocking and raising the loading dock door, Davis threw a light switch, revealing long rows of pallets, each stacked eight feet high with boxes of paper plates, cups and towels. He closed and locked the door, and stamped on the brake release pedal of a hydraulic lifter parked against the wall. Counting to himself, he pushed the lifter along the wall of pallets. When he reached row nineteen, he turned the lifter and maneuvered its long tines under the pallet. Raising it a few inches, he backed up until he could swing the pallet through 180 degrees. Then he pulled it behind him until it was back exactly where it had been before.

Davis had plenty of room to work, because where the pallet in the second row should have been, there was only a large metal plate set in the floor. Near the edge was a small hinged panel, which he unlocked with a key to expose a biometric security pad.

When Davis pressed his thumb against it, he heard a familiar click. Stepping back, he watched as the plate swung slowly upwards, followed by the telescoping ends of a ladder extending up from a deep shaft barely illuminated in red light. Grasping the ladder firmly, Davis descended through twenty feet of reinforced concrete while the door overhead swung silently closed above him. At the bottom, he remembered to don a pair of sunglasses before opening an unlocked door.

As usual, even with this precaution the bright lights in the enormous room beyond nearly blinded him. But soon he could clearly see the endless rows of floor to ceiling metal racks crammed with identical gray boxes. Each box displayed a row of rhythmically blinking lights, and sprouted a bundle of brightly colored wires that ran down into conduits embedded in the floor.

The room hummed purposefully with the sound of thousands of cooling fans, one to a box. Davis felt more than heard the other vibrations that filled the room, generated by the pulse of the thousands of gallons of cooling water that every minute coursed through the collectors lining the walls of the room, absorbing the waste heat that the racks of computer servers threw off. No heat signature would give this facility away from above; once warm, the coolant was directed to the water intake of a nearby power plant, happy to take the pre-heated water from wherever it was that it came from, no questions asked.

Walking along the perimeter of the room, Davis could look down through the open metal grid of the floor at the first of many additional tiers of computer servers. But that always made him a little dizzy, so instead he looked out for the guard he was relieving. No surprise – there he was, heading Davis's way, more than happy to call it a day. When they met, the guard stopped to slip on the coveralls he carried over one arm. Like the semi-automatic pistol the guard wore in a shoulder holster, they were identical to those that Davis also wore.

"What's the weather like?"

"Sucks. Sleet and more of the same predicted till morning."

"Figures. Tomorrow's my day off."

With that, the other man was on his way. In a few minutes he would drive off in the truck Davis had parked outside.

Well, the weather won't be bothering me in here, Davis thought. The room was climate controlled to within a tenth of a degree of a chilly 54 degrees Fahrenheit, and well-insulated by the bomb-proof walls and roof installed above. It had taken two years for a fleet of delivery vans to carry all the dirt and rock away that had been excavated from beneath the warehouse. The same vans had returned with cement, steel, and, eventually, those thousands of servers, accompanied by technicians to set them up. The process had been tedious, yes, but not a single satellite picture had ever shown a trace of the ambitious construction project proceeding underground.

Of course, the effect worked in both directions. With no links to the outside world other than a voice line to his supervisor, the whole bloody world could come to an end and Davis would be none the wiser until after his shift was over.

Davis walked up a flight of steel stairs to the bullet proof, glass-walled security booth attached to the wall overlooking the room. His major challenge for the next twelve hours would be to stand watch in that booth without falling asleep. There'd be hell to pay if he did, because another guard, in another security room far away, would be watching him on a video screen.

The row of displays in front of Davis allowed him to see every inch of the outside of the warehouse complex. Racked on the wall behind him were a high powered rifle and a shotgun, but it wasn't likely he'd ever need to use them. One flip of the large red switch in front of Davis would flood the server room with enough Halon gas to not only put out a fire, but asphyxiate any intruder careless enough to leave a gas mask at home. Not for the first time, Davis wished that the house where he lived with his wife and their two small children could be as well protected.

But the government didn't put as high a priority on protecting suburban starter homes as it did on safeguarding its most critical computer network facilities. Some storage facilities, like those serving the needs of the Pentagon and the National Security Administration, were located not far away at Fort Meade. Others, like this one, were scattered far and wide, hidden in plain sight but highly secure nonetheless. No way was anyone going to crack this nut. He was dead certain of that.

If Davis had been able to electronically monitor what was happening on server A-VI/147 on Level Three, though, his confidence might have taken a hit. True, concrete and steel walls, surveillance cameras and Halon gas were more than adequate to protect the physical wellbeing of his facility against anything short of a direct hit by a "bunker busting" nuclear weapon. But the data on the facility's servers had to rely on virtual defenses – firewalls, security routines and intrusion scanners.

And those defenses hadn't been enough. Someone had gotten inside.

1

Meet Frank

THE NEXT MORNING, a morbidly obese Corgi named Lily was sniffing a tree on 16th Street, in the Columbia Heights neighborhood of Washington, D.C. A cold, insistent drizzle fell on her, but Lily didn't care, because Lily was sniffing at her favorite tree. Indeed, the meager processing power of Lily's brain was wholly consumed by sampling the mysterious scents wafting up from the damp earth, for this was also the favorite tree of every other dog in the neighborhood.

Something was nagging at the edge of her senses, though.

"C'mon, Lily! Hurry up!"

Lily turned her head. The annoying distraction was coming from the person at the other end of her leash, someone with sockless feet jammed into worn, black loafers. Above bare ankles, a pair of pajama-clad legs disappeared into a rumpled raincoat. She saw there was an arm holding an umbrella, too, and under the umbrella, a stubbly, forty-something face topped by thinning black hair. Lily decided that the face did not look happy.

"Ah!" she thought. "That would be Frank." Relieved that the distraction could be ignored, Lily returned to the important work at hand.

"*C'mon, Lily!*" the voice said again.

The fact that Frank's face was unhappy was unremarkable. Even in pleasant weather, Frank tended to dwell pointlessly on the minor miseries of his life. Not long ago, those miseries had become much less minor when his mother Doreen entered a retirement home. After helping her move in, Frank took a deep breath and prepared to leave. No use dragging things out, he thought. Transitions are difficult and best dealt with quickly.

Still, it was sad. His mother was standing by the doorway of her new apartment, lower lip a-tremble and Lily held tightly in her arms. It was clear that she was rapidly nearing her emotional limits. Better hurry up.

"Well, Mom," he said, "I guess I'll be leaving now."

Then it happened. With a lunge, Doreen thrust Lily into Frank's arms. He stepped back with surprise into the hallway, too horrified to allow himself to grasp the obvious, while struggling to maintain his grip on the suddenly manic animal.

"The home doesn't allow pets," his mother blurted. "I could never have signed the lease if I hadn't known that Lily would be safe with you. Now don't you worry; I've made you her legal guardian, so it's all set. Now go! Get out of here, before I change my mind."

Frank desperately wanted her to change her mind. But his mother had already shut the door in his astonished face. He stared blankly at it as the enormity of his plight sank in. Now what? Lily was just three years old, and acknowledged his existence only by barking. He heard his mother sobbing piteously on the other side of the door. He felt like crying, too.

That had been two long, loud months ago. Only recently had he progressed from the denial stage to active mourning.

"*Come on!*" Frank hissed. At last, Lily turned away from her tree. She looked up at him reproachfully, and barked.

"Okay, okay," Frank said, fumbling in his pocket. He held a dog treat up for Lily to see. "*Okay?*"

Satisfied that her efforts would not go unrewarded, Lily began looking for just the right place to do what finally needed to be done. At last, she squatted, looking blankly ahead. Frank sighed with relief.

A blue plastic bag inverted over his free hand, Frank scooped up Lily's grudging gift. He handed over the treat, jerking back with his fingers barely intact.

Isn't that just the story of my life? he thought bleakly as Lily happily consumed her treat. Every day I give her a cookie, and every day she gives me a bag of shit.

Trudging home through the rain, Frank reflected that his day generally went downhill from here.

* * *

Lily shook herself mightily inside the foyer of Frank's dingy apartment house, wetting what little of Frank that was still dry. Satisfied, she planted her substantial hindquarters firmly on the floor, looked up at Frank, and barked. Frank sighed, picked up the still-wet dog, and labored his way up the stairs to his second floor flat.

As he climbed to the top, Frank's rising eyes met a pair of fuzzy pink slippers, a floral house dress, and then a pair of folded arms draped with a bath towel. Just above them, he knew, would be the perpetually hostile face of his across-the-hall neighbor. As that scowling visage hove into view, Frank once again noted the uncanny resemblance his neighbor bore to North Korean president Jong Kim-Lo. Only with hair curlers.

"Morning, Mrs. Foomjoy," Frank offered as Lily twisted wildly in his arms. He deposited the dog at her feet.

"Shame on you!" Mrs. Foomjoy barked as she knelt to massage Lily with the bath towel. "Poor, dear wet baby!" she crooned.

"It's raining, Mrs. Foomjoy," Frank observed. "Lily hasn't learned how to use the indoor facilities yet."

"Then why she not wear the lovely rain jacket I give her?" she snorted. "What is *wrong* with you? You don't deserve dog like this!"

Frank couldn't have agreed more. Lily groveled at Mrs. Foomjoy's feet, and then leaned to one side until gravity obligingly rolled her onto her back. The dog gazed up with adoring, goggle eyes as Mrs. Foomjoy rubbed her stomach.

His neighbor grabbed the leash from Frank's hand when she stood up. "I see to welfare of this dog!" she snapped, shutting her door loudly behind her. Frank stood suddenly alone in the poorly lit hallway, a warm, blue plastic pendulum swinging slowly from side to side in his hand. Relieved, he entered his own apartment and quietly shut the door.

Frank hung his dripping raincoat on a hook in the linoleum floored hallway inside. At one time, his apartment's décor might have charitably been described as "Late-Twentieth-Century Divorced Middle Aged Male." Now the most obvious theme was random clutter. He poured a cup of coffee and sat at the small table in the small kitchen. Before him the large screen of his laptop stared blankly back at him. With resignation, he turned the computer on.

Normally, the sound of a computer booting up would have struck him as cheerful; the imperceptibly soft whir of the cooling fan spinning up to speed; the blinking, blue light that assured him that the device was powering up; the screen phosphorescing into life with a pearly glow. After all, information technology – IT – was not only his profession, but the primary foundation of his existence.

Email was Frank's preferred link to the outside world, providing a social firewall between him and the random messiness of direct human contact. Frank was convinced that digital relations were far safer than their in-person analogue. Electronic communications brought him as close to his fellow man as he usually wished to be. Any more intimate than that, and things were apt to become at best unpredictable, and at worst, well, he'd been *there* all too often before. You never got enough time to think before things started spiraling out of control.

Which brought him back to the night before. Be honest, he mused ruefully. You got what you deserved. Or didn't get what you didn't deserve, to be more precise.

He stared at the keyboard. Should he check his email or shouldn't he? The rational side of his brain said, yes, what's there is there. Deal with it.

But the other side of his brain had a different opinion: "Go back to bed," it whispered urgently, "It's Sunday. You don't have to deal with anything today."

That was true. And who knows what might happen by Monday? There could be a typhoon tonight. Or maybe giant pterodactyls would erupt from a wormhole next to the Lincoln Memorial, scattering screaming tourists towards the safety of nearby Metro stations. That side of his brain was lobbying strongly to take two aspirin, pull the covers back over his head, and let reality take care of itself for another twenty-four hours.

He sighed and made up his mind. Might as well see sooner rather than later what people from his office had posted on line about the night before. A few clicks later and he was at the Facebook page of Mary, the sullen receptionist. Yes, there were pictures from the party. Lots of them. Later would do just fine after all, he decided. He snapped the laptop shut without turning it off.

The sad thing was, for once he had actually been looking forward to the Library of Congress IT Department Holiday party, even bringing his daughter Marla with him, a Georgetown University grad student. He appreciated the great impression she always made on his co-workers. Unlike her dad, Marla was self-assured and sociable. She worked the crowd like a pro, chatting and shaking hands, poised and laughing. How could he feel anything but proud? It was hard not to drink a bit more than usual as he watched her from the security of the bar in the rear of the function room.

More to the point, Frank had been looking forward to making Marla feel proud of her old man as well. Everyone knew that George Marchand, the Director of IT at the LoC, was going to announce his choice to head an important security initiative mandated by the Cybersecurity Subcommittee of the House Committee on Science and Technology. Frank figured he had the spot all sewn up. After all, he was – or at least at one time had been – a recognized cybersecurity innovator; a McArthur Foundation "Genius" Award recipient, no less, in recognition of his widely acclaimed creative work in the early days of computer networking.

So when George stood up and tapped on his glass, Frank sat up straighter. He listened impatiently as his boss welcomed the spouses, thanked the staff for their work that year, and told a joke at his own expense. At last, he began to make the announcement that Frank was waiting for.

And then it happened. One moment Frank was looking sideways to see the reaction on his daughter's face when his name was called, and the next he was hearing someone else's name ring out instead. And not just any name, but Rick Wellesley's – "only out for himself" Rick, a self-satisfied slug of a middle-manager who had never had a creative thought in his life. Someone who had even briefly reported to Frank when he first came to work at the LoC. *Rick Wellesley?* How could this be happening?

But it was. There was Rick, standing and basking in the applause, glancing briefly and triumphantly in Frank's direction. Frank was stunned, his face burning. And then he was angry. Without a word to his daughter, he stood up and marched to the bar, turning his back on the party as George finished his remarks. Knocking back another drink, Frank now felt foolish as well as angry. Everyone was probably looking at him, but he was afraid to turn around and find out. He sulked at the bar until Marla came looking for him.

Sitting now in his kitchen, Frank felt his face grow flush again. After all, everyone had expected the job to go to him. Then, with a wrenching feeling, he had a worse thought – what if no one had expected him to get the job? Maybe he was the only one in the whole damn department who hadn't seen it coming. Maybe everyone had been laughing up their sleeves as they watched him bask in his expected glory, just waiting for his jaw to drop when he realized that he had been skunked by Rick.

Of course that had been the case, he thought wretchedly. He was sure of it.

* * *

And why not? What had he really done in the last twenty years? Sure, he'd become a star at the Massachusetts Institute of Technology – "MIT" to anyone in the know. He'd enrolled at the age of sixteen after skipping two years of middle school. Not that skipping a few grades was unusual at MIT. As an undergraduate, he'd become part of Project Athena, an ambitious effort to create a distributed computing system for the whole university. Of course, the goal for the project's corporate sponsors was to use MIT as a testbed. Later, they hoped to productize the design and make a ton of money.

For some reason, Frank had intuitively locked onto the security challenges that such a system would present. He already had privileges to use MIT's gateway to the government-funded Advanced Research Projects Agency Network – the now-famous "ARPANET" that was the precursor to the Internet. Only select institutions had access to it then, but Frank immediately grasped where Project Athena and the ARPANET together could eventually lead. It hit him between the eyes that this was the start of something big. Linking terminals together around a campus was today's goal, but the next step would be to connect those networks together, using ARPANET technology.

That sounded awesome, but how would you restrict access to any particular data to one person, and not let it be seen by everyone else? MIT was already a hotbed of hackers. If students were going to great lengths now to break into restricted sections of university computers just for fun, what would criminals, or enemy countries, not do to break into classified computers, once someone had linked them all together? Frank tackled that issue with gusto, if not discipline. He was a big picture guy, and what a big and exciting picture it was! The idea of wide area networks was brand new, and big ideas were needed to make sense of it all; the details could come later. When Frank graduated, he stayed on at MIT, nominally in a PhD program, but for all practical purposes he lived at a terminal in the Project Athena lab, surviving on coffee and code like so many other young computer engineering students back in the day.

Luckily for Frank, he found a mentor – an engineer on loan from one of the sponsoring companies. Surprisingly, the two hit it off, and the older man reined in the younger one enough to keep Frank's ideas from flying off into too many directions at once. He also insisted that Frank get his best ideas recorded in some sort of coherent order. Often they talked until all hours, the older man channeling Frank's enthusiasm and helping him follow his insights down the most productive paths.

Frank never completed his doctorate, but he did finish his Masters thesis – and by anyone's account, it was brilliant. He anticipated just about every security challenge that would arise over the next twenty years as the Internet took off. He also suggested most of the solutions that were later refined and implemented to deal with a massively networked world. Even today, his thesis remained an obligatory foundational reference in just about every new network and Internet security paper that was written.

Frank's thesis also brought him to the notice of the mysterious keepers of the MacArthur Fellows Program – the unknown judges that every year contact a select group of exceptional individuals they have decided, "show exceptional merit and promise for continued and enhanced creative work."

Receiving a MacArthur Fellowship had been the high point of Frank's professional career. But as a practical matter, it also brought an end to it, because the payments of $25,000 every three months for five years gave him the freedom to do whatever he wanted to without ever having to acquire the discipline of making his way in the world. It also allowed him to get married.

It was not helpful that what Frank wanted to do usually changed every other week. It wasn't long before his work at Project Athena suffered. He no longer listened to his mentor, and his assigned tasks no longer got done. Instead, he plunged from one question that intrigued him to another, never getting very far along with any of them.

Like many people whose intellectual abilities matured before their social skills, Frank developed an abrupt and assertive manner that helped mask his discomfort around others. That was unfortunate, because his new–found fame encouraged him to become even more obnoxious than ever. Soon, the other guys in the lab were annoyed with his failure to meet his commitments, and also sick of hearing his latest revelations about security – or about any other topic on which he had decided he was now an expert.

Eventually, it was his mentor who took Frank aside and told him that if he didn't shape up, his days in the lab were numbered. Frank didn't take that well. What right did some middle aged, middle-management type with a degree from a state school in the Midwest have to tell a certified Genius anything about anything?

Quite a lot, Frank now reflected, gazing at his closed laptop. Like the immature idiot he was then, he had cleared his things out of the Project Athena lab the same day his mentor had called him out and never returned. Eventually, the MacArthur Fellowship money ran dry, and with a wife and young daughter, Frank had to get more serious about working. Or at least he should have. For a while, his thesis and MacArthur reputation carried him from job to job. But when the bottom fell out of the economy, employers received a flood of great résumés for every job they posted.

By then, of course, Frank's résumé was also getting pretty long in the tooth. He had no "continued and enhanced creative work" to show for his five years of subsidized, random behavior. He'd never published another paper, and it was others, and not Frank, who turned his thesis ideas into real protocols and products. As the jobs got scarce, reference checks counted a whole lot more, and the feedback about Frank always came back the same: brilliant, arrogant, unfocused, unreliable. That was more charitable than what his soon-to-be ex-wife had to say. But he hadn't listened to her, either.

Frank usually tried not to think much about the years that followed: the start-up that had signed him up as Chief Technical Officer and the VCs that fired him; the time spent without a job at all; the rut he fell into for years after his wife moved out with their daughter, when he said the hell with everything and everybody. That time was a blur of punching the clock in whatever high school, small business or municipal IT department would take him on until he got fired again, then waiting until his unemployment ran out before finding something else he could do in his sleep, until even that became too much to bother with.

Through all that time, though, industry insiders still sought Frank out, so he maintained a low-key consulting business on the side to make sure he could always cover his child support payments. Among the elite in the world of security, Frank still had the reputation of a wizard, able to come up with the kind of insights that would make the most impenetrable problems suddenly transparent. An emailed plea for help describing something dense and dark that had already defied all of the usual solutions would reliably generate a response from Frank an hour or two later, usually beginning, "It strikes me that…" and ending with, "I suggest you try…." Invariably, what Frank suggested worked. But requests for his ongoing assistance went unanswered.

It was his daughter Marla that finally set Frank back on his feet. One Friday when he was once again out of work, he picked her up for their weekend together. But something was wrong; his normally chatty preteen wasn't saying a word. As they walked, she looked down at her feet. Then she looked up as if to ask him a question, only to look down again. After a while, Frank got irritated. "Marla, if there's something you want to ask me, just ask it already!"

But Marla still paused. Finally she said, "Dad, you know I'm in a computer class now, don't you? It's something you have to take in seventh grade."

"Yes," he said, surprised. "So?"

"Well," she said, and stopped. He waited, now curious.

"Well," she started again, "today we went on a field trip to the computer department of a big company, and we all had to sign in and wear these name tag things. One of the people that worked there gave us a tour, and when she saw my name, she asked if I had a father named Frank, so of course I said yes."

"Uh huh," said Frank, not liking where this was going.

"Well…" Marla paused again, and then the words came rushing out. "She said that she went to school with you and you were the most brilliant person she had ever known and that you'd gotten a big award for being a genius and she wanted to know what you were doing now." Marla stopped abruptly for a long moment. "And I didn't know what to say."

Frank wished this could be all over, and quickly.

But, Marla, of course, needed an answer. "Dad, the guide said you used to be somebody really important."

Frank felt like he was dangling at the end of a rope, turning slowly in the breeze. He looked away, and tried to think what to say. What *could* he say? And then, with all of the disarming innocence of a child, Marla finished for him.

"Dad, she wasn't telling the truth, was she?"

Frank couldn't breathe. His daughter thought so little of him that she had to believe that the guide was thinking of someone else? Or was it that she would be too ashamed of what he had become to be able to deal with the truth? He felt sick.

By then, they were standing in front of the door of his cheap apartment building. The traffic rushed past the garbage cans and trash piled up on the curb, and Frank took it all in. The sights, the smells, his life – they all fit together perfectly, didn't they? Still, he couldn't think of a word to say.

Finally, Marla put her hand on his arm. "It's okay, Dad," she said softly. "Let's go upstairs."

That had been ten years ago. The following Monday he sucked it up and called his old mentor, George Marchand, and asked for a job. George was the head of the IT department at the Library of Congress now, and Frank called him out of the blue to ask if they could get together for coffee.

George had been as gracious as Frank had been uncomfortable. Frank had sent his résumé along by email, for what it was worth, and George cut straight to the chase after the opening pleasantries.

"You know I'll need to bring you in at the bottom, Frank. Can you deal with that?"

Frank was prepared. "Sure, sure, George. I'll be fine with that." George nodded, brows furrowed. Then he changed the topic.

"How's that cute goddaughter of mine these days? I can't even remember the last time I saw Marla."

"She's great," said Frank, suddenly determined; it helped to remember why he was sitting there. "Just great. We get together every weekend. She's in seventh grade now. She's smart as a whip and gets straight As."

They chatted about family for a few more minutes, and then George looked at his watch. They both stood up, and shook hands.

"I won't let you down," Frank said as he looked George in the eye for the first time.

"I know you won't," his new boss said. But Frank could tell he was only being polite.

* * *

Sitting in his kitchen, Frank reflected that he'd been as good as his word. But not much better, he made himself admit. Yes, he'd rarely missed a day of work, and no one could say he hadn't earned his paycheck. And yes, he'd earned every promotion he'd been given.

But the promotions had been few, and the last one had been awarded seven years ago. Frank still had tremendous insights into IT architecture, and he remained as interested as ever in new developments in security. His cubicle at the LoC was stacked high with articles covered in scribbled notes, and he read voraciously online as well. For anyone in the office with a thorny problem, Frank was the go-to guy who could always solve it, provided he was allowed to tackle it alone. Sitting at a keyboard, Frank was still The Man – the tougher the problem the better, just bring it on.

Three hours, eight hours or twenty hours later, he'd still be turning it over in his mind until suddenly an elegant and creative solution would spring to mind.

Management level work, though, was something else again. Every time George gave him a shot at a long term project with a couple of others to supervise, Frank could never pull it all together.

Half the time, he'd be up in the clouds thinking big thoughts that went beyond the task at hand, and the rest of the time he'd be down in the weeds, diving down rat holes to solve problems that could easily be ignored. The folks he was supposed to be supervising never knew what they would be doing from one day to the next, or what, if anything, Frank did with the work they submitted. Inevitably, George would have to take the project back. It didn't take long before the big projects stopped coming, and Frank settled into the solitary niche where he had stayed ever since.

He wasn't done beating himself up, though. Admit it, he demanded, you were relieved when the projects stopped coming. You've been marking time for years now, and that's all you'll ever do. What right did you have to think George would throw this project your way?

But this had been a *security* project, damn it. That (and the drinks he'd had last night) were what had led him to corner George later on in the cloakroom.

"I'm sorry, Frank," George had said, wrapping his scarf around his neck. "I thought about letting you know ahead of time, and then I didn't. I guess I should have."

"That's not the point, George! Rick can't find his own ass with both hands in a well-lit room. What were you thinking?"

George buttoned his overcoat, and reached for his hat. "Of course Rick can't hold a candle to you when it comes to security, Frank. There's nobody I've ever worked with who has the insight and ideas that you do. And everybody knows nobody covers his butt like Rick."

Frank let his breath out with a rush of exasperation as George settled his hat on his head. "So then why did you pick him?"

George squared off to Frank as he pulled on his gloves, looking him straight in the eye.

"Frank, you may know security, but when it comes to understanding people and how to manage them, you haven't got a clue. Yes, Rick is one hell of a weasel. But you can always rely on a weasel to watch out for himself. That means that if you give him a job to do and tell him his job is on the line, well, by hook or by crook, he'll get it done. And I can't say that about you."

Well, what could Frank say to that? He'd asked George for an explanation and now he'd have to listen to it.

"How many chances have I given you over the years, Frank? I can't remember, can you?" Frank looked away.

"You're twice as smart as I am," George continued. "You should have had my job by now! But that's never going to happen unless you grow up and learn how to perform. If you thought I'd stick my neck out for you with Chairman Steele grandstanding in the House, looking for the next poor bastard to eviscerate in front of the cameras during a public committee meeting, well, you're just delusional. Good night, Frank."

There hadn't been anything Frank could say to that, of course, so he was relieved when George turned and walked away. Furious at himself, Rick and George, in that order, he stalked back to the bar.

Frank decided that was as much of the night before as he was up to reliving; he'd leave the scene with Rick for his next exercise in psychological self-flagellation. It had all escalated so stereotypically anyway; Rick's approach and his smarmy condescension, Frank's insult in response. Okay, enough.

He felt the anger well up again, and with it, a sudden sense of purpose. Screw the jerk; just because Rick got the project didn't mean that Frank couldn't still show him up. After all, Frank had been so sure he had the spot in the bag that he'd already started writing up a proposal with his plan of attack outlined. No way was Rick going to be able to pull this job off; George would realize that soon enough, and then there'd be no one to turn to but Frank.

He snapped open his laptop and punched the keys with fury, rushing through the complicated log-in sequence that would take him into the heart of the LoC's system, where his proposal was archived. Highlighting the file name, he hit the Enter key, leaned back, and waited for the proposal to display.

Except it didn't. Frank leaned forward and poked the Enter key again. Still nothing. Perhaps his laptop was frozen. But no – he could still move his cursor.

Then Frank noticed that something on the screen was changing: the background color was warming up, turning reddish, orange and yellow, as if the sun was rising behind it. Now that was different! Frank watched with growing astonishment as the colors began to shimmer, and then coalesced into shapes that might be flames.

Yes, flames indeed – but not like a holiday screen-saver image of a log fire – this was a real barn-burner of a conflagration!

Frank wondered what kind of weird virus he'd picked up, and how. After all, he was an IT security specialist, and if any laptop was protected six ways to Sunday, it was his. So much for whatever he had planned for today; he'd have to wipe his disk and rebuild his system from the ground up.

He was about to shut the laptop down when he saw that the flames were dying away. Now what? An image seemed to be emerging from behind the flames as they subsided. Frank leaned forward; the image became a tall building – maybe some sort of lighthouse? Underneath, there was a line of text, but in characters he couldn't read. Truly, this was like no virus he'd ever seen or even heard of before. He reached for his cellphone and took a picture of the screen just before it suddenly went blank.

Frank was impressed. Whoever had come up with this hack certainly had a sense of style. A weird one, but hey, graphic art of any type wasn't the long suit of most hackers.

Frank got a pad of paper and a pen from his desk and punched up the file directory again, highlighted his proposal, and pressed the Enter key again. This time, he would watch more closely and take notes.

But all that displayed was a three word message: "File not found."

Frank tried again – no luck. He did a search of the entire directory using the title. Nothing. His proposal was gone.

Now he was alarmed. After all, the directory he was staring at was in the innermost sanctum of the Library of Congress computer system, and the LoC was the greatest library in the world. Within its vast holdings were books that could be found almost nowhere else on earth. Recently, the Library had begun digitizing materials, and then destroying the physical copies. If someone had been able to delete files in the most protected part of the Library's computer system, what else might be missing?

Frank raced through a random sampling of sensitive directories, and then let out a sigh of relief; it was hard to tell for sure, but everything seemed intact. He checked the server logs for the Library's indices, holdings and various other resources; everything appeared to be undisturbed, with no unusual reductions in the amount of data stored.

Frank drummed his fingers on the table in the cramped dinette. How to go about figuring this one out? Then he remembered his cellphone, and sent the picture of the screenshot to his laptop. The picture wasn't great, but once he enlarged it he could tell that the characters were Greek. He cropped the image until just the text remained, then ran it through a multi-script OCR program to turn the picture of the Greek characters into text. Finally, he pasted the text into a translator window. No luck – all he got was a "cannot translate" message.

Frank's fingers started drumming again. He reopened the drop down menu of languages in the translator screen and noticed that another language option was "Ancient Greek." He highlighted that choice and hit Enter. This time, the screen blinked.

Frank looked, and then he blinked, too. But the translation still read the same:

**THANK YOU FOR YOUR
CONTRIBUTION
TO THE ALEXANDRIA PROJECT**

* * *

Buy *The Alexandria Project* from your favorite online book store or at http://andrew-updegrove.com/alexandria-project/

To find out about new releases and special offers, sign up for the Friends of Frank newsletter at http://andrew-updegrove.com/newsletter/